Love Inherited

A Highland Romance

Cristine Eastin

Published by Cristine Eastin, 2018.

Love Inherited
Copyright © 2018 by Cristine Eastin
All rights reserved. No part of this book may be reproduced or transmitted in any form or by any means, mechanical or electronic, without written permission from the author.

Love Inherited is a work of fiction. Places, characters, names, organizations, and events are either the product of the author's imagination or are used fictitiously. Any resemblance to persons living or dead is coincidental and unintended by the author. Any references to historical events or real locales are intended to give the fiction a setting in historical reality.

Scripture quotations are taken from the *Holy Bible.*
New King James Version®. Copyright © 1982 by Thomas Nelson. Used by permission. All rights reserved.

New International Version®. NIV® Copyright © 1973, 1978, 1984, 2011 by Biblica, Inc.®. Used by permission. All rights reserved worldwide.

Cover design by Jason Pape, Papesite Creative, LLC
Photo background © Eric Limon/Shutterstock
Photo hands © Ersler Dmitry/Shutterstock
Print ISBN-13: 978-0-9994827-1-1
ISBN-10: 0-9994827-1-8
eBook ISBN-13: 978-0-9994827-2-8
ISBN-10: 0-9994827-2-6
Library of Congress Control Number: 2017916316
Contemporary Christian Romance
Visit the author's website: CristineEastin.com[1]
Published by Cristine Eastin

---

1. http://cristineeastin.com

Dedication

In memory of Joyce,
with gratitude for her prayers.
A bruised reed he will not break...
—Isaiah 42:3 NIV

Chapter 1

Hope for her mother's love should have died by now—yet there it was—that little flip in her stomach as she unlocked her mailbox. Was she an optimistic pessimist, China wondered, or just a fool? She grabbed the fistful of mail and snapped the box shut, October snow swirling around her boots like winter wasps.

China MacLeish juggled her way through the door of the three-story Chicago brownstone, bumped the door shut with her hip, and dropped two string bags of groceries on the hall bench. She switched on the track lighting and did a quick scan through the mail, checking the return address names. Nothing from Margaret MacLeish. Her mother's name remained the same, but the husbands and addresses changed with the seasons.

Happy birthday.

In forty-one years, what had she gotten from her mother? Boarding schools and a small trust fund. Maybe her mother had forgotten she had a daughter.

But the truth stung—her mother hated her.

China slapped the mail on the bench and blew a worn-out sigh. Seven o'clock and no Brian. Last night he showed up at ten. Working late, he'd said.

She shrugged off her coat and piled it on the bench. No longer much interested in dinner, she carried the groceries to the kitchen, the sharp tap of her stiletto heels on the tiles punctuating the emptiness of the place. At least the fridge held evidence that Brian still lived here: leftover sushi and a splash of crusted milk on the shelf.

Straightening up from the vegetable bin, her shoulders complained of a day too long on the computer. Dinner could wait till after a hot shower.

She hung her coat in the closet and stood in front of the open door, torn between pressing her nose to the collar of Brian's cashmere topcoat and shoving the coat aside. She didn't have the energy to be mad—not till she got these heels off.

WRAPPED in a bath sheet, China contemplated swiping her hand over the steam-drenched mirror but didn't feel like tracing the lines of Brian's infidelities etched in her face. She smoothed moisturizer over her taut cheeks and down her neck, putting an extra dab on the faint crow's feet that grew like cracks in ice.

She worked the snarls out of her hair and braided it into a damp rope. Turning to get her fleece robe off the back of the door, her hand stilled mid-reach. Brian's robe hung next to hers. The gray terrycloth, familiar to her touch, smelled of him too. China blinked twice, then remembered she was mad at Brian and plucked her own robe off its hook.

Lavender-infused air trailed after her down the stairs as she padded in slipper-socks to the kitchen.

China crammed the spinach and carrots through the juicer and stirred in a little honey. Dinner-in-a-glass for one by firelight. How romantic.

She picked up the mail and headed to the living room. She set the glass of vegetable sludge on the marble-topped coffee table, aimed the remote at the fireplace, and settled on the leather sectional.

Thumbing through the mail, a return address in Scotland jolted her—*Anderson Macaslan Group, Balmhain House, Edinburgh*. Her mother was from Scotland. Somewhere. A frown grew and her breathing constricted. Anything to do with her mother was trouble.

The dagger letter opener slit the linen envelope with a harsh *ffht*. China withdrew one sheet of heavy stationery, crisply folded in exact thirds. Embossed in gold under the address—*Legal, Wealth Management, and Tax Solicitors*. Her fingers stiffened as she read.

The letter dropped to the floor, and China stared at the flames, frozen in place.

Before she could absorb what she'd read, Brian's key grated in the lock, and the front door clicked open and shut. A chill came in with Brian, but his footsteps came no closer than the hall. China listened to the silence, waiting, her back to him. If he wanted to resume last night's argument—fine.

"This isn't working for me anymore," he said. "I'm moving out."

"What?" Her voice sounded small, and she refused to look at him.

"Sorry, China. I'll just get a few things tonight. I'll get the rest of my stuff this weekend."

Her mouth opened, but no words came out before she heard him hustle up the steps to their bedroom.

China drew her feet up and tucked them under a pillow. It had never gone this far before; he'd never actually left. She clutched her robe collar tight under her chin and waited for him to come down and talk about it.

Ten minutes later, he thundered down the stairs. She could feel him standing behind her.

"I'm leaving now."

A silent scream filled her throat, her eyes riveted to the flames.

"I want the ring back."

She'd heard this before. "No. It was a gift."

He called her that ugly name and slammed out. All that was left of Brian was the scent of the expensive duty-free cologne she'd bought him.

China slipped the large, flawed diamond solitaire off her finger and plopped it in the untouched vegetable muck. She snatched up the letter, crushed it into a ball, and whipped it where Brian had stood. He knew it was her birthday.

CHINA'S bed was a mess: wadded up Kleenexes, a bag of bagel chips, a plate of half-eaten hummus and celery sticks, and her laptop. She sat cross-legged in the middle of the rumpled comforter—phone at her ear.

"No, seriously, I've inherited this huge estate in Scotland. A place called Craggan Mhor." China shifted the phone to her other ear and brought her shoulder up to hold it in place. She tapped on the keyboard and sent a link to Stacy. "Isn't that about the most unappealing place you've ever seen?"

Googling Craggan Mhor turned up images of a not-very-grand house of indeterminate age that appeared to cringe below a looming cliff in the distance. Vacant-eyed windows reflected light and nothing else. There was no landscaping except for two urns of geraniums by the front door. An expanse of lawn stretched in front, bounded by a dribbling creek to one side. But there wasn't much information about the place.

"Stacy, are you there?"

"Yeah. Are you sure this is legit?"

"As much as I can be. I've searched just about everything I can think of. The lawyers sure are real. Sorry, *solicitors*." She rolled the *r*. "Some big deal law firm in Edinburgh."

"Who did you say this was? An uncle?"

"William MacLeish, my mother's brother. I didn't even know she had a brother."

"Why didn't your mother inherit the place?"

"I have no idea. Would you give my mother anything? Even the time of day?"

"Good point. What did Brian say?"

"Pardon? Who?"

"Oh, it's like that again. Are you two fighting?"

"You could say that. He walked out. I think he means it this time." China reached for a tissue and dabbed the corners of her eyes. The guy wasn't worth any more tears. But the tears kept leaking out.

"I think I'll call the lawyers." She searched for the international time zone map. "What time is it in Edinburgh?"

"Six hours ahead."

"Too late for today. I figure I'll go over there, put the place on the market, and get this over with as fast as possible."

"What did you say it's called?"

"Craggan Mhor. No idea what it means."

China heard the front door. Just like Brian to come back unannounced.

"Gotta go, Stac. The wolf's at the door."

Cornered in her bedroom, China snapped the laptop closed and stuffed the tissues under the bed.

She was ready for him when he walked in the room. But before she knew it, she'd grabbed the bag of chips and flung it at his head. He dodged back out to the hallway.

"What are you doing here?" China leaped off the bed and followed the bag of chips, crunching dried bagel under her bare feet. "Did what's-her-name let you out for the day? I don't see your leash."

"Hey, I thought you'd be at work. I came to get some more clothes."

"You get out!"

Brian caught and held her wrists as she came at him. "I've got a right to be here. My name's on the lease."

"You've got no right, you cheating—"

"Now look, China, we've been through this a dozen times." He leaned back to avoid the spray of her fury. "I don't love you anymore."

"Don't love me anymore?" She yanked her wrists out of his grasp and drew back a hand to slap him.

Brian dodged her swing, then sprang forward, stopping just short of her. "What's the matter with you? Can't we do this like civilized people? After all these years."

"We were engaged—to be married." She lunged at him, but he pinned her in his arms. She tried to stifle gulping sobs and hiccuped.

"Sorry, China. I've got nothing more to say."

She squirmed free, and like a broken spring, she thrust him away, sending him staggering back a step.

"Get out!"

China whirled into the bedroom and, with all her anger in it, slammed the door. She listened, her back pressed hard against the door—as if she could stop him from coming in. His footfalls thumped down the carpeted steps. She expected the front door bang to shake the entire house. But there was silence.

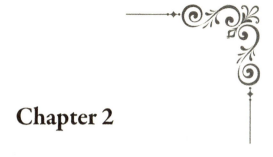

Chapter 2

The steely Scottish Highland light scarcely touched the corners of the study in Glengorm House. Sir Duncan Eideard Armstrong Sinclair, 10th Baronet, Laird of Fionnloch, drummed his fingers rapid-fire on the desk, the rest of him immobile as stone. On this desk his ancestors had written agreements with crofters, counted out rents collected, written love letters to sweethearts—and under this desk he had played as a child while his father worked. Now Duncan readied to do battle, hands poised over the computer keyboard.

Harriet, I forbid you to come here. Duncan shouted through his fingertips.

This is not a good idea. You left. Walked out eighteen months ago, haven't contacted the children but twice. You know very well the boys will be away at school during those dates. Do you plan to ever see your children again? No, you cannot just waltz back here as if Glengorm House were still your home. You filed for divorce. Let's get it over and done with.

Furthermore, when the boys were home for autumn holiday weekend, Callum asked me where you lived. I had to say I didn't know. Somewhere in South Africa, I thought. Fancy that, your son doesn't know where his mother lives!

The words blurred on the screen. The impossibility of being father *and* mother to his boys ached in his bones. Not that Harriet had been much of a mother. But a mother who tried now and again was better than silence.

I can't think what you're playing at. Reconciliation isn't your style. I gave up hoping you'd come to your senses. And I wouldn't take you back now if you crawled to me on broken glass!

He sat back, arms folded across his chest, and glared at the computer screen. Who was this woman who had borne his children? Running off with the chap they met in South Africa. He jabbed a finger in the direction of Enter, wanting to drive home the point. Instead, he placed the cursor right at the top, dragged the blue highlight down the whole lot, and whacked Delete. Knowing Harriet, it would just give her fuel for an argument, or worse, she'd ignore it. Regardless, Duncan knew she'd arrive and let herself in the front door, the poor driver staggering in her wake under a load of cases. He'd just have to deal with her when she got here. Best give his solicitors a heads-up that this divorce was likely to get messy.

Duncan closed his eyes and skewered them with his fingers, swiped a tear toward the bridge of his nose. He smacked his palms on the desk and pushed back the chair, got up and strode from the study, leaving the paneled double doors standing open behind him. Since he could no longer ring up William MacLeish, a good gallop on his own would have to do. But a ride was a poor substitute for a friend.

NIGHT Rogue nickered at Duncan and turned toward the opening stall door. The sweet scent of oat straw rose from the fresh bedding. Soft snorts and a squeal came from the other horses farther down the row of stalls.

"Hey, Ro, how's my boy?" With one hand, Duncan rubbed the stallion's neck, and in the other, he held out a pony nut on the flat of his hand. The horse lipped the treat and it was gone. Ro nudged Duncan's jacket pocket.

"Aye, you'd eat all I'd give you, wouldn't you? More pig than horse you are." Ro tossed his head. Duncan raised a hand and slowly brought it to the horse's forehead. He rubbed his knuckles on the white star between Ro's eyes.

Duncan clipped the leadline to Ro's halter and led him out to the crossties in the barn aisle. Running the curry comb down the tall Irish Thoroughbred's neck, Duncan worked his way to the horse's hindquarters. Donnie was a first-rate groom, but when Duncan had the time, he liked to groom Night Rogue himself; it settled both of them.

The black stallion was Duncan's favorite horse, a fiery eight-year-old that Duncan had raised from a weanling. Truth was, Duncan liked him feisty and often let Ro run till he tired himself out, and then they had a nice hack. Ro was, without a doubt, the finest horse for miles around, and no one rode him but Duncan. Callum wanted to, but Duncan said not till you and Ro are older. He wanted his son in one piece to one day inherit the estate.

Ro stamped a white-socked hoof.

"Now, boy, you know we're not done yet." Duncan ran a hand down a foreleg. Ro picked up his foot, and Duncan whisked the hoof pick round the frog in two quick flicks of his wrist.

Duncan led Ro, saddled, bridled, and gleaming like a moonless night, out to the mounting block in the stable courtyard. Donnie appeared from somewhere in the barn to lend a hand and hold the reins while Duncan mounted. "Have a nice ride, Sir," he said.

Duncan could feel Ro's muscles bunch as they approached the track leading into the hills, and he kept the stallion to a sedate walk

"Not yet, my boy. You know how this goes. Past Donnie's cottage, then we fly."

They passed the jump arena, and Duncan let Ro out to a high-stepping trot. Donnie's cottage—then Duncan touched his heels to Ro's sides—and fly they did—down the lane, up the rise in the undulating valley, past the small loch, splashing through the shallow ford in the burn. Duncan kept to the lane, always kept to the lane, for fear of rocks and holes that might kill them both.

They galloped hard, Ro's hoofs thudding like an army bearing down. Duncan raised off the saddle a bit and flowed with the rhythm of the stride as Ro ran the race with no finish line.

At last, Ro slowed, and Duncan brought him down to a trot, then finally to a walk. Ro's huffing breath formed a cloud around them in the chill air.

"Aye, we both needed that." Pleasantly winded, Duncan stroked the horse's sweat-flecked neck.

A red squirrel dashed across the path, and Ro shied sideways a couple of steps. Not coming close to being unseated, Duncan calmed the nearly shivering horse with his voice before they moved forward again.

The clip-clop of Ro's hoofs on the dirt track added to the surrounding Highland music: water rushing over rocks in the burn alongside, the trickled song of a dipper hunting for insects on the bank, the piercing shriek of a buzzard.

Duncan never took for granted the beauty or the grandeur of the 65,000-acre estate he had inherited. Nor did he think lightly of the responsibility that came with it. Sometimes it was all a bit overwhelming. But after eleven years as laird, he had got the hang of it, though occasionally he wondered if it would come to renting out the Great Hall and Ballroom for weddings to help the place pay for its keep.

His thoughts returned to what he was avoiding: Harriet. There wasn't a thing he could do but continue to wear out his knees in prayer.

Duncan turned Ro down the track that led back to the stable and forced himself to think about the afternoon ahead. Back to work. He could forget his cares in his botany laboratory. Better to contemplate yams—coming up with a more drought and disease resistant strain. And he made a mental note to check on preparations for the interns next term; the greenhouses would be ready for replanting by then.

Ro's horseshoes clattered over the cobblestones in the stableyard, breaking Duncan's reverie. Duncan reined up when he saw John Keith leaning against the old Land Rover, a foot propped against the door behind him. John looked none too pleased, slapping his dusty cap against his leg. These were difficult times at Craggan Mhor. Duncan had tried to caution William that his scheme for the inheritance of Craggan Mhor might go wrong, but William had been adamant. Craggan Mhor was to go to his niece, Margaret MacLeish's daughter, an American—leaving John to manage the estate—and Margaret's daughter. Duncan feared the daughter might prove to be as much trouble as the mother.

Chapter 3

Sylvie Blair clutched her thick cardigan closer, wishing she'd grabbed her windproof macintosh for the walk from Craggan Mhor to home. She hurried along in her trainers, stepping across the wee wooden bridge over the burn running with snowmelt from up the mountain. Snow-sugared mountaintops to the east of Fionnloch foretold an early winter. The sea pounded cold to her left, and Sylvie shivered, a rare thing for a Scotswoman. A strand of hair blew loose from her French twist and swept across her face. She'd forgotten her hat too.

"Andy, ye wee beastie, now don't be gettin' away." A little white rump, not far above the ground, bounced along the footpath ahead of Sylvie—the short, stout tail a metronome for his pace. The dog turned his head to the sound of his mistress's voice, then set his black nose back to the trail of something that apparently had veered down to the beach.

"Andy! Come back here. Right now." Andy launched off a rock, all fours in the air for a moment like a bounding lamb, and pelted off.

"Treaties!" That got Andy's attention and, finally, his obedience. He scuttled back to Sylvie, plopped himself at her feet, and looked up expectantly.

"You are a naughty boy," Sylvie said, reaching a treat down to the wagging Westie. "You stay with me." She poked her index finger in his direction, giving him a stern look. And he did for the remainder of the walk to Sylvie's cottage, the first cottage in a connected row of five at the south edge of the village, just up the hill from the sea. The cottage held its back to the sea, protecting the front garden from winter hoolies that blew in off the Minch.

Sylvie unlatched the rusted iron front gate. She noticed the sorry-looking flowerbeds she hadn't got to yet. It had all been a bit much lately, William dying and all. She felt tears rising in her throat but tamped them down; she didn't want to worry her mother-in-law. The yellow-painted door of the stone cottage creaked on its hinges as she twisted the iron latch ring and pushed it open.

"Come, Andy." Sylvie patted her leg. Andy left the hole he'd stuck his nose in behind the hydrangea bush and rushed in past her.

"Hello, Mum, it's me. Just popped home to make your tea."

"Oh, hullo, dearie." Nan leaned on her walking stick, turned, and stumped to the kitchen.

Wisps of hair escaped the little bun at the nape of Nan's neck and framed her face in a white mist. She probably didn't notice, not seeing well. She kept putting off having her cataracts seen to.

"Ye needn't bother, ye ken. I can manage," Nan said.

"I know, but I like fixin' your tea. And it's good to get away from the house now and again."

"Aye. How is't up to the hoose these days?"

"Empty, Mum, very empty."

"Aye." Nan took Sylvie's hand and patted it gently. "But China will be here soon. She should be a great comfort to us all."

"Mum, I'm that worried about China. What if she doesn't come? What if she's angry? William did leave her in a bit of a tangle an' all with the will."

"Dinna fash yourself, dearie. The Lord has it in hand." Nan winked a cloudy eye. "I canna believe I'll feast me eyes on the wee lassie again. 'Tis an answer to prayer to be sure."

"Aye." Sylvie smiled. "Here, Mum, sit ye down while I put the kettle on." Sylvie wrapped a shawl round her mother-in-law's shoulders and gave her a squeeze.

"Andy, go to bed." Sylvie pointed, and Andy hopped into his wicker basket and out of the way. "Did Murdo come by?"

"Aye, I put the milk in the fridge. And there's one o' cream."

Sylvie took the gold foil top off the cream bottle and decanted the thickest cream at the top into the small flowered pitcher.

"Murdo said as his mother's doin' poorly. I'll pop round an' see her tomorrow." Nan's hands fluttered lightly in her lap, seeming to want her knitting.

"Would you like me to go with you?"

"Nay, I can manage. I'm no blind yet. As if I dinna ken this village like the back o' me hand after these eighty years."

Sylvie poured the tea and slid the sugar bowl toward her mother-in-law. Nan picked one lump with the sugar tongs and dropped it in her tea with somewhat uncertain aim.

"Tae the Father who sought me," Nan said. She dropped a second lump. "Tae the Son who bought me." A third. "Tae the Holy Spirit as taught me." And she stirred in the blessing.

"Mum, do you think you should finally have your cataracts seen to?"

"Maybe. I've been prayin' on it." Nan set her spoon on the saucer, and a furrow grew between her eyes. "Jimmy came by earlier. Said to tell ye as he saw your brither in the village. Down the pub Gordy was."

"Och no, not again. Haven't we got enough?"

Sylvie hurried through her tea to get back to Craggan Mhor. She'd yet to put out a cold supper for Angus and finish up the grocery order. She didn't like to leave Nan to deal with Gordy when he turned up.

THUDS against the cottage door announced Gordy's arrival, and Sylvie lifted the latch. "Come in with you, Gordy. Dinna be standin' out there all night. You'll catch your death. Ye great numpty." Blootered again he was.

Gordy slumped against the doorframe, his blue eyes bleary with drink, and his nearly black hair looking a fright. He draped his arms over Sylvie's shoulders, as if to hug her, but couldn't quite manage the clinch.

"How's mah big sister been? I havna seen ye in a long, long...long time. Where *have* ye been?"

Sylvie averted her nose from the blast of beer-breath. "Sit ye down, and I'll get some tea." She shook her head at Nan, puffed out a breath, and said in a low voice, "Och, the sloppy drunk or the monster drunk. From the looks of him, someone down the pub tangled with the monster."

Nan smoothed Gordy's hair back from his eyes and crooned a prayer over him. "God o' Light, God o' Love, God our Provider, be wi' your son Gordy tonight an' always."

Gordy's head lolled back, and he managed a wet, crooked smile. Nan patted his cheek, the side not bruised, and said, "Where've ye been, eh? Missed my favorite Gordy." She gently ran her finger over the bruise, feeling for deeper damage. "Och, fistycuffs again. I'll warrant t'other chappie came oot the worst."

Sylvie wrapped Gordy's hands round a mug of tea. He drained it, like one more pint.

"Now come along and sleep this one off." Sylvie urged him up and guided him to the sofa where he'd spent many a night. "You'll be goin' back to Glasgow in the morning."

Settling a knitted throw over her brother, Sylvie fretted. Gordy must not be here when China arrived.

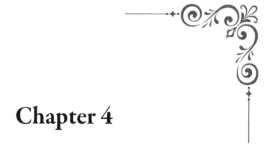

Chapter 4

China stepped out of the van, glad to have survived the careen over the Highland roads. So this was Craggan Mhor. She fisted the hand not gripping the handle of her rolling carry-on. Her spiked heels teetered on the packed gravel of the drive.

The stop at the solicitors' in Edinburgh still rankled. Mr. Anderson had told her she was stuck with this place. Not only stuck…She couldn't stand to think about it.

The driver dropped China's suitcase on the steps of Craggan Mhor, tipped his cap to her, and hastened away. She didn't move. The wind blew her hair across her face, and she spat away the ends that snagged in her lipstick. The house looked no better up close than it did in pictures.

A black and white collie-type dog rounded the house and charged China. She drew up her hands.

"Fly, come away wi' ye." A bandy-legged old man in a tweed jacket and filthy cap came around the corner of the house from the back. "Nae need tae be afeart o' her. Can't ye see she's waggin' her tail?" An impatient jab of his hand in the dog's direction indicated he thought China was some kind of dimwit for not seeing the dog's tail wagging.

"I'm not stupid. I can see that." She lowered her hands, and the dog thrust its nose at China's hand. China flicked her wrist, dismissing the dog.

"Who are you?" she said to the old man.

He eyed her. "Who's askin'?"

"China MacLeish, the new owner of Craggan Mhor." Maybe, she thought.

"Angus Ritchie, at your service." He spat to one side and left, back the way he'd come, his dog trotting after him.

China threw a cold scowl at his back. If he was an employee, he'd be the first to go.

She glared at the gray and red granite house, shaded black with age. An estate in Scotland with more acres than she'd ever heard of in one parcel—26,000. And she didn't want it.

November in the Middle-of-Nowhere, Scotland. There wasn't even an easy way to get here. From Edinburgh she'd had to take a train to Inverness, then a nightmare of a drive with a maniac van driver who had no respect for the center line, when there was one.

She turned away in disgust—and dropped her carry-on. She swept the hair out of her eyes so she could get a better look. The sea. Craggan Mhor was on a bay of the sea. She hadn't expected the house to be right on the water's edge. The sea undulated back and forth, rocking patches of seaweed up and down. China took a few steps on the lawn toward the sea and turned to look back at the house. And then she saw the rest of the house. What she thought was a large house was only the side of the house. The long, *very* large house faced the sea, with the main entrance on the side.

A woman came out the front door, leaving it standing open. She appeared to be in her 60s: sturdy shoes, a sturdy skirt, sturdy cardigan, but uncommonly dark hair for her age. The old man followed behind her, grabbed China's suitcase, and hauled it inside.

"Och, my dear, I'm so sorry I wasn't here to greet you. You must be China." The woman rushed up to China and reached a hand, as if to stroke her arm, but then withdrew it. "Silly me. I'm Sylvia Blair, but do call me Sylvie. Everyone does." The woman thrust her hand forward to shake China's.

China took her hand and gave it a quick shake. "Yes, you must be Mrs. Blair. Mr. Anderson told me you were the housekeeper here."

"Well, yes, housekeeper, cook, general dogsbody." The woman stood blinking and grinning at China. After a moment she bent to retrieve China's carry-on. "Do come in. We're that excited to have you here."

China followed, pulling her heels out of the grass with each step till she reached the gravel drive.

Next to the potted geraniums, two stone lions sitting on their haunches flanked the stone archway around the front door. Carved Celtic knotwork decorated the stone. China walked in, and the housekeeper closed the oak door behind her.

A long tartan-carpeted corridor stretched before her, and a grand oak staircase curved down to the entry hall, the worn carpet continuing up the stairs. Glinting claymores, daggers, and old brass-studded leather shields hung high on the walls, making quite a display of antique armaments.

"You must be tired, dear. Let me show you to your room. I hope you don't mind, but I've put you in your Uncle William's room. It's the finest."

Up the stairs and into another hall carpeted tartan, a door opened onto a cavern of masculinity. Dark green everywhere, accented with dark brown and occasional peeks of dark gold. A walnut four-poster bed dominated the room, and a massive armoire took up much of one wall. It was awful.

"I'll show you round the house after teatime. Would you like to take tea in your room?"

"What? Oh. Yes, please."

"Right."

"Mrs. Blair, what time would teatime be?"

"Och, now's as good a time as any. It's nearly four o'clock. I'll just go and put the kettle on." She turned to go, then stopped. "It's so good to see you...Miss MacLeish."

SYLVIE daubed at a tear with a corner of her apron, lifted the kettle off the Aga burner, and poured the hot water into the teapot. She popped the cozy on the pot and returned the kettle to the burner. Andy leaped out of his basket and ran to the back door. A scratch at the door on the outside, and Fly wriggled through the opening door faster than Angus could get it fully open.

"You mind your muddy boots, Angus Ritchie. I've told you a thousand times."

Angus took off his wellies and set them beside the door, coming back in his stockinged feet, one toe sticking out a hole.

"Ye'd think you're the ruddy queen of Craggan Mhor." Angus gave her a wink. "And so ye are. It certainly willna be Miss High-an'-Mighty."

"You mind your tongue. She'll hear you."

"And what are ye doing with holes in your socks. Leave them with me tonight, and I'll give 'em a wash and a mend." Sylvie slipped her pinny apron off over her head and hung it on a peg. "You could do with a good woman, ye ken."

"Aye, there were a time I coulda. But ye'll do." With a grin, Angus tossed his cap on a chair at the small table and sat in the other. He raked his hand through his wispy hair, which didn't straighten it any. "An' where's that tea, then?"

"Just you hold your horses. I'm taking tea up to China, then I'll be back." Sylvie set two fresh scones on a flowered plate and lifted the tray which held a porcelain teapot and cup and saucer, cream and sugar on the side, and butter and jam in pots. "Help yourself to a scone. I know ye will anyway. In the warming oven." And with a sideways glance at Angus, she carried the tea tray up the back stairs.

She tapped on China's door with the side of her foot.

"Come in." China sat on a chair by the window facing the sea, her still-packed suitcase open on the bed.

"I've brought your tea, Miss MacLeish." Sylvie set the tray on the small table.

"Thank you." China got up and looked at the tea tray. "Have you got any lemon?"

"Lemon?"

"Yes, you know, a slice of lemon."

"Nay, I'm that sorry, I dinna believe I do. I can get a lemon in the village tomorrow morn."

"Doesn't matter. I'm not much of a tea drinker anyway."

"Right. Shall I come up at half past four? Then I can show you round the house. I'd say for you to come down to the kitchen, but ye might get lost." Sylvie chuckled at her joke. China returned an anemic smile. "Well, I'll leave you to it." Sylvie could feel herself blush and nearly spun off balance in her haste to leave.

In the kitchen, Sylvie made tea for Angus and herself. "I say, Angus, that one's going to be a tough nut to crack."

Angus had already eaten most of two scones. "If ye ask me, I think Mr. William was off his nut, givin' this place tae someone as knows nothin' about it. She no even heard o' Mr. William MacLeish. Off his nut, I say."

"I don't recall askin' you." Sylvie gave him a thin smile. "Are you sayin' William didn't do right?"

Angus made a gravelly sound at the back of his throat.

"Eh?" Sylvie pressed him.

"Naw. Ye auld besom."

Sylvie humphed and set Angus's mug of tea on the table.

Angus dropped a bit of scone on the floor between the dogs. Andy dove for it, sending the dogs into a kerfuffle and causing Sylvie to step aside or be tripped.

"Eh, ye dafty," said Angus, reaching a piece of scone to Fly. "Ye always get your bit o' somethin'. Here ye go." He held the bit away from Andy and popped it directly into Fly's mouth. He chortled.

"Troublemaker." Sylvie pointed Andy to his bed. "The both of you."

Angus grinned.

"Where's John got to? I expected him in for tea," Sylvie said.

"He's oot the back in the office. Likely gettin' his desk cleared off afore Her Ladyship arrives."

"Now you stop that, Angus. I mean it. It would really hurt her feelings if she heard you."

"An' just what would she do aboot it, eh? Nothin'."

"Never you mind about that. It's no good making bad blood."

"Well, what'd he want to go an' have an American relation for? We dinna need no Yankee here." He gulped the last of his tea.

"Leave it be. You know the story. 'Twas none of his doing. We need to make China welcome."

"Och." Angus flipped his cap on his head, shoved his feet into his boots, and stomped out the door, Fly close on his heels.

With a weary sigh, Sylvie eased herself onto the chair Angus had vacated, paying little attention to the whiff of horse and damp earth Angus left behind. She stole a few minutes of quiet to sip her own tea, but Sylvie felt precious little peace. That kernel of dread lodged under her heart refused to budge. Best to trust the Lord, as Nan said, for Sylvie felt a bit like she'd run up against a stone in the dark.

Her tea finished and the scone crumbs scraped into Andy's bowl, Sylvie made her way up the back stairs and knocked on China's door. "I've come to collect the tea things, Miss MacLeish."

The door opened, and China, wearing tight jeans, an expensive-looking sweater, more sensibly-heeled boots, and a thin frown, stood back to let her in.

"I'll just run these down to the kitchen, then I'll be back to give you the grand tour."

Sylvie noticed the half-cup of cold tea and only one scone nibbled at.

MAYBE a grand tour but certainly not a grand house. It needed a lot of work. China trailed after the housekeeper but no longer paid much attention to the narration. She couldn't wait to unload this place—fully furnished. Let all the overstuffed, just-a-little-dirty furnishings be the new owner's problem. The lawyer must be mistaken; she had to be able to sell. And the idea of having to live here—that couldn't be legal.

"...And this stair leads up the back to the third floor where the servants' rooms were. But now—"

"Mrs. Blair, could we end the tour, please. I'd like to rest."

"Certainly, dear. Only I thought you might like to meet John Keith before he goes home for his supper. But never mind, there's tomorrow."

"Who's John Keith?"

"He's the factor, the estate manager. Knows everything, he does."

"Oh yes, I want to speak to him—and now. Where will I find him?"

"Out the back in the estate office. The stone building with the blue door. I believe he's expecting you."

The office was on one end of a long outbuilding.

China knocked.

A powerfully built man in rough brownish tweeds opened the door, his square head topped with neatly trimmed silver waves. A big man, he filled the doorway.

His weather-ruddied face crinkled into a smile. "Ye must be Miss MacLeish. Welcome." He stuck his bear paw of a hand in her direction. "John Keith."

China put out her hand and he grasped it, so firmly she nearly winced.

"Come in, come in," he said.

The office was a mess. If he expected her, cleaning up hadn't been part of his preparation. And if this was how he took care of the estate, he might be next on the list, right after that old man and his dog.

"Sit you down." John Keith moved a stack of papers and made a place for her on a chair to the side of his desk. He sat at the desk and swiveled to face her.

"Mr. Keith, I'll get right to the point. I don't want this place, and it's my intention to sell it as fast as I can."

He rested his elbows on the arms of his chair, laced his fingers, and drummed his thumbs together, a low humming noise deep in his throat.

"Did you talk to the solicitors, then?"

"I did, and they told me the condition of my uncle's will. But that just can't be legal. No one can make me live here."

"Aye, Mr. William's wish was that you live here."

China glared at him, her chin stuck slightly forward.

"Miss MacLeish, I assure you, Mr. William's will is perfectly legal—every condition of your inheritance. I helped him write it."

"I'll get a lawyer, and I'll fight living here. At the very most I'll come here once a year if I have to. I live in Chicago."

"Beg pardon, but you can't."

"And what do you mean *every* condition of the inheritance? There's only one: I have to live here."

"Did the solicitors not tell you? You must live here for *one year*—one year continuously—before the property actually belongs to you."

Her fair complexion turned five-alarm-red; she could feel it.

"Mr. William provided for a verra generous allowance for you during that year. And as factor of the estate, I'm responsible for the runnin' of the estate and seein' to any bills. So you needn't worry about that."

"I'd be a prisoner? That's crazy. I'll contest it on the grounds that he must not have been in his right mind."

John Keith smiled. "Nay, not so bad as that. Mr. William realized you'd need to live a normal life, so he provided for holiday time to do as you wish." The estate manager picked up a pen and fiddled with it, twirling it in his fingers.

"Did the solicitors not tell ye the other conditions?"

China lifted a wary eyebrow at him and waited.

"You canna make any changes on the estate till after ye take ownership. Not in the house, the workings of the estate, not the staff. No changes at all."

"What?" The word burst out in a rush of hot breath. "Why didn't they tell me all this? I'd have gone right to the lawyers next door."

"Maybe they didn't want to see you spittin' snakes."

"And I want that rude old man fired. He's the one 'spittin' snakes', as you so colloquially say."

John Keith sat back.

"Miss MacLeish, this has got to be quite a shock for you. I had no idea ye didn't know the particulars before you arrived. Mr. William drew up his will out of his love for ye."

"Love?" China stood so abruptly the backs of her legs hit the chair seat, almost toppling it. "We are done here." She slammed the door on her way out.

ONE faint bar of cell phone reception. Not enough to call Stacy.

"Mrs. Blair, is there *anywhere* in this place I can get cell phone reception?" China stood in the kitchen, one hand on her hip, the other clutching her useless cell phone, and faced Sylvia Blair who was mashing something orange in a bowl.

"Why, yes, there are several extensions. Would you like me to show you to Mr. William's study?"

A landline. Of course. "No, thank you. I think I can find it. Off the foyer in the turret, isn't it?" She'd almost forgotten what a regular phone looked like.

"I'm afraid mobile reception is a bit chancy out here. There's no problem in the village though."

"Great," China muttered, not quite under her breath.

China sat at the battered antique mahogany desk in her uncle's study. The desk chair squeaked as she swiveled to look out the window in the turret. Nothing but dark glass. Faded hunter green velvet drapes framed what in the daylight must be a view of the sea. A leather Chesterfield love seat provided a place in the alcove where Uncle William would have watched the sea changing moods. Two tartan-covered wing chairs faced the fireplace, and a hint of sweet smoke clung to the room.

This was her uncle's study, and there was evidence of him everywhere—of the family she never knew existed. If she thought about it, she'd explode.

She picked up the phone receiver and dialed Stacy's number, but the call wouldn't go through. Everything was so difficult.

Back to the kitchen she marched to find Mrs. Blair again.

"Do you have a phone book?" She could feel the muscles of her face tightening.

"Top right drawer of the desk, dear."

Dear? She'd deal later with how familiar Mrs. Blair was with her. Dialing all the codes, she finally got the call through to Stacy.

"Stac, I think I'm going to lose my mind. You wouldn't believe all the constraints dear Uncle William put in his will. Apparently he loved me so much he thought he'd make my life miserable."

"Try me."

China spat out all the restrictions.

"You're kidding? Can he do that?"

"Apparently. At least according to the estate manager who colluded with him. My first call tomorrow is to those weasel lawyers who sent me out of the office not knowing the full story. To come here and make a fool of myself."

"Well, what if it's true and all the conditions are legal? What will you do?"

"Do? Well—explode. That's what I'll do."

"I think you'd better think about that. Exploding sounds messy."

"Stacy, you're my best friend. Help me out here."

"I am. This may be legit. And if it is, you need a plan."

"I'll sue them."

"Really? That takes a lot of time and money. Do you think they'd draw up an unenforceable will?"

China bit her lip. What a horrible thought. "That never occurred to me." China stared at the cold fireplace.

"But these people here—they're so rude. And they all knew my uncle—and I didn't."

"This is going to sound trite, but you could get to know them."

"This is the place my mother grew up, for heaven's sake. It's like there are ghosts everywhere, and if they're like my mother, they're not friendly."

"All I'm saying is, give this some thought. It may be workable. A year isn't that long, and you've got a lot of money at stake here. Look, I've gotta run. I'm at work."

"Oh, sorry, I forgot there's six hours difference."

"Cheerio."

"Brat. Love you, Stac. Seriously."

China stared out the window into darkness. The sea was the only thing she wanted to look at. She pushed back and strode out to the foyer, grabbed a coat off the hall tree. Six o'clock, and it was blue-dark night. Light from the house windows lit her way across the lawn as she walked to the water's edge.

She pulled the green oilcloth coat tight around herself. The half-cape over the shoulders flapped in the sharp breeze blowing off the sea. Her hair flew in tangles.

A jetty extended out and curved sideways into the sea forming a small breakwater. Waves lightly slapped against the stone. Farther out, beyond the sheltered bay, China could see breakers rolling, the crests tipped with faint light. She stepped gingerly along the jetty, not wanting to misplace a foot and end up soaking wet. She sat on an iron bollard, arms wrapped around herself to keep in her heat. It was bone-numbing cold—the kind of cold that goes through a body and out the other side.

What was she going to do?

Freeze to death anyway, that was one certainty. How could anything good come of anything connected with her mother? But maybe she was no better than her mother. She'd been rude, had wanted to laugh in John Keith's face when he said her uncle loved her. Still, Stacy had a point. It's a lot of money. A lot of money.

What would Jane Eyre do? A bittersweet snort escaped, and China smiled on one side of her mouth. That had become her watchword all those lonely nights at boarding school—when Mrs. Fisher had gone home, her teacher and friend—and there was no mother.

Jane would most certainly be civil, but she would not be pushed around. China still missed Mrs. Fisher, missed the faithful letters all those years.

"Miss MacLeish?"

China jerked and almost slipped off the bollard.

"Sorry, I didn't mean to startle you. It's only, I wanted to let you know your supper will be ready in a quarter of an hour or so." Mrs. Blair stood several feet from China, clutching her cardigan closed against the wind.

"Thank you. I'll be in shortly." China gathered her hair into one hand and held it back, clearing her vision. Something about this Sylvia Blair looked familiar. But that couldn't be.

"Oh, Mrs. Blair,…where do I go?"

"To the main dining room, dear. I've got it laid out all nice for your first dinner here."

First of not many, China thought.

THE meaty aroma reached all the way to the front door. China could have followed her nose and found the dining room, just off the kitchen.

The large dining room had several unused tables against one wall and a picture window overlooking the sea. Lights of the village glittered in the distance. A table for four directly in front of the window was dressed in starched white linen and set with fine sterling and crystal—a place setting for one. China seated herself, and Mrs. Blair appeared with a plate of steaming food.

"I've made a nice roast and neeps and tatties for you. I didn't think you'd be ready for haggis just yet." She winked.

The orange mash smelled familiar. "What are neeps?" China asked.

"I believe you Americans call them rutabagas."

Mrs. Blair crossed to the sideboard to fetch a bottle of wine and poured for China to taste.

China swirled the wine in her glass and took a sip. "Yes, thank you. That's very good."

After filling the glass, Mrs. Blair turned to go, then turned back. "Miss MacLeish, would you like me to join you? I didn't want to presume, so I laid the table for yourself. Only I hate to see ye eat alone."

"No, that's fine. I'm okay."

"Well, then. I'll be in the kitchen if ye need me."

China chewed her roast beef, dry to the taste, though it was drowning au jus and so tender she could cut it with a fork. Eating alone was no good. She'd take Mrs. Blair up on her offer.

When China walked into the kitchen, Mrs. Blair and Angus Ritchie looked up from their supper at the little table by the window. The collie darted to China's side.

"Fly, come away wi' ye." The old man poked a finger to the floor beside him.

She hadn't counted on *that man* being here. She couldn't very well expect him to remain sitting by himself. "Mrs. Blair, I changed my mind. Would you still like to join me?...And, Mr. Ritchie, I suppose you might join us too."

"Naw, I'll bide here wi' the dogs," he said.

Good, thought China.

"If you don't mind, I'd like that." Mrs. Blair picked up her plate and glass of milk and followed China. "You lot behave yourselves," she said in the direction of Angus Ritchie and the dogs.

China and Mrs. Blair chatted as they ate.

"How long have you worked here, Mrs. Blair?"

"Och, I started as a wee thing. Just a girl. Maybe eleven or twelve years old. Cleaning after school. Then at sixteen I came to work full-time. Mostly in the kitchen."

"And now you're the housekeeper?"

"Aye, if it's to do with the house, I look after it. But I've got young girls to help with the cleaning. I enjoy the cooking, so I still do most of that. There's nothin' better for showing God's love than putting food in front of a person. Och, but I've said too much." Mrs. Blair seemed nervous, dabbed her napkin at her mouth.

"But who do you cook for now? You said Mr. Keith goes home for his dinner."

Sylvie sighed. "It's Angus and me now and whoever else I can offer a meal to. But then, it's right busy during the season."

"You knew my uncle well?"

Mrs. Blair snatched in a small breath. "Aye, that I did."

"What was he like?"

Mrs. Blair took quite a deep breath. "I believe you're askin', would you have liked him? And aye, you'd have liked him very much. He was a lovely man." She folded her napkin. "And now, if you don't mind, I'll tell you more about Mr. William another time. I need to see to the washing up and get home to Mum."

"Sure."

"Excuse me, then. And thank you for asking me to sup with you. I enjoyed it."

China smiled and nodded. Me too, she thought.

THIS time she was prepared for the cold, wrapped in a wool tartan blanket she'd found at the foot of her bed, and she had a flashlight. If she was going to be alone, she might as well be truly alone on the end of a pier in the Middle-of-Nowhere, Scotland—and have a good pout. She sat on the stone, her back against the bollard. The lights of Fionnloch defined the shoreline off to the right. A dark line of trees formed the left boundary of the bay—and then the sea, black and shushing her with the soft sound of waves receding over stones.

"Now, Jane, you must know I'm none too happy about this state of affairs," China whispered to no one. No one but Jane Eyre, her kindred soul. China smiled. This had started around age eleven when Mrs. Fisher had introduced her to Jane. The conversations with Jane used to go on just long enough till China was reduced to giggles and just got on with whatever was going on—usually something to do with her mother. China stared out to sea, out to nothing, deliberately trying to forget the hulking house behind her.

China sat up straighter and peered at the sky. A shimmering luminescence appeared and brightened as she watched.

"Oh my gosh," she said out loud.

The night sky intensified into neon green, streaking down in sheets that undulated in a cosmic breeze. The light danced and ducked, hanging over the edge of the village and out to sea. An enormous comma formed at the bottom edge of the sheet. Then folded back on itself. Then stretched out in a long curve and shot splinters of light up to the heavens.

On and on, the light dancers swept through the sky. China's teeth ached from being clamped against the cold. She might never see this again and hated to go in. Finally, she could stand it no longer. She had to get warm.

Her hand on the great oak front door, she looked a last time at the show. She'd at least remember this night.

Closing the door seemed to echo much louder than it should have. Was there no one in the house? She walked down the central hall to the kitchen. Maybe Mrs. Blair was still here.

"Oh, I didn't know you were here." China addressed Mr. Ritchie who was slurping tea perched on a stool like a wizened crow. Fly jumped up and wagged to China, poked her wet nose against China's hand.

"Aye, I'm just leavin.'" He scowled, making no eye contact. "I stay oot the back, next to John's office. Keep an eye on the place an' such."

"Oh." China didn't know whether this was supposed to be a conversation or a trap.

"I dinna want ye to think you're all alone here. Nae need tae be afeart. Sylvie bade me tell ye."

"Well, thanks for letting me know." Maybe he wasn't so bad after all.

"No like I care a bittie bit if the faeries carried ye off." He flipped his cap on his head and started for the door, leaving his mug on the butcher block. "Come, Fly." He opened the door, and the dog darted into the night.

China jammed her hands on her hips. The old…

"An' the kettle's hot. Make yourself some tea," he said, his back to her. He whisked a cookie tin off the table and walked out without shutting the door.

She'd definitely find a way to get rid of that insufferable little gnome. She shut the door firmly and looked for a key to lock it, but there was no key, no bolt.

She didn't really like tea, but she was chilled way past the bone. And annoyed. Teapot, tin labeled *tea*, silver strainer. She should be able to figure this out.

She carried a mug of tea to the lounge, at least that's what Mrs. Blair had called it. Living room, whatever.

She opened the door and was enveloped by warmth and a sweet smell. A fire glowed in the hearth. Bricks of something—peat, she guessed. To the side of the fire there was a copper bucket filled with the bricks, and China lifted another peat brick with the tongs and laid it on the fire. The fragrant smoke ran up the flue. Thank you, Mrs. Blair.

China curled up in the soft-cushioned kilim-print sofa facing the fire, covered her legs with the plaid throw, and pulled another throw off the back of the couch for her shoulders. She reached for her tea on the coffee table and wrapped her fingers around the warmth of the mug.

On the table was a book bound in brown leather with gold lettering: *The History of Fionnloch*. China groaned. Were they all doing this on purpose? Making a pitch to her? She bet Mrs. Blair had flipped the switch on the Northern Lights on her way out the door.

Sipping tea, reading a book in front of a peat fire. Not too bad. But she was leaving by the end of the week.

At midnight she closed the book, having read it cover to cover. She left the lights on in the lounge and went up to bed, leaving hall lights on in her wake.

She tried not to think about sleeping in a dead uncle's bed.

Turning back the down comforter, she noticed the sheets: fine cotton in a bright floral pattern, mostly blues and yellows, ironed crisp. These were surely not Uncle William's sheets. More of Mrs. Blair, no doubt. That was nice of her. But China wasn't buying it.

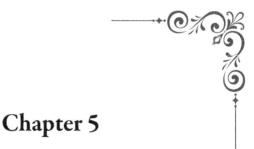

Chapter 5

Duncan turned the Land Rover onto Colinton Road and headed in the direction of the M8 bypass around Edinburgh, Merchiston Castle School receding behind them.

"But, Dad, why?"

Duncan answered the question for the third time. "Ross, I told you, I think you should see your mother."

Callum plugged earbuds into his phone. "Not like she wants to see us. If she did, don't you think she would have?"

"Don't be unkind. She's still your mother. It's just for the weekend." Duncan wasn't about to let Harriet sail in and not see the children. Not that he blamed the boys for preferring to play rugby with their mates than see their mother. He himself would rather be doing just about anything than see Harriet. Her Ladyship was due to arrive by lunch tomorrow.

Yesterday he had met with his solicitors in Edinburgh. The divorce was proceeding and, with luck, would be final by the end of the year. But now Harriet was coming to Glengorm. For what? One last farewell? He hadn't told the boys about the divorce yet. Let them have a weekend together anyway. Hopefully she could be decent to them—loving was too much to hope for. In his last email to Harriet, he'd threatened to reconsider his financial agreement if she said anything to the boys about the divorce. She'd agreed. He'd have to take her at her word—but snakes bite.

He was heartbroken for the boys.

"Dad, are you and Mum getting a divorce?"

Duncan shot a glance at Ross in the rearview mirror. His youngest son was the image of his mother: blond when the sun bleached his hair and the same finely chiseled mouth and nose, both in perfect proportion.

An answer stuck in Duncan's throat, and he watched in the mirror as Ross wiped a tear—helpless. His son was only ten.

"It's okay, Dad. We can talk later," Ross said.

Callum didn't say a word, trying to act like a fourteen-year-old man. He kept his eyes on the traffic ahead.

The four-and-a-half-hour drive to Fionnloch seemed an eternity with two unhappy boys, but it couldn't be helped. Duncan did the best he could: a stop for lunch in Aviemore, but mostly, he let the boys be, allowing them more earbud time than usual.

He couldn't shake thoughts of what in the world he was going to do now. The divorce would legally take care of itself; the settlement would be largely cash, in addition to giving Harriet the London flat. Fortunately, his inheritance of Glengorm House and a wise prenuptial agreement locked up the estate and the furnishings. One doesn't go breaking up the family estate just because a marriage ends.

He had feared it would come to this when she met that South African, the two of them locked in a primal mating dance that had an inevitable conclusion. No entreaty or threat Duncan tried made any difference. At least the other time Harriet had strayed, that he knew of, she'd eventually come to her senses, and they were able to carry on as if nothing had happened. But it had. And though he loved her, he'd formed an armor of pride around himself. How could a man not? He'd never trusted her again. And when she spent weeks on end in London, he stopped asking what was going on. The trip to South Africa had been an attempt to spend time together. Fine job that turned out to be.

He just wished this were over. His heart ached. When Callum was born, he had determined he was going to be a good father, which did not include divorce. But was divorce any worse than an unloving mother? Harriet was a Venus flytrap: giving off a sweet odor, luring victims into her deadly maw.

Duncan tapped Callum's leg. "If I can hear it, it's too loud."

Callum didn't miss a head-bobbing beat and turned the music down.

Duncan followed the A832, through Kinlochewe and onwards. Brown remnants of the heather bloom covered the hillsides. Off to the south, the grandeur of snow-topped Beinn Eighe made him wistful for a serious, muscle-taxing trek. Ross was still too young to tackle the mountain, but maybe he and the boys could do some hillwalking below the snow line. Passing along this mountain corridor always made him want to stop the car and strike out into the hills. Another day.

At last they turned into the drive to Glengorm House. Duncan's heart swelled. This place was so dear to him. And all the dearer because he knew Callum and Ross loved it as well. The mile-long lane wound through Scots pines and crossed the River Slee before opening to the grand entrance to the house.

Harriet's Jaguar was parked in front.

She came out the front door in jodhpurs and riding boots and waved to the boys. "Hello, darlings."

Duncan leapt from the car to face her. "You weren't due till tomorrow."

"Don't be owly, Duncan. What does it matter?"

The boys greeted their mother with polite hellos, which Harriet returned with a stiff hug and air kisses.

"I was just going for a ride. I'll see you for tea. Lovely to see you, children." And she got in the car and drove to the stable farther down the lane.

Callum turned to his father and made a gesture with his hands outstretched, palms up, and shook his head. "Brilliant," he said, hanging every bit of sarcasm on the word he could muster. "Just brilliant." He flung his satchel over his shoulder and stalked into the house.

Duncan put his arm round Ross's shoulder. Ross threw his arms round Duncan's waist and buried his face in his father's jacket front.

HARRIET peered over the rim of her whisky glass. "I'm not a monster, you know."

She put on that feigned demure look that revolted Duncan. They faced each other in front of the fireplace in the Drawing Room, separated by much more than the massive coffee table between the sofas. Duncan set his jaw. What she was asking was outrageous.

"I just thought it would be a way to see the children. And keep up appearances," Harriet said.

"Divorce. But you can stay here when you bloody well like?"

Motherly love? Surely not. He didn't trust her one whit. She'd never shown the boys much affection.

"Harriet, what are you playing at?" He feared he might crush the crystal glass in his hand and set it on the table.

"Nothing, darling. I just want to come home for a visit. Now and then."

"This isn't your home anymore. You've made that abundantly clear."

"But it is. And I want a few of the things from here."

She held his gaze in her inimitable way: part sweetness, part insolence. This really was too much. There wasn't a thing but her remaining clothes that he'd let her walk out with.

"Absolutely not. Our prenuptial agreement was quite clear that this estate remains entirely intact in the event of our divorce."

"But I thought you might let me have a painting or two in lieu of some cash. The little Stubbs in the dining room would be lovely. And maybe the Raeburn on the stairs."

"You must be mad."

"Not yet, but I can surely get there."

"Don't threaten me, Harriet."

"Why not? It's always worked before." Her smile dripped vinegar.

"Divorce means done. I'm enforcing the entire agreement."

"Speaking of enforcing, darling, I intend to enforce my right to keep my title."

"You can't. Not if you're Harriet Hetherington-Wells again."

"Well, that's the point, isn't it? I intend to keep your surname. That way I'm still Lady Sinclair, even if you remarry. But the thought of you remarrying. Honestly, darling. You're far too Christian for that."

"Stop calling me darling. That endearing term hasn't meant a thing from your lips since...well, not in a long time." It took all he had to remain seated. He was not going to let her best him. Trapped—that's what he was. It was true, there wasn't a thing he could do about her title. How he wished he'd married a Sassenach with not only her own money but her own title.

"And I think the children's mother should have their surname. Don't you, darling?"

Duncan nearly came up off the sofa. "I will not allow you to use the children in your games," Duncan said, though it ground his molars to get the words out.

"It's the only way I can get what I want." She coyly slid a finger around her ear, pushing her hair behind.

Fists clenched in his lap, he wished her at the bottom of Fionnloch Bay, God forgive him. How could he have been so blind? When they met, she was exhilarating and had seemingly been besotted by him as well. Their marriage was bliss—until Callum was born—then the layers fell away revealing the real Harriet. Ross had been a mistake, according to her. But his boys were the light of Duncan's life. He'd die for them. And here he was, about to die a little.

"I'll allow you to come here and see the boys. As long as it isn't disruptive to them." Or to me, he thought.

"Well, that's a start. Then maybe we'll see about the paintings," Harried said.

He scowled at her.

Undeterred, she persisted. "If not the paintings...you won't sell Blue Duchess, will you?"

She actually had a look that could be interpreted as genuine concern. It must have slipped past her awareness. That was it—her horse—the blue roan mare. Harriet's prized jumper. He'd let her wait for his reply. He picked up his glass and sipped the whisky with a leisurely air he did not feel.

"Well?" she prodded.

Playing her game rankled like a swarm of bloodsucking midges. "Take her with you, if you like." One less reminder of you, Duncan thought.

Harriet's shoulders actually sagged in apparent relief. He wished he'd see the same emotions for their children.

"The thing is, I can't take her to South Africa. And I'm not in London enough to board her there. She'd be best looked after here. She adores Donnie. Do you mind awfully?"

Mind? Since when did she care what he minded? But really, the horse was the least of his problems with Harriet.

"I mind a great deal. I mind that you've been unfaithful as a cat in season. I mind that you don't seem to give a fig for your own children. I mind that you never tried to make a go of our marriage. Yes, I mind." He let that settle with her. Let her worry for her horse.

Then, when he hoped she'd squirmed a bit, he delivered his decision. "Duchess can stay. For now." A tear slid out the side of one eye; he ignored it. "It is best for the horse." He was angry to the point of barely able to contain himself.

"Thank you, darling."

He set the glass on the table dangerously hard and stood. "And now, if you'll excuse me, I've had all of this I can take.

"And, Harriet, I hope you'll spend some time with the boys this weekend. They're here to see you, even if you're really here to see your horse."

He turned away—but then turned back. "Please."

"We can talk about it at breakfast. Maybe the children would like to go for a ride."

Chapter 6

What was that awful screeching? Bagpipes! China launched herself out of bed and fumbled with the brass finger-rings on the window, finally tugging it open. Icy drizzle sprayed her face. Leaning out, she yelled in the direction of the front lawn "Stop that! Now!"

Angus Ritchie marched around in a circle below her window, cheeks puffed out, squeezing on that infernal bag.

"Mr. Ritchie, *please* stop that noise! Are you nuts? It's six a.m.!" She imagined her fingers clasped tight around Angus Ritchie's chicken-bone neck.

The man revved the pipes even louder.

She hated this place. She hated her uncle. And she hated bagpipes.

"Stop!" China covered her ears.

He whipped the mouthpiece aside and shouted back at her, "Mr. William said as I'm tae play the pipes at six a.m. sharp every morn o' life, come hell or high water. Or come some glaikit Yank." He spat and resumed the screeching.

"I don't know what you just called me, but we have not had the last of this discussion."

Red-faced and blinking in the mist, Angus Ritchie yelled up at her. "Stupid. That's what I called ye. A stupid Yank."

China whirled from the window. She would not take this from Angus Ritchie. And today was the last day she intended to be jolted awake by something that could hardly be called music, more like the yowling of six cats with their tails tied together. She didn't care if the sainted William MacLeish ordained the pipes to be played every single morning of life. Reasoning with Mr. Ritchie had failed—treachery might be necessary. After all, *she* was the owner of Craggan Mhor now, like it or not. And she did not.

ONE night in this granite dungeon felt like a month. China hadn't unpacked much more than her toiletries and a couple sweaters and a pair of jeans, hoping she could get on a plane back to Chicago and forget about Scotland. Soon.

Still cold in the thickest sweater she had, China stood in the hallway and counted the doors from the top of the stairs. Last night she'd opened three doors before finding this bedroom. Then she noticed that each door had a brass plaque on it with the name of a bird; her room was "Sea Eagle." She made her way to the kitchen—so far away, she couldn't smell coffee till she got closer.

"Good mornin', dearie." Mrs. Blair handed China a mug of deep black coffee. "I heard you comin' down. Did you sleep well?"

A white terrier looked up from a basket at the side of the enormous old stove and put his head back down.

"I wouldn't know. If I did, it was wiped out by those *horrible* bagpipes. Really. How can anyone stand it?"

"Och, doesn't Angus love to play those pipes though."

"He may love it, but I'm going to wring his neck or slit a hole in the bag."

"Milk?"

"What?"

Mrs. Blair nodded toward the mug clutched in China's hands.

"Oh, no thanks. Black for me."

China sat at the small table, hunched over her steaming mug.

"Here, dear, sit in this chair by the Aga. Warm you up in no time it will."

China cast a questioning glance at the housekeeper but did as she suggested. China held out a hand to see just where the stove was hot, but the heat seemed to be radiating all over.

"Aye. Take your slippers off and warm your toes on the tile."

She slipped off her felt slippers. The heat of the floor tiles by the stove warmed her feet but did nothing to thaw her anger at Angus Ritchie.

Mrs. Blair lifted a huge burner cover on the Aga and commenced cooking China's breakfast.

"Pork patties or black pudding this morning?"

"Black pudding?" China asked.

"Blood sausage."

The mouthful of coffee almost dribbled down the front of China's sweater as she composed herself.

"Just eggs and toast, thank you."

Mrs. Blair flapped her apron at the dog who had roused himself to beg. "Out. Away with you, Andy." She sent the dog outside. The drizzle had stopped, but low hanging clouds remained.

Settled on a stool drawn up to the butcher block table in the center of the kitchen, her back to the warm Aga, China sopped up egg yolk with her toast.

"It might be a lovely day to meet the laird, don't ye think?"

"No, I don't think so. I've got some reading I'd like to do." Or twiddling my thumbs by the fire. Anything but meet the locals. It doesn't matter—because I'm leaving, she wanted to scream. Didn't they get that?

Mrs. Blair smiled at China, cracked an egg into a well of flour in a bowl, poured in milk, and began mixing the dough with her hands.

"Eh, Sylvie, what's for breakfast?" Angus Ritchie and his dog came in the kitchen door, leaving it standing open. "Och, I didna ken *you* was here."

The little man snatched his tweed hat off, revealing sparse tufts of gray hair. He eyed China suspiciously and backed a step. The terrier bounced in the door and ran at the collie; muddy paw prints trailed both dogs. Angus Ritchie set a battered black case along the wall.

Mrs. Blair closed the door. "Angus, sit ye down. I'll just get your tea." Plopping the dough into a buttered stoneware bowl, she covered it with a tea towel and set it on the shelf above the Aga.

Angus Ritchie sat at the small table by the window. China fixed him with a black look intended to turn a man to jelly. But he ignored her.

"Do you think you can call me stupid and get away with it?"

He sipped his tea. Looked out the window.

"Angus! You never!" Mrs. Blair shook a floury finger at him.

"Eh! She was screechin' oot the windae at me."

"*You* were the one screeching," China shot back.

"The two of you. Please stop this quarreling."

China stood and poured herself another cup of coffee, turned away from the nasty man before she said something she regretted. This was ridiculous. She was the owner, for heaven's sake. But maybe diplomacy was worth a try.

"Mr. Ritchie, I know we already talked about the pipes this morning but please, *please* stop."

She knew by his hardened look this was not going to work.

"Naw. I already told ye, your uncle made a decree that the pipes should be played under his bedroom windae as long as I draw breath an' can make the pipes sing."

So much for negotiating.

He took a loud slurp of tea and, with a low whistle to his dog, stomped out the door.

"He means nothing by it. Give him time," Mrs. Blair said.

China would give him forever, since she was out of here.

A bell rang in the kitchen hall.

"Excuse me, dear. That'll be the peat bricks delivered. I'll just be a moment."

China eyed the black case by the door. She guessed it was the pipes, and she was *not* going to listen to them tomorrow morning.

She picked up the case by the makeshift rope handle, though she knew she shouldn't, and went up the back stairs to her room. Let him ask for the things, then we'll see about negotiating.

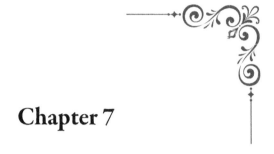

Chapter 7

The sound of Harriet's unmistakable voice mingled with the smell of manure in the barn. Duncan stopped short.

"There, Ro, you just put your head down, and we'll get this bridle on. Be a good boy now."

"What do you think you're doing?" Duncan strode down the barn aisle and snatched the bridle out of her hands. Night Rogue threw his head as high as the crossties allowed, a wild look in his eyes. "Are you mad? Or just stupid?"

"I wanted to ride."

"And what's wrong with *your* horse? The one you were making such a fuss about last night."

"She's not groomed. You know I don't like to ride a dirty horse."

"Well, get her out and bloody well groom her."

"I can ride Ro. You know I'm a fantastic rider."

"You may be *able* to ride him, and you may not. And you know it. However, you *cannot* ride him. He's *my* horse, and I forbid it. That's never changed."

"Listen to you. His Lairdship has spoken." Harriet whirled away, leaving Ro in the crossties. "Right. I'll just ride Duchess in her filthy state."

Duncan stroked Ro's neck, calming the horse, and preventing his own hands from shaking.

"I don't suppose you'd like to ride with me, darling? The boys didn't want to come out with me. For old times' sake?" Harriet turned her doe eyes on him. He used to melt under her gaze; now he despised—and pitied her. He couldn't blame the boys.

Duncan stared her down. "What are you playing at, Harriet?"

"Nothing. Can't I just go for a ride?" She stamped off to Duchess's stall and flung the door open, getting control of herself just in time to avoid spooking the horse.

Seeing the old impetuous, unpleasant Harriet allayed his fear that she was playing some togetherness card in her game, for surely there was some kind of game. Harriet's rules.

"All right. I'll ride." Ro could use the exercise. At least Ro would enjoy being out with Duchess. And he wanted to play this out. See what Harriet was up to.

"Thanks, darling. Oh, could you be a dear and fetch my saddle?"

"No."

"Fine." She crosstied Duchess in the aisle and stormed off to the tack room.

Duncan stepped outside and rang Callum on his mobile.

"Callum, Dad here."

"Dad, I know. I see your name here on my phone."

Duncan chuckled. "Yes, I know you know. But it's what we say, you know. Never mind the caller ID. Anyway, I wanted to let you know your mother and I are off on a ride. Won't be more than an hour."

"Really?" Callum's tone rang hard with sarcasm.

"Be charitable, Callum. Though I understand your point, I still don't think you ought to say it. She is your mother."

"Really? Can't prove it by me."

"We'll talk later.

"What are you and Ross doing?"

"Homework."

"Really?" Duncan hoped his son heard the humor in his voice. "Good lads.

"How about we go out in the boat this afternoon?"

"Sure. That'd be great. Can Trooper come with?" Enthusiasm edged into Callum's voice.

"Find his life vest and he can. I think it's in the gun room, in the locker with the ropes." Duncan wasn't keen on taking the Labrador with them, but he wanted the boys to have a good weekend, and if they wanted Trooper along, then so be it.

Duncan tacked up Ro, paying no attention to Harriet—or so he wanted her to think. There was something in the back of her devious little mind, he thought, as he led Ro out to the stableyard.

Harriet started to hand her reins to Duncan, obviously expecting him to hold Duchess while she stood on the mounting block. He gave her a pointed look, clearly meaning no.

"A leg up, then?" she asked.

She was insufferable. He shook his head but cupped his clasped hands for her to place her knee and hoisted her into the saddle. He had a fleeting thought of sending her over to the other side. It was the closest he'd come to touching her in a very long time.

Duncan grasped Ro's saddle and flung himself up in one fast and furious motion. Ro threw his head, and Duncan quickly settled the black.

Harriet trotted Duchess out of the stableyard and started up the lane, looking as if she were being judged on equitation, racking up the points with each flawless rise to the trot. It wasn't easy, watching Harriet from behind, remembering one of the many things he used to find so alluring about her.

He kept Ro well back to start. Ro knew who was boss, but it was good to remind him now and again. Duncan let him out to a trot at Donnie's cottage. Harriet looked over her shoulder, no doubt expecting Ro to come thundering up behind. Not today.

The long-legged horse quickly closed the distance to Duchess, and Duncan eased him abreast of the mare. Ro and Duchess nickered at each other. Whereas Duncan might have previously commented on the horses' affection for each other mirroring that of Harriet's and his own, he now swallowed a bitter taste. It didn't seem that long ago. Really, it wasn't. Two years.

"See. This isn't so bad, is it? Though how Duchess can be seen out with these filthy legs, I don't know. What do you pay the stable boy for anyway?"

"It's Donnie's day off. And we didn't expect you yet. Remember? I didn't know you'd be riding your horse yesterday, getting her up to her hocks in mud, did I?"

Harriet urged Duchess into a canter, and Duncan gave Ro the command to canter as well. Both horses settled into the easy rhythm.

Harriet looked over and, with a sly smirk, said, "Do you want to do a little cross country and jump the stone fence?"

"No thanks." In recent years, everything had become a competition with her. A ride was no longer a ride but a run for a medal. "You know there are a lot of rabbits on the hill."

Harriet leaned forward in the saddle and urged Duchess into a gallop. Duncan followed. Ro pulled ahead in a few strides and would have run all the way to the top of the mountain if Duncan had let him. But when Duncan realized he'd got caught up in the chase, he slowed the big horse. Harriet passed them, mud flying off Duchess's hoofs.

He let her go. He was not racing today. Nothing to be won. Game over.

Duncan turned Ro for home. Harriet could come in on her own time. Ro tossed his head and fought the bit a little before leaving Duchess.

Briskly walking back, for Ro had no slow gait in him, several minutes later, Duncan heard Duchess behind them.

"You're no fun." Harriet reined Duchess in and pulled alongside.

How does one reply to that? With silence, he guessed.

"Well, thanks for riding with me." Harriet patted Duchess on the neck.

Duncan silently prayed: Lord, help me get through this. Help my sons.

He wanted to weep, but he swallowed his tears and, with them, his pride. This weekend was for his sons.

"Would you like to go out in the boat this afternoon with the boys and me?"

Chapter 8

"Mr. Keith, we need to talk." China accosted the estate manager as he crossed the graveled expanse behind the house.

"Miss MacLeish." He touched the bill of his cap in greeting.

"I need to see the books for the estate." She dared him to defy her with a look that would not be refused.

"Certainly. I can give you the login instructions and all the passwords you'll need."

"Um, sure." She had expected a stack of dusty ledgers but, on the computer, so much the better. Bring it on. She was going to figure out the secrets this place held. Why so much money? Put numbers in front of her, and she could make them squeal for mercy.

"Best if you use the laptop in Mr. William's study. Sylvie can show you where it is. I'll email the links to you if you give me your address." He took a small notebook and pen from his breast pocket and stood poised, waiting for China's response.

"Sure. I guess." And she rattled off her email address. She was having a little trouble getting in step, having expected the business practices to be as antiquated as the property.

"And now, if you'll excuse me. I need to check on the horses," he said.

"Horses?" China blurted out, sounding way more enthused than she would have liked, but she couldn't help it.

"Aye. Horses." The estate manager chuckled. "You like horses, then?"

"I might." She hedged. "Depends on the horse."

"Come with me."

"You mean...I have horses?" She'd never gotten to have her own horse; she'd always ridden her friends' horses.

"Aye. Three and a bit. You'll see."

"But..." China looked around, not seeing any indication of horses or barn.

"Down the lane to the back here. We'll take the Defender, but you can also take yon footpath." He indicated a path through a thick waxy-leafed hedge at the side of the building that housed the estate office.

Three and a bit. China turned that one over in her mind.

John Keith strode to a wooden paneled garage door and folded back the two sides revealing a very old, very dirty, blue vehicle that looked like it belonged on safari—or a scrap heap.

"Hop in."

China walked around to get in the passenger side.

"Nay, the other side. Did they not tell you? We drive on the left here."

"I knew that. Unlike what Mr. Ritchie says, I'm *not* stupid." China flipped her hair over her shoulder for emphasis.

John Keith started the Defender, slammed it into gear, and backed it out, the diesel engine complaining mightily and giving off fumes that certainly weren't legal in the States.

They turned left onto the lane. But then Mr. Keith turned left again down another lane China hadn't noticed on the drive in. A bumpy lane. China braced a hand on the dusty dashboard.

"I hope there's a bumper sticker on this thing that says: My other car is a Rolls."

"Nay. William had a real fondness for old Gerty here."

"Dirty Gerty is more like it."

"There is an old Ford Anglia. Needs a bit of work, but I reckon I can get it running."

China sighed. There wasn't much convenient about Craggan Mhor so far.

The lane curved to the left, revealing the barn. China caught her breath. The barn was beautiful. They drove into the courtyard of the U-shaped stone building. Chickens scurried, flapping and clucking.

The barn, made of flat-cut stones in shades of cream and gray, with an occasional black and red stone, was more beautiful than the house. Three chimneys capped the slate roof, and the doors and windows were trimmed in fresh green paint. The shape of the barn looked like it had been added to over the years, starting with the center section and extending forward on each side.

"Come this way, lass."

He led off to the side of the barn. China trotted after him, eager beyond belief to see the horses, *her* horses.

"This here's Bess," he said.

In a paddock stood a tall, swaybacked black Shire, her long white fetlocks stringy with mud. She nudged John Keith in the shoulder, and he pulled something out of his pocket and held it out to her.

"Sugar lumps for the old girl."

China knew horses, and this was a very old, very happy horse. She could tell the horse and John Keith had a special bond, and it made her think a little more kindly toward the gruff estate manager.

"Aye, she's the last of the working horses. William certainly didn't think he'd be the one goin' first." He patted Bess's neck, sending up a small cloud of dust. "Och, she's a mite dirty. I'll have one of the lads see to her."

"She's what? Maybe thirty? Surely you were working with tractors by then."

"Aye. Tractors. But William, he loved his horses."

"I see...But if Bess is the bit of the three and a bit horses, where are the others?"

He smiled and headed off behind the barn. A fenced pasture connected to the barn at the back. He let himself in the gate and held it open for China. "You stand here," he said, and he entered the barn through the wide double doors that stood open.

A sharp whinny and a kick to a stall door made China want to run in the barn and see for herself.

After several agonizing minutes, John Keith emerged holding the lead ropes of two horses—one on either side of him—a pair of dappled bays. The taller gelding had a white blaze down his face and four white socks; the mare had a star between her eyes and three socks. And clearly, both horses wanted to be out of the barn. They barely minded their manners: heads raised high, ears scissoring back and forth. They were magnificent.

China clapped a hand to her mouth to stifle a shout and started laughing behind her hand so as not to frighten the horses. Words wouldn't form.

"Well, come here, then, if ye know horses. Give me a hand."

China started off running but quickly got hold of herself and slowed. He handed her a lead rope. She searched the horse's liquid dark eyes for a sign of acceptance, then let it smell her hand. She reached out and ran her hand down the horse's neck and onto its warm chest. The horse didn't flinch.

"I'm going to turn Major loose, so mind yourself." John Keith led the horse a few steps away and unclipped the rope.

Major took off at a dead run, tail streaming like a flag. The mare threw her head and swung her rear around. China tugged on the leadline. The estate manager was quickly at her side and took the rope from her. China was all grin.

"What's her name?"

"China."

China looked at John Keith, who was smiling as broad as could be. "China?" She felt a flush rising up.

"Aye. Your uncle named her."

China didn't know whether to be angry or touched by the gesture.

He released the China he held by the rope, and they watched her fly off to join Major in a race around the pasture.

All inheritance confusion fell away, and China was the horse-crazy twelve-year-old again. "I'm...I..." Her hand at her mouth stopped her words.

"You like them?" John Keith asked.

"Oh yes. I like them. But these two and old Bess. I don't mean to be greedy, but is there a third horse?"

He laughed. "Aye. You're lookin' at it. China's in foal. That's the three and a bit."

A foal—a baby. "When's it due?" she asked, a grin all over her face.

"Mid-April thereabouts."

That seemed a long time away.

China and John Keith retreated to outside the fence and continued to watch the pair enjoying their freedom. The horses, her horses, slowed as they continued to circle the pasture. They trotted side by side, shaking their black manes, blowing and snorting.

China leaned her forearms on the upper fence rail, entranced.

John Keith reached in his pocket and held out his flat palm. The gelding veered toward him and the treat. The mare made another small circle. He handed China a treat to offer the mare. It worked like a charm, and China-the-horse came to lip the treat off the palm of China-the-overwhelmed-woman. The mare bobbed her head, and China reached to scratch behind the horse's ear.

China's smile faded. These horses would be sold too. Her thoughts reeled. Part of her refused to believe the insane conditions of the will; part of her knew she was doomed to a year here if she wanted the money. This was all too much. The sale of the estate, back to Chicago...a long time.

She set her jaw and looked away from the horses. "Thanks. Thanks a lot. But, if you don't mind, I'll go back to the house and start looking over the estate accounts. Where's that footpath you mentioned?" He pointed the way, and she left him with the horses. He could obviously manage. "Send me the account links and passwords as soon as you can please."

"Oh, Miss MacLeish. Would you like a drive round the estate tomorrow? Thought you'd like to see it."

"Sure." She threw a backward wave at him, part goodbye, part dismissal.

"Nine o'clock all right?"

"Sure."

ANGUS Ritchie's howls carried out the closed kitchen door, across the gravel yard, and to China's ears as she was almost to the opening in the hedge behind the house.

"I'm tellin' ye, Sylvie, I'm callin' the constable is what I'll do. It's thievin' plain an' simple it is."

China couldn't hear Mrs. Blair's response before Angus ranted on.

"Naw. I know 'twas her. She's the only one low enough tae steal a man's pipes. Ye can't trust those Yanks. Where is she?"

The kitchen door whipped open, and Angus Ritchie came roaring out, pumping his short legs in fury. China turned to hide in the hedge. Too late. Both dogs raced toward her, yapping with delight.

"There ye are, ye wee limmer. What d'ye mean stealin' me pipes."

China turned to face him as he bore down on her. "Mr. Ritchie, I—" She thought he'd stop well short of her, but he came right up under her nose.

Spittle flying, hands clenched at his side, he swore at her and screeched, "Where are they?"

"Mr. Ritchie, you—"

"Those pipes were my father's an' my father's afore him. An' ye've nae right." He looked like he might burst into tears.

The little man's face was several shades of red, and China feared not only for her own cleanliness, as froth flecked her jacket, but that the rat of a man might keel over right there. Not the way to get rid of him that she had in mind.

She drew herself up and shouted at full voice, "Mr. Ritchie, stop!"

He abruptly closed his mouth and stepped back a couple steps, then continued to work his mouth like a beached carp.

"I couldn't get you to listen to me otherwise, you—"

"Angus, China, come to your senses will ye?" Mrs. Blair ran out the kitchen door, gravel scrunching underfoot, apron flapping.

"She started it, Sylvie. It's no my fault. She admitted it. She took 'em."

Sylvie turned to China and gave her a questioning look. "Did you really?"

"Oh, for heaven's sake," China said, exasperated, "I'm just trying to get some peace, and he wouldn't listen to me."

"Ye took his pipes?" Sylvie looked incredulous.

"Yes. Yes, I did."

"See. I told ye. I'm callin' the constable."

"Angus, hold your horses a wee bit. I'm sure you two can work this out."

"If she gives 'em back an' gives 'em back now!"

China tried again. "You—"

"I ken ye'd be trouble. Just like your mither." Angus Ritchie glared at her, white globs at the corners of his mouth.

It was China's turn to go red. She tensed and her eyes went hot; she nearly went for the man's neck.

"Wheesht! Stop it, the both of ye!" Mrs. Blair put up her hands like two stop signs shaking in the wind. "This is no way to behave. I'm goin' back to the kitchen to put the kettle on, and I expect the both of you in for a civil cup of tea verra shortly. I mean no disrespect, China, but do ye *both* hear me?" She turned and marched back to the house, patting her thigh at her dog. "Andy, come along. You get yourself in and *now*."

China stood there and didn't know whether to spit or grin. What a ridiculous situation. Angus Ritchie stood his ground and glowered at her.

"Well, you heard the boss. I guess we'd better work this out." China tried humor. Yelling was getting nowhere. "Mr. Ritchie, I'm sorry I took your pipes, but please, you can't play them so early."

"I can do as I like. As Mr. William likes. An' he said as I was tae play them at six a.m. right under his windae every morn." He jabbed his chin in China's direction like the deal was settled.

"Mr. William isn't here now. I am. And I say you cannot."

He looked like he'd been stung. Tears did well this time, and he roughly swiped at his face with his wool tweed sleeve.

China sagged, sensing this war was rooted in something she couldn't fix. She hadn't meant for it to go this far.

"Look, of course I'll give the pipes back to you. I'll get them as soon as we conclude this. I never intended to keep them." Though she had thought of throwing them off the nearest cliff. "But would you please compromise on this? Please don't play them under my window so early. Would you agree to that? A little farther away and a little later?"

Angus Ritchie worked his mouth like he had a mouthful of pebbles.

"It'll only be for a week or so. I'm leaving as soon as I can."

"Eh?" He brightened. "But I thought—"

"Don't think, Mr. Ritchie. It'll get us both in trouble with Mrs. Blair...Well?"

"Since ye put it that way, I guess I can give the old pipes a rest for a few days. The rain's no good for 'em any road."

"Thank you, Mr. Ritchie. You're a tough little nut."

"An' you're a nutter...Miss MacLeish, Your Highness." His chin jutted out, and there was no evidence of humor in his weather-crinkled eyes. "I ken ye canna give me the sack, so you're stuck wi' me." He gave a little chortle in his throat.

China narrowed her gaze at him. "That's true. Your Mr. William saw to that. But how about we try not to make the next week miserable for each other?" She finished the sentence to his back as he headed to the kitchen door.

"Tea?" he yelled. "Sylvie's waitin'. Bit early, but there ye have it." He whistled for Fly and spat.

China didn't hurry. She stood in the middle of a mess in the Middle-of-Nowhere, Scotland, and wondered how in the world dear Uncle William could have thought this was a good idea. But it was a lot of money.

She stood still and listened—no sound but the wind in the trees and the sea shushing just out of sight. She took a deep breath of the chill, damp Highland air and felt her heart rate calm. The high-pitched shrill of a bird of prey cut through the quiet. China watched for a moment as piles of gray and blue clouds shifted across the sky, then shoved her hands in her pockets, and started for the kitchen.

Apparently her mother couldn't wait to get away from here forty-one years ago.

Mrs. Blair glanced up from pouring hot water in the teapot when China walked in. Fly got up from her bed by the stove and wagged over to China and immediately poked her nose at China's hand. China gave the dog a quick pat on the head and flicked her fingers, telling it to go away. Fly flattened her ears against her head and wagged to her bed, looking back at China as she went.

Mrs. Blair stood, her hands clasped over her middle, looking like now *she* might cry.

"Please, Mrs. Blair, could we not discuss this any further. I'm going to get the pipes. Then be done with it."

"Aye." Angus Ritchie reached for a scone.

Mrs. Blair gently smacked his hand. "You wait till Miss MacLeish gets back."

Andy rose up on his hind legs and pawed the air. "Away with you, ye wee beastie. You could do with bein' a bit more timorous." She reached in her apron pocket and tossed a treat to the dog.

China opened her mouth to speak—something about dogs in the kitchen—but changed her mind and left to retrieve the vile pipes.

Chapter 9

Duncan cast off the rope and stepped onto the foredeck of the *Hattie Lea*. Callum put the old girl in reverse, easing them out of the marina. Duncan thought he really should sell the Aquastar, but *Hattie* and he had grown up together. And one doesn't want to be without a boat when living by the sea. He pushed away the memories of the times he and Harriet had spent on the boat. It wasn't a comfortable boat to sleep on, but it had two narrow berths in the cabin—and a door. Duncan glanced at Harriet, a black and gold Hermès scarf tied around her neck, and shook his head for no one to see. They were still husband and wife—but strangers.

Harriet and Ross sat on the bench seat running along the starboard side, Trooper in his life vest between them. Duncan sat on the blue padded seat beside Callum at the helm. The old Aquastar 20 could never have been called luxurious, but she was seaworthy, to a point. Today the sea was fairly calm, and there were no worries. This was an outing he and his family had taken countless times. Maybe it was foolish to go out so late in the year, but he couldn't think what else to do. One last charade at being a family.

Callum pointed the bow of the boat out toward the dome-shaped rocky island of Timcheall a mile and a half off shore. Puffins nested in the cliff, but otherwise, the rock was uninhabitable. Tour boats were allowed to cruise by, and tourists could gawk at the puffins through binoculars, but the island was restricted. It was to the south of the island where Minke whales were often sighted.

Duncan stood, a hand braced on the cabin roof for support against the fore and aft pitch of the boat as they motored out.

"You're doing a smashing job, Capt. Callum." Duncan tousled his son's russet hair. Callum grinned at his father, the first smile of the weekend he'd let slip.

"Dad, could I have an orange squash please?" Callum said.

"I'll get it, sweetie." Harriet flipped the cooler open, twisted off the top of the drink, and jumped up to hand it to Callum before he could fully form the grimace he was working up.

"Thanks, Mum." At least Callum had the grace to say it.

The boat took a bigger wave, sending Harriet lurching forward into Duncan. He couldn't help but put his arms around her to steady her. That or step aside and let her go overboard. Spray arced off either side of the prow and blew a mist back at them. Trooper barked at the offending sea.

Duncan caught Ross looking at his mother and him. Ross's expression seemed somewhere between sadness and hope.

"Harriet, you never were much of a sailor." He released her, feeling a bit like his hands had come away scorched.

"No, darling, that's what I had you for." She slicked her dampened hair back from her face, emphasizing her astonishingly high cheek bones.

Duncan wiped his hands down his thighs. "Captain, take us round to the south side of the island, and we'll see what we can find."

"Aye, aye, Sir."

"Harriet, how about those sandwiches?" He tried to muster a pleasant face but failed.

"Ever giving orders, aren't you? You don't know where they are?"

She just relentlessly rankled. Couldn't she just get out the bloody sandwiches and feed lunch to her boys? Be a proper mother? He tried to give her opportunities, but she too often failed to do the right thing.

Yet, she flopped open the hamper lid and fetched out the sandwiches, handing Duncan his sandwich last. Cheese sandwiches. Well, she'd made an effort. There was no Branston pickle on his, so obviously Harriet made these herself rather than ordering the lunch from Janet.

"Boys, tell me what you're up to at school. Playing football still?" Harriet said.

"I play rugby. Going on four years," said Callum between mouthfuls.

"I got a first in history," Ross piped up.

"A first. And at nine years old. Imagine that."

"I'm ten."

It was painful to watch the farce.

Ross gave part of his sandwich to Trooper and got another for himself.

"I'll take over the helm if you want a break, laddie."

"Aye, aye." Callum scooted over on the seat, holding the wheel till Duncan had it.

The November sea was unusually cooperative today, not kicking up a fuss like she could. Duncan slowed to an idle and scanned the sea for any sign of whales or dolphins.

Seeing the telltale signs of a dolphin pod, he eased the boat closer, keeping a distance so as not to disturb the animals. But it wasn't dolphins. What was causing the disturbance in the water?

"Dad!" Ross shouted and pointed, fear written large in his eyes.

An enormous gray body rolled over in the sea, mouth yawning wide to entrap scores of mackerel in a gulp. A whale was rounding up his dinner, circling the school till he could take a big bite of a ball of fish.

The whale arched and dove, exposing its length as it disappeared. It must have been seventy feet long. The slender body and its great length marked it as a fin whale, a whale Duncan had seen only once. This was a rare day.

Trooper set up an insane barking, and Harriet tried to silence him with a hand clamped around his muzzle. Trooper shook her off and continued sounding the alarm.

"Aw, cool!" Callum yelled, as the whale breached again. It pirouetted and did a graceful bellyflop.

The sea once more roiled with fish as the whale circled its prey—the roll, the gulp.

"Dad! It's gonna ram us!" Callum gripped the edge of the cabin roof with both hands.

The whale sped in their direction faster than any whale Duncan had ever seen, its back just above the surface of the water. Ross screamed and clung to Trooper, who would not stop barking. Duncan kept the boat steady, hoping to cause no movement to attract the whale's attention.

The whale suddenly veered off, well short of them, and resumed feeding.

"I think that's quite enough excitement for one day." Duncan turned the boat round, much relieved. "You boys just saw something special. That's a fin whale. I've only ever seen one."

"Let's get out of here." Ross looked ashen. His teeth chattered in spite of the thick wool sweater he wore, a waterproof jacket, and his life vest over all that.

"Aye, aye, First Mate." Duncan poured as much speed into the old boat as she had and put some distance between them and the frenzied whale.

Callum took the helm again when they were clear of the whale. Behind them they could see the feeding roundup still going on.

Trooper put his front paws on the railing and launched himself over the side.

"Dad!" Ross screamed hysterically, arms flailing.

Instantly, Duncan dove in after Trooper.

"Duncan, you bloody fool!"

He heard Harriet's shriek just before he hit the water.

Duncan bobbed up in his life vest and swam toward Trooper. Waves washed over the furiously paddling dog, the surf pulling Trooper away from Duncan. The dog's orange life vest made him easy to keep in view, but Duncan didn't think he was getting to the dog fast enough.

Callum cut the engine to idle and steered the boat round to get close. The waves kept trying to separate the boat from Duncan and Trooper. Harriet stood poised to toss the life ring.

Finally, Duncan reached the dog and grabbed the handle on top of the life vest. He tried as best he could to keep the dog's head above water and one-arm sidestroked to the boat.

When in range, Harriet flung the life ring out to Duncan. It splashed down within three feet of him, and Duncan quickly grabbed hold.

Harriet pulled them toward the boat.

"Ross, throw the ladder over the side," Harriet barked.

Duncan climbed partway up the rope ladder, then heaved Trooper up and into the boat, dropping him on the bench seat till he could climb in and lower the dog to the floor.

Trooper lay still, his eyes vacant.

Ross was frantic and bent to cradle Trooper in his arms.

"Hey there, laddie. I need some room here." Duncan gently grasped Ross's shoulders and moved him to the side.

Ross sat back, tears streaming.

Duncan gathered the big dog into his arms and, with as much force as he could, whipped the dog's head downward, hoping the swallowed seawater would come up. It did, and Trooper began struggling to get loose from Duncan's hold. Duncan carefully laid the dog on the deck. Ross squeezed his dog in a hug till more seawater appeared. Trooper drew in huge gulps of air, raised his head, and licked Ross's face.

Duncan sat down hard on the floor of the boat and leaned against the bench. He was cold. He could feel Harriet's eyes on him from across the boat.

"Could you please…" It was an effort to form the words, he was so cold.

"I'll get it." Harriet came back from the cabin with a blanket. He took it from her and wrapped it around his shoulders.

"Take us home, Callum." Duncan thanked God Trooper was all right. To be sure, they'd stop at the vet's on the way home.

They docked and tied up. Duncan lifted Trooper out of the boat and set him on the pier. The dog didn't look much the worse for his perilous swim—a bit like a drunken sailor, but he was navigating.

As they walked back to the car, Harriet more or less beside Duncan while the boys walked ahead with Trooper, Duncan said, "Thanks for throwing the life ring to me."

Harriet gave him her slyest of smiles. "What about the Clarkson? It's only a little painting."

He had been cold before, but he now felt frozen to his marrow. So she thought doing the right thing warranted a reward.

He said nothing, but he reckoned the painting would be gone with Harriet tomorrow.

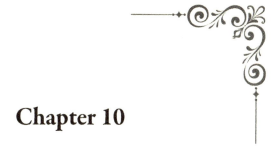

Chapter 10

Sylvie lifted the carved wooden box out from the bottom of her dowry chest and set it on her lap. She traced her fingers over the center Celtic design, the Trinity knot: Father, Son, and Holy Spirit. And, William had said when he gave the box to her—Sylvie, William, and our heavenly Father, tied together as one.

Only when Nan was snoring to rattle the windows did Sylvie take the box out, not wanting to be discovered daydreaming over the mementos that were not from Nan's own son. But Nan knew the way of things. Sylvie had loved Ranald well enough, but he was not the love of her life. The whole village knew that—as did Ranald—but, good man that he was, he had said it was all right by him.

The intricate knots twining around the lid had no beginning and no end. Chip carved and sanded smooth they were, first by William's hands, then by her fingers following the design over these many years.

She pulled the pin out of the loop and lifted the brass hasp. The box was only little, no bigger than a biscuit tin, but large in her heart. Carefully, mindful of the old hinges, she opened the lid—and smiled. Now that William was gone, this was all she had left of him, except for his old jacket he gave her. She hadn't taken or asked for anything when she readied what was now China's room, not wanting to make a show of it. All of William's things were in the attic waiting for China to decide about them; it wasn't Sylvie's place.

Sylvie knew every item in the box. Memories of promises. Then—a promise broken—along with both their hearts.

Not tonight. She wouldn't lay out the bits and bobs of a love tonight. She closed the lid and laid the box in its place for another time.

Chapter 11

Not this rattletrap again. John Keith held the passenger door of the Land Rover Defender open for China. A relatively clean towel covered the seat, but the rest of the vehicle was as dirty as it had been the day before.

The weather was—Scottish. A fine mist spotted the windshield, and a white cloud mass hid the tops of the mountains. Only a fringe of snow showed at the edge of the low-hanging murk.

"I'm glad to see you dressed for the occasion." John Keith smirked and pointed at China's smart leather boots, the ones with the low heels.

"Why? I don't get what you mean," she said.

"I'll be back in a flash."

He left her standing beside the car, truck, whatever it was, and disappeared into one of the several doors in the long stone outbuilding.

"These should do nicely." He lifted the back window and tossed in a pair of green rubber boots, mostly clean. Then he handed her a smelly tan jacket.

She wrinkled her nose.

"It's a waterproof," he said.

"Whatever," China muttered. She thrust her arms into the sleeves, got in the filthy car, and slammed the door, the clang of uninsulated metal sounding cheap.

John Keith threw two long walking sticks in the back with the boots and climbed in. The diesel engine grumbled like a garbage truck.

"We must be going on a serious expedition. Did you bring the food and water?" China eyed the estate manager.

"In the back." He jerked a thumb in the direction.

They took a narrow gravel road away from the house out the other side of the gravel yard. China noticed the shotgun clipped into the gun rack on the underside of the roof over John Keith's head. She suddenly realized she didn't know this man with whom she had just gotten into a vehicle. Maybe this wasn't a good idea.

He chuckled. "It's not loaded. But I always take it with me."

"Well, that's a relief. You're not some psychopathic killer, I hope?"

"The ammunition's in the back with your wellies." Again a barely stifled laugh.

"Not funny, Mr. Keith. I don't think you appreciate how strange...all this is for me. I was kidding, but for all I know, it could be true."

"Aye, I do, lass. But what's to be done. Your mother apparently didn't tell you about...all this."

"Not a word. But that's typical." She stopped. She was not about to confide in the help.

The Defender bumped over the end of the graded gravel, causing China to brace a hand against the dashboard. This line also seemed to demarcate the end of the pine trees around the house. Ahead, China could see little but scrubby bushes, rocks, and a few strangled pines here and there. The road continued on as a rutted track.

"I heard you and Angus nearly came to blows yesterday."

China couldn't believe her ears. "That's probably none of your business."

"Miss MacLeish, there's one thing you need to understand. They're my friends. We don't just work together. And Sylvie and Angus were both very upset."

"Did you get me trapped in this bucket to lecture me? If so, you can stop and let me out right now." China reached for the door handle.

"Eh, now. Don't get all twisted up. I meant no offense. Only this has all been verra difficult. All the way round. But I'll say no more."

"Good." China breathed hard but let it pass.

"I only want to show ye the grandeur of what your uncle left to you."

"I started looking at the accounts last night, and I have a few questions."

"I expect that's an understatement." He shot her a wry look. "After tea I'll have the time, if that's a good time for you."

"Tea? Don't you people use a clock? Am I supposed to know when tea is?"

"Six o'clock, lass. Always six o'clock or thereabouts. Unless you're in England, then it's four o'clock."

China shook her head and gave John a look half questioning, half not caring.

"In Scotland we working folk call our evening meal tea. I expect we want to be different from the English."

"But Mrs. Blair seems to produce tea any time of the day or night."

"Aye, that Sylvie knows a cuppa's like a pat on the hand and a smile."

They curved around a rock outcropping, and John Keith stopped the Defender. Before them, a river, about a stone's throw across, twisted through the valley like a brown rope. Farther upriver a terraced cascade thundered into pools on its way down the hill.

Everywhere she looked China saw a postcard picture of the Highlands.

John Keith got out and stood peering at the river, so China did the same. The river seemed to boil in dark pools below the bigger rocks.

"Your salmon rights."

"What?"

"Your salmon. Next to the laird's own River Slee, this is the best salmon fishing. And no one can fish here but you say so, and they pay you. That is, I should say, I manage all that for you."

She looked more closely at the river and saw lots of salmon, maybe hundreds. "Impressive." Fish.

He opened the back of the Defender and took out the walking sticks and the green boots. "Here, put these on. You'll be glad of them."

He rested his opened shotgun over his left arm and stuffed a few shells into his shooting vest. And handed her a bottle of water.

Without a word China pocketed the water bottle, shed her fancy boots, and put on the green rubber things. She was getting tired of asking questions and, for now, would just follow along. About time she got some exercise anyway.

John Keith handed her a walking stick and struck off down the path along the river. A tall man, his stride wasn't easy to keep up with, even for China, who took pride in her fitness.

The path wound through the scrub, dead brown blossoms giving away that earlier the entire area must have been a purple glow of heather. Her shoulder brushed a tall spiky bush that snagged her scarf. Grumbling about her uncle and this place, she slapped at the branch and came away with a scratched hand.

John Keith looked back. "Mind the gorse."

He suppressed a smug look, she knew he did, and she wasn't happy about this whole thing. Though she did admit—to herself—this place was a good definition of barren beauty.

As they walked, the estate manager reeled off statistics about the estate: 26,000 acres, salmon yield, spawning season, grouse, red deer population, stalking season. Something about stags and hinds.

His voice faded to a hum, and with every step, China found herself looking more intently at her surroundings. This could be hers. Or she could sell it. She wondered what the fair market value was. She'd soon find out when she got hold of those attorneys. Surely the stipulations of the will couldn't be legally binding.

After twenty minutes of a steady uphill march, they reached the top of the waterfall. If John Keith was still talking, China couldn't have heard a word above the roar of the falls. Silver and pink salmon leaped up the cascade, some not making the next level and falling back to try again. Sequined bodies flashed and strained with the effort.

Amazing. The salmon were majestic in their heroic race to spawn. She wanted to reach out and give them a boost.

"Aye, they're quite a sight. We're a bit late today. They're more active in the early morn and evening. We could come back later, if you like." He grinned.

China returned the smile, in spite of herself, but declined the offer, for today anyway.

"Take a good look round you. This could be all yours, lass."

"Mr. Keith, my plan is still to sell. But we really need to look at those accounts."

"Aye...ye ken, China, your Uncle William was very fond of you."

She shot daggers at him, her eyes suddenly dry and hot. "Mr. Keith, I'd like you to address me as Ms. MacLeish. I am your employer, you *ken*. And, no, I don't know that my uncle cared one bit about me.

There was never any evidence to suggest it. He's nothing and no one to me."

He held her gaze and rubbed a hand over his chin.

"Do ye not know, then?"

"Know what?" She could feel the heat rising up her neck.

"You were born here."

"What?"

"Aye."

"Oh, you mean, I was born in Scotland?" She waved her hand as if at a troublesome gnat that wouldn't go away. That was impossible.

"Nay, I mean you were born *here*. At Craggan Mhor."

Her grip tightened on the walking stick, and she stood unblinking, her mouth open.

"So ye ken, it's difficult not to be familiar with you since we've all known ye since you were a bairn. Heard your first cry Sylvie did." He turned away from her, trained his attention to the top of the waterfall.

He must be lying to her. Trying to get her sympathy. Get her to stay so he could keep his job.

The falls roared inside her head. China tried to deny the truth of his words—but she couldn't—and the truth crashed down on her. It was far more likely that her mother was the liar. How like her mother to keep this secret from her. A trembling sigh rolled out, low and soft. She had a home and a family—and she never knew it.

John Keith turned back to her. "So ye ken, China...if I may call you so, we would all like it very much if you'd give it a try. Even if you're prickly as the gorse." He chuckled. "Bide the year. Then see."

She blinked. Then turned to look again at the salmon struggling up the falls. She was sure Angus Ritchie didn't share the sentiment.

"Sylvie can tell ye more. But I think you've had enough for the moment, aye?"

China murmured an aye and turned to stumble down the path, her vision blurred by tears.

But her passport said she was born in Akron, Ohio. And she had a security clearance with the US government. This must be wrong.

JOHN Keith hadn't said a word to her on the drive back to the house. China went around to the front entrance, hoping to slip in unnoticed. She quietly shut the front door.

"Oh, hullo, Miss MacLeish. I was just coming to clean out the ashes in the lounge." Sylvie stood in the hall wearing an old flowered apron, the loop-over-the-neck kind, and carrying a brass bucket. A kerchief covered her hair.

China knew her eyes were red, and her shoulders sagged with the weight of her mother's lie. She glanced in Sylvie's direction but couldn't meet her eyes.

"Call me China, I guess." China shrugged off the raincoat, hung it on the hall tree, and trudged up the stairs to her room. The room she was sleeping in. Her dead uncle's room.

She fell face first onto the bed and sobbed—stupid, wracking sobs she didn't even try to stop. She beat her fist, just once, on the comforter. This was all her mother's fault. China wished she'd never been born—at least not to Margaret MacLeish.

A light tap on the door brought China to her senses. She grabbed a tissue from the box on the bedside table and mopped her nose and face.

"Come in."

Sylvie entered with a small tray holding a cup of tea and a cookie. "I brought this for you." She set the tray on the bedside table.

China sniffed in response. She hated crying.

"Did John tell ye, then?"

China nodded, hung her head, and ran both hands through her hair.

"I didn't think ye knew. But I feared bein' the one to tell you. I knew it would hurt."

China's coffee-colored hair fell in a veil around her face. Did she have no privacy? Everyone knew about her but her.

"Your Uncle William asked me to give this letter to you when ye knew. He so hoped you'd come."

China took the letter from Sylvie's outstretched hand. The heavy parchment envelope was addressed to Miss China MacLeish, written in a scrolled hand.

"I'll leave ye to it, then, shall I?" She turned to leave.

"No, stay." China reached out a hand to Sylvie and quickly dropped it to her lap. "Please."

Sylvie eased into the old armchair near the bed.

China turned the letter over to find it sealed with hard wax bearing the imprint of what looked like a crest. She slid her finger under the flap and broke the seal. Another letter, and her fingers were trembling again.

My dearest niece, China,

This letter may come as a shock to you. You may not even have known of my existence, but you have been in my heart and in my prayers since the day you first drew breath.

Until now I have honored my sister's wish that I not attempt to contact you, however, the Lord has impressed upon me that I must now break that promise. Forgive me. I should have broken it long ago or never agreed to it in the first place.

I had hoped to meet you one day. When we meet, however, it will be in heaven, as by the time you receive this letter, I will be with the Lord. I have instructed my solicitors to find you and carry out the particulars of my will. You are my sole heir.

Dear China, again, forgive me if the stipulations of my will seem strange, even disagreeable to you. By now you will have met the staff at Craggan Mhor. Please know that they have been family to me and I to them. I pray that in time you, too, will come to love Craggan Mhor and the people of Fionnloch.

I have ever wished the situation to be different, but the Lord promises to bless beyond what we could ever hope for.

Your loving uncle,
William Charles MacLeish

Tears dripped off China's chin.

"All right, dear?"

"All right?...I have so many questions. Who was my mother? Who was my uncle? And who *am I*?" She smoothed the folds of the letter back in place and scrutinized Sylvie. "And who are *you*? Mr. Keith says you heard my first cry."

"Aye, that I did. I assisted Granny Nan to birth ye."

"Granny Nan?"

"My mother-in-law. She's been wanting to see you something fierce. Will you come by this afternoon? She'd be right glad of it."

China let out a mighty sigh, which she hoped didn't sound rude, but she was way beyond the end of her rope, dangling somewhere between red-hot mad and absurd hope. She fought both and searched the room for some clue as to what was going on, but of course, she found none.

"I suppose I could. Where does she live?"

"With me. Andy and I'll walk ye there. Directly after dinner, aye? Lunch you call it."

Sylvie smiled and reached over to pat China's hand. China flinched and withdrew her hand but managed to return a weak smile.

"Can I get ye anything?"

"No, I'm fine." Which was ridiculous. "But thank you."

"I'll be in the kitchen if you need me."

Wordlessly, China nodded. She watched Sylvie all the way to the door.

Her hand on the doorknob, Sylvie turned to China and said, "Your uncle was so proud of you. Having a fancy job with the US government and all."

"How did he know that?"

"He googled ye, of course. He used to say you were likely as canny with the stock exchange as he was."

All China could do was give her head a rueful shake, but it didn't clear her confusion.

"Mind, he would have been proud of you no matter what ye did." Sylvie smiled again at China as she closed the door behind her, the kind of smile that could melt tough skin.

China unfolded the letter and read it again. *Your loving uncle.* She lay back on the comforter and studied the geometric shapes of the embossed ceiling paper, trying to calm her mind. She didn't want to grieve an uncle she didn't know. And she still didn't know if she wanted this place. It was all so complicated. Her home was Chicago. She had a job at the Securities and Exchange Commission. And she had friends.

But one thing she knew—she was not going to let her mother mess *this* up.

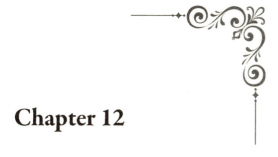

Chapter 12

Sylvie fretted. This meeting could go very badly if China was to be overwhelmed. That China could be a mite crabbit, Lord love her. Sylvie so wanted Nan to not be hurt—again. At least she'd rung Nan to let her know they'd be coming sometime after dinner. Nan would no doubt be tidying up, not that their cottage was ever untidy, unless Gordy was there. And one never knew when that penny would turn up. She'd sent Gordy packing, but he was like an elastic band, and it worried her.

"There you are, dear." China appeared in the kitchen, dressed in jeans, a thick sweater, the green waterproof, and her trainers.

"Is this the appropriate footwear? Seems I haven't picked the right shoes yet."

"They should do nicely." Andy stood at the kitchen door, stumpy tail wagging, his eyes on Sylvie. "I won't be a minute."

Sylvie hustled down the back hall to where she kept her coat on a peg. She hoped China wouldn't remark about the overlarge tartan jacket she wore, as William had given her his old coat. Maybe she shouldn't wear it, but it had so much good left in it. And it felt ever so good to wear.

"Off we go, then." Sylvie opened the door and let Andy out. He ran ahead toward home. "This Scotch mist just will not let up, but I reckon we won't get soaked. You've quite adopted that mac."

They set off on the path through the pine trees, walking side by side, Andy bouncing ahead. When Andy charged into the underbrush, Sylvie let him go. There was no keeping the little hunter on the path. He'd come when he was ready; he'd never yet missed a meal.

"Tell me about your mother-in-law. Nan, is it? Or should I call her Mrs. Blair?"

"Granny Nan she's called. By the whole village. She's like a gran to all since she birthed so many of the bairns for nigh on fifty years."

"But isn't there a hospital?"

Sylvie laughed. "Aye, in Inverness. But babies won't wait, and you don't want to be driven' the road to Inverness in the middle of the night with a woman screamin' her head off in the back seat. There's a long tradition of midwifery in the Highlands."

China nodded but seemed distracted. So Sylvie didn't gabble on.

"You mean I really was a home delivery? At Craggan Mhor?"

"Aye."

"Who's my father?"

Sylvie nearly tripped over a pebble. "Well, now..." She cleared her throat, clutched her handbag a little tighter—anything to not answer China's question.

China stopped and faced Sylvie just as the path came out of the trees and started along the shore. The sea breeze snagged her hair and blew it across her face. "Mrs. Blair...Sylvie, who is my father?"

"Och, my dear, I'm afraid I dinna rightly know. Your mother wouldn't say. I'm that sorry." Sylvie reached for China's hand, but China stiffened, and Sylvie withdrew her hand.

She hated to lie to China, though it wasn't really a lie. Margaret refused to name the lad, but every tattling woman in the village assumed the father was Gordy Campbell and said so. No wonder the poor girl fled. There was never any doubt in Sylvie's mind that her brother was China's father. And to see her now, a grown woman, there could be no doubt. Sylvie hadn't seen Margaret in so long, it was hard to say if her daughter resembled her, but there was no mistaking the good looks of Gordy about China. Those glittering deep blue eyes. The dark Campbell hair.

China struck off down the path, a stiffness to her stride that warned to leave her alone. Oh, Lord, please don't let her hurt Nan, Sylvie thought.

Finally, Sylvie had to hail China to let her know to turn in at the cottage with the yellow door on the left. Andy was already sitting at the gate, so there wasn't much doubt where they were going—if China was looking.

China turned and faced Sylvie once again. "I want you to know that this is very difficult for me, more difficult than I could have ever imagined, but I'm really looking forward to meeting Granny Nan. You don't need to worry."

Sylvie exhaled a breath she didn't know she was holding. "Thank you, dear." And she gave China a smile she hoped would reassure and warm her.

Sylvie led the way to the front door and let them in, halloing to let Nan know they'd come.

"In here, dears."

Granny Nan sat in the wooden rocker by the fireplace. Her face lit like a torch in the night at the sight of China, though Sylvie knew Nan couldn't make out the details of China. Nan could see what she needed to see all right—the face of a much-loved child come home.

Nan stretched out both hands to China. "Och my Lord, 'tis good to see ye, China dear, my dearest wee bairn."

China graciously put her hands into the aged hands of the woman who birthed her and smiled a tight, nervous smile. Nan held on to those beloved hands, now the hands of a woman, not a little child. Sylvie wiped at a tear. It had been so long; it was hard not to feel bitter toward Margaret. All the hurt was so unnecessary. But, the Lord willing, maybe hearts could mend. Here was a bit of joy.

"I'm so pleased to meet you, Mrs. Blair."

"Och, call me Nan."

"Granny Nan, I hear."

"Aye." Nan let out her sweet laugh. "Ye've finally come home."

At that, China's face reddened and tears welled. She dropped to her knees in front of Nan, their hands still clasped and resting in Nan's lap. In a cracked voice China said, "Granny Nan, I don't know what's going on. Please help me understand."

Nan squeezed China's hands, then lifted her own hands and cupped them around China's face. She smoothed the dark hair back from China's brow, gently caressed her cheek. The creases under Nan's eyes glistened wet as she drew nearer to China and kissed her forehead.

"May Christ an' his saints stand between ye an' harm." Nan breathed the blessing on China.

China's shoulders shook, and she buried her head in Nan's lap. Sylvie turned and left them together—at last.

"Come, Andy. Let's go make tea."

MEETING Granny Nan had been a shock, and China needed some time alone to clear her head and try and wrap her brain around all Granny Nan had told her. The stable seemed as good a place as any. China-the-horse nickered at China-the-woman—the confused woman. She slipped her hand through the fence rails and held out a sugar lump for the horse.

The mare came to China, lipped the sugar off her hand. China stroked the horse's neck and murmured soothing words.

No wonder the sight of Granny Nan had felt like a warming ray of sunshine. As a baby, she had bounced on Granny Nan's knee and taken her first steps toward her. What else would feel familiar?

Her mother had made such a mess of everything. China already felt like a motherless child—but to have been ripped from a family who loved her—she didn't know if she could ever forgive her mother.

Margaret MacLeish, never one to do the right thing, certainly not the hard thing, had left Craggan Mhor as soon after China's birth as she could and was not heard from till she turned up a year and a half later to take China away to the States. It baffled China how her mother had gotten a US passport for her and obliterated all traces of her Scottish birth. China would probably never know the answer, since that would require talking to her mother.

A bump from behind startled China. Fly had pushed her behind the knees, nearly sending her against the fence. The dog looked up at China, obviously pleased with herself. Fly panted and her tongue lolled out the side of her mouth. She was covered in mud up to her belly.

"What do you want, you filthy dog?" China looked around, hoping not to see Angus Ritchie. It seemed the two went together like flies and manure.

Fly gave one sharp bark and again poked China with her nose.

"Go away and leave me alone."

A crunch of gravel, and Mr. Ritchie appeared. "Hey, ye're wanted up tae the hoose. John said I should fetch ye." The loathsome man turned around, whistled for Fly, and was gone.

John could have called her if this place had been civilized enough to have cell phone service.

She turned back to the horse, not ready to run when called. This feeling of being the outsider was infuriating when it had once been her home. So far, she had gotten nowhere in changing anything about the stipulations of her uncle's will. They were all legal and binding. Binding her to Craggan Mhor, at least for a year, before she could fully inherit the house and the money—the staggering amount of money. She wasn't sure it was worth it...but meeting Granny Nan today…no, seeing her again after so many years, was breaking China down. Why had her mother taken her away from that dear woman? Her life could have been so different. She could have been loved.

There really wasn't much choice. And a hundred unknowns to deal with.

But for sure, if she stayed the year, this horse had to have a different name. That was an easy one. Charlotte. She'd wished her own name was Charlotte. Jane Eyre would have liked that name. China smiled at the silly thought of her imaginary childhood friend.

"I *would* like to see your baby in the spring." China patted the horse, then made her way "up tae the hoose."

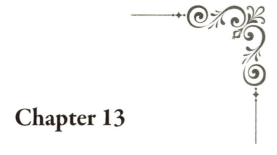

Chapter 13

One more night and she'd be going home. John had asked her yesterday, straight talking he called it, was she going for good or coming back to fulfill the stipulations?

Coming back, she had said.

But nothing was signed in her blood yet. She could still think about it. And think she would.

The sun shone in a faded blue sky for the first time since she arrived. China set out with a walking stick and a bottle of water, following the track John had taken her on to the waterfall. She wore the wellies just in case.

For an hour she walked: through the valley, then up the hillside, skirting outcroppings of gray rock, past a small loch in between the hills. She stepped over oily ooze trickling across the track to the burn on the other side. This time, she wove her way around the gorse bushes with their spikes. If she followed the track and just turned around and went back the way she'd come, she should be all right. Craggan Mhor was long out of sight, and she couldn't see another sign of habitation as far as she looked in any direction—nothing but barren beauty. John had shown her several cottages on a map of the estate, but they were hidden in the trees or over the hill to the west.

The chill Highland air was intoxicating, especially since she now knew it was the first air she'd breathed. Nan told her she had always wanted to be outside and had to frequently be coaxed away from the front door.

China stopped and listened. Water tumbling over rocks. A piercing whistle from a soaring bird.

Singing? Surely not. But the longer she listened, the more sure she was. It was coming from over the hill to her left.

She followed a narrow path through the heather to see if she could glimpse the singer without being noticed.

As she crested the hill, she saw a man standing on a rocky ledge jutting out over the valley. Though he was distant, she clearly saw that he wore a kilt and stout hiking boots. Arms stretched straight up in surrender, he sang a mournful song in a language she didn't recognize, his voice rich and deep. Then he lowered his still outstretched hands, as if to receive something, and fell silent. Mesmerized, she watched the breeze ruffle through his dark hair. But she couldn't see his face.

He turned in her direction and she panicked. His big yellow dog bounded toward her. The man whistled. She did not want to be seen, much less talk to him. She had intruded, been rude. China darted back down the path, the dry heather raspy as she brushed by.

She held the walking stick like a carried spear and scampered as fast as she could down the hill. She hoped the dog had turned back. Not another man and his dog.

When she reached the track to Craggan Mhor and recognized a landmark or two, she breathed easier. But she couldn't get the man out of her mind. First of all, was he on her land? Why was he there? And what was he doing?

The more she thought about it, the more uneasy she became, and she looked back but saw no one. She hadn't expected to be followed, but this was all strange—every bit of it.

China propped the walking stick against the wall by the kitchen door, wiped her boots on the mat, and stepped into the warm kitchen.

Sylvie was kneading bread on the long butcher block. "Have a nice ramble, then?" A wisp of hair flopped over one eye, and Sylvie swiped it aside with her wrist.

"Sylvie, out on my walk just now, I saw a man in a kilt standing on a rock—singing, of all things. Dark hair. Do you know who that might be?"

"Well, this *is* Scotland, so any number of men might be in a kilt, ye ken." Sylvie chuckled and winked. "Was he a good lookin' man? As good lookin' as they come?"

"I don't know. I couldn't really see his face."

"Well, it's likely ye met the laird."

"The laird?"

"Aye. His estate runs alongside Craggan Mhor, and it's likely he was out for a ramble. A great trekker, he is. And quite the horseman. You'll meet him properly soon enough I'm sure."

"Sylvie...I've decided to come back...stay the year."

Sylvie clapped her hands to her cheeks, leaving two floured handprints. She grabbed China and hugged her to near suffocation. China laughed.

Flustered, Sylvie let her go. "Och, sorry, dear. I've gone and got flour all over ye."

"Doesn't matter," China said, dusting herself off. "I'd better go talk to John. There's a lot to take care of to make this happen."

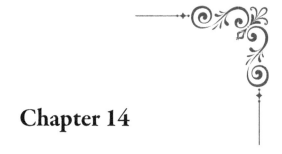

Chapter 14

Duncan pulled the bell ring by the front door of Craggan Mhor. He would have gone round to the kitchen as he often did, but as this was the first time meeting the niece, he thought he'd better make a proper entrance.

Sylvie opened the door, clutching her apron behind her. "Och, Duncan laddie, you've just missed her. Truly. John's left to drive China to Inverness not a quarter of an hour ago."

"That's too bad. I thought it was high time I came round to meet my new neighbor." He knew he didn't sound particularly genuine.

"Well, never mind. She'll be back afore Christmas." Sylvie's smile threatened to split her face, and Duncan thought she might break out in giggles.

"Oh, really?" Though it didn't surprise him. Even a fool wouldn't refuse all that money.

"Come in, come in. You must stop and take a cup of tea with me."

"Wouldn't miss it. And one of your scones, if you please."

"Aye." Sylvie gave his arm a pat and led Duncan to the kitchen.

He hadn't called in at Craggan Mhor since the reception after William's funeral. Truth was, he'd been too busy, but he'd thought often that he wanted to.

"How are you keeping, Sylvie?"

Without looking up, Sylvie continued to lay the tea things on a tray. "Och, well, the roof's not leaking."

He needn't press her. He knew her grief.

"Anyway, China will be comin' back soon. That'll be grand," she said.

When they'd settled in the lounge, Duncan asked, "Does this China MacLeish have long, dark hair and a skittish way about her? I thought I saw a woman yesterday when I was hiking. She darted away like a hare when I looked in her direction."

"Aye, that would be her. She went out for a ramble yesterday morn."

"Actually, she caught me psalm singing." He gave a wry grin. "I wonder if she thought her neighbor crazy."

"Aye. She did wonder ye might be a bit doolally," Sylvie said, tapping her temple.

Her smile faded, and she reached over and patted Duncan's hand. "I pray for you an' your laddies every day of life, ye ken."

"Aye." Duncan bit into his scone, chewed slowly, and swallowed a mouthful, hardly tasting Sylvie's lemon oat scone. His boys were never more than a breath away from his thoughts.

Chapter 15

China stood, stupefied, in the middle of her townhouse living room. Brian had cleared out all the furniture, every rug, every speaker from the sound system. All that was left were some pictures on the walls. That was it. Fury spun her toward the kitchen. Maybe he'd left the garbage bags.

She unhooked each of the framed photos and tossed them in the garbage bag—the photos of Brian and her that at one time had meant something to them, had meant they had a life together that they cherished. No more. She got the insult: take everything but leave what meant nothing to him. She was less treasured than a leather sofa and a sound system.

Outside, she whipped open the lid of the trash bin. It cracked a satisfying *thwack* as it slapped back against itself. She ceremoniously held the trash bag high over the empty bin and let it drop. The sweet sound of shattering glass. She rolled the bin out to the alley where the waste removal people would do just that, remove the waste.

China marched back to the house, ready to face whatever was left.

It wasn't much—the bedroom furniture, some kitchen stuff, the red leather hall bench, and a lamp here and there.

A note lay on the kitchen table weighted down by the salt and pepper shakers. Pay him the half of the trip to Italy she owed him, he'd written in his lefty scrawl. She ripped the note into small pieces, then ripped those pieces smaller. He could wait till forever before he'd see that $4,000. As far as she was concerned, he'd more than hauled off his share. She'd have to deal with the lease later.

Brian was making this easier. He surely didn't mean to make anything easier for her, but she'd have to start over, so why not in Scotland? A forty-one-year-old woman with no furniture to her name. What she did have was going on Craigslist tomorrow. She'd sleep on the floor before she'd sleep in that bed again. But better to never sleep here again.

She got Stacy's voicemail. Not surprising since it was Saturday night.

"Stac, can I come stay with you? Brian cleaned me out, and I can't stand the thought of being here anyway. I know you'll say yes, so I'm coming over. I've still got your key. Hope you pick this up before you get home. Thanks. Love you."

OVER the next few weeks she checked things off her list: done, sold, thrown out, packed to ship, packed to store.

Her job was the main problem, other than the fact that this whole thing was insane. One doesn't just walk away from a good job at the Chicago Regional Office of the US Securities and Exchange Commission. As Securities Compliance Examiner, she'd be up for a promotion to supervisor next year and a nice raise. She was hoping for a leave of absence until she could serve her year's time and get the place sold. But then, she might not need a real job if all that money was still there in the Financial Times Stock Exchange. She'd nearly giggled when John Keith called it the Footsie.

Apparently Uncle William was some stock exchange wizard. Everything he touched turned to pounds sterling. Well, she was no slouch herself. She did know stocks.

She booked a ticket to Inverness with an open return. One way, no way. If she got there before Christmas she could get this year over with.

Pulling books off the shelf in the third-floor study, China found an envelope sticking out the top of *Gone Girl*. She'd never read the book but thought it was an appropriate place to stick the last letter she'd gotten from her mother. There had never been an email. No doubt her mother refused to learn the computer.

She couldn't remember what the letter said; her mother never had much to say and didn't say it often. This letter was dated two years ago. China unfolded the letter and read it. The usual news—she was married again, had moved, and, "PS Miss you." What was this—the fourth marriage? China had lost count since the husbands' names never mattered, and she'd only met one of them. He had come to school with her mother to pick her up and take her somewhere for the summer. He had seemed like a nice man. But he must have had a screw loose to be with her mother.

Santa Fe, New Mexico. China stuffed the letter back in the envelope. Why not? She decided to write to her mother at this address. At the worst, it was a waste of a stamp. Maybe she wanted to gloat that she'd inherited the family estate, not her mother. Maybe she wanted to let her mother guess at how many of her secrets she'd found out. The Mother of Secrets. She found a pad of paper and a slightly grimy envelope in a kitchen drawer.

Mommy dearest.

She tore up that piece of paper, but it felt good to write it.

Mother,

Just a note, in case this finds you, to let you know I'll be at Craggan Mhor, if you want to find me.

She signed it *C* and stuck it in the envelope.

She tossed her mother's two-year-old letter in one of the boxes of clothes to be shipped over—though she didn't know why she was taking any of her heels or anything nice. It seemed she'd be dressed in layers of wool to her eyeballs and tromping around in those wellie things. But she couldn't just throw away her mother's last known address.

Never let it be said, she thought, that her mother had the corner on erratic behavior—she, China MacLeish, was about to embark on an adventure, even if reluctantly—cut loose, thanks to a faithless fiancé. China stacked her statistics texts and her economics books in a box labeled for storage.

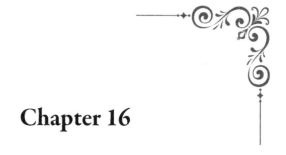

Chapter 16

"Mair pepper. It definitely needs mair pepper." Nan bent over the steaming pot of Scotch broth, blowing on a wooden spoonful of the hearty soup.

Sylvie smiled. "If the first spoonful wasn't peppery enough for ye, it's sure the second willna be."

Nan turned and pointed the now-empty spoon at Sylvie. "I think I'll get me eyes done. I'm that sure I want to see my wee China as best I can."

Again Sylvie smiled. "I've booked you in a fortnight from now. I knew you'd want to go through with it this time. You'll be seein' right as rain when China gets here to stay."

"Here to stay, is it? Och, I'll believe that when I see it. Here for a year any road. An' I'll be grateful tae the Lord for every day wi' her. Seems such a short time ago she was but a wee bairnie on my knee. Such a dear she was."

The wistful look on Nan's face evaporated, and she eyed Sylvie. "Eh, were ye goin' to tell me I was havin' the cataract surgery? Or just drive me tae hospital an' hand me off?"

Nan's wry smile said she wasn't serious, and Sylvie gave Nan's shoulders a side-hug squeeze. "I was going to tell you soon enough that you could cancel again if ye really wanted."

"Nay, 'tis time. I'm afeart o' the knife to me eyes, but the Lord will see to it."

Sylvie drew back the lace curtain at the window facing out to sea. "It's blowin' a hoolie." Her brow furrowed, though she knew they were safe in the sturdy little cottage.

The wind-tossed waves pounded on the shore with a rhythmic *whump*, a menace Sylvie knew all too well. The sea took her Ranald. His fishing boat was found the next day after the storm, but the Minch didn't give up his body for several days. Duncan had gone to do the identifying and spared her. But storms made her uneasy still.

"I'm goin' up to rest a bit." Nan grabbed the railing up the steep steps and made her way to her room, the smaller of the two bedrooms in the two-up two-down cottage. Sylvie watched her to the top of the stairs. For her age, Nan was fairly spry and determined, but she didn't see well what with those cataracts. It seemed Nan had always been here, though it was just the ten years since Ranald's father died. Such a joy she was, praying her way through the day, and a smile most always lighting her face.

When Sylvie heard Nan snoring, she went to her own room and took the carved wooden box from its place in the chest. She laid out the contents of the box on her bed and set the empty box on her bedside table next to the photo of Tom. Her dear Tom, the joy of her heart—and her greatest grief. How could Margaret MacLeish have left her child that first year and a half and even then, when she'd taken China away, not cleave that wee girl to her heart? She had her Tom barely twenty years before he was gone.

Eyes closed, Sylvie murmured her constant petition: "Circle me, Lord, keep peace within." Peace, aye. But understanding may never come.

Sylvie rested her hand on the slim book of Robbie Burns's poems, the brown leather soft from William's and her hands. Though she knew the inscription in her heart, she turned to the faded writing: *I will luve thee still, my Sylvie, till a' the seas gang dry.* A sad smile warmed her, and she carefully set the book aside, drifting her fingers back through the small mound of sea glass on the bed.

She scooped up the bits of colored glass and sifted the memories through her fingers. Satiny to the touch, their cutting edges polished off, they spoke of walks along the shore, William dashing to retrieve a glass jewel before the sea took it back—time together. The cobalt piece was her favorite, probably part of an old remedy bottle. She rubbed the smoothness of it.

Sylvie looked up and snapped her fist closed round the glass—caught. Nan stood in the doorway. How could she not have heard Nan get up?

"I'm..." Sylvie's hand fluttered like a moth not knowing where to go.

"There now, child. No to worry." Nan's kind smile let Sylvie know she was forgiven—had done no wrong, even. "I've ken many a year aboot your wee box. Ye left it oot one day. Mind, I didna open it. I thought 'twas likely from William."

Nan sat beside Sylvie on the bed and took her hand.

"You're sae dear to me. I dinna begrudge ye your memories o' William, ye ken. Ye were good to my Ranald an' he to you."

"Aye." Sylvie could find no words.

"It's been a hard time of late, aye." Nan squeezed Sylvie's hand still clutching the blue glass. "I'll leave ye to it."

Nan stumped down the stairs.

Sylvie picked up the framed photo of her darling Tom—so proud in his uniform, so young—and she could no longer hold back her quiet tears.

Chapter 17

A road sign told her she was on the A832, but China had no idea where she was. On the way to a year at Craggan Mhor was all she knew. Jet-lagged and sick of her stomach rolling on these twisting mountain roads—on the wrong side of the road—China braced a hand on the side of the seat as John took another curve too fast. The Ford Anglia was no more comfortable than the Land Rover Defender and wasn't much cleaner. What was the hurry to get her prison sentence started?

John had left her alone for the last half hour. He tried to get a conversation going but must have given up. She knew he was trying to be nice and make her feel welcome, but she wasn't in the mood. Faces of granite wall whizzed by, blasted away to make the road. Now a fence, then a white house close by the road, and a frequent view of a stream tumbling alongside the road.

The car slowed, and John pulled into a gravel parking area, switched off the engine. "There's the view ye want. Loch Maree." He exited the car.

China stepped out of the car and looked where John pointed. The wind tugged at her hair and blew it across her face. Once she cleared her vision, she noticed a ribbon of twisty road ahead of them—a long, twisty road. At the foot of the valley lay a silvered loch the color of a salmon's belly. A few weeks ago, she must have been by this spot but had no recollection of it. For all she knew, she might not have even looked around, upset as she was at being here. Today the sky was a hundred shades of gray, clouds piled upon clouds driven by the wind, but the air was cold and crisp on this mid-December day. And she was once again upset at being here.

She gave John a tired smile. "It is beautiful. You'd make a good tour guide—or a salesman." Her smile quirked.

"Feel free to make yourself comfortable, madam." John made a sweeping gesture in the direction of two porta-potties.

China rolled her eyes at him.

"Gents on the left, ladies on the right," he said.

"Ladies are always right." As China turned toward the blue box, the wind combed wintery fingers through her hair.

Back in the car, China pulled the door shut with a creak of hinges and a hollow *clunk*. "How much farther?"

John pulled onto the road and jammed through the gears. "Not much farther, aye." He passed a delivery van between curves.

A sign pointed left to Fionnloch. The narrow two-lane road forked and continued winding. So far, she'd not seen a road or a path in Scotland that went straight or level for very long. They drove on through more twists and turns.

"John, I have to tell someone, or I'll blow up." China stared straight ahead, though her insides were a crooked mess. "I'm really nervous about this."

"This?"

"Yes, *this*. This is crazy. Living in Scotland for a year. Being the owner-in-waiting at Craggan Mhor. Not one thing and not another."

John laughed. "Owner-in-waiting, is it?"

She wanted to go on about how awful it was to be moving into her uncle's home. An uncle she never knew but might have liked—if she'd had the chance.

"Ye ken, we all want you to do well and be happy. Nay, truth be told, we want you to stay, even after your year is up."

China snorted. "Even Angus?"

"Give him time."

"Yes, I'm sure you'd rather have me than some absentee Englishman. Or worse yet, some Arab sheikh moved in with his harem."

John set his jaw. "We'd manage, aye."

China could see she'd gone too far. "Sorry. Just my frustration talking."

"Do ye often speak before ye think?"

Now it was her turn to be offended. But it was true. Too often she did. Rather than let him know he'd hit the mark, she chose silence.

But John didn't let the silence alone for long. "Remember, I said we Scots like straight talking?"

"Yes." China kept her eyes on the road ahead.

"Let's talk straight, you and me. It's no good the owner not trusting the estate manager, and I need to know I can trust you as well."

"Trust? What's that?"

"Look, China." John pulled off into a wide spot along the roadside, jerked the parking brake on, and turned to face her, his arm flung back over his seat. "I ken your mother well, and she gave you a raw deal in life. But I dinna have the time nor the inclination to put up with your tantrums. You're a grown woman, and I expect ye to behave like one. Nay, I *want* ye to behave like one because I dinna want your mother to stamp ye with her way of bein'. You can trust me, so act like it till ye do. Am I clear?"

China's mouth fell open and her eyes widened at this huge man taking up more than his share of the tiny car. No one had ever spoken to her like that. The smell of his tweed jacket—outdoors, barn, and diesel—seemed too close. She'd just been lectured by an employee. And it was fine. It was. What choice did she have? Besides, she was too tired to argue, especially when he was right.

"Clear." She turned back to looking out the front window. Her chin crept forward.

John put the Anglia in gear. "My father was the factor before me, and I've worked on the estate since I was a grouse beater at twelve, ye ken. Anything else you'd like to know?"

"No, not right now, thank you." China folded her hands in her lap and smiled accidentally. If John saw it, that was all right. The more she knew of this rough, but obviously capable man, the more she respected him. No wonder her uncle had entrusted the estate to him.

China recognized the low granite wall in hues of red, gray, and black flanking the lane on the right. The darkened bronze plate bolted into the wall read *Craggan Mhor* in large letters.

A small crowd hung around the front entrance of the house. Fly and Andy barked and circled around the car as John drove in; Sylvie and Angus shouted at their dogs to come away and stop that racket.

Who were all these people? And there was Granny Nan sitting on a bench beside the door.

She eased out of the car, but before she'd fully straightened up, Sylvie had her in a tight hug.

Fly wouldn't stop barking and head-butted China's leg.

"Fly, get away." Angus shouldered his way past China and slammed the passenger door shut. He waved Fly off. "Ye keep this up an' I'll gie ye away to *her*, then where'd ye be, eh?" He went around to the back of the car, yanked China's other suitcase out and set it beside the one John had already deposited on the gravel drive.

"Och, my dear, we're that glad to see you." Sylvie held both China's hands clasped between her own.

"I...well, I'm glad to see you too." Stupid thing to say, but she felt like she had a spotlight on her. She bent closer to Sylvie and lowered her voice. "Sylvie, who are these people?"

"Why, these are all the folks who work here at Craggan Mhor."

At least a dozen people smiled at her, the men standing with caps in hand. She faced them, a smile frozen in place. Recognition seemed to flicker in the eyes of the older staff, but China looked away. Most likely they were strangers who had known her.

China went to Granny Nan and bent to kiss her leathery cheek.

"My wee lassie," said Nan, leaning on her walking stick.

"Oh, please don't get up," China said.

"Nay, 'tis good for me." China and Nan embraced, till Nan held China at arm's length and studied her face. "'Tis sae sweet to see ye, dearie."

"Granny Nan, what happened to your eye?"

"Och, I had the cataracts done while ye were away. Just a bit of bruising, aye. An' now I see ye fine. 'Tis a miracle really." Nan stroked China's cheek with bony fingers.

Sylvie appeared by China's side. "I know you're tired, but your staff wanted to greet ye properly."

My staff. Strange words to hear. She had an administrative assistant at the SEC, but *staff*...that sounded odd.

Sylvie introduced each person. All shook hands and welcomed her with a little nod. Several looked like high school kids. Apparently, there was someone to do everything at Craggan Mhor. China would never remember all their names just yet, but she'd remember the work and weather etched on their faces and callused hands.

The line of cedar trees on the far side of the stream slowed the wind but didn't stop it, and a gnawing damp blew down the collar of her leather jacket, threatening to chill her to the marrow. China cupped her hands and breathed a bit of warmth into them.

John said, "Well, that's us off, then." The staff again said their welcomes and dispersed to wherever it was they'd been before China arrived. John helped Nan to the car.

Angus disappeared with her suitcase and left the front door open, Fly following after him into the house. John hefted the remaining suitcase like it was half its weight and went in, still leaving the door open.

"I've got your room all ready for you." Sylvie clasped China's hand. "Did ye have a good flight? Och, but you must have had a lot to do since we saw ye last." Sylvie looked flustered and dropped China's hand. China was too tired to give it much notice. "There's me chattering on like a magpie." Sylvie picked up China's carry-on bag, went to the door, and motioned China to enter. "Come ahead."

John hustled past Sylvie on his way out. "I'll just run Granny Nan home, aye?"

Sylvie nodded at him, then turned an entreating look to China.

"Thank you, Sylvie. This was very sweet of you." They all no doubt thought it was a homecoming, but she'd make no promises beyond a year from now. As far as she was concerned, home was still Chicago.

Sylvie set China's bag outside the bedroom door and opened the door to Uncle William's room. With not one ounce of enthusiasm, China stepped into what felt like a one-way plank off a ship.

But...this wasn't Uncle William's room. There must be a mistake. She hadn't seen this room before.

China turned to Sylvie. "What?..."

"I took the liberty of having your room redecorated. I hope ye like it." Sylvie was now quite flushed, her eyes searching China's face.

"But I thought I couldn't change a thing for a year."

"Well, I talked to John, and he thought it perfectly reasonable to make a few changes in your uncle's room. To make you more comfortable, aye."

China could have been standing in her own room—actually, the bedroom of her dreams—walls washed in her favorite shade of sea blue-green, carpet the color of sand in shadow, and no curtains on the window. The inviting bed, piled with pillows in floral and seashell prints, had an upholstered headboard in buttoned and tufted aqua velvet. Gone was the two-ton walnut four-poster.

"How?..." A grin plastered her face.

Sylvie laughed, clearly delighted. "I rang your friend Stacy. She told me what ye liked."

"How did you get her number?"

"Do I look so old I canna figure out technology? You left the door open to William's study when you were on the phone. Well, I couldn't help but hear ye talking to someone called Stacy, so I checked the phone records. I'm that sorry if it was a bit devious, but I wanted you to be happy. Make ye welcome. Do ye mind?"

"No, Sylvie, it's perfect. Really beautiful. Thank you. But I'll get after that Stacy. We've had a no-secrets rule since our school days." China felt a flush warming her cheeks. "I don't suppose this should count though." She didn't often know so much kindness all at once. At least not since her teacher Mrs. Fisher.

China drank in the transformed room for long seconds, then turned toward her suitcases which were on luggage racks next to the walnut armoire.

"Well, I'll leave you to it, then." Sylvie took a couple steps into the room and set China's carry-on down. "If there's anything you'd like to change here, you certainly may." She quickly turned and left.

"Sylvie," China stopped her. "Thank you."

"Aye, you're welcome. Ye are." Sylvie quietly clicked the door shut.

China walked over to stand in the bay window of her room and looked out across the lawn to the jetty and the sea. She'd always wanted to live where she didn't need curtains, where she could fall asleep with moonlight dusting her face and the morning sun warming her awake.

But there was probably never a time here when clouds didn't obscure everything in the heavens above.

Chapter 18

"You canna be here, I'm tellin' ye. Not now." Sylvie twisted her apron in her hands.

Fists balled at his side, Gordy faced his sister. "If she's my daughter, I wanna see her."

Sylvie stepped back, the sitting room in her cottage seeming way too small to contain the anger in Gordy. Yet she knew his anger was at Margaret, had always been at Margaret. It's just that everyone around him got the lashing of his tongue and, if he was drunk enough, the sting of his fists should a poor devil be fool enough to cross him.

The stench of last night's bender hung on him. It was a miracle he still had his job in Glasgow, but then, dock workers were known for being a rough lot. Maybe the boss turned a blind eye.

His face was near purple. "I have a right."

"Aye, ye do, Gordy." Sylvie reached out to touch his arm, but he pulled away. "But can ye give it some time? You're a chancer now. It's too soon. Let her settle in, get to know us, then—"

"Shut it, Sylvie. I willna. 'Tis forty-one years, an' I'll lay eyes on mah daughter."

"What if you frighten her off? You'll have only yourself to blame for that, eh?"

Gordy stormed out and slammed the door hard enough that the knocker clattered as it bounced against itself. Sylvie heard his truck roar to a start; pebbles flew as he swung round and peeled away back to the village—back to the pub.

She was worried Gordy would make a bigger muddle than he could handle this time. But she was more worried for China, the poor wee lamb. This was none of her making.

THE man across the street stared at her too intensely. China's hand rested on the door to the Wildcat Coffee Shop: the Best Coffee in the Highlands, according to the sign. John had dropped her off, to get some local culture, he said, while he had some business in the village. The tall, staring man had a mass of dark hair falling in messy waves almost to his shoulders. His biker leather jacket hung open, and his jeans were ripped at one knee—the kind of rip that didn't look like he'd paid extra for it. China quickly looked away and entered the coffee shop.

John had warned her this was a quirky place. The first thing she saw was a scruffy mounted Scottish wildcat in full snarl, white plaster showing through in a chip on the nose. And under it, a sign in large lettering: Thursdays Save the Wildcat Day. In smaller letters: 10% of Profits go to Wildcat Haven.

There was stuff everywhere: on the walls, the ceiling, and on the floor between the mismatched tables and chairs. There were license plates from several countries, skis, photos of mountain climbers, India print hippie cloths draped over a couple sofas, a toy mountain cable car strung in a corner, a ratty stuffed badger with a sign posted over it indicating Wednesdays were Save the Badger Day—and more.

But the smells coming from the counter drew her like a sleep walker. Chalked menu boards high on the wall listed pastries, sandwiches, and meat and fish pies. The caramel-colored cake drizzled with buttery goo called to her.

"Can I be helpin' ye, then?" A young woman with a tattooed sleeve and light brown white-girl dreads over a foot long looked inquiringly at China.

The woman said something else unintelligible. "Excuse me?" China said.

"Och," said the tattooed girl, and she slowly formed each word again. "I said, 'Is this your first time tae the Wildcat?'"

"Yes."

"Sae, ye mun be the American, aye."

China sniggered. Did everyone know who she was? "*The* American? Am I the only one to come in here?"

"Naw, but we dinna see mony come the winter, ye ken. An' you're expected, ye ken."

"I ken." China returned the girl's warm smile. "What's your name?"

"Alex. Alex Wylie."

"Mine's China MacLeish."

"I ken." Alex flashed a crooked-toothed grin at China.

"What's that?" China pointed at the brown cake in the square pan.

Alex said something, but all China understood was "puddin'."

"Pardon?"

Alex rolled her eyes with a friendly smirk and once again spoke slowly. "Sticky toffee puddin'."

"I'm sorry. Must be my ears. We are speaking the same language, aren't we?"

"Naw, I speak Glaswegian."

"Did you say, 'Norwegian'?" China asked, smiling.

The woman frothing milk at the coffee machine tipped her head toward Alex, nodded, and made a funny face.

China took her Americano and dessert to the sunroom attached to the side. The glass-enclosed room overlooked Fionnloch Bay and the islands in the distance. A sign taped to the glass almost caused her to spill her coffee in a spasm of laughter: Unattended children will be given espresso and a free kitten.

She chose a table in the corner. This was all right—sticky toffee pudding overlooking the sea.

A shape loomed beside her, and she looked up, the fork still in her mouth. That man was standing so close to her, she smelled oil on his clothes. His face was that of a rough, older man, and China didn't like the looks of him. Her instincts told her from years of big-city living not to speak first.

"China MacLeish?" said the man.

She chewed her bite of cake and took her time, though the cake suddenly tasted dry. "Who are you?"

"Name's Gordy Campbell."

His stale beer breath almost made her flinch. "Move along please, Mr. Campbell." She forced herself to look him in the eyes.

"Eh?" An ugly glower contorted the stranger's face.

"I said move along."

Feigning nonchalance, China reached for her coffee. Breath exploded from the man, and her hand jerked, splashing coffee into the saucer. He turned on his heels and left.

China looked at Alex, who was drying a glass and staring after Gordy Campbell, lips pursed tight.

On her way out to get a ride back to Craggan Mhor with John, China stopped at the counter. "Alex, who's that man, that Gordy Campbell?"

"All I ken is ye should stay well clear o' him."

China nodded and left. She didn't need this.

John pulled into the parking lot and shoved the passenger door open for her.

"John, who's Gordy Campbell?"

"Eh? Gordy Campbell? Why?" John shot her a look that unnerved China.

"He was staring at me on the street, and he came into the coffee shop. He wanted to talk."

"Ye stay well away from him, lassie. Well away."

"He knew my name."

"Aye, the whole village knows your name. He's a bad lot, that Gordy Campbell."

China swallowed hard.

"You tell me if he comes round again, ye hear?"

John gripped the steering wheel with tense hands and drove them back to Craggan Mhor, a muscle on the side of his jaw twitching.

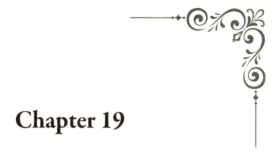

Chapter 19

A week here, and she might go crazy.
China roamed the house and the stable, fed sugar lumps to the horses. She wanted to ride, but John hadn't had time to take her. Riding alone wasn't a good idea, not knowing the horses or where she was. And all the rocky hills looked alike and dangerous. She wasn't afraid, but she wasn't stupid. And the weather was unbelievably terrible. Clouds often hung down into the valley—clag, John called it—obscuring anything that might have been beautiful in an endless drizzle.

Thank heavens for Stacy. Phone calls had been a lifeline to China's life in Chicago. Except she wished Stacy hadn't said anything about Brian. Apparently Brian was trying to find her, but Stacy wasn't helping him.

After again looking at Uncle William's stock portfolio, it was beginning to sink in just how much money he had made on the Footsie. She closed the laptop and walked from the study down the long green tartan-carpeted hall into the kitchen to look for Sylvie.

"Och, there ye are. I was just thinkin' maybe you'd want to have a wander down to visit with Nan for a bit."

China leaned against the kitchen doorframe.

"What are ye doin'? Waitin' for an invitation to come in?" Sylvie chuckled and wiped her hands on her apron. "Warm yourself by the Aga." She waved at the black cast iron stove with the two large gleaming burner covers on top.

China moved to stand with her back to the stove. "I don't want to bother Nan."

"No bother. She'd be ever so delighted to see you. I'll ring her and let her know you're comin'. Won't take a minute." Sylvie sat at the small desk crowded with a laptop and boxes of papers and receipts. The old dial phone made a whirring noise.

"It's me, love...Aye, a bit later I should think...I'm sending China round to see you, if that's all right...Aye, I told her so. She'll be there directly, I should think...Aye...Bye now."

"All set. She's thrilled to bits."

"Thank you, Sylvie. I admit, I'm going a little nuts. I need to find something more to do."

"Well, it's Christmas is coming next week with all the parties. And there's the lovely Christmas Eve service at the kirk."

"No, I don't think so. Besides, I haven't been invited." China felt a ridiculous lump in her throat.

"Och, no one needs invitations in Fionnloch. It's a small village and everyone's invited. They all assume you'd be coming. Why, there's a party right here at Craggan Mhor on Hogmanay—every year."

"Hogmanay?"

"New Year's Eve."

"I'd rather not this year, if you don't mind."

Sylvie looked taken aback. "I'm that sorry, China, but this year the party's already set." She gestured to the computer on the desk. "I've already placed the grocery order. Maybe next year you can change it...if ye like."

"Oh, I forgot. I'm Mistress of Nothing for a year." Bitterness about this arrangement overtook her sometimes.

"It's a grand time, it is. And you'll meet the laird, aye. He always comes with his family."

"Great. Can I have a headache that night?"

"If ye like, but no till after the laird's been here." Sylvie winked. "Then Ne'er's Day the laird hosts the games at Glengorm House. The entire village turns out for that."

China's shoulders slumped. "Oh, Sylvie, can I just cancel out on the holidays? Please? This is too much."

"Away with ye now. Nan's waitin'. Take a torch with you as you may be coming back in the gloaming. I'll have your supper waiting for you." Sylvie handed China a flashlight and went back to beating whatever it was she was making in the large crockery bowl.

"Dinna forget your mac, aye. It's by the front door. An' keep your eye on the weather. Call for John to fetch ye if need be."

China certainly knew the whereabouts of the raincoat by now. She donned the coat and slipped into the wellies, then closed the heavy front door behind her. The door was never locked.

By now she knew the way to Granny Nan's, having visited there twice.

The sea was wild. Even in the relatively sheltered bay where Craggan Mhor sat, the sea threw itself against the jetty. Behind the jetty, closer to the house, the restless sea tossed wavelets in random patterns. A storm was coming, but if she stayed inside because of the weather in the Highlands, she'd never get out. She wished she could drive. Not that she wanted to drive on the left, but it was better than being on foot or at the mercy of getting rides for the next year. She twisted her hair in a ponytail and set out on the path. She had maybe a couple of hours to avoid the worst of the storm.

Insistent barking grew closer, and China turned to see Fly bearing down on her at a flat-out run. The dog nearly plowed into her legs and nosed her hand—tongue hanging out, panting and wiggling all over. Fly took off ahead of China and chased a squirrel up a tree. The dog ran back and fell into step, trotting beside China. Fly looked up at China, and China could have sworn the dog visibly grinned.

She stopped and reached to pat Fly's head. "You'd better get back. Angus won't like this." Fly begged with her nose for more, which China obliged. "Don't tell anyone, but I really like dogs." China put her hand on the dog's head, stroked her thumb between the dog's eyes.

China kept walking, thinking Fly would turn back, now she'd got what she came for, but she didn't. They walked on a bit farther together. Then came a barely audible whistle, and Fly wheeled and charged off toward the house.

China couldn't see Angus, which was just as well. With a sigh, she turned back to the path to Nan's. Her mother had given away any animal she'd ever loved. First it was the golden retriever puppy that had been a bribe to spend the summer with her mother at that Colorado commune. Then it was the kitten she'd found in the window well of the house next door in Minneapolis. She'd never really had a pet. The goldfish at school didn't count.

Nan opened the door before China knocked.

"Come in. Come in, my dearie." Nan grabbed China's hand and pulled her down to kiss her cheek.

Granny Nan smelled of powder, the kind Mrs. Fisher had in a round box on her bathroom vanity.

China carried the tea tray into the sitting room and looked around while Nan poured the tea.

"Who's this?" China asked, picking up a framed photo of a young soldier in desert fatigues.

"Och, that's my grandson, Tom."

"Sylvie's son?"

"Aye."

"Is he in the service?"

"Killed in the Gulf War, poor laddie. In the Black Watch, he was. Like to have broke Sylvie's an' my Ranald's hearts. Mine too, aye."

"I'm so sorry." China swallowed hard and set the photo back on the mantel. "I didn't know Sylvie had a son."

"Aye, the light of our lives Tom was."

Sadness must have drawn many of the lines in Nan's face, yet her eyes held a sweet softness. China thought such a great grief might make a woman hard, but Sylvie had that same sweet look.

"Would ye like a McVitie's biscuit, dear?" Nan offered a plate of plain cookies.

They sipped their tea, and China ate two of the graham cookies.

"Nan, please tell me more about my time with you. Tell me what we did, what I was like."

"Ye dinna remember a thing, eh?"

"No, not a thing. Just this weird sense that I'd seen you before when we met in November."

"Well, ye were but a wee thing when your mither came for ye. I've been waitin' for ye to ask. An' here I've got a few photographs tae show ye, aye." Nan reached over to the side table and picked up an old cookie tin.

As they looked at each photo, China alternated between joy and tears. Nan showed her the love she must have known as an infant and young toddler—love from Nan and her family, and all the people of Fionnloch—for there were photos of lots of different people holding her and playing with her. A collie dog, much like Fly, was apparently a constant companion.

The shutters rattling on the sea side of the cottage signaled to China that she'd better be going. It was dark twilight already. She kissed Nan on the cheek and thanked her.

Glad she had the flashlight, China hurried back to Craggan Mhor. The first drops of cold rain bit at her face. She was sorry she'd left the wide-brimmed hat on the hook by the front door. When she reached the house, her hair was nearly soaked. The soft light through the closed living room drapes was a welcome sight.

She entered the house and stamped off the rain, then hung the raincoat on the hook where it dripped onto the rubber tray below. She toed off the wellies and was about to put her own shoes back on when she heard Christmas music coming from the living room. A soft hum of voices accompanied the music.

China slicked back her wet hair and crept to the living room door.

She stood in the doorway, stunned by what she saw, and all she could think to do was run.

THE Christmas tree reached all the way to the tall ceiling. Gold balls and silver stars dotted the evergreen; garlands of red berries and fat red tartan ribbons hung festooned on the branches, and a shower of tinsel blanketed most of the tree. At the top, an angel in glittering white held an electrified candle aloft. White lights glowed all over the tree.

Heat surged through China.

Sylvie held out a hand and a smile to China, and China took a step back.

"It's only three days till Christmas Eve, and we wanted to surprise you," Sylvie said.

Andy let out a sharp bark. Fly was nowhere to be seen.

Several of the staff were present, and all looked her way, all smiles. John was up a ladder, draping tinsel that a woman she didn't recognize handed up to him. A girl who did the cleaning held a bundle of the stuff and was spreading it over the lower branches.

"I...I didn't..." Words refused to come out around the swelling in China's throat. A recoiling deep in her heart terrified and taunted her. Flooded with longing, yet fearing disappointment, her defenses screamed at her.

She turned and bolted to the front door, pushed her feet into the wellies, tore the dripping mac off the hook, and ran out the door. She didn't know if she closed it but didn't look back.

Down the path to the stable she ran. She veered onto the track out to the river and into the hills, running in the heavy wellies. Her hair was now thoroughly soaked, rain streaming into her eyes.

Stopping to catch her breath, she looked back in the direction she'd come. No one followed her. She didn't expect it, yet she was surprised. Why didn't they? Then she felt foolish for even wondering. The pain in her chest felt like it would crack her ribs–or break her heart.

In the dark, she jogged on toward the sound of the cascading falls; cold rain pelted her head. Why she'd ever agreed to this whole scheme didn't make any sense. These people were strangers, yet she'd moved in for a year like they were family. It seemed like a whole lot of pretending by everyone. She'd been fooled before—not this time.

China stuffed her freezing hands in the mac pockets. And found the flashlight. The white beam lit the deer trail she'd followed weeks ago that had taken her to the edge of the neighbor's property. The slick mac slid past the gorse thorns, and she kept going, up the hill. Hot tears diluted in the icy rain. She wanted to get away from Craggan Mhor, but she couldn't.

Up she climbed till she reached a pile of rocks. The path through the rocks grew narrow and indistinct, even in the light of the flashlight. She didn't remember this spot from her previous walk. The night thickened around her, the clag settling over the hill, and she realized she'd soon not know up from down. Suddenly, she was afraid.

Surely they would look for her. A sob escaped. She was acting like the child John had said he wouldn't tolerate. Running off like this was a tantrum, and she'd found out long ago that tantrums never worked. Why would they look for her?

When she turned to follow the trail back, her toe caught on something, and she fell. With a cry, she hit rocks beside the path, and the flashlight flew from her hand. She heard it bounce on the rocks before wind and rain tore away all other sound. No light showed her where the flashlight had landed, broken.

China knew she was hurt. She sat up slowly. Her head hurt; her hand felt like she'd run it through a meat grinder, and her hip hurt. But the pain in her ankle stabbed at her stomach, and she feared she'd vomit. Fresh tears stung. Rain seeped in at her collar, wetting her sweater, and she shivered, feeling very much like an abandoned child.

She didn't know how long she sat there, but the reality of being alone, cold, wet, and injured in the wilds of the Scottish Highlands was sinking into her fogged brain. She had to get back. China grasped at the rocks around her, but her hands wouldn't cooperate, too stiff with cold to hold on. She tried to push herself up, but when she put weight on her ankle, she cried out and fell again, this time onto her knees.

"Help!" Desperate, she yelled into the murk. Desperate enough to choke back the lump of hurt and anger in her throat. "Help me, please!"

She yelled till her throat was raw. The wind took her words and her panic and threw them back at her. She scooted backwards into a cleft in the rocks which might afford some shelter, but not able to see beyond five feet in any direction, she had no idea where she was.

She'd just have to wait. Her panic was now complete.

And she was so tired.

So cold. So very cold...

A blinding light...and hands lifted her.

She struggled, speechless, against the nightmare. What was happening? Furious barking surrounded her, filled her head.

A man's voice soothed, "There, there. I've got you now. You'll be all right."

Before she felt any weight on her throbbing ankle, she was swept into strong arms.

Someone tucked a blanket around her, and she was borne off by a stranger. He must be a stranger—she smelled a hint of unfamiliar cologne. China let her head rest against his hard shoulder.

DUNCAN waited for word on how the runaway niece fared. He sat in the deep wing chair beside the peat fire, his stockinged feet stretched out before him, a cut crystal glass of whisky in his hand. He'd helped himself to whatever was in the decanter on the sideboard. Lagavulin by the dark look of it, William's preferred whisky. He swirled the liquid and watched the legs run down the sides of the glass. The Christmas tree lights flashed a kaleidoscope in the facets of the crystal.

He missed William. They had spent many an evening in this room, enjoying a dram. William was like a brother. They were so like-minded: about their faith, about friends and family, love of country. And where they differed—politics—it had been a source of heated discussions and much laughter.

And now, here was this foolish niece of his come to take over the estate. Duncan feared for what would become of Craggan Mhor, though he knew he should trust William and John when they got their heads together. They rarely made a mistake in judging character and making decisions concerning the estate. William had done so much to set things right at Craggan Mhor. The MacLeish name no longer had people talking behind their hands. But tonight might start the tittle-tattle all over.

Duncan flexed his aching shoulders. He wished the woman hadn't run so far. He wasn't young anymore, and he was sore from carrying her. He'd thought of throwing her over his shoulder like a sack of flour to carry her more easily. Not that she weighed much. He had to admit, when he laid her on her bed looking for all the world like a drowned kitten, that she was an attractive woman. Beautiful, in fact. He wondered if she was named China for her pale porcelain skin.

When she had opened her eyes and gazed up at him, he knew she didn't see him, barely conscious as she was. But her dark indigo eyes and thick black lashes were startling, like rare jewels. Maybe all beautiful women were trouble.

Really, she was fortunate Fly and Angus had found her. If he reckoned right, she fell near the cliff at the bottom of which her great-grandmother was found.

Dr. Reza was with China. Duncan had told Sylvie he'd wait till there was word as to how she was. Sitting here was as good as sitting at Glengorm. Sylvie was so worried, it was the least he could do for her.

Duncan sipped the whisky and thought again of what he'd been grappling with when the call came that China MacLeish was lost in the storm. He'd come straightaway to help with the search. Now his thoughts returned to his sons. His heart ached for what they were going through. And he didn't know what to do. Not for sure.

The front door shut with the sound of heavy wood, and Duncan heard the doctor's car drive off. The howling wind had stopped.

"Och, Duncan, you are a dear." Sylvie dropped down on the sofa. "The doctor said it's just a bad sprain. Lots of scrapes and bruises, but she'll be right as rain." She flapped her hands off her lap. "I guess we don't need more rain at that, eh?"

"You're the dear one, Sylvie." Duncan pitied how exhausted she looked.

Sylvie waved the comment off.

"Why did she run off do you suppose?" Duncan asked.

"She came through the lounge door there, saw the tree and us finishing up the trimming, and just bolted like a rabbit. I wanted to surprise her. Do you think she didn't like it?"

"I doubt it had anything to do with the tree."

"Did ye say she was near the cliff?" Sylvie asked, worry creasing her brow.

"She was."

Sylvie shook her head, grim-faced.

"Does she know?" Duncan asked.

"About her great-grandmother and all?"

Duncan nodded. "And all. She may know nothing of her kin since it seems Margaret brushed away all tracks leading back to Scotland and Craggan Mhor. At least that's what John told me."

"Aye. I hate to bring it all out, but I fear she'll hear it in the village. It's best if it comes from me, aye."

"Will you tell her all of it, Sylvie?"

"Och, that's a verra big mouthful to swallow, ye ken."

"As you say, you don't want her hearing it in the village."

Sylvie sighed. "Aye, you're right. But she's no going to like hearing it."

"I'll be off, then." Duncan tossed back the last of the whisky and set the glass on the side table. "Don't get up. I'll see myself out." He pressed a staying hand on Sylvie's shoulder and squeezed gently.

"Nay, I must go up and see to the ice on China's ankle."

At the front door Duncan slipped on his wellies and retrieved his rain gear. It was late, and he had a lot to do in the lab tomorrow. All this drama made him weary. He couldn't say that he was prepared to get on well with his new neighbor; he'd probably give her a wide berth.

SYLVIE climbed the stairs. She was only sixty, but at this moment, she felt every one of her years as weights on her feet. No, the truth was, the weight of it was all she needed to tell China. But no rush. China wasn't going to be out and about in the village for a few days.

Sylvie stopped. But it was almost Christmas. And people might come here to visit. She'd have no wagging tongues telling China about her great-gran. Sylvie clutched her cardigan closed across her chest. What would she do? And this was not the lovely Christmas she'd hoped to give China. This would not do. She'd have to sort this out.

The door to China's room clicked quietly as Sylvie opened and shut it. Soft light shone from the lamp on the dressing table. The redecorated room looked so very different from when she had nursed William. In truth, she had wanted the room changed as much as she had assumed China would.

Sylvie shifted the ice pack on China's ankle and tucked the comforter around her shoulders. Sylvie sat in the chair beside the bed, a too-familiar feeling, but at least the chair was different.

China slept. Her dark hair, nearly dry now, lay in tangles on the pillow. Sylvie couldn't help herself—she got up and laid her hand on China's forehead, smoothed back her hair, and whispered a prayer over her. "Lord, may you be with this dear one in sleep and in waking through the days of her life. Thank ye for bringing her to us. Keep her near you. Keep her safe, aye. Amen to the Father, amen to the Son, amen to the Holy Spirit, three in One."

China shifted her hurt foot in her sleep. Sylvie removed the ice pack and set it in the sink in the bathroom. Let the anti-inflammatory do its work now. She snapped off the light and started to take herself off to the lounge but changed her mind and came back to the chair. She couldn't leave her niece now. She'd watch a while and make sure the wee lamb was all right. And Sylvie settled to her familiar bedside vigil.

Sylvie woke, startled by a noise. She looked up to see China leaning against the bathroom doorframe.

"I didn't mean to wake you. Sorry," China said.

"Och, no bother at all." Sylvie was quickly on her feet to help China back to bed. The pale pink and blue light coming in at the bare windows promised this would be a rare day.

Supported on one side by Sylvie, China hobbled back to bed.

"How do ye feel, dearie?" Sylvie fussed over the rumpled bed.

"Like I was dragged a mile behind a truck."

"Aye, I can well believe it."

"What happened?"

Sylvie glanced at China, dismayed that China might not remember the events of last night. And that she might have to recount them. And tell China more besides.

"What would you like for breakfast? Yesterday's porridge is as good today. And it's quick."

"That would be fine. And coffee, please. Black. Lots of it." China settled back into the freshly fluffed pillows. "And, Sylvie, we need to talk."

"Aye, that we do."

Chapter 20

There it was—a divorce for Christmas. *Nollaig Chridheil.* And a Happy New Year.

Duncan threw the envelope into the center drawer of his desk and whipped the drawer closed, in danger of cracking wood were it not so stout.

He'd told his solicitors to get this over with, but it was still a shock that it could move through the legal system so fast. Apparently Harriet's side had been cooperative. And why wouldn't they when he'd given her more than a fair settlement, in light of how unfair the whole business was.

Where were the boys? He desperately needed to be with his children. Home for the holidays, they had no idea this news was coming, and he wasn't about to tell them and spoil Christmas. There would be time enough to tell them before they went back to school mid-January.

Duncan called Ross on his mobile. Ross answered after several rings. "Where are you, laddie?"

"Out in the stable grooming the horses with Donnie."

"Fancy a ramble? Is Callum with you?"

"Aye, Da."

Duncan smiled into the phone. Ross often lapsed into the vernacular when he spent time with Donnie. Duncan didn't mind. Nothing wrong with his boys sounding like Scots.

"Aye to the ramble? And to Callum with you?"

"Aye." Duncan heard Ross yell to Callum. "Da's asking do we want to hike with him."

"I'll have Janet pack a lunch for us and meet you in the kitchen. About a quarter of an hour?" said Duncan.

"Aye."

An amused "humph" escaped from Duncan. Ross wasn't usually so short on words.

Duncan hurried to his bedroom where he changed into his kilt and thick wool knee socks. He slipped his sgian dubh in at the top of his right sock, the hilt of the knife sticking out. Though it was cold, he preferred to wear his father's old green Sinclair kilt when he hiked. It made him feel right with the land and right with his clan. He pulled a bulky cream wool sweater over his head. No need for a mac today. The weather was fine. Work in the lab could wait.

Janet clucked when Duncan walked in the kitchen and announced that he and the boys would be taking a picnic to the hills. He knew she wasn't really upset; he saw that smirk as she went for the rucksack in the pantry.

Duncan's mobile rang, and he stepped outside to take the call. Glasgow Police. He didn't have to think twice before he turned down the forensic botany job, though it did sound interesting. Occasional work for the police was challenging, but at the moment, there was too much going on.

By the time Duncan concluded the call, Janet had prepared their lunch and was standing with her hands on her hips next to the bulging rucksack on the butcher block.

"There ye be. Ham an' cheese sandwiches, apples, plenty o' chocolate, an' a flask o' tea. Should do ye nicely, aye?" She folded her arms over her ample middle.

"Och," she clapped her hands. "I near forgot the boiled eggs."

"Perfect. Thank you, Janet," Duncan said.

"Nay bother. 'Tis a braw day for it," she said, wrapping the peeled eggs in greaseproof paper.

"Hey, Dad." Callum rushed in the kitchen door, Ross directly behind, both boys breathless and red-cheeked.

"Hey, boys." The sight of his boys swelled Duncan's heart.

Janet reached to pinch Ross's cheek, and he ducked out from under her hand.

"We'll be back for supper." Duncan threw the rucksack over one shoulder and made for the door.

"Aye, ye will, or it's cold neeps an' tatties ye'll be gettin'."

In the gun room they laced up their hiking boots while Trooper danced from one front paw to the other. They set off in the Range Rover to park where the track ended and the rocky path into the hills began. Stalkers used this path, which was just about wide enough for an all-terrain vehicle laden with a deer.

Duncan set an easy pace. The legs of a ten-year-old needed to be the mark of how far and how fast they could go. Ross showed signs of being a first rate hillwalker, but it would be a year or two before he'd join Callum and himself on the lower slopes of Slioch.

Callum darted past and took the lead in their single-file march along the pebble-strewn path through the heather. Duncan smiled. He was never happier than in the company of his boys. He turned and let Ross go ahead. No need for the youngest to be last.

The ground was level for a distance, and they came to the bridge over the River Slee that tumbled through the valley. Resonant thumps sounded from the timbers as they trod onto the bridge.

"Poohsticks!" shouted Ross.

Callum rolled his eyes, and Duncan shot him a good-humored warning look to play along with his younger brother. They had played this game since the boys were little.

They all broke off branches of heather and stood ready at the upriver rail. The dipper feeding along the river's edge flew off and shrilled a protest.

Ross called the start. "Ready. Steady. Go!"

They dropped their heather sticks into the river and rushed to the other side to see who had won.

"Trooper! No!" Callum called the dog away from jumping in after the sticks.

"Drat! I forgot what my stick looks like. I don't know who won," Duncan fibbed. "We'll have to do it again."

The next time Callum forgot, and they had to play a third time. And so it went through five rounds.

"Had enough?" Duncan showed Trooper a stick and flung it into the river for the dog to fetch. "Let's try and make the lochan for lunch."

A fish eagle soared overhead, riding the air currents. Trooper bounded out of the water and shook himself. Callum had to leap aside or be drenched. And he laughed.

"I'll show you where I saw a badger sett the last time I was up this way." Duncan led off down the path.

Stunted juniper trees dotted the hills amongst the rocks. The rush of the cascading Slee faded to the background.

Callum whistled a tune, then stopped. "Dad, I don't suppose Mum is coming home for Christmas?" Undisguised sarcasm tainted Callum's question.

Caught off guard, Duncan cleared his throat before answering. He had been trying to forget that he was now a divorced man. In Christmases past, Glengorm had buzzed with Harriet's relatives, most of whom had two or three noisy children, and it had been a grand time—except for Harriet's mother, Cruella de Vil.

"No, she won't," Duncan said, his voice a bit thick.

"Then what are we going to do? Christmas is only two days away." Callum didn't seem overly concerned that his mother would not be here. It was no different from last year.

"Church Christmas Eve, of course." He was at a loss after that; he realized he hadn't planned anything. This Christmas seemed lonely beyond belief, even worse than last year—not that he missed Harriet—he found her absence a blessed relief for the most part. But he knew it wasn't right for the boys. He thought the boys would have heard from their grandparents, but it seemed the cord had been severed and tossed away. By tomorrow he'd look for a box delivered to the door from Harriet's parents. Gifts for the boys, if last year indicated how it would go. Grandparenting by FedEx.

"I don't suppose you want to open gifts, eh?" The boys cheered their yes loud enough to startle any badger that might have been lying at the mouth of its sett.

"Then we'll do that Christmas morning, as usual." Duncan shifted the rucksack to the other shoulder not because it needed shifting but because he needed to think of what to say next to his children who deserved a happy Christmas. "To be honest, I haven't given it much thought. I'm so sorry. It's been a bit hectic."

"That's okay, Dad. I understand."

Callum seemed so much the young man. But he was the one Duncan worried about most. He was angry. Not that Duncan blamed him. He was sure Callum knew the truth of why there was a divorce, though he'd never let on to the children. He could see it in Callum's eyes, especially when he had looked at his mother when she last visited. Betrayal.

"What if we help serve the meal at the Heritage Centre? Then we'll come home and have our Christmas dinner that Janet's preparing for us." It seemed absurd, the three of them having Christmas dinner around the huge table. "Shall we invite Janet and Tolly to join us? I know their son is away."

"May I invite Donnie?" Ross jumped with enthusiasm.

"Absolutely." Duncan hoped they all could come on this short notice, or it would turn into yet another disappointment. "That's settled, then. I know Janet's been dousing the Christmas pudding for weeks. One for you, and one for me." Duncan winked. The one for him was drowned in whisky; the one for the boys was drizzled with orange juice. "And I know she dropped the coin in the batter. We'll see who's lucky this year."

Duncan took a metal cup from the rucksack and stepped just off the path to dip branch water from the small burn gurgling over rocks. They drank their fill of the golden peat-tinged water before moving on.

"There! There's the badger sett." Callum pointed up the hill. The hole with a mound of dirt in front of it was hard to see.

"That it is, laddie. Good eyes." Duncan clapped Callum on the shoulder. "Looks like fresh dirt. The ladies at the Wildcat will be glad to know Glengorm is doing its bit to save the badger."

"Let's go." Ross moved on down the path. "I'm hungry." And, Duncan thought, Ross probably didn't like the idea of a badger charging them.

Loch Fuar nestled in a bowl between the hills. A cold, deep loch, it was no more than two acres in surface. And it was a favorite spot. A rocky ledge thrusting up and out over the edge of the lochan was where Sinclairs had picnicked for as long as Duncan could remember. Likely long before that.

Trooper immediately took a running leap into the loch and emerged to shake cold water in an arc, just missing them. Duncan and the boys clambered up the well-worn side of the ledge where the granite formed steps of a sort, and Duncan laid out the lunch on the table rock.

Booted feet dangling over the ledge, which wasn't so high that Duncan worried, Ross shared his bread crusts with Trooper.

"Dad," Callum said in a serious tone Duncan didn't often hear from him. "I don't want to go back to school. I want to stay here with you."

Mid-chew, Duncan stared at his son, then swallowed hard. "Why, laddie? You can't just not go back to school."

"Yeah," Ross chimed in. "Why do we have to? What's wrong with the school here? Josh likes it fine."

In truth, Duncan had been grappling with the thorny issue of the boys' schooling. Merchiston Castle was one of the finest all-boys public schools in Scotland, and he'd broken with Sinclair tradition by sending the boys there instead of to Eton College in England. He wanted his children educated in Scotland. Harriet had fought him on this, but he had been adamant. Yet, he wanted Ross and Callum near, and just now, Edinburgh seemed half a world away.

He'd gone so far in thinking about this as to talk with the headmistress in Fionnloch. Fionnloch schools were top notch. He felt snobbish thinking it, but it would be unprecedented for the laird's children to attend local schools past age ten. A move, however, that he was willing to make if it meant his boys were better able to weather this divorce and their mother's scarpering off.

Duncan took another bite of his sandwich and chewed slowly, eyeing the two boys who seemed to be in league on this.

"I'll tell you straight, then. I've been thinking about it."

Both boys leapt to their feet and cheered. Trooper barked along.

"Hey, now. You don't need to go off the ledge about it." He'd had no idea this had been brewing in those little heads of theirs, but he wasn't surprised; Ross had seemed depressed and Callum so angry.

"But," Duncan said, and the boys stopped celebrating—Trooper did not. "I think you should finish out the year at Merchiston. Then start Autumn Term in Fionnloch."

"Promise?"

"Callum, I promise as best I can. I'll make an appointment to talk with Merchiston admin when I take you back after break. They'll be sorry to see you leave. You've both done well there. I'm proud of my men."

"Aye, Da." Ross puffed out his little-boy chest.

Duncan grinned at Ross and shook his head. "You're a rascal."

But then he fell solemn. "Not a word of this yet. Agreed? I need to trust you on this. I don't want village tongues wagging with Sinclair business till it's all settled. And I mean it, aye?"

"Yes, Sir!" the boys shouted in unison.

"That's more like it. And it's *Sir Duncan*, if you please, ye wee tumshies." The boys tackled their father, sending Trooper into gales of barking, and they all tumbled in a happy scrum—till Duncan remembered there was a ledge nearby and sat up, laughing. "We'll talk more on this. I promise."

They had eaten and rested long enough; Duncan could see the cold blooming on the boys' cheeks. Apple cores and sandwich wrappers stuffed in the rucksack, flask drained and stoppered, and they were off, back to Glengorm. Ross and Callum scampered ahead; Trooper raced after possible rabbits, and Duncan took up the rear, his kilt swaying at the back with the easy downhill walk.

In the distance, a russet shape moved up the hill—a stag. Duncan watched as the red deer ascended with slow, stately steps. It stopped and looked their direction, huge antlers pivoting in the light. Then the monarch of the glen resumed his climb to the top of his kingdom.

"'The earth is the Lord's and everything in it,'" Duncan murmured. "Aye, it is."

Chapter 21

The peat fire sent up lazy flames; the Christmas tree glowed and shimmered, and China sat with her foot on an ottoman in the living room. She finished the last bite of fruitcake Sylvie had brought her and set the plate on the side table.

Christmas had been a disappointment. But then, China had come over to Scotland at this time expecting just that. Better here where she was a stranger than back in Chicago where she had been hoping to plan a wedding with Brian. Her disappointment was with herself, and now she had an injured ankle to show for it. Running away like that was the most juvenile thing she'd done in a long time. She was no longer ten years old when, oops, her mother had said, something's come up, and I'll see if Mrs. Fisher can keep you over Christmas break.

That had crushed China's little-girl heart. And one day during that long school holiday, sitting next to Mrs. Fisher on her scratchy brown couch, China had cried it out. Mrs. Fisher said to her: "Your mother loves you. She just gets confused sometimes. It's not your fault."

Mrs. Fisher had included China in everything, right down to the same number of gifts under the Christmas tree that the grandchildren got. But China was an outsider, and the Fisher family was not her family. Yet it was the greatest and most painful kindness China had ever known—until now.

Sylvie had done her best to make Christmas special. The tree was lovely. And the Christmas dinner Sylvie brought for her from home was thoughtful. But China knew Sylvie had a life outside of Craggan Mhor and didn't expect her hand held. She wasn't an invalid; it just took her a little longer to get around. Sylvie had apologized all over herself, but China assured her she'd be all right on her own. It seemed the entire village went to church Christmas Eve. A sprained ankle had been a good excuse to miss something she didn't want to do anyway.

John and his wife had come to wish her Merry Christmas. China hadn't known John had a wife. Fiona was very nice: buxom and tweedy, red-haired and freckled.

China half-expected other visitors but wasn't really surprised when no one came, given the stunt she'd pulled. They probably thought she was nuts.

The surprise had been Angus. Christmas Eve after dinner, Angus had sauntered into the living room, Fly at his heels, and announced that he'd leave Fly with her for the evening while he was away at kirk. He signaled Fly to go stay by China, clapped his cap on his head, and left.

Fly was ecstatic about the arrangement. And so was China.

For the longest time Fly sat with her head in China's lap, brown eyes studying her. China stroked Fly's head, dug her fingers in the dog's fur on her neck and shoulders. Fly stuck her nose under China's hand if she stopped petting, demanding more. It was good to have a dog, even if only a borrowed one.

Fly eventually lay down in front of the fire. She stretched out on her side, feet to the fire, and slept. Her paws ran after sheep, and she let out sleeping-dog woofs, then lapsed into soft snores. China read.

Around ten o'clock, Fly heard a whistle, shot out the living room door, and tore down the hall.

China had hobbled up to bed, alone in the house on Christmas Eve. But she knew Angus and Fly weren't far away out back.

But the holidays weren't over yet. This dreaded Hogmanay party at Craggan Mhor was coming up in a few days. She flexed and stretched her ankle, not nearly as sore now, and wondered what she would do with herself for the evening. The TV lounge was an option, but the BBC was a reminder that she wasn't in the USA.

China was already sick of sitting, doing nothing but reading or familiarizing herself with Uncle William's stock portfolio. She finally understood what was going on with it. William MacLeish had been one of those rare stock market geniuses. And legally. She had verified that right away. She wished she could have picked his brain to know how he did it.

After the holidays were over, she needed something to do for a year, or she would go nuts. The portfolio was far too complicated to manage on her own, and the investment firm Uncle William hired just after he was diagnosed with pancreatic cancer seemed to be doing a good job.

Andy's bark roused China from her thoughts.

Sylvie stood in the doorway. "I'm off now. Is there anything else I can get for you?"

"Sylvie, are you avoiding having that talk with me? I wasn't so delirious I forgot about it."

"Avoiding? Nay...well, aye, probably." Sylvie picked up the empty plate and started for the kitchen.

"I need to know about my family."

Sylvie stopped, her back to China. "Aye, I knew you'd want to know."

"I have so many questions."

Sylvie faced China, her eyes and mouth pinched at the corners. "Ye ken, I'm just the housekeeper. I don't know that I have the answers ye seek."

"You are not just the housekeeper. I can tell. It's like you were part of the family. John too. When, Sylvie? When can we talk?"

Sylvie sighed noisily. "Well, now's as good a time as any. I'll ring Nan and let her know I'll be a bit longer. No need to keep you waiting."

Back from using the phone in the kitchen, Sylvie settled into a wing chair, her back a bit straighter than usual.

"Now, then. What would ye like to know?"

SURE they weren't being overheard, no windows were open on this nippy day, Sylvie fretted to Nan as they walked to the shops. "Och, I dinna know if I've done right, telling China."

"She had a right tae know aboot her kin. It's important, ye ken. 'Tis part o' who she is—what lives in her bones," Nan said.

"But such a hard story. And I didn't know what to say about her mother. Margaret left so young and in such a state. Does Margaret have the madness, or was she just young and foolish? I hated to say one way or the other. Though William thought she did."

"Did ye tell her o' her great-gran, then?"

"Och, no. I couldna bring myself to tell her all that. Maybe I should have. But I was so afraid, the night she ran off, to hear she'd been near the cliff where they found poor Una MacLeish all twisted on the rocks below."

"Aye, I mean ye no pain, dearie, but ye know as well as any the cost o' the MacLeish madness."

Nan's words stung. But not so much as many years ago when William had been firm that they could not marry for fear of passing the madness on to their children. Sylvie and William had cried in each other's arms, seeking comfort that could never come, and vowing to be friends to their dying day. In all those years, she and

William had never so much as touched, not till the end when he lay dying.

Nan rested a gentle hand on Sylvie's arm crooked over her shopping basket. "Aye, that Lachlan MacLeish was surely one o' the meanest men tae walk these parts. God rest his soul. His bairns shrank from his shadow. At least William's father kept himself an' his rages locked in his study, smashin' only glasses."

"Did ye tell her o' Gordy?"

"Nay. That may have broken her. In truth, I didn't tell her overmuch. I didn't want to upset her again."

They were coming to the shops now, and people were about; Sylvie said no more. Yet she knew in her sorry heart that she'd have to tell China more.

IF China thought she needed a job to do, she certainly had one this week. Sylvie had China set up in the kitchen on a stool at the long butcher block table—beating batter, steeping oats in Scotch whisky for the Atholl brose, mixing up the non-alcoholic ginger wine, shaping the shortbread, rolling out crusts for the meat pies. China had never seen so much cooking going on.

She normally ate healthy, but since she'd been here, she'd been too exhausted and consumed with all the changes to give it much thought. If she made New Year's resolutions, eating healthy again would be near the top of the list—right after getting back to Chicago by next New Year's Eve.

Three more girls from the village came to help with the cleaning, making five girls going over Craggan Mhor from top to bottom. Apparently, cleaning for the new year was a tradition.

"Fruitcake. Finally, something that looks American." China watched as Sylvie took a large tray out of the larder and set it on the table.

Sylvie chuckled. "Aye, but I'll wager you don't have a coin for luck in your black buns. We're a superstitious lot, ye ken." Several cheesecloth-wrapped cakes reeked of booze. She set a bottle of Scotch and a jar of orange juice on the island. "But it's for fun and sticking with the old ways we do it now, most of us. There's no doubt the Lord's our protector to be sure."

China smiled but had nothing to say on the subject.

Sylvie spooned Scotch over all but two of the cakes, which got the orange juice treatment. "For the bairns, ye ken."

"What a waste of good Scotch," China said.

"Nay, this is the whisky I cook with. Whisky for the guests is on the sideboard in the lounge.

"Check the pies, would you, dear?"

China wrapped a heavy pot holder around the oven handle and peeked at the pies. "Not quite golden brown yet."

The Aga fascinated China: a half-ton monster of a stove with two huge covered burner plates on top, constantly on, fed by fuel oil. The warmth and quaintness of the stove drew China like a magnet whenever she was in the kitchen, which was often, if she wanted to talk to Sylvie, which she did.

"You say you do this every year?" The aroma in the kitchen was a pungent mixture of meat, sugar, and alcohol. China scooped out a fingerful of shortbread batter and popped it in her mouth.

"Aye, this was your Uncle William's favorite party. He loved Hogmanay. Making people welcome and starting the year with the Lord's blessing."

"Blessing?"

"William prayed a blessing on the guests."

"Surely I'm not expected to—"

"No worries. The laird will do the honors this year."

The laird? Which was worse? "I suppose I'll have to meet him."

Sylvie rewrapped the sticky fruitcakes, then washed her hands under the tap in the three-foot wide sink.

"Well, my dear, you already have met the laird."

China shot Sylvie a sharp look.

"Aye. He carried you here the night ye ran off. Fly may have led Angus to you, but it was Duncan brought ye back."

China wanted to shrink away, slip into next December if she could, but she was up to her elbows in stiff shortbread batter. The bitter taste in her mouth blocked any words.

Had he seen her that day when he was singing in the hills? No doubt he thought she was nuts—like her mother.

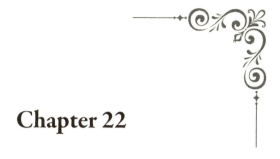

Chapter 22

A single candle glowed in the window to the side of the door. Duncan and his sons stood outside Craggan Mhor, waiting. They were a splendid trio in full Highland dress of the clan Sinclair.

Cheers rose from inside. Party whistles blew. It was the new year.

Duncan nodded. "Go ahead, Callum. It's time for your first first-foot."

Callum shifted the basket of gifts to his left arm, stepped up to the door, and pulled the bell ring. The chatter of voices stilled. John Keith opened the door and said, "Welcome to you. *Bliadhna Mhath Ùr.*"

A crowd pressed in behind John to see the first-footer. China hung at the back Duncan noticed.

Callum stood tall and delivered his greeting in a loud, clear voice. "A happy Ne'er's Day tae ye, and God's blessing." He grinned. And Duncan clapped his son on the shoulder.

"I'm not very dark-haired, but will I do as your first-footer?" Callum asked John.

"Aye, laddie, you're a fine first-footer. You don't look like a Viking raider to me." John shook Callum's hand and pulled him into the crowd. "Come in. Come in. You ken what to do."

Callum made his way through the group, basket on his arm, kissing all the women on the cheek and handshakes to the men. His own cheeks flared red, and his grin was constant, apart from when his lips were puckered in a kiss.

"Your turn as first-footer will come." Duncan tousled Ross's hair.

"I hope I want to kiss girls by then." Ross made a face like he tasted something sour.

When Callum had finished the round of kisses and handshakes, John held out his empty glass into which Callum poured a dram of whisky from the bottle in his basket. John handed Callum a glass of ginger wine, and they had the first toast to the New Year. Callum raised his glass and declaimed the traditional Hogmanay toast. "A guid Ne'er to ane an' a'! Lang may yer lum reek."

"Aye," John said. "Here's to fuel for the fire and a good smokin' chimney."

Duncan was proud of his young-man son.

Callum passed his basket of cakes and chocolate to Sylvie, giving her an extra kiss on the cheek.

Highland music swelled from the stereo, laughter popped out over conversations, and the *tink* of glasses rose above it all. Duncan moved around the room, greeting as he went. A few of his own staff had come to the Craggan Mhor Hogmanay party. William would have enjoyed the sight of a crowd having a good time in his house.

"Sylvie, would you introduce me to the new mistress of Craggan Mhor?" Duncan was fairly certain China MacLeish had no recollection of laying eyes on him.

"Aye." Sylvie searched the party. "Where can she be now?"

"There, by the window. Isn't that she?" A willowy form in a tight navy blue dress to her knees stood gazing out the bay window in the lounge. Duncan followed Sylvie to where China stood, her back to the party, apparently watching the guests reflected in the dark windows.

Sylvie lightly touched China's arm. "China, I've someone as I'd like you to meet."

China turned, and Duncan felt the room spin a bit. The woman had the most arresting eyes he'd ever seen—deep blue sapphires, flecked around the pupil with bits of amber the color of Cairngorm stones. And now, when those eyes were actually focused on him and not dimmed by hypothermia, he nearly gasped for breath.

Her lips were a pale pink with just enough fullness to not appear perpetually pouty. And her hair fell in tumbling espresso waves over and past her shoulders. He wasn't prepared for how beautiful she was. Duncan tried not to focus on the neckline of her dress. He felt a fool.

"I'd like ye to meet Miss China MacLeish, mistress of Craggan Mhor," Sylvie bubbled with obvious pleasure. "And this is Duncan Sinclair, Laird of Fionnloch."

"Mr. Laird." China flushed a nice red that complimented her dress. "I think we've met." She didn't smile. Didn't offer her hand. The sparkle he'd seen in her eyes for a moment faded, and she took a small step back.

Sylvie stood, lips parted, looking quite gobsmacked. "Well, I'll leave ye to it, then," she said and fairly ran from them.

"Miss MacLeish." Duncan gave a polite nod. "Yes, we have met. Although you're a bit dryer than when I last saw you." Duncan flashed her his most affable smile.

"I suppose I should thank you," she said.

He waited. He noticed a hint of a frown as her gaze drifted to his grandfather's sealskin sporran hanging from a silver chain round his waist.

She took a sip of her drink and looked away. "So, thank you."

"My pleasure."

"I doubt it," she said. Still no smile.

That was enough of this. She obviously wore her beauty like a suit of armor, and he wasn't interested in jousting. He'd done the proper thing and introduced himself. "Pleasure to meet you, Miss MacLeish." She nodded, and Duncan went back to the party.

The party continued into the night with singing and laughing. Occasionally Duncan was aware of China but made no further effort to speak to her. He found Ross fast asleep on the sofa in the TV lounge, Andy curled beside him.

At Sylvie's signal, Duncan prayed the New Year's blessing. Then John raised his strong baritone voice, starting them off on "Auld Lang Syne." Forming a circle, they all crossed arms and clasped hands, swaying to the familiar strains of the Robbie Burns song. Sylvie made a place for China, and to the woman's credit, she sang along on the refrain.

Duncan heard a banging on the front door, and since he was closest, he stepped out of the circle, crossed the foyer, and opened the door to see who the latecomer might be. There stood Gordy Campbell. The man reeked of spirits.

"I wanna see mah lassie, aye." Gordy listed to one side.

Duncan barred the way. "Gordy, now is not the time."

"I'll no be put off, d'ye hear?"

Gordy wanted to come in, that was clear, but he would have had to thump Duncan on the shoulder to do so—and Duncan was not moving. Duncan stood to every bit of his height and breadth, knowing that even a fool like Gordy Campbell was unlikely to try to get by him.

Duncan stepped forward, causing Gordy to stagger back two steps, and closed the door behind him, leaving him outside with Gordy.

"Tell you what, Gordy, why don't you go back to Sylvie's cottage and sleep it off? I'm sure there's a better time to meet Miss MacLeish. Talk to Sylvie about it."

Gordy gave a low mean-dog growl.

"And, Gordy, don't think about making trouble at Glengorm House tomorrow. I'm asking you. All right?"

"Aye, His Lordship always gets his way, ye Sassenach-tainted scunner."

In a flash, Duncan's hands found Gordy's shirt collar and twisted. "Don't you ever speak to me like that again. You hear? And if you cause trouble for Miss China MacLeish, you'll have me to answer to. Aye." He shook Gordy loose.

Cursing and spitting, Gordy backed away. Duncan readied for a charge that didn't come. Gordy staggered to his truck, and Duncan waited till he spun his tires on the drive, and his old truck roared down the road and out of earshot. This was surely not over.

Duncan hated to put a damper on the party for Sylvie, but he had to warn her that her brother had shown up, drunk, and that he might be trouble. At the very least he'd be sleeping on her sofa when she got home.

He didn't like it, but he'd have to be involved for Sylvie's sake.

Best warn John as well. Gordy Campbell was no harmless drunk.

LAST night, when China had turned and come face-to-face with His Lairdship, she was almost knocked speechless. What a ridiculous cliché of the romantic Highland hero. She'd never seen such a good-looking man.

And she took an instant dislike to him. A man like that must be insufferable.

She was really irked that she'd let him disturb what little sleep she got last night. Like some adolescent, she'd dreamed of him, standing on a heather-covered hill, hand outstretched to her.

It didn't help that for the half hour after she got to bed she couldn't drive the picture of him out of her head. Tall, much taller than Brian. Polished mahogany hair just long enough to be soft, with a silver dusting at his temples. Kind green eyes. A nose carved by Michelangelo. Lips...He was the kind of man you wanted to look at, not talk to. And she'd done just that. Probably not very nice, but she was going to keep Duncan Sinclair, Laird of Fionnloch, a long arm's length away.

And now she was on her way to Glengorm House for the New Year's Day festivities with Sylvie and Nan. Not her choice.

In Sylvie's little car, they crossed a bridge over a shallow, rippling river.

"Is this the driveway?" China asked. There was no sign of a house yet.

"Aye, 'tis a mite long. Glengorm's up the valley a bit."

"Sylvie, why didn't you warn me about the laird."

"Warn ye?" Sylvie gripped the steering wheel of the Morris Minor and shot China a concerned look in the rear view mirror. "Why on earth?"

"About how good looking the man is."

Chuckles floated back from Nan in the passenger seat; she certainly wasn't deaf, and Sylvie gave a hearty laugh.

"I did, ye ken. 'Good lookin' as they come,' I said. And the nicest, aye."

"Nice?"

"Aye. He's been underfoot at Craggan Mhor since he was a wee thing. He and William were great friends. Though William was a good bit older."

"There." Sylvie waved ahead. "There's the manor house."

A great whitewashed stone house stood at the back of an expanse of lawn, a drive circling around the front. It looked baronial in the extreme. At least twice the size of Craggan Mhor.

Parked cars lined the drive and formed rows in a marked area of the lawn. It looked like a medieval fair in full swing. Bright tents. Banners. Smoke from huge grills. And games. Small children, maybe four- and five-year-olds, were lined up to begin a race at the far end of the lawn.

China stepped out of the car and helped Nan out. The smell of grilling meat teased her nose and drew a groan from her stomach.

A starting pistol fired, and the children were off, fists pumping. Cheering parents crowded the sideline. The red-headed child in the lead stumbled and fell; she'd lost a shoe. Her dad jumped in to fix the disaster, and the little girl charged on to shouts from the crowd, crossing the finish line last, but happy.

China raised a fist and cheered before she knew what she was doing. Nan smiled at her and took her arm. "Let's get a bite to eat, shall we? Feed that noisy wame o' yours."

Everyone they passed on the way to the food tent stopped to greet Nan and Sylvie—and China. China couldn't understand everything they said, but they sounded friendly. It was uncomfortable, but China pasted her smile on and plowed ahead.

Until. A woman smelling in need of a bath, with frowzy salt-and-pepper hair, wrapped her arms around China. "Och, there ye are. Ye were just a wee bairn that last time I laid eyes on ye. Ye've grown, aye. I dinna guess ye'd remember me. Franny Dalrymple? Has your mother spoke o' me? We were pals, aye."

China untangled herself from the woman's arms. "Pleased to meet you." She stepped back; Franny advanced with her.

"I hear you're back to take over at Craggan Mhor, eh?"

"Excuse me please." China stepped around the smelly woman and leaned in to whisper in Sylvie's ear. "I'm going for a walk. Be back in a bit."

The man she'd seen at the coffee shop, that Gordy Campbell, stood at the edge of the woods. He turned and disappeared into the trees. She walked the opposite direction.

CHINA opened the laird's stable door. Not something she'd ordinarily do, entering where she wasn't invited.

A low nicker greeted her, and she walked in, leaving the door open behind her.

The stable smelled of horses: a hint of manure but mostly hay. Her eyes adjusted to the dim light. The barn was spotless. Stalls of heavy wooden planking, topped with iron horse-prison bars, lined both sides of the aisle.

Another nicker from the first stall on the left. "Night Rogue," read the polished brass plaque on the door.

"Pleased to meet you, Night Rogue." China stroked the muzzle that poked through the bars. The horse tried to lip her fingers. "I'm afraid I don't have anything for you, boy."

The tall black horse arched his neck, did a turn around his stall, and came back to her. "Showing off, huh? You're a beauty." The horse snorted and tossed his head. "I'll bet you are a rogue."

A shadow fell into the aisle and startled China.

"I see you've made friends with my horse anyway."

China dropped her hands to her side, caught by Mr. Laird himself where she had no business being.

"I'm...I'm so sorry." She wanted to bolt but already felt enough of a fool.

The laird strode over to the stall door and laid a hand on the horse's neck. "You like horses?"

He was so near to her she got the scent of his cologne. It smelled familiar. And today he was dressed in jeans, turtleneck sweater, and a tweed sport coat—still dangerously good looking—and so tall.

"Again, I'm sorry. I'll be going." She started to leave, but he reached out a hand and grasped her arm, gently. She looked at him and again couldn't mistake the kindness in his eyes, even in this light. He quickly released her.

"Miss MacLeish, could we start over? Last night wasn't a very good start, and after all, we are neighbors, so we might as well be friends."

Friends? A man wanting to be friends was usually code for something else on his agenda. But she was a little short on friends here.

"I suppose we might as well. It might make my year go faster to have at least one friend."

"Good." He flashed her a smile that brought out a ridiculous, but alluring, dimple on the right side. What more? She expected to hear a *ping* as a starburst glittered from his smile.

"Your year, eh? William told me about his unusual arrangement for your inheritance. Then you mean to stick with the year?"

"Yes, and I'll try to be gone as much as I'm allowed in that time...if it's any of your business."

"Steady on. I meant no offense. I'm sure it's very difficult to be in this situation."

"You have no idea."

He broke the eye contact that was making her uncomfortable and turned back to his horse.

"I was asking: Do you like horses?"

"I do. In fact, I've discovered that I have three and a half of them. And I'm thrilled. I can't wait to ride."

"Ah, yes," he said. "China...your mare is bred to Ro."

"Charlotte. I can't have a horse with my name. One named China is bad enough. Uncle William probably thought I'd never show up to claim her."

"He did, actually. He always hoped you'd come. One day. But he'd hoped to meet you when you did."

"You know, Mr. Laird, I can only take very small bits of all this at a time, and I've just about reached my limit here. But I don't want to do the childish thing and run off again. Ever. So, if you don't mind, I'll excuse myself." She spun on her heel to leave.

"Call me Duncan. Please."

China turned back to him, and in the light coming in at the stable door, she thought she saw a man who really did want to be friends—or he was flirting with her. He had an ease about him that both drew and repelled her, but he had Sylvie's endorsement, and that meant something. She poked her chin out a bit. "China," she said.

"China...would you like to meet the other horses? As long as you're here."

Loneliness pulled her back in, curiosity found her standing next to him.

"How's your ankle, by the way?"

"Nearly healed. Thank you. I hardly even limp."

"We should ride soon. Do you think you'd be up for that?"

Words China had been longing to hear—from someone. "Yes, please. I think I'll be ready in about a week." She couldn't help smiling.

"Right." They walked along the row of stalls as they talked, and China admired Ross's Highland pony and Callum's bay gelding.

A flashy blue roan poked her nose between the bars, and Duncan reached up and rubbed her black face. "And this is my wife's horse, Blue Duchess. Quite the jumper."

"Your wife?" China asked sharply. She had assumed he was divorced, having no wife with him at the party last night.

Duncan looked stricken. "Sorry. I forgot. We're divorced."

"You forgot you're divorced?" Icicles hung on her words. Was this a game for him?

"Just recently."

She drilled him with her eyes—waiting.

"A few days ago actually. Not my idea."

"So you still love her?" China wanted to get this charade over with. She didn't have time for men with wife-baggage, as friends or anything else.

"Oh, no. Believe me. Nothing like that. It's complicated." He ran a hand through his hair.

"It always is." Did he think she was stupid?

"Look, China,...if I may still call you that?" He thrust his hands in his jacket pockets and made unwavering eye contact. "I really do mean I'd like to try and be friends with you. Just friends. And if you're not interested, I understand."

This whole thing was ridiculous. A gorgeous man with his hands in his pockets, gazing into her eyes, flashing a winsome dimpled smile, thinking of her feelings. As if under a spell, she couldn't say no. She expected someone to pop up and say the day was almost done; Brigadoon was about to vanish for another hundred years, and she'd better get out of town.

"Okay," she said. "Call me when you want to ride. I guess I'll ride my gelding, Major."

"Good. Now then, shall we get back to the party? If we walk back together, we'll set tongues wagging for sure. You game?" He grinned. That dimple again.

An easy laugh bubbled out of her. Ridiculous. "I sure am." Her stomach growled.

"First stop, the food tent, aye?"

They were out in the gray daylight now, the noise of a game played with sticks coming from the lawn. Duncan turned to her. "You *can* ride, can't you? I wouldn't ask, but Ro's full of himself, and he'll expect a bit of a run."

China gave him a sly sideways look. "We'll see, won't we?"

HE didn't know why he'd tried so hard with that China MacLeish woman. He could have let it alone, but he had to go and ask her to ride with him. Shades of the past coming to haunt him.

Duncan stretched his legs to the fire blazing in the grate of the enormous fireplace in his study. He settled into the old wing chair, the shape of his father, and now his own shape, imprinted into the leather. The gray granite mantel supported by stone Highland warriors on either side of the fire reminded him of his heritage, his responsibility, and he often sat here to think. The Sinclair crest carved in a large oval frontispiece below the mantel never failed to stir him. Several generations of fires had darkened the rooster in the crest, no matter how much cleaning was applied, but the motto stood clear: Commit Thy Work to God. Duncan knew it in the fiber of his being.

He picked up the small pitcher of branch water on the side table and dribbled a bit into his whisky. He swirled the amber liquid in the cut crystal glass. A Scotsman's guiltless pleasure. He savored the first sip as it warmed his throat.

A new year. The old year gone. And with it the life he knew, that he had expected. He never intended to be a divorced man.

His children, dreaming good dreams in their beds he hoped, had no idea yet that the divorce was final. He'd have to tell them soon. Living in a village and being the laird certainly made communication amongst the family a priority. His father had instructed him that it was better to hear the truth from family than to hear some version of it on the wind in the village.

Duncan was never one to worry overmuch about decorum as he was raised to do the right and proper thing. Marrying that wild Sassenach was as close as he ever got to rebelling. But his parents had come round and accepted her into the family; Harriet had looked good in the family photos. No one outside the bounds of their bedroom walls had known quite how wild Harriet was—that was, until their fights about her other men had rung through the halls. A man couldn't help but doubt himself when his wife strays.

A tear slid down Duncan's cheek. It could have been such a good life. He put his hand over the ache in his heart—the ache for his boys.

He got up and set his empty glass on the table from where, by the time he came down in the morning, it would be cleared away. He'd long ago stopped tucking the boys in, but tonight he had a desperate need to feel the warmth of his sons as they slept.

Duncan climbed the stone stairs, past the family armaments and paintings on the walls. He'd moved the boys down to this floor after Harriet left. He wanted them nearer to him.

The old house made sounds like a body: the tick of the longcase clock resonating in the stone all the way from the foyer, the soft sigh of steam in the radiators. He listened at Ross's door. Silence. Then turned the knob.

Ross was fast asleep, curled on his side, the duvet bunched round his ears but tucked away from his face. His mother's face. The fine Hetherington-Wells nose and the soft lips gave Ross the look of a child younger even than ten.

Duncan smoothed Ross's fringe off his forehead, rested his hand on his son's blond head. Ross was warm as stones in the sun.

"Hey, Dad." Ross stirred.

"Hey, laddie. I didn't mean to wake you."

Ross rolled over in his single little-boy's bed and was asleep again; he might not have been awake at all.

Duncan bent to kiss his son's forehead, tucked the duvet back in place, and quietly left the room.

At the end of the hall, Duncan heard music on the other side of Callum's door. He hoped it wasn't through Callum's ear buds, or his son would be deaf as a post by the time he was sixteen.

Duncan lightly rapped his knuckles on the door.

"Yeah?"

"It's Dad." Duncan opened the door and peeked in. "I came to tuck you in." His grin forestalled any protestations from Callum. Duncan was relieved to hear the noise coming from a speaker by the bed and not from Callum's head.

"Can't sleep?"

Callum stood in the middle of his room in sweatpants and his Merchiston Castle rugby shirt. No doubt Duncan had interrupted an air guitar session.

"Naw. All wound up from the games, I guess."

"That was a smashing party, wasn't it? Good job the rain held off till the very end." Duncan smiled at his son—athlete, scholar—heir to Glengorm House.

Callum plopped in the middle of his large bed and sat cross-legged. "Dad, tell me, man to man, when are you and Mum getting divorced? Don't give me any more lame answers."

Duncan sat on the edge of the bed. He hadn't wanted to tell the boys just yet, but he wasn't going to lie to Callum.

"It was final a few days before Christmas."

The edgy silence weighed on them both; Duncan could see it in his son's tight jaw.

"I'm sorry, Callum."

"I hate her." Callum pounded a fist on the bed.

"Now, Callum..." Duncan tried to put a warning in his voice, but he also knew he had to just let Callum be angry for now.

"This never would've happened if she hadn't run off with that pillock. Why'd you let her?"

Let her? Duncan reeled. Did Callum blame him?

"Callum, I—"

"You should have gone after her," Callum ranted, red-faced.

How honest did he want to be with his fourteen-year-old son?

"I did."

"You did? When?"

"Right after she left. Within the week I went to South Africa and confronted them both."

"And?"

"And what? Is this really what you want to hear?"

"Yes. Otherwise I'm left to guess."

"Well, let's just say, I came back with sore knuckles and left him with a bloody nose."

Callum gaped at his father. "You hit him?" His mouth quirked at the corners.

"I'm not proud of it. And I'm not saying it was the right thing to do, but I was so angry. So hurt." Duncan could feel himself tightening, and he wanted to stop this conversation.

Callum studied his father's face, and his own face slowly crumpled into the anguish of a child left by his mother.

"She's a..." Callum hung his head without finishing the sentence.

Duncan put his hand on Callum's shoulder. "I promise you we'll get through this." Callum's shoulder shook, and Duncan pulled his son to him. Callum didn't resist and fell into his father's arms. Duncan pressed his cheek to his son's head, blotting his own tears in Callum's hair.

Chapter 23

China gripped the handle of the door to the charity shop. She needed a job or go crazy, and Sylvie had arranged this meeting with Maude Grant, a woman of means and determination who ran the local charity. Volunteering wouldn't tie China down.

"Alex, I didn't expect to find you here." A familiar face. And familiar tattoos.

The server from the Wildcat looked up as she bagged a sweater for a customer and pushed her dreads over her shoulder. "Hiya, Miss MacLeish, I'll be wi' ye in a bittie bit." Alex whisked the two coins off the counter, plopped them in the till, and shut the drawer. "There ye go, love. Ta-ta, now." She handed the bag to the elderly woman who cast a shy glance at China and scurried out of the shop. China was about to say hello, but the woman was halfway out the door.

Alex grinned at China. "Guid tae see ye again, Miss MacLeish."

"Call me China, please."

"Oh aye, China it is, then. Say, how'd ye get that name any road? 'Tis a bit unusual, eh?"

"So's my mother."

"Right, then." Alex arched a knowing eyebrow and let it pass. "You'll be here tae see Maude, eh?" Though it was cold outside and not very warm in the shop, Alex wore a short-sleeved sweater that showed her tattooed arm.

"Yes. I have an appointment with Maude Grant."

"An appointment, is it? Follow me, aye." Alex started off toward the back of the shop, past rows of sweaters and jackets; she parted a beaded curtain and walked through into a hallway. China followed close behind and wondered if she were entering into a time warp back to the 60s. Alex motioned to an open door on the left. "Miss MacLeish. Miss Grant. I'll leave ye tae it."

A brown-and-white spaniel greeted China with a wet nose to the hand before China could get her hand extended to Maude Grant.

A bulky fifty-something woman rose up behind a desk cluttered with papers, food cartons, and a few mugs. Maude Grant was dressed like she had just come in from hunting: shooting vest over a green sweater and khaki trousers. Her graying red hair hung in a chin-length bob with straight-across bangs, several decades out of style. Maude clomped around the desk in heavy boots and came to a stop close to China. She pumped China's hand in a firm grip. It didn't matter that China was momentarily speechless since words gushed from Maude.

"Welcome, China. Do you mind if I call you China? No, of course you don't. So good of you to come."

Maude's refined speech was a shock.

"I knew your mother. Well, she was a bit ahead of me but never mind. Would you like a cup of tea? 'Course you would." Maude flipped the switch on the electric kettle and wiped the insides of two mugs with the almost clean tea towel hanging on a nail. "Milk and sugar?"

"Just plain, thanks." China inwardly groaned. She still didn't really like tea.

"Hmm." Maude opened the dorm-sized fridge and took out a small pitcher of milk and poured some in both mugs.

"Sylvie tells me you're bored and need a job."

"Well, I—"

"No, more to the point, she says you're a financial whiz and could do wonders here."

China had a hard time believing Sylvie would be so blunt, but if she had, it was the truth. "Miss Grant—"

"Maude. Call me Maude. And this is Spanner." The dog looked up and beat his tail against the bed he'd gone back to. "Sylvie's a dear. 'Course all she said was would I meet with you? But I guessed the rest. Working for the Chicago Security and Exchange Commission and all, you must be a genius. Just like your uncle."

"I need to do something useful. Yes, I want a job. Though, of course, you don't have to pay me." China rushed to get the words out before Maude began another monologue.

"Do you want to work in the front with the customers? Or in back with the financial end of the stick?" The kettle clicked off and Maude poured water over tea bags in the mugs. "I must say, I could use help with the accounting." She handed a mug to China.

China quickly fished out the tea bag, dropping it on a plate beside two other used tea bags and set the hot mug on the desk. "May I sit here?" She indicated a chair that needed to be cleared of a few papers and a leash.

"Certainly, certainly." Maude transferred the mess to her desk. She sat in her wooden swivel chair, planted her feet wide and leaned forward, elbows on her knees. "Truth is, we could use your help wherever you'd like to offer it."

"I can offer you three mornings a week for now." China wasn't about to tell Maude how little she had to do. "What if I do both jobs? With the customers and with the books." It couldn't hurt to meet some of the villagers, and the accounting for a place like this couldn't be difficult.

Maude clapped her hands. "That would be grand. Just grand. When can you start? I'll put you on with Alex to show you the ropes in the shop. Then the next day I'll show you the accounting. I never could make much sense of it. Your Uncle William was a dear and a help to me. Since he...well, it's been in a bit of disarray of late."

China had a wary feeling about this, but she smiled and stuck out her hand to shake on it. "Next Monday morning?"

Again Maude pumped China's hand as if she were hoping for water. Spanner jumped to his feet and waved his flag of a tail.

"Monday next. Half past eight work for you?" China nodded and pulled her hand free. Reaching to pat the dog on the head was as good an excuse as she could muster to get out of Maude's grip.

"I'll find my way out. And thanks for the tea." China had forgotten to take so much as a sip of the milky stuff but didn't want to prolong this meeting another second.

Back in the front of the shop, Alex motioned China over to where she was straightening sweaters on their hangers. "Ye look a bit like a landed mackerel, aye," Alex said just above a whisper.

China gave a small laugh, mostly through her nose.

"She's awright, Maudie is. A heart the size o' the moon," Alex said.

"You work here too?" China asked.

"Work? Naw, it's a lark, helpin' the grannies. Maudie runs the food bank too, an' I take a bit o' food round tae folks. Volunteerin', same as yourself."

"Good for you. Sounds like you'll be training me next week. You think you can put up with an American?"

"My specialty. You'll be here a year, eh?"

China looked at her, a bit startled and not very pleased. "Is there anyone in this town who doesn't know everything about me?"

Alex twirled a dreadlock between her fingers. "Probably not, aye."

"Yes, one year. Which is up precisely eleven months and a week from now."

"Aye, that's wha' I said too."

China shot her a mildly quizzical look.

"Four years ago." Alex waggled four fingers in the air at China.

If China had known Alex better, she would have grabbed at Alex's fingers and stopped the taunting, good-natured as it was. Maybe she should make hash marks on her bedroom wall, counting down to December 15.

JOHN held out a set of car keys and jangled them at China. "I've not got time to be your chauffeur, so here, Madam, are the keys to your kingdom."

When John had driven her to the charity shop yesterday, China could tell that the day was coming when she'd have to drive herself. John had seemed distracted and not his usual bantering self. She took a gulp of coffee, eyes leveled at the keys.

"Well? I'm a busy man, ye ken."

"What? Now?"

"Aye. Unless you're too busy." John's mouth quirked. "Or do you have a date with the laird, eh?"

China set her cup on the butcher block and gave an imploring look to Sylvie, who was up to her elbows in flour, to rescue her from this man.

"I've put the sign on the back of the car." John dropped the keys in front of China.

"Sign?"

"Aye, the sign. In this country it's a big *L* for learner. You get a big red *Y* for Yank."

Sylvie looked up. "You never."

"Nay, just funnin' with Her Ladyship."

China didn't mind a bit when John teased her. When Angus called her names, it rankled, but she could do nothing about it, though she'd noticed that Angus wasn't as much in her face as he had been.

"Let me get my jacket." She started for the pegs by the front door that held jackets and rain gear.

"You can drive a manual transmission, can't you?"

Her step hitched. Fortunately, her back was to John, or he'd have seen the momentary panic. She didn't own a car in Chicago, hadn't driven since the rental car on vacation in Belize with Brian, and was never very good with a stick shift.

She waved a nonchalant hand back at him and kept on going to fetch her jacket. "Of course," she said.

Shut in the little Anglia with John in the passenger seat, China gripped the steering wheel. The engine hummed but sounded small. How did a man who could have bought a car company with the money he had drive around in this tin bucket? Uncle William must have been a caricature of the thrifty Scot.

China put the gear shift in reverse and let out the clutch. Instead, the car lurched forward and died. John laughed. Fortunately, they were in the middle of the gravel yard behind the house with no solid objects near.

"Don't you laugh at me. I mean it, John." Everything was backwards—working the gears with her left hand, sitting on the wrong side of the car. At least the gas pedal was on the right, or she'd have been pushing and stomping randomly, hoping for the best.

"Many apologies." He snickered and guided her through the gears. "Putter around the yard here a bit before you tackle the open road, eh?"

Fifteen minutes later, no longer jerking and grinding to find the gears, China thought she had it licked.

"Right. Out to the lane, then." John made a show of jamming his cap on tighter.

Driving down the lane, China got up to second gear.

"Take the turning to the stable here. Practice parking, reversing. Just jockey the old girl round a bit, ye ken."

His bulk was too much in this car, and she could barely turn to look behind without bumping him in the shoulder.

"You're lookin' a bit grim there, Miss MacLeish."

"Button it, John. Or you can walk." China shot him a faint smile between maneuvers.

After several minutes of pointing the car this way and that, China wanted to stop and give her horses carrot treats from the bag Angus kept in the tack room, but John said he didn't have time.

"Now it's out to the road," he said.

"Are you sure? In traffic?"

"It's not Chicago, ye ken."

"I don't drive in Chicago. Matter of fact, I don't own a car."

He threw up his hands and dramatically looked heavenward. "Och, now ye tell me."

"So this is enough for today?"

"Nay, lassie. You're doin' fine. Turn left, aye."

Stopping at the end of the lane, China looked before pulling out on the road.

"Eh!" John slammed a hand against the dashboard, and China stamped on the brakes. A delivery truck whizzed by, veering to miss them. Too close.

Bug-eyed, she said, "Sorry. I didn't see him."

"You'll be fine. Just remember to look opposite to what you do in America. Traffic comes from the opposite direction, aye. Look right first. Then left. Then right again. Right, left, right, ye ken."

"I ken, ye ken." China felt a little foolish. Seriously determined now, she looked *right*, then eased into the road. Up to third gear.

"See ahead there? He's pulled to the side, waitin' for you to pass."

Sure enough, the road wasn't wide enough for two cars. China feared she'd never get home alive, so all her thoughts about surviving the year didn't matter since she'd never see Chicago again; American killed driving on the left.

John nodded at the other driver as China crept by. It was difficult to judge where the left side of the car was, and the Anglia lightly scraped the ivy-covered bank hemming the road in. This really shouldn't be that hard, China thought, as she set her jaw and drove on.

At the T intersection John told her to turn left toward the village. At least this was a two-lane road with a familiar center line. Look right. China eased the clutch out, gave it gas, and tootled down the road to the village. Fourth gear felt like flying. She grinned, but didn't take her eyes off the road.

"Aye, lassie, now you're drivin'."

China wiggled her fingers to prevent them falling asleep for lack of blood from the death grip she had on the steering wheel.

"Pull in just here to the grocer. Sylvie asked us would we pick up some milk."

No problem. China parked and exhaled a big breath.

"Come on." John stood in the parking lot, car door open, waiting for her to do the same.

"I'll wait here."

"Nay, come in."

China didn't know why she just willingly trundled after John and did what he said, but she did.

"Mr. Chandra, this is Miss China MacLeish. Mr. William's niece, ye ken." John had his coins out and was paying for the milk.

The Indian man behind the counter gave a little half-bow toward China, his palms together prayer-like. "Wery pleased to be meeting you," he said.

"And you, Mr. Chandra."

"You like here? Scotland wery nice, no?"

China smiled. "Yes, it's nice. Cold, but nice."

"Not so cold like Chicago, I think."

Inwardly, China stood dumbfounded at the relentless lack of privacy, but outwardly, she smiled.

"Well, that's it for us. Ta-ra." John picked up the milk and gestured China ahead of him, holding the door for her.

"Nice to meet you, Mr. Chandra." They nodded at each other.

In the parking lot China held the keys out to John.

"Nay, yer doin' fine, lassie."

"Please, John. I've had enough for one day."

"Well, all right. You've done well...for a Yank."

They were back to Craggan Mhor in a fraction of the time it took to get to the village with China driving. Twice China had to close her eyes while John zoomed by a car waiting in the wide spot in the road or backed up to a passing place as fast as he'd been going forward.

"How did it go, dear?" Sylvie took the milk from John.

"I never thought I'd say this, but I need a cup of tea." China collapsed onto a chair at the table by the kitchen window. "Please."

"Right you are, then."

John handed China the keys to the Anglia.

NIGHT Rogue thundered down the track to Craggan Mhor that connected the estates. Duncan gave the stallion his head and they flew up a hill. This should settle the boy so he'd behave, just in case China MacLeish wasn't a confident rider. Duncan knew Major was a steady horse, having ridden with William many times, but Duncan didn't want to take a chance.

Duncan slowed Ro to a collected canter as they crested the hill and started on the downslope. The Highland winter palette of browns, grays, and dull greens washed the hills. Bunches of steel-tinged clouds dotted the white sky. No rain today, at least not till after dark. The wind played in Ro's mane, flicking strands at Duncan's hands on the reins.

Ro's rolling canter covered the mile and a half of Glengorm land till Duncan was on Craggan Mhor land. This was the shortest route between the estates. Going by way of the roads, it was closer to six miles door to door.

With the boys back at school, Duncan had immersed himself in work at the lab the past week. Three interns were due to arrive in a fortnight, and Janet was doing her obligatory complaining about extra work, more mouths to feed, and loud music. But she hummed through her day, getting things in order on the third floor. Duncan enjoyed it when the interns descended on Glengorm; the house seemed less empty. That would soon change with the boys at home, attending school in Fionnloch. Yet it troubled him to take Callum out of Merchiston. There was Callum's future to think of, and his future was not that far away. Ross was another matter; he was still a young lad. Duncan had hesitated to send Ross off to board so young anyway. And he needed to remember to have the heating seen to in one of the greenhouses.

Ro snorted and shied sideways, nearly unseating Duncan. A stag bounded across the track and disappeared into the gorse. Ro tucked his haunches, crab-walking backwards a few steps in high gear. "Easy, boy. Sorry, I wasn't paying attention."

Duncan lightly tapped the horse with his riding crop and urged him forward. "Walk on." Ro complied but stepped gingerly, ready to bolt, his ears twisting forward and back. No sound but the wind and the red kites whistling to each other. The big horse shivered, and Duncan soothed him with his voice. Ro flicked an ear. Softly, Duncan sang his praise to God. *"Leig h-uile càil a bheil anail an Tighearna molaidh.* Let everything that has breath praise the Lord." Ro tossed his head, then settled, ears forward. And Duncan joined his voice with the wind.

Ahead, Duncan saw a rider approaching. He couldn't make her out yet, but he assumed it was China. The rider appeared to be rising to the trot, but of that he wasn't certain either. What he was sure of was that the rider looked like a sack of potatoes on top of a bay horse.

He urged Ro into a trot. The distance quickly shortened as Ro high-stepped closer to China and Major.

China pulled Major up and waited.

The two horses touched noses and snorted, Ro arching his neck, clearly the boss.

Duncan chuckled. "Sorry, I shouldn't laugh. Not much of a greeting. It's only…well, that's quite a riding getup."

China returned a grin with a saucy edge to it. "You don't like it?"

She looked like she had commandeered whatever hung on the pegs at the stable. The tan canvas jacket might have been William's, maybe even John's, it was so large on China. The sleeves covered her hands on the reins. The brown velvet riding hat came down over her ears, but at least she had it securely buckled. Her dark hair hung in a ponytail, smashed flat by the hat. Tight jeans disappeared into her smart knee-high boots.

"There's a shop in Inverness that can get you kitted out for riding in style. Not that this isn't a stylish look, mind you." He couldn't suppress a smirk.

China waved a hand at Duncan, revealing dirty string riding gloves a size too large.

"Riding is just one of many things I wasn't prepared to do here in bonny Scotland."

"I expected I'd have to ride all the way to the stable to fetch you," Duncan said.

"Angus gave me directions. Turn left at the fork. Though I wouldn't have been surprised if he'd sent me to the edge of a cliff."

Duncan wanted to chide her for being hard on an old man who missed his employer and friend, but now was not the time.

"How are you and Major getting on?"

"He's a nice ride. I took a few laps around the paddock to get the feel of him before we headed out."

"Well, what say we ride a bit? That's a good way," Duncan pointed back the way China had come. "If we take the other track at the fork you passed, it goes up a hill, then flattens out in a high valley."

China wheeled Major and took off at a brisk trot, posting perfectly, as best he could tell with all the canvas obscuring her form.

Ro danced in place before Duncan let him follow.

When Duncan came alongside China, they slowed their horses to a walk. "I see you *do* ride."

"Yes."

"Just yes?"

"Yes." She grinned at him and took the lead as the hill steepened.

"Ro won't like this." Duncan had to be firm to keep Ro behind.

"He needs to adapt."

Duncan shook his head. This was beginning to sound like the tune he and Harriet had danced to. Next, they'd be racing, with China having no hope of beating Ro. Harriet always had to win, and whether she did or not, she had a way of making it seem like she did. Everything was a competition with her.

Duncan fell silent. He kept Ro back enough to not trouble Major. And didn't trouble himself to talk to China. Maybe this ride wasn't a good idea. Why was he trying to be so nice to her?

At the top of the hill China stopped and craned her neck around. "This really is beautiful."

Duncan pulled up next to her and rested his hands on the pommel of the saddle. He'd spent his life in the Highlands, when he wasn't at school, and he never tired of it.

"Yes," he said, not looking at her but looking to the hills.

"Just yes?"

"This is all Craggan Mhor land, as far as you can see ahead and to the right. To the left is Glengorm land. The nearest village that way," Duncan gestured ahead, "is twelve miles."

China was silent.

"It's yours...if you'll have it," Duncan said.

She gave him a stony glance. "I wasn't looking for a sales pitch."

Duncan felt a knot in his throat. "Sorry. It's just that Craggan Mhor meant so much to your uncle."

"Well, I don't think I could build a shopping mall here. Too rocky, don't you think?" A faint smile softened her features again.

Duncan noticed that she had applied just a minimum of make-up—maybe a bit of color on her cheeks and a sheen to her lips. And he decided not to play any word games.

"Craggan Mhor is Gaelic, isn't it? What does it mean?" she asked.

"Big rocky."

China's tinkling laugh was a surprise.

"That's an understatement, if I ever heard one."

"Oh, you can't even see the biggest rocks from here. That would be where Fly found you. And where—" Duncan stopped himself. Her family tales were not his to tell.

"And?"

"Where you sprained your ankle. How is your ankle, by the way?"

"My foot's jammed in a stirrup, so it must be doing fine, thank you."

"Fancy riding up to the waterfall? I think Ro and Major would like a bit of a canter. If you're up to it, that is."

"Mr. Laird, I'm so happy to be riding again. It's been a long time."

"You don't seem to have lost the knack. Where did you learn? Your mother?"

"Good grief, no. I've never seen her on a horse. Strike that. I've never seen her much at all. I learned to ride at my friend Stacy's. I spent summers with her family. That was, after the disaster of a summer when my mother dragged me off to a commune in Colorado. But I won't bore you with all that. It bores me."

"Right, then. Let's ride."

Duncan gave Ro the cue, and the horse surged into an easy canter. Behind him, Major beat the canter rhythm in counterpoint. And China let out a joyous-sounding laugh.

Duncan pulled up well away from the tumult of the waterfall and patted Ro's neck, the horse's ears pricked straight forward at the roar of water. China soon drew Major alongside, and both horses blew with the effort of the canter, Major clearly having worked harder than Ro. China stroked Major's neck and crooned her appreciation to him. This woman obviously knew horses and was a pretty fair rider.

"My waterfall?" she said.

"Aye. You have three."

"Then there's one I haven't seen. Three waterfalls, three and half horses."

China lengthened her hold on the reins, letting Major lower his head, and seemed to be taking inventory, studying the land. They sat with only the sound of the waterfall for a time and let the horses rest. The horses put their noses to the ground, but there was no grass to be had on the rocks.

"My feet are getting cold," China said.

Duncan looked at her fashionable boots. "I don't doubt it," he said with a grin.

"Best I could do for now." She grinned back. "Or I could have worn the spiked heels."

"Ladies first." Duncan offered her the lead on the way down.

"Oh, go ahead. I can see Ro's not the kind of horse to follow."

When the path widened, they rode side by side, mostly silently. It was good she didn't seem to feel the need to chatter constantly; he liked that in a friend.

At the fork, they stopped.

"Thank you, Mr. Laird. I enjoyed our ride."

"My pleasure. I'd be happy to see you all the way to the house."

"No, it's fine. I don't think I can get lost from here." China turned Major toward Craggan Mhor and started down the track.

"China..."

She stopped and turned in the saddle to face him.

"May I see you again?"

"Are you asking me on a date, Mr. Laird?"

"Date?" Taken aback, he hadn't thought of it that way. Then he noticed her frown forming. "Well, yes, I suppose I am. Dinner? Saturday?"

She laughed that tinkly laugh again, turned, and threw a backward wave. "Call me."

He watched as she walked Major on toward Craggan Mhor, still looking like a large sack of potatoes astride the horse.

Duncan turned Ro toward home. "Steady on," he said to his horse.

CHINA rang up the basket-load of dishware and children's clothes Mrs. Pakulski deposited on the counter. The woman hadn't been in Fionnloch long. China was able to gather that much in the couple of times she'd been in the charity shop; the woman spoke little English.

China bagged the plastic Little Mermaid plate and bowl. "You have a little girl?" China smiled at the woman.

Mrs. Pakulski held up three fingers. "Boys." Two fingers. She pointed to the plate and bowl. "Masha birth day."

"How old?" China asked.

Four fingers.

Mrs. Pakulski, a woman maybe in her late thirties but looking ten years older, dug in her purse and offered a handful of coins for China to take what was owed. "How much?" Noticing the woman's purple-rimmed eyes, China took only a small portion of the money, though what Mrs. Pakulski held out was £2 short. "Tank you." Her smile quivered just slightly.

"Where do you live?" China asked the question slowly.

"Mmm?" Mrs. Pakulski inclined her head, obviously trying to decipher what China had asked.

"Where you stay?" China pointed at Mrs. Pakulski and made a gesture of laying her own head on her pillowed hands, thinking the woman might get the idea of where she slept.

"Oh." And the sentence continued in Polish with nods and waves of her hand in the direction of the small caravan park up the hill and down the road more than a mile, behind the pig farm. "Beggs," she ended.

Beggs Farm was a large pig operation, well outside the village, that employed a number of Polish immigrants. The Polish women were easy to spot when they came in the charity shop; they were friendly, in a hesitant sort of way, and dressed in layers of fairly shabby clothes. Most were quite thin. The children they had in tow weren't dressed warmly enough, and all of them had chapped rose-bloomed cheeks. The men didn't come in the shop.

"You have a nice day, Mrs. Pakulski."

The woman nodded and smiled a big gummy smile. She backed a couple of steps before she turned and left the shop, setting the bells on the door jingling. No doubt she was walking home.

China immediately turned and marched to Maude's office.

"Maude, we've got to do something more for the Polish people at Beggs Farm."

"What? Oh, China, I didn't know you'd come in for your shift."

Maude was a perplexing woman. China had waved hello to her when she came in an hour ago. But then, Maude often seemed to not notice things, like the boy who stashed a book under his jacket right under Maude's nose and sauntered out the door. Maude did, however, get a tremendous amount of work done.

"Beggs Farm? Oh, you mean the caravan park?"

"Can we take them some food or something?"

Maude looked up from the computer screen and pushed her reading glasses down her nose. "Aye, well, we do that once a week. But we can do it twice a week, if you like. Talk to Alex. I believe she's due to be going out there tomorrow."

The food pantry was behind the shop and busiest on Wednesday, with payday not until Friday. People could come in a back entry and not be seen on the High Street. Deliveries to certain people were scheduled for Tuesdays and Thursdays. Alex drove an old delivery van around the narrow lanes as far away as twenty miles. China had gone with her twice already and was astonished at how and where some of these Highlanders lived. It was like going back in time fifty years. By the end of their delivery day, China and Alex were full to the brim with tea and biscuits, and the old folks they visited had groceries for a few days.

China didn't know the Polish community at Beggs Farm was on the schedule. She'd see if she could go along with Alex tomorrow.

The bells on the front door jangled.

"Best get back to my post," China said. But Maude was already studying the screen. "By the way, I'll be gone for a couple weeks the end of the month." Maude didn't look up. "I'll send you an email." China looked cross-eyed at Maude, who of course didn't notice, stifled a chuckle, and went back to the shop, now no longer empty of customers.

"I thought I'd find you here Monday mornings."

"Mr. Laird, what are you doing here?" China stepped behind the counter to put something solid between this man and her. He was dressed in jeans, a cabled wool sweater, and one of those suede-elbow-patch jackets rich people wear in the country, only his looked well-worn.

"Me? I'm here quite regularly, actually. I just haven't had much time lately. I came to talk to you about dinner."

"I have a phone. Aren't you afraid of starting rumors."

He smiled and that dimple poked in.

"Yes, but I was across the way and saw you here in the shop a few moments ago, and I thought I'd pop in and set the time. Anyway, I learned long ago that the gossip goes on whether the Sinclairs do anything to warrant it or not, so no need to bother about it."

"You know, you don't sound very Scottish."

Again that dimple. "Thanks to public school on the Queen's doorstep."

China shook her head like he'd spoken jabberwocky.

"You call it private school. Eton College. At the foot of Windsor Castle."

"And that explains it?"

"Aye. School of princes and future prime ministers. Now, about that dinner. Saturday? Shall we say seven o'clock?"

"Sure. What shall I wear?"

"You look fine the way you are."

She knew he wasn't flirting, he wouldn't be fool enough to do that here in the shop, but it certainly felt like it.

The door bells sounded again.

"Morning, Kathy." Duncan greeted the young woman who came in holding a toddler by the hand.

"Mornin' to you, Sir Duncan." She bobbed her head, then gently swiped the child's hand from his runny nose.

China widened her eyes a bit at Duncan and tried really hard to stifle her snicker. He smiled back with a shrug and a tilt of the head.

"Miss MacLeish." He gave her a nod.

"*Sir* Duncan."

He turned and left. China couldn't help staring after him, just briefly.

Chapter 24

Sylvie slid the fish pie into the Aga's simmering oven and shut the door. She wiped her hands down her apron and was about to put the kettle on. An early cup of tea would be just the thing—have her tea in peace before Angus came wanting his as well. Andy looked at her from his basket and wagged.

A pounding rattled the kitchen door, and Sylvie's hand flew to cover her heart.

"Sylvie, I know you're there." Gordy's voice rose above the racket.

Scared nearly half to death, she opened the door before the noise brought all the staff running. Holding the door, barring his way, Sylvie faced her brother. "Gordy, whatever are ye doin' here? You canna be makin' such a ruckus."

"I came to see mah lassie, an' I willna be denied this time."

He pushed his way past Sylvie, and short of being knocked to the floor, she gave way to him. He slammed the door behind.

Andy sat to attention but didn't leave his basket. He let out one sharp bark followed by a low growl, his lip curled.

"I've told you, love, give her time. Don't come thrashing your way, trying to get into her life. You'll scare the livin' daylights out of her."

"Time enough. I say 'tis *now*." He banged a fist on the butcher block.

"John willna be pleased with you."

"I dinna give a tinker's what John Keith thinks o' me."

"You didn't used to be so hard, Gordy."

"What's going on?" China appeared in the kitchen and sucked in a breath at the sight of Gordy. Her expression changed to that of the rabbit trapped between running or freezing before the hawk strikes.

Gordy stared back at her, the dark cloud of a pending storm on his face.

Sylvie wrung her hands and her apron together. There was nothing for it. Gordy would get his way.

"Miss MacLeish, this is Gordon Campbell—my brother."

"Dinna Miss MacLeish me. She's mah lassie. She's mah China." Gordy whipped his cap off and gripped it in his fist. "An' I mean to claim what's mine."

"Eh?" Sylvie was confused.

China didn't look away, unblinking and silent.

Sylvie put a hand on her brother's arm, trying to quell the storm. "Gordy, ye ken, it's never been sure."

"Just look at her." Gordy shook off Sylvie's hand. "I'm sure. I'm her father, ye ken." He gestured wildly at Sylvie. "Look at yourself, if ye've a doubt."

China stood straight. "You're my…father?" she whispered, sounding tight and brittle.

"Aye, you're mah daughter. So what's yours is mine by rights," he roared. "High an' mighty heiress owes her da summat for his trouble." Gordy made a move toward China, and Andy stood in his bed and set to barking.

"Get out!" China's voice cut through Andy's racket. "Get out, or I'll call the police and have you thrown out!"

"Eh?" His face contorted with fury.

China flew at him.

Sylvie thought her heart would stop—or break. She was terrified China would hit Gordy. Heaven help her then. But China shouldered past him to fling the door open.

"Get. Out!"

Gordy slowly turned and faced China. They wouldn't back down, neither of them. Sylvie didn't know whether to step between them or cry out. Tears of fear trickled down her cheeks. "Oh please, in God's mercy, would ye stop. The both of you."

"Ye've nae seen the last o' me, lassie." Gordy yanked the door from China's grip and slammed it closed behind him. Andy stopped barking as soon as Gordy was gone.

"Och." The squeak barely escaped Sylvie's lips. She clapped a hand to her mouth and looked at China who stood before her, rigid as a board. Sylvie reached her hands out to China, but she couldn't erase the damage Gordy had just done.

China seemed to recoil and, with a look that Sylvie couldn't read, turned and fled.

Sylvie stood, numb, till she heard the bang of China's bedroom door—then silence in the house. It was no good running after her now. Let the poor lamb be for a bit. And Sylvie had to collect her wits.

"Och, Andy, whatever shall we do?" Andy bounced out of his basket and rushed to Sylvie. He raised up on his hind legs and stretched his front paws toward the ceiling. "Aye, laddie," said Sylvie, tears streaming down her cheeks, "it's prayer we've got."

CHINA got up from the chair in front of her bedroom window where she had been sitting, staring at the dark green sea gently splashing at the breakwater. She grabbed another Kleenex, opened the door to Sylvie's soft rap, and walked back to the chair without saying a word.

China could feel Sylvie standing near but didn't turn to look at her.

"I don't blame you, dear, if you're angry with me," Sylvie said.

"There sure have been some things you haven't told me."

"I'm so sorry. I only ever wanted you to be hurt no more. I was going to tell ye, but the time wasn't right."

China blew her nose. The tears would not stop leaking out.

"May I sit?" Sylvie asked.

China nodded.

Sylvie pulled a chair over from the vanity and sat, not too close to China.

"So you're my aunt?" China continued to scowl out the window.

"Aye, dear, I am. Your mother would never name him, but I think there's no doubt that Gordy's—"

"No! He may have fathered me, but he's *not* my father. Never will be." She clenched her hands in her lap. "All those years. He could have found me, but he didn't." China spat the words like venom.

"For that matter—why didn't you—or dear Uncle William try to find me?" A bit of shredded tissue fell to the floor, and China turned her red-rimmed eyes to Sylvie.

Sylvie's own red eyes met China's. "A foolish promise given foolishly. William said as much in his letter to ye. Your mother made William promise to never contact her...or you. He regretted that promise in his deepest heart, but he honored his sister's wishes. And I honored William."

"So Gordon Campbell is the man I've seen staring at me, like some stalker."

"He's no a bad man, your father—"

"*Don't* call him my *father*! Ever. I swear I'll be out of here on the next plane."

"Sorry, love, it slipped out. Too many years of holdin' all this in my heart." Sylvie's voice wavered. "And whether or no you wish to remain here is entirely your decision. But ye ken, China, we all want you to stay. *I* want you to stay. More than my heart can say."

A hard silence hung between them, alive enough to give out its own sigh. Still Sylvie sat, hands laced together in her lap.

China writhed inside, twisted by longing to know and a rage she could hardly contain.

She could finally stand it no longer. "So tell me. Tell me everything. About my family. About me. I've never known a thing."

Sylvie cleared her throat, and in that moment before Sylvie replied, China feared she'd say no.

"Well, now, that may take some time. Would you be willin' to hear it in two parts—over tea and after supper? There's a fish pie in the oven."

"Of course." China squinted at Sylvie. "But I mean everything. I have to know...Please."

"Aye, I promise. Hard as that may be for ye to hear." Sylvie nodded, tight-lipped. "Let me just pop down to the kitchen and fetch us a cup o' tea."

"I'll come down. It's warmer in the kitchen."

Sylvie left for the kitchen, and China opened her mouth to draw in a deep breath, then sighed it out till it stuck in her throat. She had always hoped to one day know the truth. And she had known it would be a cruel truth.

China put the chairs where they belonged and pulled the newly installed drapes closed against the draft. She splashed water on her face, grabbed a pocketful of tissues, and went to join—her Aunt Sylvie—in the kitchen.

China's heart ached: a terrible ache and a good ache. She walked on wooden legs down the stairs and along the hall to the kitchen.

Fly sprang up, nearly bending herself in half to rush at China. The dog leaned against China's leg and wagged in ecstasy when China reached down and stroked her head.

The electric kettle clicked off, and Sylvie poured the boiling water into the porcelain teapot, swirled the water around, and emptied it into the sink. She set the pot on the butcher block and faced Angus, one hand planted at her waist. "Are you finished with your tea, then, Angus?"

"Mmm?" Angus swallowed his mouthful of oatcake and looked at Sylvie. Then he looked at China. "Oh aye. I'll just be off." He tossed down a gulp of tea, popped the last bite of oatcake in his mouth, and nearly jumped up from the table. A slap to his leg, and Angus and Fly were out the door.

"Right, then," Sylvie muttered to herself and finished making the tea.

"I must look terrible. Angus looked like he'd seen a ghost." A thin smile creased China's lips.

"Och, you know men and women's tears."

Sylvie cleared away Angus's tea and laid out tea for them using much prettier dishes.

Settled at the table by the window, the aroma of the fish pie filling the kitchen, China listened as Sylvie started at the beginning of her story—China's story—a story she had both longed to hear and dreaded for as long as she could remember.

Chapter 25

Her great-grandmother had been pushed to her death from this spot. China stood at the top of the cliff and dropped a handful of earth as a remembrance to a woman who, until yesterday, she had never heard of.

She said a prayer, not because she prayed or even knew how to pray, but because Sylvie had told her that Una MacLeish was a devout Christian. When she'd said amen, China brushed her hands together, but the damp dirt clung to her palms in streaks.

Una MacLeish was found by her son, Uncle William's father, well after dark when she should have been home. There she lay, her body broken on the rocks, her husband on his knees beside her, sobbing and wailing. Lachlan MacLeish had appeared to be praying fervently, bobbing up and down, hands clasped tight. He said his wife had slipped, but folks thought they knew otherwise. A man given to black rages, he often left someone hurt: a servant limping, his children bearing red marks only the nanny saw, his wife with a swollen eye.

China was learning too much about her family. The family curse—or so it was said. Sylvie had certainly left out a lot to spare her the hurt, and maybe that had been best until now.

Last night China had lain in bed, awake and stunned. She must have slept eventually because she dreamed, a dream that woke her with a dry gasp of breath that set her coughing. Just as well she couldn't remember the dream.

When she thought of it all together—her great-grandfather, her grandfather who disappeared into his study for days at a time, her mother's erratic behavior—it all made sense. But naming a problem didn't make it any less damaging. How could her Uncle William have come through all that and been so loving?

China clapped her hands against the cold. She'd forgotten her gloves.

Sylvie was right—she would have liked Uncle William. Sylvie talked of him like he was a saint. A kind, generous man who was a friend to all. He had never married, apparently afraid to pass the family mental illness on to his children.

China had done nothing but think for the last many hours. But thinking only goes so far—she'd always had to just straighten up and get going again.

A dimly felt smile crept over China's lips, and she turned her face to the wind to let her hair flutter behind. She had an aunt. Tears pooled and dropped, chilling her cheeks. Her mother may have given birth to China, but Granny Nan and Sylvie had given her life. No wonder Sylvie had been so overjoyed to see her when she first arrived—China was her niece. She and Sylvie had gotten a laugh amidst their tears, remembering the scene in November. China regretted treating Sylvie like just the housekeeper; anger at the situation was no excuse for rudeness. But after an apology, there was nothing more to say but to now enjoy the truth of it.

Joy swelled in her battered heart.

China turned to pick her way down the rocky path, past where she'd twisted her ankle. The sky boiled in shades of gray, and the clag hung over the tops of the mountains. She knew not to leave it too long, or she might be caught in the thick mist.

In the distance, she noticed movement. A black horse raced on the track she would soon be joining. Mr. Laird on Ro, of course. She hurried to try and be on the track when he got there; he was coming on so fast. Duncan was up off the saddle, leaning forward, letting the horse run.

China arrived at the intersection, breathless, in time to wave at Duncan.

Duncan slowed Ro and waved back. He pulled up near to China, and Ro tossed his head and huffed, clouds of the horse's breath rising. Duncan kicked his feet out of the stirrups and jumped off the horse. His face was flushed poppy red, and he wore a grin that made his dimple a crater. Duncan flipped the reins over Ro's head, gathered them up in one hand, and started toward China. Ro fidgeted and danced, still apparently wanting to run.

"Now *that* was a ride," Duncan said, puffing with the exhilaration of the gallop.

"You certainly are a good rider, Mr. Laird. But I do believe you're trespassing." China smiled up at him.

"Didn't anyone tell you? We have public access to private land—footpaths and bridle paths and such. Bit of a nuisance for the landowner at times but, overall, a grand plan. Feel free to ride on Glengorm land any time." He gave a couple hearty pats to Ro's neck, then wiped his hand down the horse's mane. "I didn't expect to run into you out here."

"I needed the air." China barked a humorless laugh. "I met Gordon Campbell yesterday."

"Ah." Duncan frowned and his mouth tightened in obvious displeasure.

"So I suppose I don't need to spell out the ugly details," China said.

"No. But I'm glad you told me. He's a man you need to know the whereabouts of."

"Sylvie told me everything."

"You mean..."

"Everything...back to my great-grandmother."

"You must have been to the cliff, then."

She nodded.

"Let me walk you home. It'll do Ro good to cool down."

"But won't you get caught in the mist."

"No bother. I'll ring Donnie and have him bring the horse van round. The mist may hold off, but I think Ro has had enough for one day."

They fell into step together, Ro clopping alongside them. China liked how easy it was with this man.

"Mr. Laird, do you remember me from when I lived with Granny Nan?"

"Only vaguely. I would have been in knee pants still and much more interested in my mates and my pony."

She slipped into silence with her mixed up thoughts. The presence of this vision of a Highland laird in his riding gear and his midnight-black stallion was too much on top of everything else she'd just had flung at her. Something about this guy was a force to be fought off or fallen into, and she was in no mood to do either.

"China,..." Duncan broke the silence, "your family has had its troubles to be sure, but let me tell you, your Uncle William was one of the finest men I've ever known, or hope to know. He was friend, uncle...even father to me."

"I'd be happier to hear that if I'd been given the chance to know him myself."

"Aye. William longed for that."

China walked along, her hands clenched in her pockets. "I don't know how to talk to you or Sylvie...Aunt Sylvie, or anyone else, for that matter. Anything I have to say you probably already know...And I don't know *any* of you."

Duncan stopped on the track and faced her squarely. "We don't any of us know you now. That's who we want to know—China

MacLeish the woman. It had been forty years since anyone here laid eyes on you."

"But don't you think people look at me and see my crazy mother...or that loathsome drunk?" China looked off to the hills, her face feeling stretched tight.

"To be honest...I think people waited to see. But now it's clear you're neither. You're your own woman. If you knew that in Chicago, you'll know it here. Besides, if I thought you were like either your mother or Gordy Campbell, I wouldn't be standing here with you."

A tear slid down China's cheek, which she hoped he didn't notice. She felt gratitude to Duncan she could not, would not, express.

He put his fingers under her chin and gently tilted her face up till their eyes met. His kiss was soft and sweet. And he managed to avoid bumping her with the bill of his riding helmet. Their lips were cold from the chill air, but her face burned.

Ro quickly ended the kiss by tossing his head, tugging at the reins Duncan held.

"Steady on, boy." Duncan turned his attention to the horse and ran a hand down the stallion's neck.

The unexpected kiss left China a bit dazed, her lips still stupidly parted.

Duncan wiped his hand on his breeches, cleared his throat. "What say I get you back?"

"Sure." She searched for more words but couldn't find any she wanted to say, so she walked beside him, silently. She thought he might take her hand, but he didn't.

Their dinner date should be interesting.

Chapter 26

Duncan parked the Jaguar in front of Craggan Mhor. He'd rarely driven this car, but he had to admit, he rather liked it. Harriet had gladly given it up in lieu of cash. At least it didn't smell of her perfume, or he'd have sold it straightaway. Nothing held her scent anymore; she'd been gone so long.

He found himself eager to see China again but was on edge. This seemed reckless.

Whatever had possessed him to kiss her? Of course he knew why he'd done it—China MacLeish was positively alluring. Tears in those sapphire eyes had undone him. And blast if he didn't really like her. But he could kick himself for kissing her when she was most vulnerable. That seemed patently wrong, and he'd apologize.

At the front door he pulled the bell and waited.

China opened the door. She was stunning: her remarkable hair a heap of waves falling past her shoulders, a fashionable bad-girl leather jacket over a steel-blue cashmere turtleneck, and skinny black jeans. He needed to stop the mental inventory.

He must have been standing with a daft look on his face because she said, "Mr. Laird?" as if she wondered whether he thought he was at the wrong address.

"You look lovely," he said.

"Gee, thanks. I wasn't sure where we were going, so I thought this would be okay."

"Perfect." A schoolboy blush warmed his collar. Maybe he no longer knew how to talk to women.

"Let me get my purse. I'll just be a sec. Come in." She closed the door behind him and disappeared up the stairs. He recognized the smart Chicago boots that appeared to double as riding boots.

He looked around at the familiar house. Nothing had changed. But then, he knew it wouldn't have. Even the same macs hung on the pegs by the door.

He tried not to stare as she came down the stairs, the lady of the manor. China tossed her hair aside as she slung her purse strap on her shoulder.

"Now this is what I call a car," she said, stopping to take in the silver Jaguar. "Honestly, I can't believe Uncle William drove that Anglia. He could have had any car he wanted."

"Aye, William MacLeish was a verra thrifty Scot, to be sure." Duncan troweled on the accent. "I wouldna be surprised if ye found a bag o' soap slivers in a cupboard."

She laughed her trickly laugh.

"This side," he said. "Unless you want to drive."

"Sheesh, you'd think I'd have this by now. I do drive, you know. I've been driving to the village quite regularly."

"So I hear."

She shot him a quirked, squint-eyed smile. Neither one of them had much privacy in the village. That's just the way it was. Which was one of the reasons he was driving them over to the Blade and Bear in Strathmuir.

Duncan opened the door for her, and she swept by him, her scent tickling his nose.

The Jaguar motor purred like a large contented cat, and Duncan turned the car round in the drive, rather enjoying the feel of all that pent-up horsepower. He was keenly aware of China as well, so close in the car. Her spicy perfume made him want to put his nose to it like Trooper scenting the wind.

He turned onto the single-track road and tried to get his hormones in check.

"So where are we going?" she asked.

"I've booked a place I think you'll like. Old world charm, excellent food, and no one there will know you."

"Don't tell me we'll have some privacy?"

China gasped as Duncan pulled rather sharply into a passing place to let another driver by.

"Oh, trust me, there's no real privacy within one hundred miles of Fionnloch." He glanced to the side to gauge her reaction, and in the lights from the dash, he saw that she was looking intently at him.

"You really are a public figure, aren't you?"

"Not so much as just from a very old land-owning family."

"How old?"

"More than three hundred years."

He turned north onto the main road to pass through Fionnloch and on out to the peninsula beyond.

"My family used to own the whole of the village of Fionnloch and collected rent from the villagers as tenants. My great-great-grandfather allowed the villagers to purchase their cottages at a fair price and own them freehold. He said God had blessed him, and he wanted to bless the village."

Duncan took a deliberate chance in mentioning God to China; he didn't want to hide his God.

"I feel pretty blessed by God too." He didn't look at her. "I'd like to be the kind of laird Eideard Sinclair was." He feared he'd said too much. He'd at least keep his full name to himself just now, though he wanted to tell her that he was named for the great man. And that her great-grandfather had bought the Craggan Mhor land from his family.

They rode in a bit of an awkward silence for a time. Comments here and there. Nothing more of importance.

"Here we are." Duncan pulled into the car park to the side of the Blade and Bear. "It's a little quieter off-season."

"I like it." China got out just as he was rounding the car to open the door for her. She stood looking at the painted sign above the door. "A bear brandishing a claymore. Cute."

"'A claymore.' I'm impressed."

"I'm not illiterate, ye ken."

"Clearly."

Duncan gave his name at the reception desk, and they were shown to the table he had booked. Duncan appreciated this place for the small alcoves. This particular walled nook afforded a view of the coal fire in the grate of the enormous hearth without being roasted out. Velvet-cushioned benches along the wall on the two long sides of the small table made the nook snug. A window of wavy-glass diamond panes set on the outside of the thick walls created a shelf where a single taper burned in a brass candle holder. Two red glass votive candles marked the center of the table.

This was far more romantic than Duncan had intended.

Drinks in front of them and locally caught salmon ordered, Duncan laced his fingers and rested his hands on the table, hesitant to meet her eyes.

"China, I have an apology." He ventured a look at her.

Tilting her head to the side, she didn't say anything. For such an outspoken woman, she had a bit of an unnerving way of seeming to size one up and wait.

"I'm so sorry I kissed you."

"Oh?" And she waited again, cocked her head to the other side.

"No, that came out wrong. Sorry." This was not going the way he planned. "What I mean to say is, it was rather bad timing. And I apologize."

The server arrived at the table and set bowls of sweet pea cream soup in front of them.

When the server had gone, China seemed to study her soup. She picked up her spoon, dipped it into the soup, and let the spoonful of steaming pale green liquid fall back into the bowl.

"So you're saying you did like it?" she said without raising her gaze.

Duncan's pulse thumped in his ears—a warning bell he tried to ignore.

She lifted her chin and regarded him with those astonishing eyes. Tread carefully, he thought.

"Yes." He couldn't lie.

"Just yes?"

He smiled slowly at her. This had gone far enough, and he reined himself in. "Tell me about what you're doing at the charity shop. Maude tells me you've actually explained the accounting to her."

"Yes. Changing the subject are we, Sir Laird?" China gathered her hair in one hand and got it out of the way of eating soup. "I enjoy working at the charity shop."

Duncan inwardly sighed; he'd just averted breaking his ankle in a rabbit hole.

They chatted through the soup course. She asked if he knew about the Poles at Beggs Farm. Without telling her the particulars of his benevolence in the village, most of it anonymous, he did tell her that he worked closely with Maude Grant concerning the needs of the villagers.

Their entrée arrived; he noticed she declined a second glass of wine.

"I'm going back to Chicago in a couple weeks."

"Pardon?" He hoped his astonishment didn't show—but his fork did stop midway to his mouth.

"I can, you know. I'm not totally imprisoned. The will stipulates that I can leave for two weeks up to four times in the year."

"Ah yes. I'd forgot."

"I suppose you knew."

"Yes, William told me all the particulars. In fact, he showed his will to me. I read it."

"For your approval, I suppose."

"Something like that. But you knew John and I were both aware of William's wishes."

"I'll be staying with my friend Stacy."

"In Chicago?"

"Yes."

"But I thought you have a flat in Chicago."

"I gave up the townhouse. Not much reason to keep it. Brian pretty much cleaned it out before he left."

"Brian?"

"Oh, I suppose you don't know." She appeared to be pleased about that. "My fiancé. But that's very over. Come to think of it, maybe that's something no one here knows about."

So China had lived with a man to whom she was engaged. He didn't want to know any more about that just now.

"What about your job in Chicago?" he asked.

"Right now I'm on a leave of absence. LOA officially. Sounds like MIA, missing in action." She quirked her mouth. "But I don't have to face that yet. One of the knotty problems Uncle William handed me."

"You will come back, won't you?"

"I said I'd do the year and I will. I do keep my word."

"Sorry."

"Now your turn. How about you tell me some of your secrets?"

He thought a moment, then decided to forge ahead. "You know I have two boys." She nodded with a mouthful of broccoli. "They're away at school in Edinburgh…I'm thinking of having them home and attend the local schools. At least Ross, my youngest." He searched her face for signs of—he wasn't sure of what—but there was no flicker of shadow in her face. "They're having a difficult time…without their mother."

"I can understand that," she said.

Then he saw the cloud pass over her expression.

"But that really is a Sinclair secret."

She reached a hand and lightly touched his forearm. "I don't tell my friend's secrets either."

They smiled at each other. She was lit by the candlelight in such a way that he fancied her eyes held gold sparks. Duncan drew his arm away from her touch under pretext of cutting his fish. "Friends?" he said.

"Friends."

"Then, would you please call me Duncan?"

"Not Sir Duncan?"

"No, just Duncan."

"All right, Just Duncan."

DINNER ended with pudding, which wasn't pudding at all, but that brown cake swimming in caramel sauce she'd had at the Wildcat. Sticky toffee pudding was now at the top of her list of favorite desserts.

China excused herself. Duncan rose partway when she stood up. She wasn't accustomed to such chivalrous manners. On the way to the ladies, she admired the black timbers and thick whitewashed walls. The Blade and Bear was a wonderful place. No straight angle anywhere. She didn't know why she'd never come to the British Isles before. All her overseas travel had been to warm beaches. Ah yes…her mother. Margaret MacLeish never spoke a good word about things Scottish. China should have known to come running here.

When she returned, Duncan stood, only this time he saw her coming and stood to his full height—his sport coat emphasizing his Herculean shoulders. She had to swallow hard to counter the dumb look she could feel glazing her face. This was like a dream, and she feared she'd wake up and not remember it.

"Coffee?" Duncan asked.

"What about back at my place? I think I can find my way around Sylvie's kitchen." She thought he might refuse. In a way, she wished he would.

He hesitated, and in that moment, China wanted a hole in the floor to open up and provide an escape. Maybe she'd read him all wrong.

"Right." He folded cash in with the check and raised a forefinger to the server.

The bill settled, Duncan smiled at China and said, "Shall we?"

ON the drive back to Craggan Mhor, China savored what was quite an unfamiliar feeling. Things had never been this easy with Brian. His attention had easily and often wandered from her. He'd blame her; she blamed him. They'd both make promises—and it would start all over. In the end, she blamed herself and had given up, thinking this was just the way it was going to be, that someone who loved her some of the time was good enough. But it wasn't. She didn't hate him—there wasn't room in that space for Brian *and* her mother.

Duncan pulled up in front of Craggan Mhor. "Do let me open your door this time." And he jumped out before China could respond.

As he offered his hand to her, she couldn't help a small laugh. It was almost comical to be treated like a princess. So not American.

When China turned to look at the sea and the breakwater, she gasped, "Oh." The northern lights danced lavender and green over Fionnloch and out to sea.

"A sight that never gets old," Duncan said, thrusting his hands in his pants pockets. "God's light show for us."

They stood in silence for several minutes, watching the sheets of light fold over and back on themselves as they billowed on celestial wind, the lavender surging to red.

"You're shivering. How about that coffee?" he said.

She thought he might put an arm around her, but he didn't.

Hanging her purse on a hook by the door, she waved him toward the living room. "Make yourself comfortable in the lounge." But of course, he knew where it was. "I won't be long."

In the kitchen China flicked on the electric kettle and hunted up the French press.

She carried a tray back down the hall with the coffee pot, two mugs, cream and sugar, and a plate of mint chocolates. She set it on the low table in front of the fire.

Duncan had started the peat fire Sylvie laid before she left. The sweet reek of the peat smoke spread through the room. China noticed that Duncan had also poured himself a Scotch from the crystal decanter on the sideboard.

"Would you like a dram to go with your coffee?" Duncan held the decanter poised to pour into a cut crystal tumbler. "I recommend it." The honey-colored liquor shimmered in the firelight.

She hesitated. "Sure." But she wasn't sure she liked Scotch.

"Sorry, did I overstep my bounds?"

"What? Oh, no...I don't think so. Did you?"

"I forgot myself there. William and I often shared a dram in this room. It feels rather like home to me."

China poured the coffee, her back to him so he couldn't see her smile.

He brought her glass to the table and took a seat at one end of the long sofa, a leg crossed, ankle over knee, looking relaxed. She handed his coffee to him and snuggled into the other corner of the sofa.

"You know," Duncan said, "I haven't asked you how you like Scotland so far."

"No, you haven't."

"Well? What do you think?"

"Honestly?"

"That's preferred." He took a sip.

"It scares the hell out of me."

Duncan gulped, looking in danger of accidentally spitting out his coffee. "Can't say as that's the answer I was expecting."

"Sorry. It just slipped out. But it's the truth."

"May I ask why?"

Now she was in it, she couldn't back out, so might as well say it. "It seems I have family here—but it isn't my home." She tamped down the emotions threatening to rise. Looking away from the concern in his face helped. "But that Gordon Campbell." China shook her head.

"You don't have to talk about it. Sorry, I should have known that wasn't an easy question for you."

"I'd much rather listen to you talk. Tell me more about Callum and Ross." China set her coffee down and picked up the glass of Scotch. "You say this stuff is good?"

"Oh aye. It tastes of the Highlands itself. But sip it slowly. Let it rest on your tongue."

She took a sip and coughed at the sting to the back of her throat and up into her nose. Duncan laughed. She tried again, swallowed, and smiled at him. "I see what you mean."

"Now you're a Highland lassie. Next you'll be playing the pipes."

"No thanks. Sad to say, but I can't stand bagpipes. Angus and I nearly came to blows because he played the pipes outside my bedroom window at the crack of dawn."

Duncan laughed heartily. "Oh, I forgot. That was a tradition William enjoyed. He fancied if it was good enough for Queen Victoria at Balmoral, he'd have the same at Craggan Mhor."

"Callum and Ross?" China prompted.

NEAR midnight the fire had burned to embers, and Duncan stood to leave. China stood too and found herself very close to Duncan.

"I've had a lovely evening, China."

"Me too. Thank you so much...Duncan."

He smiled that dimpled smile, leaned over, and kissed her lightly on the lips. The kiss ended before she was fully aware she'd been kissed.

She followed him out of the room.

At the door he turned to her. "I do hope to see you again before you go to the States."

She knew he was going to kiss her again, kiss her for real this time. She stepped toward him and into his embrace. She stood on tiptoe and pressed her lips to his. He bent to her, tightening his strong arms around her. Their hungry kiss threatened to steal her breath, and their bodies softened to each other.

Suddenly, Duncan pulled away, grabbed her, but gently, by the arms, and set her away from him.

"China, I'm so sorry. I can't do this. This is wrong." He looked anguished. But she was confused. She thought this was where this was going.

"Wrong?"

He kept holding her at arm's length, as if he feared to let her go. "Yes, wrong. I'm only just divorced, and you're—"

"You should go." She twisted out of his grasp and yanked the door open, nearly clipping him in the shoulder. She stood aside to clear his way out. "See you around."

They stood and stared at each other for several eternity-long seconds before Duncan turned and left.

China pressed the door closed, breathing hard. She set her back to the door and leaned against it.

No sound came from outside; she wondered what he was doing. Surely five minutes passed before she heard his car door open and shut, not with the slam she expected. Then came the roar of the car engine and the quiet crunch of gravel as he drove away.

She was so mortified she couldn't cry.

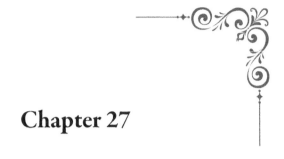

Chapter 27

In the days that followed Duncan's making a complete fool of himself, he engrossed himself in work. He took one of the forensic botany jobs Police Scotland continually dangled before him and was gone to Glasgow for three days. It was unpleasant work, but challenging, and he thoroughly enjoyed getting up to his elbows in the sophisticated police lab equipment.

Midday on Thursday found Duncan driving up the approach to Glengorm. A flash of movement drew his eye on the lane branching off to the right, and he braked to see what shouldn't be there.

Ro raced toward him, stirrups bouncing against his sides—riderless—the reins broken.

Duncan jammed the car into park and jumped out. He waved his arms and shouted, "Hey! Ro!"

Ro stopped so fast his hoofs spewed a cloud of gravel up to his belly. He reared and beat the air with his front hoofs.

Arms out to the side, Duncan advanced down the lane, trying to keep the horse from bolting past him.

"There now, boy. Easy does it," Duncan crooned to Ro, not twenty feet from him. The horse danced nervously in place, tossing his head, the reins flapping loose. As Duncan drew nearer he could see Ro's skin twitch. Blood ran down the horse's left foreleg just below the knee, and a wound oozed blood on his left haunch.

Ro snorted but let Duncan approach him. Duncan slowly reached for what was left of the reins and steadied the horse with his voice. He ran a hand down the quivering horse's neck. Ro lifted his injured foot and held it off the ground. The wounds weren't severe but would require immediate care; the cut on his rump needed sutures.

But how in blazes did Ro get here? The only possible answer was that bloody woman. He should never have agreed to give Harriet any access at all to Glengorm after their divorce. He had presumed a modicum of communication but should have known she would take advantage and serve herself rather than the children.

He punched the speed dial on his mobile to call Donnie.

Donnie answered immediately. "I'm sorry, Sir. I couldna stop her." He sounded frantic. "I didna want to disturb you."

"Well, Harriet's apparently come off, and I'm standing here in the middle of the lane to the hills holding a bleeding horse."

"Oh my Lord, I'm that sorry, Sir. I'll bring the van straightaway." Donnie rang off before Duncan could tell him the horse wasn't that badly injured. But Harriet. Now he had to find her.

He phoned the Fionnloch Police and asked them to send a search team. Then he rang Tolly to get him out on a utility vehicle to comb the route Harriet might have taken on her ride. She would have been foolhardy to get off the tracks lacing the hills because of all the rocks, but she might have done just that, and she could be anywhere.

For the boys' sake as much as anything, he said a prayer for Harriet's safety. Though he couldn't stand the sight of her, he wished her no harm.

Duncan walked the horse down the lane a bit and back to keep him from stiffening up before Donnie got there with the van. He called the veterinarian and asked him to come as soon as he could. And then Donnie was there with the van.

After they'd got Ro safely in his stall with Donnie looking after him, Duncan paced. He blanched to hear the ambulance coming down the lane, siren blaring, followed by a police car. Behind the emergency vehicles, an old Land Rover Safari pulled a trailer loaded with four utility vehicles. The volunteer search team sprang to action and was ready in minutes.

Three-quarters of an hour later, and the only radio communication was about where the team had searched and that they'd found no evidence of Harriet. She was nowhere on the usual bridle paths.

Now Duncan was worried. Harriet had her faults and was reckless beyond belief, but this wasn't like her, to be this irresponsible on a horse.

One hour into the search, word came over the radio that Harriet had been found, limping along a track close to Craggan Mhor land but heading for Glengorm, scratched face and torn breeches, holding an arm to her side—and hopping mad. She had given the men who picked her up an earful of venom as to why the bloody blazes did it take them so bloody long to get to her.

Duncan could barely summon relief before he gave vent to his fury. "Take her to hospital," he shouted into the receiver. He clicked off the radio and threw it on the floor of the utility vehicle.

Deliberately, Duncan went nowhere near the ambulance before it pulled away bearing the injured Harriet. They might as well be taking her to the insane asylum for all the sense it made for her to just show up and take his horse for a ride—his horse, which no one else had ridden.

Duncan contained his rage—he had to—he wasn't done cleaning up Harriet's mess. He invited the search team to share in a dram as thanks for their efforts. Janet went round with a tray of glasses, and Duncan poured the best whisky he had to offer—said his thanks through nearly gritted teeth.

After the team departed and he and Tolly had retrieved the Range Rover, Duncan drove to the stable to check on Ro. The vet and Donnie were just washing up after stitching the gash on Ro's haunch. The cut on the foreleg had merely needed washing, a good slathering of antiseptic, and bandaging. The injection of antibiotic would see Ro through till the vet's visit tomorrow.

Duncan stormed back to the house, changed into his old kilt, laced his hiking boots, and headed out into the gloaming to the hills behind the house. He needed to feel the chill air and work up a sweat. The moon would be dim tonight, but Duncan knew his land as a father knows the shape of the shadow of his child.

The rhythm of his stride swung his kilt side to side, sending the cold nipping at his thighs above the thick knee socks. He prayed and raged as he walked. He had never intended his life to be like this. This nonsense with Harriet would end. Divorced would now mean divorced. Harriet could not have it both ways.

And he'd been such a fool with China. How could he have kissed her like that? Like a starving man. If there had been a bed beside them, even a soft cushion, he barely trusted himself—or her. He apologized to the Lord, and he'd need to apologize to China—again—when she got back from the States. He doubted she'd listen to him this time. A friendship ruined just as it was starting.

Chapter 28

The two weeks at home in Chicago had flown by. When she had left Craggan Mhor, it felt like she'd made a prison break. But returning to Craggan Mhor—she'd never admit this out loud—it was good to be back.

China could not leave it with Duncan as it had ended before she left on her two week pass. And, if she was honest with herself, she missed Duncan. Surely they could get past a kiss that never should have happened.

She pulled the Anglia up to the front of Glengorm House. The house was imposing—not so much grand, as enormous and solid. She hadn't been here by herself and didn't even know if Duncan would see her.

China stepped up to the great double door of the main entrance, which was recessed into a large stone-arched entryway. Just as she reached for the bell chain, the door swung open.

China faced a woman of extraordinary beauty, though she was a little scratched and bruised. Her long blond hair fell silken over her shoulders, and she was dressed in fine country attire—except for the walking cast encasing her left foot.

The woman appraised China with a look of disdain. "Oh, you must be the American. The little heiress, so I heard."

China refused to back down the steps but felt pushed by the force of will coming from this woman.

"And you must be the—"

"Lady Sinclair." Still holding the door, obviously not about to let China in, Harriet smiled a sickening smile.

China couldn't resist. "Lady? That's not what I heard."

She spun on her heel and left. If Harriet had a retort, China didn't hear it. She revved the little Anglia motor and spun out gravel as she left. A Mercedes limo stopped to let China pass. In the rearview mirror China saw the limo pull up to the front door. The trunk popped open, and a uniformed driver leapt out.

Well, that was that. Mr. Laird could take a hike.

SYLVIE held the door open, gawping.

"Sylvie Campbell, don't tell me you're still here."

Margaret MacLeish stood just outside the door. Dressed in a fashionable blue-green pantsuit and red wool shawl, her highlighted brown hair falling in a curve from chin to shoulders, the woman who had caused so much trouble was now on the threshold of Craggan Mhor.

"Well, are you going to let me in or stand there with your mouth open like a fish?"

"I...well..."

"Oh, for heaven's sake." And with that, Margaret started to come in, causing Sylvie to give way or be bowled over. "Be a dear and have someone bring in my cases." She gestured to the pile of luggage the taxi driver had deposited on the drive.

"I'm famished for a cup of tea." Margaret breezed by, an unpleasant floral scent in her wake.

Sylvie watched the woman as she disappeared into the lounge, a woman she hadn't seen in nigh on forty years. This woman was older and a bit rounder but no less rude and insufferable. It could only be Margaret. Whatever was she doing here?

Sylvie advanced to the open lounge door once she'd gained a bit of composure. "It's Sylvie Blair now," she said, not to be cowed by the likes of Margaret MacLeish.

"Tea?" Margaret waved a dismissive hand in Sylvie's direction. She sank into the overstuffed wing chair, kicked off her shoes, and put her feet on the coffee table.

Sylvie turned and marched to the kitchen. And to the telephone to warn China that her mother had arrived. But the call went immediately to voicemail. Flustered, Sylvie hung up. She had to at least let John know the bad penny had turned up.

MATCHED designer suitcases in the front entryway set off an alarm deep inside China. She hoped that what she feared wasn't true.

The sweet stench of her mother's brand of cigarettes emanated from the living room.

Slowly, fists rigid at her side, China walked to stand in the doorway and face her mother.

"What are *you* doing here?" China tried to contain her anger, but since she was still mad at Mr. Laird for being an idiot and a liar, it didn't take long for her to get to *really* mad at her mother.

"And put that cigarette out. There's no smoking in my house. You know that." China was shouting by now.

"But, darling, you know that I smoke. And here I am."

The so-what-can-I-do gesture, waving the cigarette in the air, infuriated China.

"Put it out and get out!" If only she hadn't sent that note to her mother.

Her mother took a long drag and blew the smoke at the ceiling. She picked up her porcelain teacup and took a slow sip, then, taking her time, set the cup back on the saucer.

China heard footsteps hurrying toward her from the kitchen. She glanced down the hall and held up a staying hand. Sylvie halted, clutching her apron in her hands.

"Is that any way to greet your mother?" her mother said indignantly.

China wanted to smack the pout off those lips. *Mother*. A word that had always tasted bitter on her tongue. This woman had borne her but never mothered her.

China strode to the nearest window, grabbed the brass finger pulls, and yanked the window open.

She turned to face her mother, fanning the air in front of her so she could speak without choking. "I suppose you've come with your hand out too?"

Margaret rested her elbow on the arm of the wing chair and nonchalantly held her cigarette in the air like some vapid 1940s starlet.

"Whatever do you mean? I've just come to see you."

"You could have done that at any time back in the States." China was wound up for the offensive—words she'd had stored for a long time. "I'm not even sure where you live."

Margaret looked directly at China for the first time. "Too?"

China didn't understand what this crazy woman was talking about.

"You said, 'your hand out *too*.' You mean I have to join a queue?"

China *knew* it. Her mother was after money.

"Yeah, line up behind that Gordon Campbell. My *father*, right? *He* didn't waste any time beating a trail to my door." China spat the words at her mother.

Margaret stood abruptly and bumped the table, setting the teacup clattering askew in the saucer. She bent over and stubbed out her cigarette on the plate she was using for an ashtray.

"Gordon?" Her face had gone ashen and her lips resembled taut strings. She looked around as if she feared he might be hiding behind a curtain.

China studied her mother. It didn't look like Gordon Campbell was someone her mother wanted to run into.

"Seriously—why are you here?" China advanced toward her mother.

Margaret jumped like she'd gotten an electrical shock between her shoulder blades and looked at China with slightly wild eyes.

Seconds ticked by with Margaret mute. She waved a hand at an unseen gnat buzzing her head.

"Well?" China waited. She'd waited years, a few more minutes didn't matter.

Margaret seemed to shake herself out of a trance. "Is he here?"

"How should I know? He showed up at the kitchen door, wanting money. I threw him out and slammed the door behind him."

"Oh dear." Margaret absently worked her lower lip.

"What time is your train?" China had to restrain herself from giving her mother the same treatment she'd given...that man.

"Train? There's rail service here now?" Margaret looked confused.

"The one you're leaving on."

Margaret straightened up and tugged with both hands on the bottom of her pantsuit jacket. "Oh. Well, I don't think I'm leaving just yet."

China knew that look and knew there was no point in further discussion. She whirled, shut the lounge door, and walked down the hall to the kitchen with slow, deliberate steps that belied the fury inside her.

WHEN China walked in the kitchen, Sylvie handed her a mug of tea. China reached for the mug, hands trembling, and wrapped her fingers tightly around the warmth. She sank onto the chair at the table. Andy looked up from his bed, put his head back down on his paws.

Sylvie stood before China, wringing her apron tight.

"I'm that sorry, China. I tried to warn ye, but your mobile...I couldna..." Sylvie's hands flew from her apron to her face and back again. "I went to answer the bell...and there she was. After all these many years. Lord, have mercy."

China sighed a deep sigh but refused defeat. She reached up and took Sylvie's hands in her own and held Sylvie's gaze.

"It's all right."

All of a sudden, Sylvie convulsed into sobs. Between gulping breaths she managed to get out, "I havna seen the woman since she came to take ye away. The last I saw was the back of her and you reachin' over her shoulder to Nan and me."

China stood and wrapped her arms around Sylvie.

"I'm that glad you've come home, aye," Sylvie said into China's shoulder.

China released Sylvie and wiped her own eyes. With a rueful smile she said, "I never thought I'd say it, but right now, I'm glad too."

"Och, sorry for all the fuss." Sylvie took a mangled tissue from her apron pocket and mopped her face.

"I'm afraid we need a plan, Sylvie."

"Oh aye." The grave look on Sylvie's face might have been comical under less infuriating circumstances.

China instructed Sylvie to have Angus take Margaret's luggage upstairs to the bedroom farthest from China's; give her fresh towels, a sandwich if she wants one, and nothing more; lock all the doors except the lounge and the dining room, most especially, China's bedroom and William's study. They were not about to make Margaret MacLeish feel welcome.

China almost tiptoed up to her bedroom to fetch her purse and a heavy wool wrap. She was going *out*. Margaret emerged from the lounge just as China rounded the bottom of the stairs. China ignored her name being called and kept on walking to the kitchen.

"I'm sorry, Sylvie, but I'm leaving you in charge here." China tried to muster a smile. "I just can't deal with her right now. You certainly don't have to be nice to her. In fact, I suggest you stay out of her way. It goes better that way."

"Dinna fash yourself, dearie. I haven't forgot the ways of Miss Margaret MacLeish."

"I'm off to the pub. I'll eat there. It's been a day too full of impossible women."

"Eh?"

"I'll tell you later."

China opened the kitchen door to leave, and there stood John Keith about to come in.

"What's this I hear?" John looked ready to wrestle a bear.

"She's in the lounge. Have at her." And China left.

Chapter 29

By now China was more comfortable maneuvering the Anglia around the single-track road into the village. It was nearly dark, and oncoming headlights gave a little warning to quickly look for the nearest passing place.

She felt bad about leaving Sylvie but not bad enough to turn around. The Anchor would be just the place to spend the evening.

Saturday night off-season in Fionnloch was a night for the locals to enjoy their village, and the parking lot of the Anchor Inn was full. She didn't like the idea of trying to parallel park on the street. This driving on the left was still a challenge, and depth perception backwards was tricky.

She spied backup lights coming on in the parking lot and hoped someone was pulling out. One good thing today. A tight squeeze that took a little jockeying around, and she was in a parking spot.

China had long ago gotten over being a single woman alone in a restaurant. She may have been with Brian for five years, but she was often alone. His job required a lot of travel, or so he said. Her practiced death-to-men glare was usually effective, and she could get some peace, if she wanted it. Tonight she wasn't sure what she wanted, other than the delicious steak and ale pie the Anchor served. Maybe Alex and her friends would be here. They had invited her to sit with them a couple of times. Even Maude had waved her over a few weeks ago and proceeded to run a monologue.

She opened the heavy door and was met with a hubbub of chatter, laughter, and an undercurrent of Celtic rock music. Several people nodded and smiled at her. No one waved her over. And, fortunately, no sign of Mr. Laird.

"Well, good evenin' to ye, Miss MacLeish." Henry, the stout proprietor behind the bar, greeted her. His white shirtsleeves were rolled to the elbow, and he had a navy blue barkeep's apron tied around his girth. "What can I get ye?"

She leaned between two patrons and ordered a half shandy. "And can I get a table for dinner please?"

China took off her wrap and draped it over her arm. While she waited, she surveyed the room.

The Anchor was one of those two-hundred-year-old pubs, its thick stone walls slathered with innumerable coats of whitewash. Old lobster pots, oars, and floats hung from the blackened beams; swags of fishing nets draped the walls, and a fleet of intricate boat models sat on the window sills.

There was no place to sit near the coal fire in the massive river rock fireplace, so she remained standing and took a sip of her beer.

China felt a light but firm touch on her elbow.

She turned her head to see who had touched her so familiarly and looked up into the face of Mr. Laird—and frowned.

"Please, China, before you speak, could we talk?"

She didn't let up her frown much.

"Oh, sorry, that sounded rather odd, didn't it? What I meant is," and he leaned in so as not to be overheard, "I'm sorry."

She mirrored his lean-in, realizing they probably looked like ridiculous conspirators. But she didn't care. She was annoyed. "About which?"

"Which?"

"Yes," she hissed in a whisper. "Kissing me like you meant it, or the ex-wife in your house?"

He pulled back and looked astonished, or aghast, or something, before he replaced the look with his public face.

"Let's go outside. Please?" he said.

"I'm waiting for a table."

His dimpled smile appeared. "I've got a table in the other room—if you wouldn't mind sharing it with me."

"Did you not hear me?"

"I did say please."

Why was she such a sucker for this guy? "Fine."

He led them outside to the unoccupied patio garden overlooking the sea. Instantly chilled, China flung the wool wrap over her shoulders. Waves broke on the pebbled beach and sighed as they receded out to the low tide.

China refused to look at him. "I met your wife today."

"*Ex*-wife."

"Oh, really? She seemed to be at your place for a visit. How ex is that?"

"Believe me, I didn't invite her." And Duncan explained the insane agreement he'd had with Harriet about her access to Glengorm, assuming she might visit to see the children. And he explained about Harriet's injuries and how she'd received them riding his stallion without his permission.

"Well, that was a pretty ridiculous agreement."

Duncan let out a clearly frustrated noise. "At the time, I hoped it might work. But I should have known. Things will change though."

China stuck her chin out a bit. "I went to Glengorm today to apologize."

"Oh? But it's really I who should apologize. I guess I did, come to think of it." He grinned. "I do mean it. That kiss…" He cleared his throat.

It appeared that whatever else he wanted to say was stuck somewhere around his tonsils. Honestly, weren't they grownups?

Couldn't he accept a passionate kiss without blushing like a teenager? She wasn't going to make this easy for him. She waited.

"Actually, could we continue this later? I'm famished, and you must be freezing." He started to rise off the bench but sat down again when China remained immobile.

"Just what, may I ask, are we going to continue?" She gave him a piercing look meant to convey that it was time to take a stance. Was this a kissing kind of friendship or not?

He looked away and out to sea. He left the silence a moment too long, and she averted her eyes to hide her desire.

Still watching the waves, he said, "It's a friendship."

She turned to look at him, and strands of hair blew across her face. She swiped her hair behind her ear.

"Oh, you mean you don't want friends with benefits?" she said, a little annoyed.

"Something like that."

"Not very modern of you."

Again that silence.

"I don't know how to explain it without sounding foolish to you."

"Try."

"Too cold and too hungry right now." He gave her hand a quick pat. "Let's go in."

"We'll keep the gossip fires burning you know."

His chuckle had a nervous edge. "Aye, we will. But if I lived my life worrying about all the village tittle-tattle, I'd never leave the house. Besides, I want to hear about your visit to America. Your friend Stacy, is it?"

China took a deep breath and let it out before saying, "Oh, and did I tell you my mother arrived today? Here. At Craggan Mhor."

AFTER dinner, Duncan walked China to her car. The car park was now only half full. Time had slipped by as they talked.

He reached for the car door handle, but before he could open the door, she stopped, turned and faced him rather abruptly.

"Look, Duncan," she glanced around the car park. "I like you, and I'd like to be friends. But here's the deal—you can't have it both ways. No benefits? Then don't touch me. At all. And stop treating me like a date. Thank you, but I can open my own car door."

She moved to do just that. He caught her spicy fragrance as she came close to brushing against him.

"China, I'm sorry."

She whirled back to him. "Would you stop saying that?"

"But what if I *am* sorry?" And he was. Sorry in ways he couldn't quite work out.

"And by the way, I felt a little ambushed in there with you coming up to me in a public place where I couldn't be properly mad at you."

"Sorry." He smiled.

She threw him an exasperated look. "I've got nine months and a few days to go."

That pugnacious chin of hers stuck out again. Something he'd seen enough of now to be amused by.

China clamped a hand on her hip. "So...when do you want to ride next week?"

She was full of surprises. He thought she was sending him packing but apparently not, which pleased him no end. "I can't. Ro's out of commission for a bit."

"Well, can't you ride *her* horse? That seems like some kind of justice."

"I suppose. Though I think my feet would drag on the ground. Duchess could use the exercise, that's certain." Duncan shook his head, his heart not in riding the blue roan. Maybe he'd sell Duchess now Harriet had signed off on her. One less reminder.

"Well?"

"Truth is, I'd rather not. Would you like a ramble in the hills? I mean higher up. We could climb one of the smaller munros. Do you have any proper hiking footwear?"

"As a matter of fact, I picked up a pair of boots when I was in the States. I do like a good ramble, as you say. I've really come to love hiking around Craggan Mhor."

"We'll have to watch the weather. There can be snow, but it's been rather mild lately."

She pulled the wool wrap tighter. "You call this mild? This is bone-chilling." She gave a dramatic full-body shiver.

"China...I hope it's all right...with your mother, I mean."

"If I go hiking? Really, I'm past asking my mother's permission to do anything." She smiled a strained smile.

"You know what I mean."

"Can't be any worse than it's been. She won't stay long. She never does.

"Well, see you later," she said.

China got in her little car and drove off—rather well, he noted—for a Yank.

He watched her till she was out of sight. He didn't know why he watched her go, but he did.

Chapter 30

An unruly strand of hair hung unheeded over one eye as Sylvie pounded her fist into the bread dough. Margaret had been here only three days, and she was no end of trouble—like always. Demanding and unpleasant is what she was.

The front door bell rang loudly in the kitchen hallway. Sylvie looked at the clanging bell high on the wall where all the bells for each of the rooms were in a row by size. At one time she'd known the sound for each of them. The front door was the biggest and loudest bell.

Sylvie was alone in the house, except for Princess Margaret, and had no choice but to abandon her bread. She started to run her hands under the tap.

"I'll get it." Margaret's voice shrilled from the front of the house.

Fine. Let her. Sylvie turned off the tap.

Then Sylvie froze. She couldn't make out what they were saying, but clearly, Gordy had come to the front door and was now speaking with Margaret—if speaking it could be called. It didn't take long before both their voices rose to a pitch, and Sylvie heard what they were shouting at each other.

"You've got a lot of a nerve coming here. And to the front door. I thought I told you forty years ago I never wanted to see you again."

"Aye, well, here I am, an' ye'll like it."

An ominous silence followed. Then Margaret shrieked, "Get away from me!"

Sylvie was torn in pieces, not knowing what to do. She knew she should call the police, or John. But Gordy. Oh, dear Lord, my Gordy. Why did he have to be so foolish? He always was when it came to Margaret MacLeish, and it had gotten no better in her absence.

She heard the sharp slap—and she ran with dripping hands down the hall to the entryway.

Gordy stood with one hand to the side of his face and the other hand fisted and ready at his side.

He was coiling to lunge at Margaret when Sylvie cried out, "Gordy, for the love of Almighty God, what are ye doing?"

He stopped and pivoted toward his sister, his eyes those of a man raging in his drink.

"Aw, Sylvie, get your nose outta mah business, would ye?"

"Nay, I'll not." She tried to get a step closer to him. He backed up like a cornered wildcat. "Please," Sylvie said in a voice to gentle a beast, "get ye to home. Nan will make you a cup of tea, and I'll be home directly as I can, aye?"

Margaret picked up a burled walking stick from the stand in the corner and held it as a weapon. "Get out," she cried, taking a step closer to Gordy.

Oh no! Lord, don't let her. Sylvie stepped in front of Margaret and only narrowly missed a blow to the shoulder as Margaret swung the stick at Gordy.

He snatched the stick out of Margaret's grasp and stood, his chest heaving, facing Sylvie who blocked his way to Margaret.

Tears ran down Sylvie's face, and she pleaded with Gordy, pleaded with the Lord.

No one moved. Finally, Sylvie turned and faced Margaret and, with a calm she did not feel, asked Margaret to please go back into the lounge.

To Sylvie's astonishment, Margaret did an about-face, though with a look of black contempt, and sashayed into the lounge, slamming the door behind her.

Sylvie turned back to her brother.

Neither said a word, till Gordy flung the stick down and rushed out the front door, banging it shut to nearly rattle the windows.

Sylvie hardly dared leave the entryway for fear they'd be back at each other, but she had to let John know. She waited till she heard Gordy's truck spit gravel as he spun the tires in the drive and took off for heaven only knew where. She prayed he wouldn't kill someone in his drunkenness.

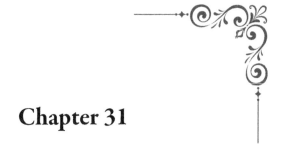

Chapter 31

"Thank you, Mr. Chandra." China stowed her wallet in her purse. She realized she hadn't even given a thought to counting out the money. Well, figuring out the money didn't mean she was staying. China popped the butter and brown sugar Sylvie had asked her to pick up into the shopping bag.

The charity shop had been busy this morning, and then it had taken her only a short time to update the accounts for Maude. This volunteering was all right. And it was a good excuse to be away from Craggan Mhor while her mother was refusing to leave. A week under the same roof with Margaret MacLeish was a trial.

Her mother had been away to Edinburgh for a couple of days. But she'd come back. Business, she said. China believed her mother planned to contest the will and had met with an attorney. She couldn't think of any other reason her mother would have come to Craggan Mhor.

The time they couldn't avoid being around each other was strained. It had been hard to avoid every dinner with her mother. Conversation was brief and superficial.

China walked up High Street to her car in the car park. Behind the row of shops, the sea beat quietly against the beach. She looked right and crossed the street.

"Hello, Mrs. Pakulski. How are you?" China said to the woman approaching with a child by the hand on each side.

"Hello, Miss MacLeish." Mrs. Pakulski bobbed her head repeatedly and smiled a rosy-cheeked smile as she passed. "Good. Good." The children turned and waved as their mama hurried them on. China was glad to see they all now wore warm winter coats, though Artur's jacket flapped unzipped.

An old gentleman clumped by in wellies. "Afternoon to ye, Miss MacLeish," he said as he touched a finger to his cap.

China nodded and smiled, not remembering his name. He smelled vaguely of fish and diesel.

Granny Nan emerged from the fish shop and looped her shopping bag over her arm. She set her cane steady and started off down the hill toward home, her face lighting when she saw China.

"Granny Nan," China hurried to her. "Let me take that for you." China relieved Nan of a bagful of what looked like tonight's dinner.

"Thank ye, dearie."

"Do you have any more shopping to do? Or can I give you a ride home? My car's just up here."

"Nay, I'm all finished for today. Twa'd be lovely."

China slowed to walk beside Nan the short distance to the car park. Nan walked with a little roll to the side like a duck with a bad leg, but she never complained.

As China pulled the Anglia up in front of the small cottage, Nan insisted she come in for a bit of lunch.

"There now," said Nan. "Just let me put these things away, an' we'll be havin' a bit o' cheese an' pickle."

"Can I help?" China took off her jacket and draped it over the kitchen chair.

"Aye, fetch that bread from the box, if ye will. Cut us a couple o' good bits."

China opened the lid of the green tin bread box on the table and took out a round loaf of bread, its split crust baked to a deep brown just this side of burned.

"Smells delicious." China cut thick slices, sending crumbs flying as she sawed through the perfect crust.

Nan waddled over with a wedge of buttery yellow cheese and a jar of something brown.

"Sit ye doon, lassie."

They sat at the kitchen table. China could just see out the small window facing the sea. The tide was out, and the waves rolled a fair distance from the cottage. She could imagine that in the worst of storms this cottage might seem perilously close to the sea, but maybe a fisherman didn't mind so much. Sylvie's husband would never have had to wait for the weather report; it was there in his backyard.

Nan bowed her head and clasped her hands, resting them on the table before her. And she began to say grace. "Dear Lord our Father, we thank ye for this day o' life."

China quickly bowed her head.

"We thank ye for your grace an' mercy. We thank ye for your Son who saved us. An' we thank ye for this food ye give tae sustain us. In the name o' the Father, an' o' the Son, an' o' the Holy Spirit. Amen."

China echoed, "Amen."

"Well now, here's a bit o' the best cheese ye'll ever taste, aye. Grant's—made right here in Fionnloch. Have ye met Mr. Grant, then? Ye'll know him by the smell o' sheep." Nan chuckled at her joke, sliced off a slab of the creamy cheese, and set it on China's plate.

"Maude's husband?" China had no idea Maude Grant was married. She'd assumed Maude wasn't the marrying kind.

"Nay," Nan chuckled some more. "Maudie's father. Old Digby's nigh on as old as me."

China nodded, her mouth full of bread and cheese.

"Be a dear an' get us a glass o' milk, eh?" Nan gestured to the little fridge in the corner. No wonder Nan shopped so frequently, the whole fridge would fit inside an American refrigerator.

"Put a bit o' pickle on your cheese there. Ye'll like it." Nan pushed the jar labeled Branston Original toward China.

A spoon stood up in the open jar, and China scooped out a thimbleful and dolloped it on her cheese.

"Mmm." She liked it; chutney disguised in a name she didn't know.

"Aye, we'll make a Scot o' ye yet."

"Don't count on it. But now I know I like pickle on my cheese."

"China, my dear, I've been meanin' tae have a word wi' ye."

"Oh?"

"Aye." Nan paused. Took a drink of her milk. "As I've told ye, I've been prayin' for ye since the moment ye were birthed."

China could feel a flush starting up her neck. Where was this going? She didn't like being preached at. But she loved Granny Nan and really did appreciate her prayers.

"Well, I was just wonderin' if ye know Jesus as your Lord an' Savior?"

The bread must have instantly absorbed all the moisture around China's tongue; she felt bug-eyed and stupid, unable to form words.

Nan reached over and gave China's hand a pat and smiled with love shining in her eyes like China had seldom seen—maybe never. But she still couldn't get any words out. Instead, she took another bite of bread and cheese.

Nan reached for a slice of bread. "Tell me a bit about your work at the charity shop, eh? Maudie tells me ye've been a world o' help to her an' that folks seem quite taken wi' ye."

China eyes resumed normal and her shoulders relaxed. "Well, I don't know about that, but I like the work. It's not work at all, really."

Dodged that one, she thought.

SWIRLS of driving mist surrounded the house in an otherworldly cocoon. Duncan pulled up the collar of his mac, tugged his tweed cap on tight, and tucked his head down against the chilled pricks of drizzle. It was but a short walk to the garage.

He drove the Range Rover to the greenhouses, which were hidden in the trees out of view from the drive. It was a good day to spend inside checking on the progress of the seedlings and see how the interns were getting on.

Though his father had harped that a laird didn't need to be employed, that running the ancestral estate was work enough, Duncan had never regretted studying plant sciences. And as it turned out, a grant to develop genetically engineered food helped pay the bills on the estate, not to mention, gave him quite a nice laboratory. Of course, he'd expected to work in the field a number of years before he inherited Glengorm, but that hadn't been the case.

Some days it seemed he'd never get all the work done. Right now he wished he hadn't agreed to present a paper at the World Hunger Symposium next year.

And he wanted to see China again—soon.

He could almost forget about her now and again. But then she'd drift back into his thoughts, and he'd see those mysterious blue eyes. He couldn't quite fathom her.

Duncan parked next to a muddy utility vehicle. One of the interns must have been out for a bit of fun.

Inside the first of the two greenhouses, rock music blared just above the level Duncan could tolerate, but he wasn't one of those stuffy botanists who believed it was necessary to play lullabies to keep plants happy. Better to have happy interns listening to the music they liked.

"Morning, Dr. Sinclair." Jeremy, the intern with the reddest hair imaginable, greeted Duncan. "Got some stats for you."

He'd ring China later about hiking. The weather was supposed to clear in a couple of days. But the Highlands was a capricious lassie who refused to commit to her weather for long.

CHINA strode down the hall clutching the key to Uncle William's study. Since her mother's intrusion, China kept the rooms where Margaret could snoop locked tight as Fort Knox. China wanted to go over the stock portfolio and check the latest transactions, as she did every day. She had a stock in mind, based on her research, that she might suggest to the fund managers.

Her mother stood in the entryway surrounded by her luggage.

"Ah, there you are. I was just going to find you to say goodbye."

"Goodbye?" A sneer threatened to curl China's lip. "We've barely said hello."

Margaret waved the pair of gloves she held in one hand in a stagy gesture. "Yes, but it's time to be off."

"It is." No disagreement there. It was so like her mother to just leave. Come and go as she pleased.

"I suppose you've finished your business in Edinburgh." China tried to hold her mother's gaze, but Margaret was elusive.

"Oh, that. That was nothing."

"I'll bet. Contesting the will?"

"The will? Heavens no...nothing like that."

"Then what?"

"Really, dear, you'll find out soon enough—if you need to know. Not to worry."

A honk sounded from the drive.

"There's my taxi now. Where's that Angus? I told him I wanted him to load my cases. He dropped them here, and *poof*, he was gone." She opened the front door and looked around for him. Instead, she pointed to the driver, then inside to her suitcases. The driver got out to do as she bid.

"I'll help." If it helps you leave, China thought. She grabbed the two smaller cases and deposited them by the taxi. It felt like the only thing she could do that was of her own free will when it came to her mother. "Where are you going?" Might as well ask. She might get an answer.

"Where indeed? Anywhere Gordon Campbell isn't."

The driver looked up at the mention of Gordon Campbell but said nothing.

Margaret lightly grasped China by the shoulders and blew European-style kisses on both cheeks but didn't more than brush China's face with her hair. That was the first touch from her mother since she'd come to Craggan Mhor. China felt a ridiculous urge to cry.

The taxi driver opened the door for Margaret and left her to see herself in and close the door while he finished loading the cases.

"Ta-ta, dear." Margaret gave a backhand wave, got in the taxi, and was gone.

China bit her lip and continued to fight tears. She turned and, in a fog of wishing this was not reality, slowly went back in the house, her house, and quietly closed the door on her mother's leaving.

What now? She should know this. It had been repeated countless times.

China lifted a thick wool jacket off the peg by the door, picked up her wellies, and made for the kitchen.

Stone-faced, China toed off her shoes and slipped into the wellies by the kitchen door. She bundled into the jacket, wrapped a scarf around her neck, and said to Sylvie without looking at her, "I'll be in the stable." And left.

Charlotte and Major nickered at her when she opened the stable door. The stable smelled of fresh bedding in the stalls and the sweet molasses-laced feed in the buckets.

"No, I'm not Angus. But I do know where he keeps the carrots."

Bess glanced China's way but didn't stop her business of pulling hay out of the net bundle tied to the side of the stall. Normally, the horses would be turned out for the day, but the weather was particularly nasty with winter clutching at this March day. And Charlotte was starting to look like a pregnant mare. John said he wanted to watch her more closely.

China fetched three carrots. She broke one into thirds and offered it to Bess, a piece at a time, on her open hand. The big draft horse's whiskers tickled China's palm. When Bess had lipped the last of the carrot and made a sloppy mess of carrot bits and spittle at the side of her mouth, China reached up and stroked the white blaze down the length of the horse's face from its forelock to its velvet-pink nose.

Major made short work of his carrot, took a quick turn around his stall, and came back for more.

"No you don't. This one's for Charlotte."

China unlatched Charlotte's stall door and entered the stall, closing the latch behind her. Charlotte was a sweet-natured horse, and China had spent hours talking to her. The horse gobbled her carrot, then bobbed her head as if to say, more please, and gave China the gentlest of shoves.

"Bad habit there, girl, but I'll let you get away with it today." China ran a hand along Charlotte's belly. She hoped she might feel the baby move. "How's that baby in there?"

Charlotte turned her head toward China and whickered.

Tears sprang up and clogged China's throat. She hugged Charlotte around the neck and pressed her cheek against the horse's warm hide, trying not to cry.

"China, dearie." Sylvie stood outside the stall. "Come." Sylvie unlatched the stall door and beckoned.

After securing the bolt, Sylvie invited China to her with open arms. China crumbled into her Aunt Sylvie's embrace, soft sobs rolling out as she gave up to the tears.

"There, there," Sylvie crooned. "Shh now, dear." She stroked China's hair.

When her tears subsided, China drew back and sniffed, mopping at her face with the backs of her hands. Sylvie reached with a tissue to dab at China's cheeks.

"You'll see, dear. It'll get better."

"Will it?" China didn't believe that for a minute.

"Aye."

"All I ever wanted was for her to be my mother. But where there's supposed to be a mother, there's a big hole."

Sylvie's eyes misted. "Aye, ye canna fill a hole with the wind. But she always comes back to you, does she not?"

China sniffed again, and Sylvie handed her the tissue. "I suppose she does."

"Then she'll be back, you'll see." Sylvie linked her arm with China's and said, "Come along. I'll fix you a nice cup of tea."

Chapter 32

The day Duncan and China were due to hike Mheall Beag was blue sky perfection—a tease of spring on a March day in the Highlands. The few mare's tail clouds held no hint of foul weather.

Duncan tossed his large rucksack in the boot of the Range Rover. He'd brought all the safety equipment, just in case, along with the usual extra jacket, foul weather gear, food, and water. Never trust the Highland weather, he learned long ago.

He hadn't been up this hill in several years, and Duncan looked forward to it. Silly, but he remembered feeling a bit proprietary the last time, looking down on Fionnloch and the expanse of Glengorm land. But that could have been because Harriet was with him, and she had made a fuss over how much they owned. To Duncan, it was more like looking at his family history through a long lens.

China should like this hike, he thought, as he motored toward Craggan Mhor. Duncan had chosen the little munro as an easy hillwalk, no more than an hour and a half up and much less coming down. Yet the view from the top was reward enough for the hike. To the east on the clearest of days, the mass of Beinn Eighe was visible, the side of the mountain that he and Callum had hiked the previous summer. And the view to the west of Mheall Beag was of distant Fionnloch laid out like beads along the shoreline.

The light frosting of snow had melted off the top of the hill days ago, but to be safe, he'd checked the weather forecast before leaving to collect China.

As soon as Duncan pulled up at Craggan Mhor, China emerged out the front door, William's small rucksack slung over one shoulder. She looked kitted out pretty well, dressed like a hillwalker, though a bit comical in William's overlarge jacket. And again, the jeans gave away her big-city lack of savvy about life in the Highlands. Tight as denim skin, they would provide little warmth, should she need it. The new navy suede hiking boots were a nice touch. With her hair in a ponytail, China looked younger than her forty-and-a-bit years.

She waved at him and stuck a hitchhiking thumb out.

"Want a lift?" Duncan automatically sprang from the car, but China had the back passenger door open and her rucksack stowed before he moved more than a couple steps.

"Boy, do I need a lift." And she tossed her ponytail over her shoulder.

He gave her a questioning look.

"I'll tell you on the way."

"Right."

Duncan drove north on the main road out of Fionnloch. Chitchat was light: the weather, the road, why did he wear a kilt hiking? She seemed a little preoccupied, but he didn't press her.

The turning to the right led them on a single-track road up through the hills. China gripped the side of the seat when Duncan veered into a passing place; a lorry whizzed by without slowing a whit. He smiled to himself at how commonplace this driving was to him.

When she released her hold, China said, "So, remember when I said my mother always leaves?"

He nodded.

"Well...she left."

"So I heard. I'm sorry."

"Dang! Isn't there anything I can tell anyone that they don't already know?"

"I'm sorry."

"And would you *stop saying that*?"

He could feel his irritation rising and had trouble keeping his voice steady. Her outburst had taken him off guard. "Would you rather I act surprised when I'm not?"

She didn't respond.

"Look, China, this is a small village and that's just the way it is. To expect it to be otherwise will just disappoint and frustrate you."

"Well, you're used to it, and I'm not."

"True enough. But realize that, by and large, people mean well."

"If they don't think I'm like my mother."

"I think they've seen enough of you by now to know that you're not."

Again she was silent. But now he could feel the tension in her ebbing.

"In fact, I think people quite like you. You're stepping into the boots of a very great man—a man who the villagers loved deeply. You even wear his jacket rather well." He hoped she'd see the truth of what he said—and the humor. He glanced at her and found the hoped-for slight smile.

"But what about all the I'm sorrys?" she said.

"You want me not to be sorry, when I am?" He tried to keep it light. "I *am* sorry for you. It's a difficult spot you're in, wouldn't you say?"

"Okay...but I don't want pity."

"Right you are, then. No pity it is." His hand twitched on the steering wheel for wanting to reach over and squeeze China's hand, but he was afraid he might get bitten. And he told her so.

China laughed that trickly laugh, bordering on a giggle, he enjoyed hearing.

Duncan turned into the postage-stamp-sized car park at the trailhead and parked the car. Theirs was the only vehicle, even though this was a popular hike. In a few weeks, with spring more securely in place, it would be difficult to squeeze the big Range Rover in.

Duncan shouldered his rucksack and handed China a trekking pole.

She took William's wool brimmed hat out of her rucksack and jammed it on her head. It came a little far down, and she looked impishly at him.

"I think you need to go shopping." Duncan gave her hat brim a tug, then put on his own wool cap.

"Maybe," she said, adjusting her hat, "but I don't want to buy a bunch of stuff I won't get much use out of."

Ah, yes—she was a short-timer. Duncan couldn't help but feel he'd got bitten after all. In many ways China MacLeish fit in here so well, it was easy to forget she'd probably take the money and run. He'd like to think she was better than that, but if he was honest with himself, he didn't know her all that well.

"Really?" China indicated his kilt. "Aren't you cold?"

"Not unless we stand around all day."

They fell into step while the path was wide enough for them to walk side by side. He remembered that Harriet had struck out ahead of him last time in her usual competitive fashion. He looked sidelong at China, but she was engrossed in the scenery.

He was indeed sorry. Most sorry that China and William never got a chance to know each other. They would have been so blessed.

DETERMINED to forget about her mother, China marched beside Duncan on the trail.

"Are we going camping?" China motioned to the backpack Duncan carried. "You didn't tell me, or I'd have brought my teddy bear."

"Just all the things that it's a good idea to have when hillwalking in the Highlands."

"In case of a grizzly bear attack?"

"It's the weather can be the bear. And the rocks. Seems they have a way of reaching out and tripping hikers."

"Got my phone." China patted her jacket pocket. "We're good."

"And how many bars do you have?" He gave her a one-eyebrow-raised look.

She whipped out her phone and punched it awake. One faint bar, probably not enough to get a number dialed. This place was maddening at how far removed from civilization it could be. She shuddered at the memory of that stormy night she'd run off into the hills and twisted her ankle. She'd made sure she was never again without her phone. But of course, if her cell phone didn't work in the house, why would it work in the hills? So all those times she'd gone off riding or hiking by herself and so carefully taken her phone with her were for nothing. She'd been foolish.

"Not to worry. I've got the radio. Never hike without it." Duncan swung his trekking pole in an easy rhythm. "But you might consider getting a different mobile. Or is that also something you might not get much use of before you leave?"

She ignored him but made a mental note to do that immediately.

Yet she was acutely aware of his every step, every swing of his kilt pleats, as he matched his stride to hers.

The pebbled path rose at a gentle incline, and a burn gurgled as the water spilled over rocks on its way down the hill. Browned plants she thought to be heather, bent by the weight of winter, waited for the new growth of spring.

Duncan stooped to examine a plant.

"Heather? Right?" she said.

"*Calluna vulgaris*. Terrible name for a beautiful plant," he said as he felt along the base of the plant stem.

"There's a lot of it. When does it bloom? The heather on the hills of Brigadoon."

"Late summer and early fall. And yes, there's an awful lot of it in the Highlands. The result of land management for hunting and grazing, which results in arrested succession of the vegetation..." He stopped and smiled up at her, his dimple flashing. "Oh, sorry. I didn't mean to bore you."

"You're not. Except when you say sorry. I've never known a botanist. Does it mean you have a green thumb?"

"It means I could make a plant grow an orange thumb, if you like."

"Why are you looking at that heather?"

"Well, you see here? You can tell that this plant is over twenty-five years old because more of the ground is exposed under the center of the plant. It's starting to die off. And see here? Seedlings are sprouting up. A healthy life cycle. And a sure sign of spring."

China looked where he pointed and saw tiny green stars of heather sprouts dotting the ground.

"And here I thought you were just a laird."

Duncan brushed his hands together to knock the dirt off and stood from where he had been squatting beside the heather.

They struck out for the top of the mountain. The path narrowed, twisting its way steeper, till they could no longer walk side by side. Rock outcroppings strewed the route, and China had to pick her footing carefully, steadying herself with a hand on rocks as the path rounded boulders. Duncan moved with the grace of a big mountain cat. They didn't talk much.

"Could we stop a minute?" This hike was more than she had tackled on her own.

"Sure." Duncan swung his pack off his shoulders onto a table-topped rock and took out two bottles of water, handing one to China.

She made a grateful noise and plunked on the rock. Duncan remained standing and swigged from the bottle.

"Not much farther now," he said, capping the bottle. "You reckon you're up for the final assault?" He grinned at her.

Stalling for more rest time, China took another sip and gazed out over the brown-green-gray patchwork landscape. In the distance, the silver sea rippled like silk all the way out to the islands.

"Where's Craggan Mhor from here?"

Duncan pointed, and China could just see the roof of the house behind the trees at the end of the path to the village. Strange to view her property from this distance and this height. There was such a lot of land around it. Those curls of smoke in the trees must be from the cottages: John and Fiona's, and those two young men from Glasgow who helped John, whose names she couldn't remember.

"Where's Glengorm?"

"You can't see it. It's in the valley up that way." He gestured to a general area that encompassed a huge tract of land of just about everything except Craggan Mhor and the village.

China stowed her water bottle in her own backpack and stood with renewed spring in her legs.

"A quarter of an hour. Tops." Duncan led out on the path.

China enjoyed watching the sway of his kilt—and tried not to wonder whether it was true what they said about men and kilts.

The path leveled out and wound around rocks on the wide plateau of the summit. Duncan stopped where taller rocks formed a horseshoe of protection around a spongy patch of coarse grass.

"How about lunch here? Do you mind sitting on the grass. Well, not exactly. I did bring a ground cloth." He dug a small tarp out of his backpack and spread it on the ground.

China sat cross-legged and felt around, patting the ground cloth beside her. "Nope, I don't feel a pea anywhere. Perfect for this princess."

Duncan joined her, the backpack between them, and began to unload the lunch he'd brought. Fresh bread, pâté de campagne, a wedge of soft brie, strawberries, and a small plastic lidded container of Branston Pickle.

She took out her water bottle and held it out to him. "Can you turn it into wine?" she said. He didn't smile immediately, and China was afraid she'd crossed some line. Maybe he was a religious stuffed shirt. "Sorry," she said.

"Not at all." A slow smile lit his eyes. "Do you mind if I ask the Lord's blessing on our lunch?"

She felt the crease between her eyes before she could stop it, but she nodded, dropping her eyes from his. Her mouth tightened. There sure was a lot of praying around here. It was one thing from Granny Nan and Sylvie, but Duncan praying made her uncomfortable.

Duncan didn't bow his head and clasp his hands like she expected; he opened his hands, palms up, as if holding something out to the air. And he spoke in Gaelic. She didn't understand a word, yet the words flowed like a sweet melody. Then he repeated the blessing in English, but China didn't understand much of that either.

"...and your love that enfolds us. In the name of the Father, and of the Son, and of the Holy Spirit, three in One. Amen."

China didn't add her amen to the prayer. Thoughts of her mother and Brian prodded her. Love meant she got left. Alone.

Duncan handed her a small loaf of bread. "Here, give it a rip."

"Thanks." She tore off a hunk and slathered on the pâté and brie, topping it with the chutney. She tried to smile at Duncan. Nothing would ever fill that hollow space in her.

"This is good. Thank you," she said.

"I'd like to take the credit, but it was Janet."

"Well, you carried it up here, so thank you."

"China, did it make you uncomfortable that I prayed?"

"It makes me uncomfortable that you ask."

"Oh, sorry." She shot him a look, and they both laughed a little. "Look, you might as well give it up. I was trained to say sorry." He held the container of strawberries out to her. "Strawberry?"

They munched for a time in silence.

A strand of hair blew across China's face, and she curved it behind her ear. "Granny Nan was after me too. Wanting to know if I believed in God. And I guess I'd rather not talk about it."

"That's fine. I don't mean to intrude."

"It's important to you, isn't it? Your faith, I mean."

"Aye, very."

She just nodded, the wind freshening on her face.

Duncan suddenly straightened, looked to the side of the rocks that sheltered them, and stood, tipping over his water bottle. He strode away from the rock shelter and looked to the east behind them, then he whirled back, his kilt flaring to the side.

"I don't mean to frighten you, but we need to leave *now*." And he bent to gather the lunch things and began stuffing them in his backpack. He took the radio out and clipped it to the belt on his kilt.

The urgency in his voice did frighten her. "What is it?"

"You'll see."

The wind lifted her loose strands of hair. She could smell a change in the air. More pungent. More moist.

In no time, Duncan had the pack secured and slung over his shoulder.

When they emerged from the rock shelter, China gasped.

A heavy mist poured like a vast waterfall over the mountain just beyond the valley behind them. Hugging the contour of the land, the fog began to collect in the valley, forming a boiling mass that would soon reach the top of Mheall Beag and do the same down this mountainside. Wind whipped fingers of the cloud mass toward them.

"Stay close to me. We need to move as quickly as we can."

"Duncan,..." But he didn't hear her strangled whisper.

No longer out for a leisurely hike, Duncan cast constant glances at the thickening fog. He looked like a worried man—and that worried her.

They weren't going to make it.

By the time they got to the narrow rocky portion of the trail, the mist crept around their feet and grabbed at their knees. They walked single file now, and China struggled to keep an eye on where she put her feet and at Duncan's back.

Duncan turned to her. "We'll have to rope together."

China shivered as much from fear as the increasing cold and tightened her grip on the trekking pole.

Duncan produced a bundle of climbing rope from the pack and quickly tied one end around China's waist. He then tied the rope around his own waist, leaving enough slack so they could maneuver, and fastened the remaining rope on a carabiner clipped to his belt.

They picked their way through the rocks, their pace slowed. She'd had no idea how disorienting a fog could be. Right looked no different from left.

Duncan stopped, and she nearly bumped into him.

"Don't worry. I know this trail like the back of my hand."

China wanted to believe him. "I thought you said you hadn't been here for some time."

"Yes, but I've hiked it a lot over the years. We'll be fine. I promise."

"Maybe you'd better pray."

"Oh, I did that already. When I first saw the mist rising up the valley." He gave her a grin. "You could pray too, ye ken."

China opened her mouth to retort, but he turned and continued their descent, and she had to follow or get tugged along.

The mist was now so dense it was an effort to make out the ground beneath their feet. China could barely see that they followed a well-worn path. Everything around them was shrouded in swirls of congealed white. The fog must be pouring down the other side of the mountain on its way to Fionnloch.

The path widened. She felt a gentle pull on the rope as Duncan pulled her closer to him.

"You won't bite if I hold your hand, will you?" he said.

In response, she grabbed his hand and held on tight.

They walked on, careful at each step. The white world held shapes yet no shapes. Never had China been so unable to trust her eyes. What she thought she saw disappeared or never materialized. She had to trust Duncan.

"What if we miss the car?"

"I don't think we will. The mist is likely to thin out a bit as we get closer to the trees and the road."

China couldn't tell whether they walked a straight line or zigzagged all over the place. It was all the same.

"There." Duncan pointed at a dark shape. "There's the car."

The black of the Range Rover loomed in the white and grew in size as they approached, but it was hard to make it out as a vehicle until they were nearly next to it.

Duncan undid the rope from China's waist. She dropped her pack, looked up into his kind eyes, and flung herself into his arms, grabbing fistfuls of his jacket. He tightened his arms around her, their jackets bunched between them. "Shhhh," he whispered.

She broke away. "Sorry." China dashed a tear with the back of a hand and turned to open the car door. It was locked. She stood, unmoving and flushed to the roots of her hair, till Duncan fished his keys from a pocket and beeped the door open. She got in and left Duncan to deal with the rope and the packs.

DUNCAN leaned his head against the headrest and let out a great sigh.

China peered out the front window into a sea of white, wishing she could take back clutching at Duncan like a wimp. "Now what?" she asked.

"Now I call Donnie on the radio. He'll worry himself to a frazzle as soon as the mist hits Glengorm."

Sure enough, Donnie's voice sounded thin with tension. Duncan assured Donnie that they were fine and that he'd radio again when they were headed back. And Duncan gave Donnie instructions to ring Craggan Mhor and assure Sylvie that Miss MacLeish would be delivered safe when the fog permitted.

"Now we wait?" China was feeling a new tension, the call of nature, and she didn't like what appeared to be the inevitable option.

"Aye, we wait," Duncan said.

"But I have to..."

Realization took a moment. "Oh, I see." He laughed. "I'm afraid you can't get very far from the car."

"I can see that." She yanked at the door handle. "No looking. And no looking in the rearview mirrors. You keep your eyes closed till I'm back in the car." She shot him a warning look as fierce as she could make it, with a slight smile.

"I promise."

For additional emphasis, she speared a finger in his direction.

"Or I could tie you to the rope again, and you could go as far as you like."

"No thank you." And out she went to do what she had to do.

As soon as China got back in the car, Duncan said, "My turn."

Necessary breaks over, they settled in for the wait. Duncan produced a Cadbury's chocolate bar and split it.

"You know, I wouldn't be surprised," China said, "if a hoary old man with lichen stuck in his long beard came lurching toward us out of the murk."

Duncan chuckled. "You've seen old Jock MacTaggart, have you?"

"Who?"

"Do you want me to tell you a ghost story?"

"A Christian telling a ghost story?"

"It's an old, old tale. Highlanders were a superstitious lot in the old days. You might say they'd pray to the Lord and then throw salt over a shoulder, just in case."

"Sure. We don't seem to be going anywhere soon."

"Weil...'twas a day verra much like this." Duncan winked at her.

"Jock MacTaggart went tae the hills above Fionnloch, as he did most mornin's, his collie, Snap, workin' the small herd o' sheep ahead. A fog, thick as anyone had ever seen, rolled in o'er the hills, blottin' oot the afternoon. Jock's wife had his tea laid oot an' scraps set in a dish for Snap.

"But neither Jock nor Snap came home to tea.

"Jock's wife sent the neighbors tae look for Jock, but the fog made the lookin' sae dangerous that folks called off the search till mornin'. But Charlie Gow, he swore he heard Jock callin' for Snap. An' Charlie, who be Jock's best friend, stayed oot till he could risk it nae longer. Callin' Jock was, said Charlie, callin' for Snap wi' a cry in his throat."

Rapt, China pictured old Jock, staggering in the fog, as lost as his dog. Duncan wove the tale, the melodic Scots burr flowing like his natural way of speaking.

"Still nae Jock. The next day the mist lifted an' the sun shone clear o'er the hielan' hills. The villagers turned oot tae find Jock. They spent the day combin' the hills.

"But Jock wasna found. No a trace of Jock, no a trace of Snap. No so much as a shred o' cloth nor wisp o' fur snagged on a bush. An' the next day they searched. An' the next. Till by week's end, hope seemed lost as the winter snow thickened upon the ground.

"The sheep were found. All deid. At the bottom o' the cliff or caught in the gorse an' twisted over.

"Charlie listened every day for the sound o' his friend, but finally, he reckoned what he hoped was Jock was but the wind sayin', 'Yer a dafty, Charlie Gow.'

"An' so folks say, on a foggy nicht such as this, they've heard Jock callin' an' cryin' for his collie dog. Some say as they've seen 'im—an old man wi' a long, white beard twisted up wi' twigs an' bracken, wearin' a ragged wool coat, his eyes red-rimmed an' pleadin.'"

Duncan stared ahead into the fog winding around the car. "An' sae is the tale o' Jock MacTaggart, a mon as disappeart in the mist."

The only sound around the car was the swoosh of the wind. A good ghost story indeed, China thought as she blinked, her eyes slightly dry from trying to spot Jock in the fog. But the veil was still impenetrable, the color darkening from white to gray as the afternoon faded.

She hated to admit it, but she had been afraid on the mountain.

"Did you scare your kids with that story?"

"I certainly did. Every time they asked for it. And we checked under their beds every night we tucked them in."

China heard the "we" and ignored it. Did he mean with his wife?

"It *is* a true story...more or less."

"Really?"

"Only it was more likely Jock MacTaggart stumbled off into the mist after too many pints, having left his dog in charge of the flock." Duncan checked the time. "But the story has served over the years to give the village children a healthy respect for the dangers of the Highland weather."

He didn't seem to be kidding. "We weren't in any real danger were we?" she asked, expecting reassurance.

He raised his eyebrows. "Let's just say, I've only seen a mist roll in and thicken up like this once before. I'd rather not see it again. The first time left one of my mates with a broken ankle, and he counted himself lucky at that."

Her mouth felt very dry. She pulled out her water bottle and took a deep swig.

"Let's have some more of that lunch, shall we?" Duncan said. "We were rather rushed. A tailgate party. Isn't that what you Americans call it?" Duncan got out and opened the trunk. China followed, her fingers curled into her too-long sleeves.

They didn't linger outside, the chill deepening by the minute in the waning daylight.

Back in the car, Duncan ran the heater while they finished their lunch. He produced a thermos of milky tea and two insulated mugs from a box on the back seat. "Janet thinks of everything."

He reached in his jacket pocket and took out a Swiss Army knife, a compass, and a pocket-sized silver flask. "And what she doesn't think of—I do." He poured a tot of the whisky into each mug. "That'll warm you up. Part of my survival kit." His dimple popped in when he grinned.

China clamped her hands around the mug like it was the last warmth she'd know and brought the steaming tea to just under her nose. She closed her eyes, feeling safe and civilized again. "Hmm." She breathed in the faintly alcoholic steam.

"I'm really sorry about this mess." Duncan sipped his tea. "I checked the weather right up till we left and there was no sign of this. But that's the way of the Highlands, I'm afraid."

"Doesn't matter," China said.

But it did matter. Here she was, nearly touching shoulders beside this man, when what she wanted was an ocean's distance between them—or nothing at all.

She'd plan to take another two weeks to the States as soon as she could. Maybe three weeks. She'd check with John; he'd know when she was allowed to leave again.

They were captive to the fog till nearly full dark when the wind shifted and blew misty tendrils back to the mountains.

They had talked and laughed—time and mist forgotten. The way Duncan spoke about Callum and Ross squeezed China's heart. He wanted her to meet them when they came home on break at the end of term in a few days. Come to Glengorm for dinner, he had said, sounding as normal as if he were asking her to coffee.

She would. She wanted to. And then she'd leave.

Chapter 33

A horse van pulled away from the stableyard bearing Blue Duchess to her new home in Peebles. Duncan felt lighter. And sad. But it was the perfect match: a willing horse and a thirteen year old girl bent on winning gymkhanas. Once he'd made up his mind, it didn't take long before his estate manager had a buyer lined up for Duchess. Duncan prayed a blessing on the girl.

Harriet would be furious—but he had no intention of telling her he'd sold Duchess.

Donnie yanked on his cap brim where a dark spot indicated he often did so. "That's a good horse, aye," he said.

Duncan watched the van till it rounded the curve heading out to the lane.

"Excuse me, Sir. I'll be cleanin' the stall, then."

Duncan nodded and walked off.

He felt a chill down his neck and turned up the corduroy collar of his mac. He jammed taut fists into his pockets. The breeze tingled on his cheeks, but he turned his face into it and made for the track that led to the unoccupied cottage about three-quarters of a mile on.

Along the way, he paused and idly touched a delicate white blossom on a blackthorn tree, drifting a finger through the tiny yellow balls of the stamen. This week was certainly a blackthorn winter, cold returning after a tease of spring. The profusion of flowers blanketing the thorny shrubs glowed in the gloom of the day, their musky scent heavy in the moist air.

The track followed the burn through the flattest part of the valley. A tea-colored torrent, the burn ran with snowmelt from the highest mountains and sounded like a distant airplane. Only a few feet across, the burn cut through the rocks and bracken, creating four foot deep banks, which were now nearly full to the brim. Goat willow trees dotted the banks, the fuzzy gray male catkins wobbling in the breeze.

Duncan hesitated at the bend in the track and turned to look at the crofter's cottage set just up the hill twenty yards away. The two-hundred-year-old whitewashed granite walls were interrupted by two small windows, one on either side of the door, and topped by a mossy slate roof.

His heart ached at the memories here.

He could let Blackthorn Cottage to tourists for a ridiculous price, or he could bunk a couple of interns here, but he kept it unoccupied. Since Harriet left.

He might have had lead boots as he trudged the last bit of stone walkway to the red-painted door.

Duncan examined a branch on the dog rose that had run riot on a trellis by the door. He snapped off a twig. The bush had died over the winter.

The iron latch creaked, and he opened the door on another part of his life—that he was here to put behind him.

The cottage was colder on the inside and smelled musty. Still as a wary fox, Duncan surveyed the cottage yet tried not to see. Blackthorn Cottage was where he and Harriet had been utterly alone.

Duncan fetched the tin of matches from the kitchen dresser, ignoring the small bedroom at the back, and bent to the task of lighting peat bricks in the fire grate. He rolled up mouse-nibbled newspaper from the basket in the corner, held a match to the edge, and gently blew on the tiny fire till the bricks ignited. Wisps of fragrant peat smoke wafted up the chimney.

He pulled the short three-legged stool over in front of the hearth and sat with his hands to the heat. The primal need for warmth. No man was different from any other. His needs. His sorrow.

And Duncan began to pray.

And weep.

DUNCAN woke the next morning, still feeling the peace of the Lord that he had when he left Blackthorn Cottage. He no longer wanted to hold the anger he felt toward Harriet—toward himself. And he'd given his burden to the Lord, asked for forgiveness. And he'd forgiven Harriet. He might need to do so countless more times, but he would.

He turned back the counterpane on the bed and padded to the window, drew the drapes aside, and let in the dim pink light of early morning. Unlatching the diamond-paned window and pushing it open, he braced his palms on the window sill and leaned out into the chill air, drawing the late March breeze into his lungs. Gooseflesh raised over his arms and chest.

Today he was going to Edinburgh to fetch the boys home for term break.

He straightened up, reached his hands over his head, palms facing the day, and said, "*Molaibh Dia ann an àirde.*" Praise God in the highest.

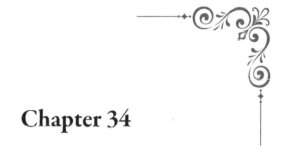

Chapter 34

Dinner at Glengorm with Duncan and his boys had been interesting. Days later China still thought about it.

And yesterday she booked her ticket to the States. In a month she'd go back for two weeks. She wasn't sure what her plan was, but it definitely included checking in with her boss; her career was important. But she didn't want to be gone for long after Charlotte's foal was born.

China drove back to Craggan Mhor following her Thursday morning shift at the charity shop. A delivery lorry squeezed past her on the road, and she didn't even shut her eyes, though she did grip the steering wheel a bit tighter. Pulling over into the passing places on the single-track roads no longer caused her heart to race.

Easing back into the road, China reflected on the dinner at Glengorm. It had been unsettling—too much like meeting the boyfriend's children.

Duncan was the perfect host, and his sons were the most well-mannered children she had met. It was all "Miss MacLeish" this and "Miss MacLeish" that, even after she'd told them they could call her China.

Uncertain who would open the door to her at Glengorm House, she was surprised when it was Duncan who swung the door wide.

"Care for a Cook's tour of the main floor before we go in to meet the boys?" he'd asked.

They'd started in the Great Hall: a jewel of hunter green damask-papered walls, three overwhelming crystal chandeliers, and a mahogany Regency dining table too long to shout down the length. Three French windows opened to the garden and were hung with red Sinclair tartan drapes topped by deep swags. The adjacent Ballroom was a mirror image of the Great Hall but without the table.

She was sure she gawked like a tourist as Duncan showed her his ancestral home. The elegance, combined with the Highland lodge mystique, was magnificent. Antlers stuck out among the gilt-framed oil paintings. One mounted stag's head in Duncan's study was particularly impressive, bagged by his grandfather, Duncan said. She noticed Duncan didn't give a lot of details and family history, but then, she didn't expect him to be a docent in his own house.

He led her to the Drawing Room where the boys sat on either end of a long sofa, its twin on the opposite side of a huge coffee table. China gulped.

Ross and Callum leaped to their feet. Duncan introduced her as "Miss MacLeish, our new neighbor, Mr. William's niece."

"Very pleased to meet you, Miss MacLeish," they both said in turn and shook hands with her. It was clear which son took after his father and which resembled his mother—though Callum's unwelcoming eyes didn't look at all like his father's.

A yellow Lab jumped up from his place in front of the fire screen and made for her. Ross introduced her to Trooper. Clearly, Trooper approved of her, wagging his entire back half.

Ross chattered away. Sitting on the Persian carpet, hugging Trooper around the neck, Ross told her of his dad rescuing the dog from the sea—not leaving out any detail, including his mother swearing at his father and then tossing the life ring to save them.

As they went in to dinner, China caught a glimpse of Callum slug Ross in the arm when he thought his dad couldn't see. Ross did a silent little-brother "What?" like he had no idea what he'd done.

Dinner was served in the family dining room, a large room with floor-to-ceiling windows that apparently overlooked the garden at the back of the house, though the heavy blue and cream drapes were drawn. Duncan said the east-facing room was lovely for breakfast and was where the family and the interns, when they were there, took their meals. And on those few days when the sun didn't shine in the Highlands, he said with a straight face, the yellow walls and cornflower blue carpet brightened the day. She might have mistaken the room for the formal dining room if Duncan hadn't already given her the tour.

Meaty odors wafted from the chafing dishes on the sideboard, and Trooper made for it, his nose pointing the way, until Duncan ordered him to his bed along the wall.

Bangers and mash. She'd had to suppress a smirk as she plopped a big dollop of mashed rutabaga and potatoes on her plate, followed by two venison sausages. Sir Duncan, Laird of Fionnloch, was unpretentious and made no apologies. Finally.

Ross was curious and fired questions at China. Did someone really take a goat to a Chicago Cubs game? Did she have a dog?

Callum was reserved, responding politely but not at length, when his father asked him to tell her about his rugby team.

She'd hit gold though, when she asked them about riding. Callum's eyes lit up, and he said he hoped to ride his father's stallion soon. Duncan rolled his eyes. And Ross described in detail learning to jump, starting with small cavaletti and working up to foot-and-a-half-high rails in the practice ring. He waved his dessert spoon for emphasis. Both boys asked about her horses.

After apple crisp and warm custard, Duncan excused the boys, who actually gave China a slight bow when they stood up to leave. Again they said, "Nice to meet you."

She wasn't sure whether or not they meant it, but it was all right either way. She couldn't blame them if they didn't.

Ross turned back as he was almost out the door and blurted, "Miss MacLeish, would you like to go riding with me?"

She'd been startled by the question and took too long to answer. Excuses were on the tip of her tongue, but she looked at his fresh little face, which was on the verge of sagging in disappointment, and said she'd love to. And she invited him over to see the foal after it was born.

"Yes!" Ross fist-pumped and scampered off, chased by Trooper.

"Care for a drink?" Duncan's dimple appeared again.

And China gratefully accepted a wee dram.

"*Slàinte*," Duncan had toasted—to her health.

And that had been that—meeting Duncan's sons—seeing Duncan as a loving father.

China turned the Anglia into the gravel yard behind Craggan Mhor.

A month yet till she could escape again to the US—get a decent haircut that wasn't eighty miles away, take in a symphony concert, and spend time with friends who already knew her faults and still chose to hang out with her at Starbucks.

She pulled the car into the garage, switched off the engine, and yanked on the hand brake. And let out an exhausted sigh.

CHINA headed to the kitchen door. She liked entering the house through the kitchen, usually greeting Sylvie, and savoring the aroma of what was cooking on the Aga.

She heard the crunch of gravel from the front of the house and turned to see a taxi driving in.

Her mother stepped out of the taxi and hailed China with a wave of her hand high in the air. Leaving the cab door open, Margaret walked toward China. She took mincing steps, seeming to be mindful of her spiked heels in the gravel.

The two women faced each other, the distance between them much greater than the five feet that separated them. Neither spoke. Margaret's face bore the strain of something.

China's stony expression betrayed nothing of the turmoil inside her. Whatever her mother was doing here, China was not about to make it easy for her. She waited.

Finally, Margaret gazed off toward the hills and said, "I only ever wanted to protect you."

She appeared about to say more but spun to leave, nearly stumbling as she did.

"Wait!" China called after her.

A paralyzing noise split the air, and Margaret spun yet again to face China, her arms flailing as she pitched backwards. Her mother seemed to fall in slow motion, hitting the gravel with a dull thud like a hundred pound sack of grain thrown down.

China screamed, a dry, choked-off cry. Her mother lay on the ground, red blooming on her coat. As China frantically looked around, she saw the taxi driver racing to them, his mobile at his ear.

Another shot fired from the direction of the woods, and China threw herself over her mother's body.

The driver pushed China toward the house, grabbed Margaret by both hands, and dragged her around the corner of the house, China scrambling after. "I've called the police. Are ye all right?"

China nodded, bent over her mother, clutching her mother's limp hand.

Margaret turned wild eyes to her daughter—shapeless words formed and died on her lips as she struggled for breath.

"Don't die. Oh please, God, don't let her die." China stroked her mother's face, smoothed her hair—then gasped when she saw that she had smeared her mother's blood from her own hands back to her mother.

China gently peeled away her mother's coat. Bloody froth bubbled from a hole torn through her mother's right breast. If she pressed on the wound to try and stop the bleeding, China was afraid she'd do more damage. She laid the blood-soaked coat back over the wound and prayed.

The driver grabbed China by the shoulders. "Is anyone in the hoose?"

Again, China nodded.

He sprinted for the front door, it not being safe to go in by the kitchen door which was only feet away.

If Sylvie screamed, the sirens drowned her out; all China saw was Sylvie running toward them.

"Oh my Lord. Oh my Lord." Sylvie knelt in the gravel beside Margaret. "You'll be all right, dearie." Margaret rolled her eyes toward Sylvie.

Sylvie grabbed China's hand. "I heard *two* shots. Are ye all right?" China nodded, and Sylvie's eyes filled with stricken tears. She stood and turned away, her shoulders convulsing with her sobs.

Police officers in flak jackets streamed from two vans that braked hard to a stop, an ambulance close behind. Rifles shouldered, ready to fire, they ran to where Margaret lay.

Sylvie turned to them and spoke in a low voice; China couldn't hear what she said.

An officer asked China from what direction she'd heard the second shot. She pointed toward the woods surrounding the footpath to the village.

Sylvie had her hand screwed to her mouth.

After that, China only saw the police as a blur of uniforms. The paramedics placed her mother on a stretcher, plastic tubes threaded into her.

"Any of her kin here?" asked a paramedic.

"I'm her daughter."

"Best come with us, then."

Sylvie stood like a statue.

In the hours from there on, China kept putting one foot in front of the other, marching through a tunnel with no end. Margaret was taken to Fionnloch Medical Centre, then med-flighted to Raigmore Hospital in Inverness. John drove China to Inverness, but for the duration of the eighty-mile-long drive, he told her nothing of what the police had found when they searched the area, even when China asked.

Duncan called. No, China assured him, there was nothing he could do right now. He too hedged on telling her anything of the investigation.

China stayed by her mother's bedside, wandered to the cafeteria for meals, and slept fitfully in a recliner in her mother's room—for three days.

Part of her mother's right lung and a shattered rib were removed. But worst of all, a thoracic aortic aneurysm appeared to be the greatest threat to her mother's life. The surgeon said it could have been forming for several years, and in her present condition, operating was inadvisable.

On the second day, her mother raised her fingers, indicating she wanted China to take her hand. China cradled her mother's hand in hers and gently stroked the blue veins on her thin hand.

Her mother spoke through a drugged haze. "I'm sorry," she said.

Words China never thought she'd hear, not from her mother. China nodded. "Shh. Don't speak. I know it hurts you." And Margaret closed her eyes again and slept.

Chapter 35

Two weeks in the hospital, and Margaret would live. China didn't give a second thought to the question of where her mother would go for rehab; she would go to Craggan Mhor. Nurses could stay at the house until Margaret was strong enough to make decisions as to where she might go from there.

As China packed the few things she'd brought to the bed and breakfast near the hospital, she thought for the hundredth time about the terrible crime.

John had finally told her about Gordon Campbell's suicide. China was astonished, and a little concerned, that she felt so little for the man. Her mother didn't say anything when John told her, her expression unreadable.

But Sylvie worried China. Dear Sylvie. China didn't know if Sylvie would want to resign her position at Craggan Mhor, or where anything stood. All she knew was that she wanted to wrap her arms around her Aunt Sylvie and comfort her.

Her mother's apology had been a hopeful note, but it would be foolish to trust her. Where had her mother been before she showed up to deliver a one-sentence speech? Was there a bomb waiting to go off in the form of another letter from a lawyer? China had no illusions that an apology would sweep away all the trampled heelprints on her heart—or that it might change her mother in any fundamental way that would make a normal mother-daughter relationship possible. Yet her mother had wanted China to hold her hand on several occasions.

Her mother hadn't talked much during the two weeks in the hospital. With pain medication and reduced lung capacity, it seemed an effort for her to talk at all. When she was forced to get up and walk, she hung onto her IV pole and shuffled the halls, reluctant at every step.

The ambulance was taking her mother to Craggan Mhor today. John would arrive shortly to take her home too. China frowned and yanked the zipper on her duffle, catching and nearly tearing her nightgown in the process. Craggan Mhor was not home, and she wouldn't even think of it that way. She was just tired.

She closed the door on all the B&B floral chintz and went to the lounge to wait for John.

BEATING powdered sugar into the butter and cream cheese, Sylvie tried not to think of Margaret on her way to Craggan Mhor. Grief weighed Sylvie down like a stone on her heart. She knew it was Gordy—the moment she saw Margaret lying on the ground—she knew. And she knew what the police officers would find. And they did.

Guilt gnawed at her like a rat loose in the pantry. She should have paid more heed to the gunshots. But shots heard at a hunting lodge were no rarity, though she later realized with agonizing clarity—they were too close to the house. Maybe if she'd been in time, Gordy would have seen her and not fired that second shot. Yet she knew that once Gordy made up his mind, there was nothing she could have done.

For the past two weeks she had stemmed the flood of mourning in a frenzy of baking, cooking, and delivering food to people. When the ambulance bringing Margaret from hospital pulled to the front door, Sylvie was icing a cake for old Flora Beaton. Andy raised his head at the sound of the door opening, then laid his head down again over his paws.

Two nurses had arrived this morning, one young and one not so young, and were settled in rooms near Margaret's. The older nurse had an air about her of a Lieutenant Colonel accustomed to giving orders.

Sylvie stood at the end of the hall, twisting her apron in her hands, and watched Margaret's entourage wheel her in. The Colonel led the way as two strapping orderlies carried Margaret upstairs in her chair, the young nurse following behind.

China came in last and stood, looking for all the world like a bewildered deer. John closed the door, leaving China standing alone.

China walked the distance to Sylvie, and Sylvie flung her arms round the wee lamb.

"I'm so sorry," China said, hugging Sylvie tight.

"Aye. Come, dearie. I'll make us a cup of tea while they get your mother settled."

AS soon as China could, she hurried to the stable to meet the new baby. The little foal looked up from nursing, bobbed her head a couple times, switched her whisk-broom tail, and went back to business. Charlotte nickered at China.

"Have you named her, then?" John came alongside China in the stable aisle.

The weariest of sighs escaped China's lips. "I haven't thought much about baby names lately."

"Aye." John unlatched the stall door and stepped in with Charlotte and the baby. "Come ahead." He gestured China in.

"Won't I bother Charlotte?"

"Nay. She's a good mum. Takes it all in her stride she does. This bein' her third foal an' all."

China inhaled the intense sweet and sour smell of horse as she slowly entered the stall.

"There now, girl." China crooned to Charlotte and laid her hand on the horse's neck. The foal started and backed away from China, but China stood still, palm outstretched to the baby. Little No-Name raised her head and gave a comical look, part curious, part befuddled.

Curiosity won out, and she minced the few steps to China, tail whipping back and forth like a windup toy. She reached her nose to China's flattened hand. No-Name snorted on China's palm and drew back, her head bobbing.

"I think she likes you." John rested his hand over the filly's withers, ran it down her back and over her rump. She kicked halfheartedly, and John repeated the move. This time she didn't kick. "There's a good lassie."

He backed away. "Here, give her a rub."

China stood still, called No-Name to her with soft tsk-tsking sounds. The little ears scissored. Head up, her forelegs shivered—and the two tiny white hoofs, with stockings to her knees, stepped forward. Her black nose reached toward China's face, and as she did so, China slid a hand to her neck.

China smiled till tears of joy brimmed. The dark baby was letting China give her a good rub. China ventured to touch the foal's face and rubbed the white star, elongated like the Star of Bethlehem. No-Name tried to nip, and China put up the flat of her hand and said, "No. That's enough of that." Baby bobbed okay. And John laughed.

"She's her da's offspring all right," John said.

Charlotte circled in the stall. Nursery visiting hours were over.

China and John continued to watch mama and baby through the bars. Baby gave a small buck but had nowhere to go and kick up her heels.

"The weather should be fine on the morrow, and we'll let them out in the paddock. Then we'll see what the wee sprite can do."

"Starry Night."

"Oh aye. That's a fine name for her."

Chapter 36

Hope and anger washed over China in waves, every seventh one threatening to knock her off her feet. Time hung suspended somewhere over Margaret's physical recovery and Margaret's moods. But always, time revolved around her mother.

The Colonel had Margaret's nursing needs ordered and carried out precisely. China wasn't needed for much, but she often chose to sit by her mother's bedside. It seemed the right thing to do, even if mostly, she read and studied the stock market.

Her mother wasn't in a chatty mood, and China didn't know how to do this time-with-mother thing. Gradually, China faded to other parts of the house and frequent visits to the stable. All other activities that had become her temporary routine were on hold. She missed the charity shop. She even missed Maude. And, of course, she had cancelled her trip to the States.

And she didn't want to face anyone in the village.

China was about to grab her jacket off the back of a kitchen chair and head to the stable.

"There." Sylvie closed the oven door on tonight's dinner. "We've got a bit of time, and you and I are goin' to the village."

"No, thanks, I really—"

"Fetch your handbag, aye." Sylvie took a sweater off a peg in the kitchen hall.

Too weary to argue, China figured she could stay in the car while Sylvie shopped.

When China returned with her purse, car keys in hand, Sylvie gently curled China's fingers over the keys and said, "Nay, we're walkin." Without waiting for China's response, she picked up Andy's leash off her desk, said, "Come, Andy," and exited out the kitchen door.

"But, Sylvie." China hustled after Sylvie, walking sideways to her, trying to get her to stop. "We'll have to walk by—"

"I ken, dearie. I ken."

Nothing was going to work with Sylvie, so China gave up and walked.

It wasn't a long way to the spot where Gordon Campbell was found. Sylvie stopped in the path, and Andy shot off into the woods.

"China, I've been to the place where Gordy took his life many a time already. Come with me, aye?"

China nodded, tight-lipped, and Sylvie linked crooked elbows with her. Together they took the few steps to just behind a boulder.

No evidence of the crime was visible, but China didn't look closely, not wanting to see what might be there. In the silence between them, China noticed stalks of May bluebells dipping in the light breeze, the quiet shush of the sea—and her numb heart.

"Oh, Sylvie," said China, pressing Sylvie's arm to her side, "how can you bear it?"

"I canna." Sylvie turned toward China, eyes glistening. "I surely cannot. Not without the Lord's help."

"Sylvie, did you..." China thought better of asking the question.

"D'ye mean, did I see him?"

China couldn't even nod, so sorry she'd asked.

"John went. He went straightaway before the police even asked me. The dear man." Sylvie dabbed a tissue to her eyes.

China's dry eyes embarrassed her, but she had no tears for Gordon Campbell.

"I dinna want you to be afraid to walk by here...to be sickened by your home," Sylvie said.

China opened her mouth to say that this wasn't her home, but Sylvie put up a staying hand. "I'll brook no argument," she said as she reached to smooth a strand of China's hair.

Sylvie's touch was soft and welcome. Tears for Sylvie stung, and China gave her aunt a sad smile. "But this is all crazy." The wind seemed to rush in China's ears. "What's wrong with them?"

"Dinna fash yourself, my dear. There's no answer to make any sense of it. Your mother's the lightening bolt and my Gordy the clap o' thunder. Ye can't have the one without the other. And once the drink took Gordy, I prayed all the more."

Prayer. Her mother had lived and Sylvie's brother didn't. Was God unfair—answering her prayers for her mother but not the prayers of a good woman like Sylvie?

"But how did he know my mother would be here? She'd left nearly two weeks before."

"It seems she flew to Glasgow and then went on to Edinburgh, near as the police can tell. It's likely she saw Gordy, but she's not saying."

"Why? She hated him."

"Aye, there's no sense to it—none at all."

"Come." Sylvie took a deep breath and straightened, smiled at China. "We've got shopping to do. Or the roast will be a brick by the time we get back." She whistled to Andy.

They continued on to the village, past Sylvie and Granny Nan's cottage. China wanted to stop and say hello to Granny Nan, but Sylvie said she was out visiting at the moment.

As they walked down the main shopping street, nearly every person nodded and smiled, including China in the greeting. Several people stopped to ask how Sylvie was doing and how China's mother was getting on.

At the market, Mr. Chandra took a daffodil from the vase of flowers on the counter and handed it to Sylvie. "I am so wery sorry for your loss," he said, bowing. And he handed a flower to China too.

Shopping done, they started back for Craggan Mhor.

"China! Hold up." China turned to see Maude Grant hustling toward them, sweater flapping open, hair sticking out like she'd forgotten to comb it this morning.

"I wondered when I'd see you." Maude grabbed China's arm and propelled her along. "Hello there, Sylvie."

"Maude." Sylvie nodded.

"Oh," Maude exclaimed as Andy circled around her, nearly tripping her in a web of leash. She grabbed the leash before Sylvie could get it and twisted herself loose.

"China, when are you coming back to the charity shop? I'm about to go barmy without you. The customers ask for you, and I simply can't remember all you told me about that infernal spreadsheet. Do come back."

"Well, I—"

"Shall I look for you, shall we say, Tuesday week?"

"Sure. I think my mother's nearly out of the woods."

"Oh good, good. So glad to hear it." And with a quick squeeze to China's arm, Maude charged back the way she'd come. "Ta-ra." She waved as she went.

"That Maudie Grant," Sylvie tittered under her breath. "I daresay as I come away from a chat with her feeling a mite stunned."

They stopped in at Sylvie's cottage, but Granny Nan was still out. China left a note.

Andy ran free from there back to Craggan Mhor, his little tail wagging in time as he bounced along. He stopped to sniff the area from where Gordon Campbell had taken aim, but Sylvie and China didn't stop.

Chapter 37

China had rebuffed his attempts to see her for the last fortnight. Duncan had intended not to press her, but he couldn't let it go. Sylvie had told him that China was wandering from room to room and beating a trench between the stable and the kitchen door.

Donnie brought Ro to the stableyard, and Duncan swung into the saddle. A ride this fine spring day would be just the thing. His plan was to rout out China and get her up on Major for a ride.

Not letting Ro out to full thunder, they nevertheless covered the ground between the estates in good time. May in the Highlands was glorious, and the footing was firm.

When Duncan arrived at Craggan Mhor, he first stopped at the stable, thinking he might find China there with Charlotte and the filly. But she wasn't. Instead, he talked Angus into saddling Major.

Leading Major along the lane to the house, Duncan went round to the kitchen door. He dismounted and tied the horses to the old hitching posts. But before he got to the door to knock, China opened the door, obviously not expecting to see two horses and him.

"Care for a ride?" Duncan handed China her riding helmet and crop.

"But I told you—"

The firm click of the kitchen door closing behind her cut China off.

Duncan laughed. "Sylvie's locked you out."

"Okay, you win."

"I wasn't looking for points but if you insist."

He gave her a leg up, and they made for the track up the valley.

It was different between them; the silence didn't feel easy like it did. But then, a lot had changed.

"You stopped answering my texts." Duncan kept Ro to a slower walk to stay alongside China.

"Sorry."

"Now you're saying sorry." Duncan tried to keep it light.

"I ran out of things to say. Unless you want to hear all the details of my mother staring at the ceiling. Or that I don't know what in the world to do with myself." Once she'd blurted that out, she said no more.

Duncan had at least twenty follow-on questions, but he said nothing. Instead, he rattled on about the boys; they would be home in a month's time, Ross to stay. China smiled politely, but he sensed her heart wasn't in this conversation. She looked miserable. Some time ago he realized that he'd do a lot to make this MacLeish woman happy in her stay here—to honor his dear friend. Then he'd realized that he liked her just for herself—that he wanted to hear her laugh, wanted to smooth away her frowns. It crept up on him, like the sniffles before a full-blown cold. But he kept his heart safely hidden.

China nudged Major into a trot and pulled ahead. Duncan hadn't quite been cut off in what he was saying, but it felt a bit like it. He refrained from comment and let her go on ahead.

She turned onto a narrower path that wound into a sparse stand of old Douglas fir trees. When they came to a clearing, she dismounted and tied Major to a tree branch.

He could play at this too. Without comment, he did the same and came to stand near—but not too near her.

"Tell me what this is?" China turned and led him on a little-used footpath. She stopped at a cluster of rocks fallen off the cliff above and pointed at a particular rock. There, inscribed, but faint, was a heart containing the letters *W* and *S*. "Do you know anything about this?"

Should he frown, or should he smile? Of course, he knew about this. But it wasn't his story to tell. He rubbed his chin, trying to decide how to reply.

"Is it *S* for Sinclair?" she asked.

"What?" At first he was confused. "You think *I* did that?" He shook his head and smiled in spite of her gravity. "No, not I."

"One of your family, then?"

"No. I can't imagine my father or my grandfather going in for hearts."

She stood with that pugnacious look, her chin jutted out a bit. She obviously wasn't giving up.

He reached up and lightly fingered the new growth candles on an overhanging pine bough—stalling. "Does it matter so much to you?"

"Yes, it does. My uncle never married, and it seems there's precious little love in this MacLeish clan. So I want to know who's carving hearts on my property. I found another one on a tree."

Duncan weighed his words carefully. "I do know about it, aye." And he hoped to leave it at that.

"Well?"

"The trouble is, I don't think it's my place to say."

China softened as she seemed to back down from what could have become a ridiculous argument. She raised her eyes to meet his, and an ache passed through his heart as he saw the sadness there.

"Please tell me," she said.

It was so difficult not to reach out and touch this woman. He fairly twitched with wanting to stroke his fingers down her cheek.

He held her gaze a moment. "You'd best ask Sylvie."

"Sylvie?" China's eyes widened and a smile grew. She whirled to look again at the etched stone. "And Uncle William?"

She didn't run, but she was in a hurry.

Duncan watched her retreat down the path back to the horses. "I'll ring you later," he called after her.

"Right." She tossed a wave back to him.

He hoped it wouldn't pain Sylvie too much to tell China of what might have been.

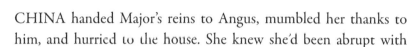

CHINA handed Major's reins to Angus, mumbled her thanks to him, and hurried to the house. She knew she'd been abrupt with Duncan, but she wanted to catch Sylvie, just in case she was going home to tea with Granny Nan.

When China burst into the kitchen, Sylvie gasped, and her hands flew off the computer keyboard, looking prepared to surrender.

Breathing hard and flushed, China stood close to Sylvie. "Why didn't you tell me about you and Uncle William?"

Sylvie's hands settled in her lap and stilled. "I...I don't know what ye mean."

"A *W* and an *S* in a heart?"

Sylvie took off her reading glasses and set them on the desk. "Och, that was a long time ago."

"I don't mean to be rude, but please tell me." China peeled off her jacket and flung it on a chair. "Here, let me make us a cup of tea." She poured water in the electric kettle, too impatient to wait for the Aga to heat up the big kettle, and set out mugs for them.

Sylvie sighed, and China turned back to her. "I don't mean to hurt you, Sylvie. Really. Never mind if it's too painful."

"It's not that...Well, yes, it is painful, but I don't mind the pain. It's part of the love. For love it was. Still is, as long as I breathe."

The bell for her mother's bedroom sounded from the row of bells high on the wall in the kitchen hallway.

"I'll go," China said, setting the biscuit tin on the butcher block. "Back in a sec."

Her mother sat in the chair, staring somewhere out the window.

"Oh, China, it's you. All the better. I think I'd like to sit outside for a bit. It's such a lovely day."

Bad timing. But then, China had been trying to get her mother to move more for the last few days. The Colonel had departed for her next nursing assignment, Margaret being that much better, and the young nurse had no ability to make the patient do anything she didn't feel like doing. And, of course, the young one happened to be out at the moment Margaret wanted the world to serve her.

China helped her mother into a sweater. The wounds were healing, but Margaret was still on pain medication and seemed to do everything in slow motion. They descended the stairs, Margaret clinging to the banister on one side and to China's arm on the other.

When they reached the entryway, China seated her mother on the boot bench by the door, said, "Back in a sec," and hurried to the kitchen, ignoring her mother's annoyed sigh.

"Sorry, Sylvie, but my mother wants to sit in the garden. Though I'd much rather be sitting here listening to you."

"Doesn't matter, dear. Another time. I'll bring tea out to the both of you."

"Thanks." And China returned to her mother. The wry thought popped in her head that she was certainly adding to the wear on the old hall carpet.

Margaret again leaned on China's arm as they made their way to the stone patio where a white wrought iron table and chairs overlooked the sea. The tide was out; green seaweed and kelp carpeted the shore, the air a pungent blend of salt and rot.

By the time they had walked the short distance, her mother was clearly distressed in her breathing. Her chest must still hurt considerably. But, settled in a chair, Margaret recovered her breath.

"I always hated this place." Margaret cast a broody look out to the breakwater and beyond to the village. "I think I hated it as much as my brother loved it. Dear Saint William."

Her mother's lip twitched unpleasantly. China thought it safest not to respond.

"Aren't you going to say anything?" her mother asked.

Then again, it was never predictable what was safe with her mother. Getting her to talk about herself usually worked best.

"How are you feeling?"

"Tired. I'm always tired. And, of course, I want a cigarette," she said with a sullen backhanded swat in China's direction.

Sylvie arrived with a tray of tea and McVitie's biscuits.

"Thanks, Sylvie." China motioned to the chair next to her. "Please sit with us."

Margaret stiffened noticeably. The lines on her upper lip deepened, like she had a lemon slice in her mouth.

Sylvie stood very straight, looking prim. "Thanks all the same, but I'd best get on with my work."

"McVitie's biscuits?" Margaret asked. "Is that the best you can do? Isn't there cake or such?" She snatched up the pitcher and splashed cream into her cup.

"China likes them, aye." And with that, Sylvie turned on her heel and left.

China wanted to crawl under the table. She poured the tea, concentrating mightily on the task, not wanting her mother to see the anger burning in her eyes.

Her mother gave her tea an irritated stir and clanked the silver spoon on the saucer. "She's so common."

The remark was barely audible but sliced through China's heart. She slowly stirred the cream into her tea and glared at her mother. "Why are you so rude to Sylvie? Can't you just be nice? Is that so hard for you?"

Unruffled, Margaret took a sip of tea before again gazing out to sea. "I think you know why."

"No, I don't. I don't know why anyone would be rude to Sylvie. She's...she's more like a mother to me than you are."

Margaret tensed, jerked her head like she'd been slapped.

China waited for the verbal beating. But it didn't come.

Margaret's shoulders deflated, and she seemed to cave into herself, her hands resting one over the other in her lap.

"Sorry," China whispered. And she was—sorry about so much.

A silence stretched taut and long between them.

"You know, China, I meant what I said."

China risked a questioning look, not wanting to continue this conversation, but not able to leave it alone either.

"I meant it—I only ever wanted to protect you...from me."

China jutted her chin out. "I don't know what that means."

"That I *am* sorry for how it's been between us. I know it's my fault."

All China could do was nod in lame agreement. Could an apology ever make it right? That would take time, and they never seemed to have that. She had hoped her mother's convalescence might be a precious time they'd look back on as a turning point in their relationship, but it wasn't. It was a series of her mother's demands, her needs, her withdrawal into herself.

Appearing transfixed by the bay, her mother said, "Couldn't you just accept me for who I am? Not who you want me to be?" Then she darted her eyes to fix on China's for a brief moment.

Her mother actually had a pleading look that nearly tripped China up. It was all about her—always had been. "I needed you, and you weren't there."

"You seemed to be fine at school," her mother said.

"I was a *child*." A sob threatened to erupt, but China tamped it down. "I barely knew you. And you kept me from my family here."

"I thought it was for the best."

"Well, it wasn't."

"I think it was." Her mother's expression hardened. "You have no idea how much better I've been as a parent to you than my father was to me. My grandfather was even worse."

"You can't just erase a child's history."

"I think I did a pretty good job of it."

China batted her hair over her shoulder. "And, by the way, how did you manage to get me a birth certificate from Akron, Ohio?"

"Oh, that was easy. Most fools will do anything for love or money. Frank thought I was in love with him, and a little money greased the way at the hospital and the courthouse." The familiar self-satisfied demeanor returned.

China readied to fire another question that had burned in her ever since being the butt of grade school teasing. "And why in the world did you name me China? What a ridiculous name."

Her mother's look turned downright sly.

"When I found out I was pregnant, I stomped straight into the butler's pantry and threw every piece of the Limoges china I could reach. And that was quite a lot."

China blinked stupidly at her mother. Her name had sprung from her mother's rage at being pregnant with her. Truly, she wished her mother had lied to her.

China let out a sigh pent up for years.

Her phone dinged, and she checked the text message.

Dinner @ Anchor? 7? pick u up D

She replied. *Yes plz!!! C*

"Good news?" asked her mother, not sounding particularly interested.

"I guess. Dinner out tonight."

"Duncan?"

"Could be."

Her mother flashed a crooked smile that looked like a dirty smirk. She didn't know Duncan at all, and China wasn't about to let her mother spoil this friendship.

Margaret hunched her shoulders forward and winced.

"You all right, Mother?"

"Just a little twinge." She put a hand to her chest and took a labored breath. "I think I'll go in now." A sharp cough seemed to intensify the pain.

"You want me to call the doctor?" Now China was really worried.

"No. It's nothing." Her mother gave one of her bossy scowls.

"It's not nothing, and you know it."

"I won't have it," her mother said in her not-to-be-denied tone.

Margaret attempted to get up and was able to rise off the chair only a little, then sank back with a peeved huff. She accepted China's arm, and they slowly made their way to the house.

China resolved to phone Dr. Reza in the morning, whether her mother liked it or not.

Once inside, China called to Sylvie, who came running from the kitchen. It took both of them to get her mother to bed, with two stops on the stairs for her to rest.

"I'll cancel my dinner tonight," China said as she poured a glass of water for her mother.

Margaret's hand shot out and gripped China's wrist, slopping water over their hands. "You will *not*."

China froze. She looked from the hand locked on her wrist to her mother's face and saw a wide-eyed fierceness she'd never seen. Her mother released her grip, and her hand dropped limp at her side.

China stroked her mother's brow, brushed the hair off her forehead. "I'm worried about you," she said.

"I'm fine." Her mother closed her eyes and seemed to relax. "Thank you, dear."

"I'll sit with you till the nurse gets back."

"Yes. Do that." And her mother was asleep, drawing shallow breaths.

AS Sylvie walked home, she wondered whatever would she tell China about the love she and William shared from the time they were children. Love that grew to desire. Desire that was never more than dreamed.

And yet, she wanted to make it plain to China that she and William had never crossed to that place from which they couldn't return, especially not after Sylvie married Ranald. It was a heartache to be borne and then to try and not think about, though she saw William daily at her work. Those first years after William declared they should not marry were agony, but she stayed on at Craggan Mhor, as much to be near William and he to her, as to continue in the only job she knew. She could see that his decision pained him. But to risk having troubled children like his father and grandfather was unthinkable to him. He wanted to spare her.

Tears of too many losses ran down Sylvie's cheeks.

She mopped at her tears, remembering William's last hours.

"Lie next to me," he had said. And she did. She curled her body beside him and laid her hand on his wasted chest, felt his heart struggling to beat. He brought his trembling hand to cover hers, and there they lay, till his heart beat no more.

But she'd not tell China all that. That was for her and William alone.

Chapter 38

Duncan speared another bite of the Anchor's specialty pork roast and smashed a few peas with it onto the back of his fork. "Ross was still talking about that promised ride with Miss MacLeish when I took the boys back for Summer Term. You made quite an impression on him."

China swallowed a sip of McEwan's ale and smiled at him over the rim of the half pint glass. "I'd like to make good on it, but I don't quite know how to do that. I guess I could ride Major over to your place, and then Ross and I could ride from there."

"Not to worry. The pony is used to being trailered. I'll bring them to you."

China sighed.

"Sometime. I know now is not the time to think about it."

That's Duncan, ever thoughtful. It wasn't that, but she didn't say so. She didn't know if it was a good idea to have the young son of a friend get all smitten with her. She knew what it was like to need a mother and come up disappointed. She changed the subject. "I'm worried about my mother," China said.

Duncan set his knife and fork on the plate. "Oh?" he said, leaning toward her.

"Her chest is still causing her lots of pain."

"What does the doctor say?"

"That's just it. She wouldn't let me call the doctor today—or cancel dinner with you. She was most insistent."

"I'm glad about the not canceling dinner part."

Duncan's eyes were kind.

"But I'm calling Dr. Reza tomorrow morning, whether she likes it or not. What really worries me is her cough."

"Do you want to leave now?"

"No, she'd probably just be upset about *that*."

"We'll leave straightaway after we've finished eating. All right?"

China nodded. "Thanks."

The phone vibrated in her jeans pocket, startling her.

China checked the number. The nurse.

"Miss MacLeish, I think you should come *now*," the nurse said.

"What's wrong?"

"Just come, aye?"

China pushed End.

"Something's happened with Mother."

"Right. Let's go." Duncan immediately rose and ushered China out, his hand at the small of her back. He laid money on the bar as they passed by. "In a rush I'm afraid," he said to Henry.

The bartender gave a nod.

They didn't talk on the drive from the pub to Craggan Mhor. China twisted her fingers together in her lap.

She rushed from the car, leaving the door standing open, Duncan right behind her.

The nurse waited in the entryway.

"How is she?" China slung her purse strap on a hook and headed for the stairs.

"Miss MacLeish,..."

China stopped, her hand on the newel post, and felt a numbness fall on her.

"I didn't want to tell you on the phone, but...your mother has passed."

"Passed?" Her own voice sounded far away.

"Aye, just before I rang you."

Duncan put his arm around China's shoulder. "I'm so sorry, China. Do you want me to come up with you?"

"What?" She looked at him, dazed, not yet comprehending what had happened. "Yes...please."

"I've called the doctor," the nurse said. "He'll be here shortly. I'll see to letting him in. And Mrs. Blair's coming directly."

The nurse stood, hands clasped at her waist, as if waiting for instructions, but China had none to give—and started up the stairs.

"Oh, and, Miss MacLeish, I should warn ye, your mother's color might surprise you a bit."

China frowned at the nurse, not understanding.

"It's the lack of blood, ye ken. She's a mite patchy."

"Thank you, Nurse," Duncan said.

Only because Duncan put his arm around her waist and gently squeezed did she move, and together they climbed the stairs to her mother's bedroom.

Before China opened the bedroom door, she turned and found Duncan's eyes with her own. He wordlessly folded her into his arms and cradled her against his chest. She was aware of nothing but his scent, his arms, and the sound of her own breathing.

When he let her go, she turned to open the door.

There her mother lay, arms resting at her sides outside the bedcovers. The alarming pale and bluish-purple mottling of her mother's skin made it unmistakable that it was over.

China approached the bed and stood looking down on her mother's impassive face.

"Would you like me to wait downstairs?" Duncan touched China's shoulder.

"No, please stay."

She bent to take her mother's hand. Soft and limp, it was cool to the touch. She let her mother's hand rest on her palm and caressed the slim-boned fingers.

Sounding dull, she heard the door open and close, Sylvie and Duncan talking quietly behind her. Then Duncan came to her, lightly kissed her hair, and whispered, "I'll be downstairs. Sylvie's here."

Sylvie touched China, a simple stroke down her arm. "How's my lamb?" she said.

Something snapped in China, and she turned into Sylvie's embrace, buried her head against her aunt's shoulder, and wept.

Chapter 39

She'd given in to a memorial service, though she had no idea if a church service would have meant anything to her mother or not. A plain beechwood box on a white-draped table at the front of the church held the urn with her mother's ashes.

China sat in the front pew on the left side of the church, Sylvie beside her, then Granny Nan. Behind her sat John and Fiona and all the staff of Craggan Mhor. She got a faint whiff of barn from Angus.

Duncan was across the aisle from her, along with the Glengorm staff. As they waited for the service to start, she and Duncan exchanged reassuring glances. Duncan was a friend unlike any she'd ever known in a man—almost as true as Stacy, but much better looking. He'd been with her whenever she needed him through this past miserable week. Stacy would have been here too, China was sure of it, but she hadn't yet told Stacy of her mother's death.

She turned to look behind at the villagers crowding the church. China leaned in and whispered to Sylvie, "I wouldn't have thought so many people would turn out for my mother."

"They're here for you, dearie." Sylvie reached over and patted China's hand.

A salty tear or two stung, and China dabbed them away.

The organ music suddenly swelled. The congregation stood and sang out a hymn China didn't know, not that she'd know any hymns, as far from church as she'd been. Sylvie opened the hymnal and pointed to where they were; China tried to keep up. The Reverend said a prayer, and the congregation took their seats again.

The service was like dancing with a partner who knew the routine—all China could do was follow with clumsy steps. She just wished it were over.

The dried up old preacher droned on about the valley of the shadow of death, his quavery voice every bit as hard to understand as Alex's Glaswegian.

Another hymn and another prayer, and the Reverend sat in the throne-like chair to the side. Duncan stood up, strode to the front, and took the place at the lectern. China didn't know he was going to speak.

"Miss MacLeish," Duncan nodded and smiled at her, "friends, we're here today to honor the memory of Margaret Vivian MacLeish." He took a small card from the inside breast pocket of his dark suit jacket and laid it on the lectern. "Margaret was older than I...and a lot more mischievous, I hear." Quiet chuckles rose. Sylvie covered her mouth with her hand, and China couldn't help but smile along with them. She bet it was true. And how like Duncan to put people at ease.

"Many of you remember Margaret. She had a vivacity about her that made one take notice. What I know of her is gleaned mostly from others' memories, people who remember her fondly."

Duncan told three stories about her mother—stories China had never heard, stories from when her mother was a young child—before her crazy moods set in and before all the hurt. She listened and met a mother she didn't know; a story of a beautiful little girl dancing at a ceilidh from first note to last; a star pupil at the primary school who enthralled listeners with a dramatic recitation of Robert Burns's "To a Mouse"; a sister who had her older brother wrapped around her little finger. Silent tears slid down China's cheeks; she swiped them away.

"Margaret MacLeish held a special place in our hearts. And though her homecoming turned tragic, it was good to have her home for a bit, aye?" Murmured aye's agreed.

"But God does not promise to deliver us from heartache in this life. His covenant with those who accept his Son as Savior and Lord reaches beyond the grave. Eternity with him awaits. Psalm 116, verse eight reads: 'For you, Lord, have delivered me from death, my eyes from tears, my feet from stumbling,...'" Duncan paused. "No more death...no more tears. Think on that."

Sylvie whispered an amen.

"The Lord knows Margaret's heart. His mercy and grace are boundless and his judgement sure. We are none of us saved by our works here on earth nor are we condemned by them...any of us."

A scowl tightened China's brow. She felt sure Duncan meant that Gordon Campbell wasn't condemned by attempted murder. Or was it first degree murder? Would the aneurysm have burst if a bullet hadn't ripped through her mother's chest? If so, God's justice must be unfair. How could Duncan believe that? He seemed so trustworthy in everything else. Before, she would have said it didn't matter, this God thing, but it did matter—a great deal. She set her jaw and listened as Duncan continued—determined to speak to him about this later.

"Imagine Margaret MacLeish in the presence of the Lord, aye? Prostrate before his Majesty and happy as a lark." Again, titters of amusement rippled through the church.

Duncan closed with a prayer, and China forced herself to say the amen.

The Reverend wiped his eyes. China wasn't sure if it was from emotion or because he had rheumy eyes. He rose and said a blessing; the service was done.

Like a wedding, the ushers had China lead the congregation out. She stood outside with Sylvie and Duncan and shook hands as people left.

The reception at the Anchor Inn was loud and too warm. China couldn't bear the thought of a reception at Craggan Mhor and had taken Henry's offer of the Anchor. China mingled as long as she could stand it, then sat in a corner with Sylvie and Granny Nan.

Eventually, people went home to their tea, some having had a bit too much alcohol, Maude Grant among them. Maude had planted smacking kisses on both China's cheeks when saying her goodbyes.

China attempted to slip out between the remaining stragglers, but Duncan caught her elbow. She hadn't avoided him exactly, just been up to her neck in the niceties of what one does at funerals. And she wasn't sure yet if she felt ambushed by his eulogy of her mother.

"Thank you for the eulogy." She gently, but firmly disengaged her elbow from his grasp. "I didn't know you were going to do that."

"Sorry. I should have told you."

"One of your laird duties?" She didn't mean it to sound snotty, but it did.

A small frown passed over his eyes, and he looked a bit wounded. "No, I wanted to do it for you. I thought you had enough to take care of."

She nodded, feeling a flush on her neck. "It was nice. Thank you."

He nodded in return.

"But we need to talk about this God thing." She surely had a welt on her head from being thumped with Duncan's Bible.

His dimple twitched. "Any time."

The drive to Craggan Mhor was lonely. Sylvie and Granny Nan had left already, and there was no one else who needed a lift. Sylvie had asked if China wanted her to spend the night. Though grateful for the offer, China declined.

Craggan Mhor was empty.

"Hey! Are ye aboot the hoose, then?" Angus's shout from the kitchen could be heard up in her bedroom where China had just changed into jeans.

"Here," China yelled over the banister.

A scramble of feet on carpet, and Fly came bounding up the stairs at her. China knelt and got a chin-slathering of doggie kisses.

"Angus?" China called. But there was no answer.

"It's just you and me tonight." She dug her fingers in the fur on the dog's neck, then sat straight down on the floor and hugged Fly to her chest.

HER mother's ashes dropped in a lacy sheet away from the cliff face, the wind catching and shredding them to tatters, till by the time they reached the rocks below, they were no more than tiny threads of the body that had been her mother. China said a prayer, as she had for her great-grandmother, to God who might be there.

This rocky promontory overlooking her birthplace was where she came to think. Tomorrow she was going back to the States for two weeks. Her last trip home had felt like she was fleeing to sanity and safety, but this time…she wasn't sure why she was going. Something in Stacy's voice had made China wonder whether this was a good idea. There were other friends in Chicago, though none she wanted to spend time with right now. Stacy was her main anchor, other than her job.

China picked her way through the rocks down the path to Craggan Mhor.

Stopping at the stable on her way to the house, China leaned her forearms on the top fence rail. Little Starry ripped around the paddock while Charlotte cropped the grass. China whistled low to Charlotte, and the mare raised her head and nickered. China fished in her jacket pocket and stuck an outstretched hand through the rails, a pony nut on the flat of her palm. Charlotte switched her tail and strolled over to the treat. The filly wheeled and darted to her mother, stopping with her tiny hooves planted firmly, bobbing her head at China.

At the sound of footsteps behind her, China turned to see Sylvie coming from the house.

"I thought I might find you here," Sylvie said. "All right, then?"

"Right as can be, I guess…It's done."

"Aye."

They stood in silence, watching the horses. Charlotte ambled off a few feet, and Starry gave a little buck and trotted to stay by her mother's side. When Charlotte stopped, the baby jabbed at a teat to nurse.

"Aye, you've got a fine filly there. She's a credit to her da," Sylvie said.

"I hope she's an easier ride than Ro."

"Aye, well, Duncan doesn't try overmuch to calm the fire in that horse, ye ken."

That was certainly true, China thought. Duncan liked Ro a spitfire.

Starry peeked her head out from under her mother's belly and made an impudent face. China rested a foot on the bottom rail, watched Major and Bess graze at the far end of the pasture.

"Did you know my mother left her entire estate to me?" she said.

"It doesn't surprise me. I know she loved you verra much."

"Here I thought she was contesting Uncle William's will, but she'd gone to Edinburgh to have her own will drawn up."

Sylvie remained silent.

"She knew she was dying, Sylvie. That's why she came here, to Craggan Mhor."

"Nay, dearie. She came to *you*."

China fought against the sting in her eyes.

Sylvie laid a hand on China's shoulder. "You'll be back, won't ye? From America?"

China patted Sylvie's hand. "I said I'd stay the year, and that's what I'll do. I can't promise more than that. I just can't." Pain flickered in Sylvie's eyes, causing the ache in China's chest to nearly throb. But she could always visit here. She knew she'd be welcome.

Sylvie straightened. "Right. I'm parched. Care for a cup of tea?"

Chapter 40

Rattling round this great house by himself was wearing on Duncan. Though household staff were always about, they had a way of doing their jobs without being seen much. The interns were back at school, and his boys weren't due home from Summer Term for another month. That left him busy doing a lot of what he didn't exactly want to be doing at the moment. He performed the duties of laird and laboratory manager without his usual enthusiasm. The greenhouse staff from the village tended to the plants quite well, but they needed supervision from him. The data analysis was complex, but he could do it in his sleep. And his estate manager ran the estate proficiently, but meetings with him were at least weekly.

Duncan buttered his toast and studied the flowers in the drizzled garden outside the dining room window. The daisy-like heads of the Red Campion waved in the wet breeze, and the Pink Pearl rhododendrons put on a show at the bottom of the garden.

But he was bored.

No, truth be told, he missed China.

It stung that she hadn't said much of a proper goodbye when she took off for the States again. He didn't know what he expected, but it was more than a phone call.

Maybe the distance was for the best. He knew the village tongues were wagging, but that was a given.

He picked up his mobile by the side of his breakfast plate. *Hello, Duncan here. Enjoying your time in the States?*

He sent the text, then cut into the slice of black pudding and sopped it around in the runny egg yolk. She'd get his text over her breakfast in a few hours.

Sort of. Her reply came straightaway.

You're up late, he texted back.

Couldn't sleep.

What does one say to that? Why? Thinking of me? Well, of course not. *Sorry to hear that*, he replied.

Sorry? LOL! ;-)

He chuckled. *Think I'll spend weekend with C and R in Edinburgh. What are you up to?*

Shopping, etc.

Fun?

No, boring. Truth.

Sorry.

More LOL! Sleep now. Goodnight. C

G'night. D

He put the phone down, leaned heavily against the chair back. Why, Lord? He didn't want this complication in his heart.

CHINA'S suitcase yawned empty on Stacy's guest bed. She might as well start packing while she waited for Stacy.

It had quickly been clear why Stacy hadn't sounded enthusiastic about having China visit. Stacy was pregnant. Tinged a shade of green till noon, throwing up every day, and boxes of saltines in the cupboard were definite clues. Not to mention that Stacy had that bloomed look China had seen on other pregnant girlfriends. After three days, Stacy fessed up, and China spent that afternoon by herself at Grant Park, walking and watching kids play around the fountain.

China wasn't sure whether she was thrilled for Stacy—or furious. The whole deal seemed wrong. At age forty-one Stacy said her biological clock had gone off with a huge *bang*, and she wanted a baby—now. So she and her friend Steven decided they'd do something about that: they started trying for a baby. With Steven and his partner, Jorge, living close enough, Stacy thought it would be ideal for all of them to raise a child together, passing it back and forth.

China wondered if she was turning into some kind of prude. What would Duncan say? She was pretty sure it was against his religion—Mr. No Benefits.

But what about the child? Stacy painted a picture of a loving alternative family. And maybe it would be. She hoped so. But China's gut told her it was mostly a self-centered decision. Yet she felt harsh judging Stacy. So she tried not to think about it, though all the heaving in the bathroom every morning made it hard to ignore.

Stacy's pregnancy hurt too. Truth was, China had hoped to have a family with Brian, but when he had said an emphatic no, she'd put it out of her mind—and her heart. And she'd come to accept living a childless life. Now it was too late for her. She was too old and had doubted she'd make a very good mother anyway. Maybe it was for the best after all, since she'd learned the secret of mental illness in her family. But she knew she would have loved any child no, matter what.

She'd had enough of this visit. Another twenty minutes at least for Stacy to finish tossing her crackers and get dressed so they could go out shopping for yet more baby paraphernalia. China felt like a bad friend, but she was just too raw after her mother's death.

China pulled out her phone and texted Duncan. It would be just before dinnertime there.

Hi, it's me. What's for dinner?
His reply was immediate. *Hello. Having fun now?*
Noooo!
Why not?
Stacy pregnant.
That's a good thing, aye?

Complicated.
I see. Sorry.
LOL. Tell you later.
There was a pause before Duncan replied.
Miss you.
Two small words. China's chest tightened, her fingers poised over the keys for several moments.
Try not to.
Sorry, too late.
Too late. That was what she'd been thinking minutes ago. It was too late.
Coming back early. A lot to do at CM. She almost typed *back home.*
When? I'll pick you up.
Thanks but already arranged with John. CU. C
D

That was probably rude, but she would not make promises—to anyone.

She was leaving on a red-eye tonight. Stacy had been a little miffed, but she'd get over it, being so absorbed with baby. Besides, neither of them would let all their years of friendship go; it would just change a bit.

China opened a dresser drawer and started packing.

But thoughts of Duncan nagged at her. It was difficult to say no to him—because she didn't want to say no—to anything he said. That tug on her heart would not go away when she thought about him. Every day. No matter how hard she tried *not* to think about him.

Maybe after the year at Craggan Mhor was over, she'd just start fresh somewhere else. She could do what she wanted to; she could work if she wanted; she could build an orphanage in Botswana. She didn't have to live in Chicago. And she didn't have to need *anyone*—ever again.

CHINA was due back tomorrow, and Sylvie couldn't remember if she'd told China that Craggan Mhor was open for guests again in a mere two weeks' time. Fishing, shooting, stalking—it was a buzz of activity round the estate till mid-February with only a few days at Christmas and Hogmanay to themselves. And strangers tramping round the house may not be to China's liking. She was certain she'd told China that last year's season had been cut short due to bereavement. Could she not have told her when it would resume?

She finished the booking confirmation on the computer and reached to stroke Andy's head. He sat on his haunches and raised his front paws in the air.

"Whatever shall we do, laddie? If I've been addlepated, there's not much can be done for it now."

Sylvie picked up her notebook and started off, to-do list in hand, to check on how the girls were getting on with the bedrooms. There was work to be done, but she couldn't shake the fear that she'd forgotten to tell China, and the poor lamb would be coming home to a shock.

Andy hopped to all fours and looked up at her expectantly, wagging his wee tail. "Nay, you stay here. You'll just be under foot." And Sylvie pointed to Andy's bed. His tail stopped, and he dutifully did as he was told. "Och, will you look at that," she said. "Where'd that obedient dog come from, then?"

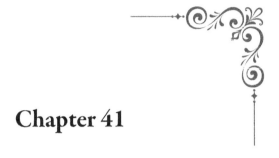

Chapter 41

A pinprick in the tender skin below her right eye, and China realized it was summer in the Highlands; the midges she'd been warned about were on the attack. She swatted around her head at the no-see-ums. Another sting to a hand. Then a jab at the back of her neck.

She was already plenty put out—now she really felt under siege. Craggan Mhor was a hunting and fishing lodge: a hotel for fat tourists eating and drinking in her house, shooting the deer she enjoyed seeing bounding through the heather, and blasting away at her birds. But she was as much put out with herself—she'd forgotten—and she didn't forget details. Of course, the attorneys and Sylvie had mentioned it. And she remembered some reference to Craggan Mhor as a hunting lodge when she first googled whether this whole deal was legitimate or not. But a *season* had an insufferable sound to it.

A stab on her cheek. She turned and ran from the burn where she was throwing rocks in with a vengeance. Just when she'd settled into a routine and had actually found aspects she enjoyed about living in this damp, nettlesome place. She wasn't upset with Sylvie or John—they were just doing their jobs—but she needed to think. And apparently, she needed to be indoors to do that today.

Breathless, China shut the kitchen door like the midges were still after her. "Sylvie," China called when she found the kitchen empty.

"In here, dear." China followed Sylvie's voice down the hallway to the butler's pantry. Candlestick in hand, Sylvie dipped a rag into the silver polish jar.

"I'm off to the Wildcat," China said.

"Right you are. See you for tea, then?"

"Unless I die of jet lag." China managed a smile. Sylvie's chuckle followed China out.

It was difficult to find a parking spot in the village. The lot in front of the Wildcat was full. China ended up in the car park a block up the hill. She backed into a space where she could just about open the door to ease out of the car.

The village had been transformed in the few days she'd been away. She had to stand aside at the door to the coffee shop while a noisy family of tourists exited. The man had a large camera bouncing on his belly, and the woman in shorts swore at her kids when one flaxen-haired brother almost shoved the other brother into China. Americans.

The busy place sounded like a call center. Alex waved from behind the counter, then said, "Next please." China got in line. Starbucks in Chicago wasn't this crazy.

"Hiya," Alex looked up from the hissing Italian coffee machine. "Where ye been, eh?" She started China's usual Americano.

"I was in the States a few days. What happened here?"

"'Tis the season, aye. Got a tour bus comin' in a bittie bit."

Coffee in one hand and a plate of blackberry crumble in the other, China looked for a seat. Several villagers said hello. She stood at the door to the glassed-in porch, hoping someone was about to leave. Rare sun beating in made the greenhouse porch stifling, but it was better than being midge fodder. A man at the corner table gathered his newspaper and left, and she grabbed the chair.

China turned so she faced Fionnloch Bay and not the crowd. Sun diamonds sparkled on an azure-green sea. The dome of Timcheall stood high and clear in the distance, smaller islands scattered around it like black pearls. To the south, Craggan Mhor was just out of view at the end of a sheltered bay. Shadows of the few puffy clouds crept over the mountains surrounding Fionnloch.

The hum in the coffee shop intensified, and China swiveled to see what was going on. A line of tourists snaked out the door. The tour bus. China watched, fascinated at how Alex and the other staff handled the orders—with big smiles to go with the dollops of clotted cream on the puddings. The locals got up, one by one, and vacated their seats, nodding and smiling at the strangers. A light-bulb moment pinged, and China realized she was witnessing an every-summer ritual. The village welcomed and made room for the tourists, an economic lifeblood to the village.

Well, that put things in a different perspective. She turned back to gazing at the sea, no longer as annoyed by the crush of people and noise, but thinking of the cash going in the till.

But why did Uncle William run Craggan Mhor as a sporting lodge? He certainly didn't need the money. And now she was stuck with it for this season. Whoever bought the place could carry on with whatever they liked; they could turn it into a meditation retreat center for all she cared.

GERTY the Defender jerked forward as China ground the gears, determined to drive the thing. Out the track toward the bridge over the river, she could do no damage but run into the heather, so John said. She found neutral, tried again, and smoothed the old bucket into first. And hit a pothole.

"There you've got it." John bounced up, his head barely missing the shotgun clipped in an overhead rack. The tracks on Craggan Mhor had clearly never seen a road grader. "Now let her rip and take her up to second gear."

China set her jaw and shifted into second. No grinding. A faint smile played at her mouth. "You don't drive this thing; you *ride* it," she said, tightening her grip on the wheel.

"Aye. She's grand."

China tried to avoid the rock ahead, but the track was a minefield, and Gerty lurched up and to the left. The truck caromed into the heather, and China jammed on the brakes.

John roared with laughter. "I was only jokin', ye ken."

"What?"

"I never thought you'd actually run us off the road."

"You want to drive?"

"Nay, you're doin' fine, lassie."

China muttered about Scotsmen, and John laughed some more.

"Put her in four low," John pointed to the selection lever, "and drive us on out of here." He made a sweeping gesture forward through the heather and back to the track.

The Defender charged slowly through the heather, rocking side to side. Scraping and an occasional bang on the undercarriage had China worried, but John didn't seem concerned.

"There now. Well done." John patted the dash. "Drive on to that wide spot, and I'll have a look-see at her undercarriage. We've no doubt dragged a bit of heather with us."

"I'm afraid I might have put a hole in her," China said, sucking in her lower lip just a little.

"A hole? Naw. She's got an armor-plated belly. Made for this sort of thing, she is."

China switched off the truck and jerked the parking brake on.

John pulled a couple branches of heather from a wheel well. Then he got down on his hands and knees to look underneath and declared her clean as a whistle.

"While we're stopped, let's see what Sylvie packed for us, eh?"

He reached behind the passenger seat and produced a thermos of milky tea and a paper sack that contained two tin mugs, a zip bag of Sylvie's oatcakes, and a small pot of strawberry jam. John pulled out a hunting knife for the jam; China tried not to think about where the knife had been.

They munched and sipped, leaning against the side of the Defender.

"Have ye thought about the coming season, then?" John asked.

"What do you mean?"

John was slow to answer. "I dinna know how to say this, but you've got a job to do."

China pushed away from the truck and stood facing John. "A job?"

"Aye. You're the mistress of the manor and guests will expect to see you from time to time. And at dinner, if they've booked to dine at the house."

China turned away and bit hard on an oatcake. No matter what John said, he was right, so she might as well save herself the lecture and think before she spoke. She chewed and swallowed, the jam-smeared oatcake tasting dry as dust.

"You mean I'm to play host...to the guests."

"Aye. That's the long and the short of it."

"Answer me this, John." China now faced him squarely. "Why did my uncle run this place as a sporting-lodge-cum-bed-and-breakfast? He didn't need the money."

John poured the last of the tea, offering to China first. "That's an easy one. Two reasons, aye. He loved Craggan Mhor, and the land and the animals need managing. And he loved the villagers."

China shot him a quizzical look.

"The people. They need the tourist traffic for their livelihoods, ye ken?" He grinned. "We employ a number of the villagers, and the venison, ye ken, goes to folks as have need of it. And William...he enjoyed havin' the company. Och, it's a grand time, the season is."

The scene at the Wildcat flashed in her brain—the bus unloading tourists with their wallets open. John had done it again. He had a way of humbling her and then grinning about it—making it clear that he enjoyed setting her straight—and that he thought she was all right—for a Yank.

She closed her eyes and tilted her face to the warmth of the welcome Highland sunlight. The people, this place—it could steal her heart—if she let it.

"You'd best get yourself a MacLeish tartan kilted skirt to boot. Fiona can point ye to a good shop in Inverness."

Now the man was directing her wardrobe selection. She cast him a sidelong pursed-lipped scowl. "I have to wear a uniform?"

"Aye, somethin' like that. For the tourists, ye ken." He grinned and stowed the thermos.

"I ken." For *one* season.

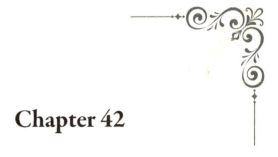

Chapter 42

Tourist season and midge season were full bore at Craggan Mhor. After three weeks of it, China moved to the rhythm of the house, rarely missing a step. Playing host wasn't nearly as bad as she had feared. Just about anyone was tolerable for a week. They were, after all, paying a fat lot of money for the privilege of tramping around the estate, pretending it was theirs for a few days. Many guests were repeaters, visiting upwards of fifteen years—mostly English, some Germans, Italians, a few Americans. Unexpectedly, she learned a great deal about Uncle William from the guests. He was indeed an extraordinary man—an uncle she would have loved, if she'd been given the chance.

Sylvie was run off her feet with the extra work, and China gladly took over the booking and most correspondence related to the guests. The house was so busy, she forgot what the solitude—and the loneliness—was like. She did miss her privacy, though. There was no more going to the kitchen in her robe for a late-night hot chocolate. At least all of the rooms had bathrooms en suite so guests weren't lined up in the hallway, waiting for the loo. It was reminiscent of boarding school days with the noise of doors opening and closing, feet thudding on the carpeted hall, and the occasional inebriated laugh.

And it was a great help that four young people from the village lived in. There was always someone to see to the guests' needs. The two girls stayed in rooms on the third floor, the old servants' quarters, and the village boys bunked in a room next to Angus's digs behind the house. Sylvie kept a tight rein.

John ran the sporting operation, but China didn't want to know as much about that. Anglers headed to the river in their Land Rovers, and ramblers struck out with topographical maps John provided. Gun season started in September.

China often thought of her mother. But how was she to grieve a mother she hardly knew?

One morning, China and Sylvie stole a rare time alone together as they walked to Sylvie's cottage after breakfast. The late July breeze through the trees meant no midges. China hadn't seen Granny Nan in two weeks and missed her. And talking with Sylvie about her mother might help. But it didn't. Sylvie sighed and didn't seem quite herself.

China let the conversation drop before she heard yet again, "But your mother loved ye." She had tried to find that love somewhere inside her, but she couldn't find a piece big enough to get hold of.

Silence walked with them for a time, except for the crashing of the sea. Once out of the trees and the sheltered bay, the weather came directly over the outer islands and the open sea. A storm was coming in tonight, and Sylvie clamped a hand on her hat before the wind grabbed it.

"You haven't told me about you and Uncle William yet," China said.

"Andy, come here, ye wee beastie," Sylvie called to Andy as he darted at a crow. She clapped her hands at him. "Come here."

"Sylvie," China prompted.

"Aye, well…I'll tell ye. It's not a secret. No secrets in Fionnloch, eh?" Sylvie's smile didn't quite reach her eyes like usual.

She drew in a big breath and let it out; her walk slowed. And she began to spin out the story of their love. The W and S in a heart. A pure love, treasured as gold. A love of sacrifice.

They stopped to sit on a bench within a stone's throw of Sylvie and Nan's cottage. Andy rushed toward the cottage, then back along toward Craggan Mhor where a red squirrel shot across the path and up a tree to sit and scold from a branch.

China watched the dog's antics and swiped away a tear. To be loved like Sylvie and Uncle William loved each other. She felt a longing ache in her heart.

Sylvie reached for China's hand and held it in the crook of her elbow. "I canna say if William was right to not marry for fear of our children bein'...well...troubled. But we both trusted in the Lord." Sylvie patted China's hand.

China placed her other hand over Sylvie's and pressed down as if firmly pressing their lives together—as family.

Surely, there was much Sylvie left unsaid, but China would never ask.

Trust in the Lord? She knew she trusted Sylvie. And Granny Nan. John...and Duncan.

END of July, and the boys had been home almost a month. And Duncan was content as a dog drowsing in the sun. Callum helped out in the greenhouses or played rugger; Ross had riding lessons or was off having fun with his mates. Trooper was forever with one or the other of the boys.

Duncan sat back and pushed away from the microscope. He rolled his chair so he could see out the window to the gathering storm. The wind whipped the spent rhododendron blooms.

Maybe he should have employed a nanny, at least for Ross, but he couldn't see the need of it really. Duncan was perfectly happy to shuttle his boys where they needed to go, and if he couldn't, he sent them off with Donnie in the truck. A little mud and manure on the wheels of his carriage never did a prince any harm. Duncan was determined not to raise snobs. So far as he could tell, their mother hadn't tainted them with her airs. And dear Janet was agreeable to the boys hovering round the kitchen—and her plates of cookies. The boys were busy and seemed content. And that made Duncan content.

Callum had agreed that he should return to Merchiston Castle. After all, his rugby team needed him. Duncan didn't like to separate the boys, but this was likely for the best. Ross had fairly skipped with excitement round the halls of the Fionnloch Primary School when Duncan took him to enroll. And since then, Ross had been jabbering at Callum in the Gaelic phrases he knew, getting ready for Gaelic immersion class. Callum had spouted back at Ross in butchered Gaelic that Duncan didn't like to point out was Callum asking for Ross to please pass the butter.

They were settling into the summer holiday quite nicely.

Only Duncan didn't feel settled in one respect—China—that MacLeish woman. Duncan's lips twitched in a soft smile, and he whispered her name.

Since she'd come back from the States, they had met as often as they could, which was less frequent in recent weeks, busy as she was at Craggan Mhor. They texted this and that. And she'd made good on her promise to ride with Ross.

But Duncan was indeed unsettled. This friend thing was wearing on him. His hands fairly tingled when he was around her for wanting to tangle his fingers in her hair and kiss her senseless.

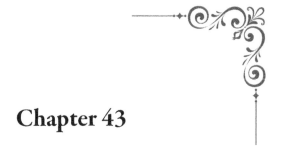

Chapter 43

The filly galloped circles around her grazing mother. China laughed. She crouched with baby-size halter in hand, waiting for Starry to come check her out. Starry did a buck and turn and started haltingly for China. Gentling training had started immediately, and Starry was good about coming for the halter and allowing herself to be led around the paddock. But at almost four months old, the baby was proving to be a little monkey. China couldn't turn her back on the pickpocket.

Starry stood one step away from China and bobbed her head, nostrils flaring and sides heaving from her run. "Come and get me," she seemed to say. China slowly stood and put a pony nut on the flat of her palm, extending it only partway, asking Starry to come closer. Bob, bob went the little head, and Starry came for the treat.

China put her arm over Starry's neck and slipped the halter on. Once caught, Starry stood like a ballerina: head up, ears pricked, toes pointed.

The halter buckled in place, China held the leadline and walked Starry around the paddock. Charlotte gave only a brief lift of her head to check on her baby. Bess stood off in a corner, head low in a drowse, tail swishing lazily. And Major eyed the cow parsley on the other side of the fence.

China was about to end the lesson when she looked up. A man leaned on the gate, one foot resting on the lower rail. She recognized him as one of the Germans who had arrived yesterday afternoon.

The breeze stirred his blond shoulder-length hair; his rolled up shirt-sleeves revealed Popeye forearms, and the shirt buttons strained across his chest. China hadn't seen any of his party at dinner last night; she heard they'd gone to the pub. Confirming that, she'd been awakened at one in the morning by a thud against the wall near her door, followed by muttered German and stifled man-giggles.

She didn't like guests traipsing freely about the property. She worried a gate might get left open. John all but said to the guests that the stable was off limits, but it appeared they would have to be more clear about this.

"You have quite a vay vis horses, Miss MacLeish," the German said.

China smiled halfheartedly. She couldn't avoid him since he was blocking her way out. "Thank you, Mr....I'm sorry, I don't recall your name."

"Faust. Diederich Faust. Call me Deter."

"Any relation?"

His smile seemed more like a leer. "No." He straightened and put a hand on the gate latch. "May I come in?"

Rather than say a yes she didn't feel, China merely tilted her head. He was probably coming in whether she said yes or not. Anyway, it was good to have Starry exposed to other people.

When the man entered the paddock, Charlotte strolled over to within kicking range. The German moved to put the filly between the mare and him. The German said something to Starry before he slowly approached her. All China understood was *Liebchen*. He held his palm out for her to sniff before laying a hand on her neck. Talking all the while, he ran his hand over her chest, down a foreleg, then down her back and over her haunch. Starry twitched and bobbed at his touch, but she didn't kick.

"She is good filly, zis one."

"You know horses?"

"*Ja*, I breed Hanoverians. Very big horses."

"She's half Irish Thoroughbred."

"A black?" He raked a hand through his male-model head of hair.

"Yes." China shortened her hold on the lead rope as Starry tried to back away. "And her sire's a handful."

"I sought so."

When Starry stood still again, China unbuckled the halter, and the filly trotted around to the other side of her mother. Charlotte nosed the filly and moved them off to the other end of the paddock.

"You have a nice place here."

"Thank you." China didn't really want to engage in a lengthy conversation and opened the gate.

The German sprang to polite action and swung the gate open wide enough for her to get through, then closed the gate behind himself. He locked onto her eyes with his too-pale-blue leer and grinned, crinkling the sun lines around his eyes. "You are very beautiful voman, Miss MacLeish." He moved closer and reached for her hand.

China busied her hands looping the leadline in one hand.

The German looked over her shoulder, and the crinkles disappeared. "Ah. Braveheart I think is looking for you."

China turned to see what was going on. A tightness grabbed deep in her chest and her face flamed.

Duncan strode toward them from the stableyard, his hiking boots crunching on the gravel and his kilt swinging wide—fists tight.

AS he approached China and the man standing with her, Duncan slowed, lest he appear too much like a charging bull. He had a crazy flash of Harriet and that bloody blond South African but got hold of himself before he rammed a fist into *this* chap's nose too.

"Duncan," China took a step away from the other man, "I didn't expect you yet."

And what exactly did that mean? He didn't know what to say. The other man stuck out his hand. "Faust. Deter."

"Duncan. Sir."

"Pardon?" The outstretched hand pulled back a tad.

"My name is Sir Duncan."

"I see."

Duncan wanted to smack the smirk off the German's face. Instead, he took the German's hand in a firm grip. The German gripped back to the point they might have started arm wrestling, but they let go before it became ridiculous.

Duncan took a step closer to China.

As did the German. "Miss MacLeish, may I dine at your table zis evening?"

Duncan almost dropped his jaw. The cheek of the man.

"I suppose." And she took a step away from both of them. "I'll tell Mrs. Blair. How many in your party?"

To her credit, she didn't sound overly keen, Duncan thought.

"Two. *Danke schön.*"

The man ran a hand through his insufferable hair like a preening cock pheasant.

"Till dinner zen." He gave a shallow bow, turned on his heel, and sauntered back toward the house.

An awkward silence remained in the German's wake. Duncan wanted to know just what was going on here.

China looked up from studying the ground and said, "It's business, Duncan."

She sounded a bit put out.

"Aye?"

She stuck her fists on her hips, halter and lead rope smacking against her thigh, her blue eyes hard. "Yes."

He'd not seen that look in her eyes, and it took him aback. In an instant, he saw himself as the rightly jealous husband—accusing China. And he felt a fool.

He sighed before he knew it was out. "I know. But I cannot abide his type. A Lothario, if ever there was one." He toed a pebble out of the dirt. "Sorry. I don't know what came over me."

Her eyes softened. "Hmm. Ex-wife maybe?"

"No doubt."

"Forget about it," she said.

He wished he could.

"He called you Braveheart." She unsuccessfully suppressed a giggle.

Duncan didn't entirely see the humor. "Smarmy git."

"Is that rude?" China smirked.

"Not enough."

"Why don't you come to dinner too? We'll be a foursome." Now she was really grinning.

"Oh, right. That would be good fun...Are you serious?"

"I am."

He laughed. "Then I will. Can't wait to see Lothario's face when I turn up."

She looped the halter and rope over the gatepost. "I'll go and change. Won't be a minute to get my hiking boots on."

Duncan watched her go, the same direction the German had taken, and he was tempted to follow. He was troubled, very troubled. Clearly, she was doing this friend thing better than he, and he'd have to either back off or...or he didn't know what.

ANGUS'S nightly call to dinner had screeched from the front lawn. The old geezer wasn't a good piper, but he was enthusiastic, squeezing away on the bag. The guests seemed to enjoy "Scotland the

Brave," some strutting in time down the hall to the dining room like the drum major at the head of the parade. To China, the noise still sounded like the shriek of very upset cats.

Dinner was only halfway through, and China was exhausted. The German's other party member was a twenty-something English woman seated directly across from Duncan, décolleté cut almost to her navel. China knew that the woman knew, that every time she cut a piece of roast, her breasts flexed and threatened to escape the tenuous drape of her dress. The woman lived in Manchester; he lived in Stuttgart. No wedding ring or even engagement ring in sight. China suspected the oily German was married with a family—a man cut from the same filthy cloth as Brian.

Duncan handled the conversation so adroitly that China resolved to give him a standing ovation later. Braveheart indeed. And Duncan managed not to drop his eyeballs in the cavern of cleavage, and he didn't dribble soup down his shirtfront.

And it was difficult to swallow around the lump in her throat. That squeeze in her chest when she looked at Duncan had risen up and lodged near her tonsils. It was getting unendurable. Maybe they needed distance, thousands of miles, to stop this ache that could come to nothing. He'd made it clear how he felt about her. And that was—back off. Yet he kept coming around. The hike this afternoon had been their usual easy time together. But they hadn't talked much.

A spoonful of dessert in her mouth, she stole a glance at Duncan, who was debating with the German about some point to do with horses. Duncan's intense green eyes spoke his dislike of the German, and his mouth twitched slightly as he listened to the man. China longed to trace those lips with a finger, then kiss them like a butterfly searching for a sweet place to land.

Duncan caught her looking. His eyes softened, and a faint smile played on his lips. Flushed, she swallowed and concentrated on the next bite of carrot cake and custard. Perhaps their friendship was explained by nothing more complicated than being the two largest landowners in the area, loneliness, and having found a trusted friend in each other away from their public lives in the village.

She could feel a slight sting in her eyes. She was not going to excuse herself and make a scene, coming back to the table with red eyes, having cried her eyes out in the privacy of her bedroom.

She really needed this sentence imposed by Uncle William to end.

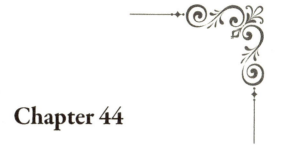

Chapter 44

With Callum back at school in Edinburgh for Autumn Term and Ross enrolled at Fionnloch Primary, Duncan had a bit more free time. He rang the Glasgow Police to see if any forensic job needed doing. He needed to get away. As luck would have it, there was a big case pending that required at least a week's work in the Glasgow labs. It would be intense, this being a particularly grisly murder that involved plant matter found on the body not matching the vegetation at the site where the victim was found. The police had to find the crime scene.

Janet agreed to live in while Duncan was gone. Gruff as she was sometimes, she loved the boys like grandchildren, and Duncan was content to leave Ross in her care. Donnie would pitch in and deliver Ross to school and wherever else he needed to go. Lately, that included hanging around the stable at Craggan Mhor, helping gentle the filly. Angus was patient with Ross, but the truth was that Ross hoped to see Miss MacLeish. Ross had developed quite a crush on China, and Duncan was concerned that Ross might get *his* heart broken as well. Maybe he'd best tell Donnie to keep Ross distracted enough that he wasn't pestering to go to Craggan Mhor in Duncan's absence.

And maybe he'd look up some old school chums while he was away. Stinky Finch and Peter Barclay were both in Glasgow, and it would be good to catch up over a dram or two.

Duncan snapped the leather valise closed and grabbed the garment bag off the clothes valet in the corner.

Things stowed in the boot of the Range Rover, Duncan got out his mobile to text China. She had been cool of late. He wasn't sure what that was all about, but he had a dread that, with December approaching and her year up in only three months, she really would leave.

Working in Glasgow at least a week. CU. D

He held the phone a few moments, hoping, but there was no reply.

Chapter 45

They had seen each other infrequently since he returned from Glasgow three weeks ago. Something had changed, but neither of them acknowledged it. China didn't know why she'd invited Duncan to dinner with the guests again; it just slipped out in a text. She knew she was not about to let her heart be trampled on again. Ever. And if that meant drifting away from the man she admired most in this world, then so be it.

He was his usual lairdly sophisticate self at dinner. And he looked the part in tweedy jacket and brown silk cravat—without looking smug. But she tried not to look at him much.

After dinner, and as little time spent with the guests having coffee in the lounge as politely necessary, Duncan asked her to walk with him.

She grabbed a coat by the front door, and he led her out to the jetty. The lights of Fionnloch twinkled in the October dark. Waves slapped a gentle rhythm against the stone breakwater.

Duncan thrust his hands in his pants pockets and stood square on to the blackened sea, the jetty extending before them. The breeze lifted his hair to the side. China couldn't read him, so she waited, thankful there was no moon and the guests couldn't see them.

Motionless, Duncan said, "This isn't working, is it?"

Iciness washed through her. "What isn't?"

A tight silence stretched too long, filled only with the splash of waves and the thump of her heart.

"This friend thing," Duncan finally said.

He wouldn't look at her, and China was glad for the veil of hair that blew across her face. She swallowed the unwanted tears.

"No, it surely isn't." She spat the words out and spun away, leaving him standing alone, as he apparently wanted to be.

"China, I..."

The wind took his words. She didn't care to hear them anyway.

"Leave me alone!" she shouted over her shoulder.

She didn't stop till she got to the stable where she let herself into Charlotte's stall. In the dark she put her arms around Charlotte's neck, laid her head against the horse's mane, and cried slow, shuddering sobs. Starry nuzzled her in the side, which did little to stop China's tears.

Chapter 46

For the next three days, China asked to be excused from any responsibilities to do with the guests. After she was done crying, she hiked, drinking in the last faint tint of the heather bloom, wanting to hold the lavender hills in memory forever. And when she'd had enough hiking, she went to Begg's Farm to visit Mrs. Pakulski, who was pregnant again. Then she stopped to see Maude.

On her last day off, China settled into a deep couch at the Wildcat with a coffee and an oat scone. She took out her phone and opened the Bible app she'd downloaded on a whim. She'd asked Granny Nan what she should read...*if* she read anything in the Bible. So she started with John, chapter 4, Jesus talks with a Samaritan woman.

She read the story of Jesus asking a woman at a well for a drink of water. Jesus knew the woman was a sinner, yet he treated her with compassion, offering her living water. China guessed that had something to do with eternal life. The woman believed the Messiah would come and explain everything, and Jesus said, "I am he."

"Ye awright, duck?" Alex put a hand on China's shoulder.

China turned brimming eyes to Alex. "What?" She swiped the tears off her face. "Yes...I think so. Thanks."

"Right, then. Mun be summat good you're readin', aye?"

A tiny smile stole over China's lips. "Aye," she murmured—it was. She never wanted to be thirsty again.

THE washing up done, Sylvie wiped her hands more briskly than necessary on the tea towel. She had to hurry back to Craggan Mhor for the dinner, now she'd had tea with Nan, and she was in a flap.

"Och, she's bein' a fool. And so is he." Sylvie gave a backhanded swat at nothing. "She's wretched without him comin' round. And he's like a moanin' coo lost in the mist."

Nan dried a plate and set it on the bottom rail of the kitchen dresser, seeming to pay little attention to Sylvie's rant.

Sylvie had gone round to Glengorm yesterday, under the guise of talking to Janet, and gone in to hallo Duncan. She'd found him sitting at his desk in that great study of his, staring out the window, all moon-eyed. He'd asked after China, but Sylvie didn't have the heart to tell him that she hadn't seen nearly as much of China either. Neither of them said it, but China MacLeish was acting like a woman who was leaving.

The towel snapped as Sylvie shook it out, folded it in half, and laid it on the grooved wooden drainboard beside the sink.

"And I canna for the life of me think why he doesn't do something about it." Sylvie followed Nan into the sitting room.

"Now, now, dearie, dinna fash yourself," Nan said. "All in the Lord's timing, aye?" She eased herself into her chair by the fire and took up her knitting: a scarf for China, blue as her eyes.

Sylvie dropped another peat brick on the fire and plopped into her chair opposite Nan. Evenings were chilly, and it would be dark before she was back at Craggan Mhor to oversee the dinner. The girls had the cooking of it well in hand, but Sylvie liked to be there. Seems she had to be two places at once when the season was on.

Sylvie couldn't let go what troubled her about Duncan and China. "I must speak to Duncan, ye ken."

"Nay, ye leave 'em be," Nan said gently.

Nan's tone might have soothed most folk, but Sylvie was not to be calmed—and she burst into tears. "I'm so sorry. It's just that..." She pulled a hankie from her skirt pocket and blew her nose.

"Aye, dearie, ye just want happiness for 'em."

Unable to say more to dear Nan, Sylvie twisted her hankie round a finger.

"Did ye know, dearie, that China might be readin' the Word, eh?" Nan's needles clicked a steady rhythm.

Sylvie jerked her head up.

"Aye." Nan nodded and smiled, not looking up from her knitting. "She came to me, it be a fortnight now, an' asked what should she read...*if* she read the Word." Nan gave a soft chuckle. "We dinna go easy, some of us."

"Lord be praised," Sylvie breathed.

"Aye, the Lord be praised in his sanctuary. That be nigh on forty-two years o' prayer mebbe answered." Nan let her needles rest in her lap and swiped a tear off her wrinkled cheek. She folded her hands over the deep blue wool, closed her eyes, and began to pray. "Heavenly Father, God o' mercy an' grace, we praise your name. We thank ye for your everlovin' kindness."

Sylvie bowed her head.

"Now, as ever, we commit China tae ye. Draw her tae ye. Aye. Draw her tae ye." Nan continued in whispered Gaelic.

Sylvie wanted to add—and let that clot-heid Duncan come to his senses. Aye.

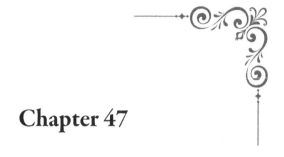

Chapter 47

Early November snow capped the surrounding mountains as China drove to the Inverness Airport. The Anglia chugged up a hill and China downshifted. Four days in London would be a good tonic—get away from the endless season at Craggan Mhor. She would have asked Stacy to meet her, but with Stacy seven months pregnant, that wasn't going to happen. Instead, she was meeting Martha, a school friend who had popped up on Facebook a couple years ago. Martha had posted that she had business in London, so China had messaged her. China wasn't sure about this, but how bad could four days be? Martha was one of the wild girls in high school and had nearly gotten herself kicked out for drinking their junior year.

To China, London had only ever been an airport layover on the way to somewhere sunny with white sand and a blue sea. She looked forward to seeing the sights. It didn't seem right to spend a year in the UK and not see London.

The flight had been a bit bumpy. Approaching Heathrow, the plane banked and dropped below the heavy clouds, revealing the familiar tower of Windsor Castle. Rain beat on the wings of the plane.

She could have taken the train into the city but decided she'd splurge on a cab all the way to the Dorchester Hotel. She and Martha were going all out. It's not like she didn't have the money, and Martha was on an expense account. She wasn't so Scottish at heart that she had to pinch pennies just for the sake of heritage.

China checked in and was escorted to her deluxe room overlooking Hyde Park. She changed into something smart, including her spike-heeled boots.

Martha had texted that she was in the bar, where China found her, one martini into happy hour and about to start on her second. The smacked air kisses and slightly slurred greeting put China off from the start. Martha had been a dormant friend for several years, and now China remembered why—she was a drunk and a phony.

Dinner was torture. Martha's account of men she'd bedded and great martinis she'd had went on, and on. China kept glancing apologetically at nearby diners. She realized she'd finally done it—turned into a total prude—and she didn't care.

Immediately after dinner, China excused herself, saying she had a headache. She was pretty sure she'd have a headache for four days.

Next day, guidebook and umbrella in hand, China happily spent the drizzly day taking in London. And the next day, and the next. London was wonderful.

Martha and she texted a couple of times, but it was clear neither of them pined for the other's company. China figured Martha had hooked up with a man and was busy.

By day, China navigated the Tube to get from the Tower of London to Buckingham Palace to Westminster Abbey. She walked from Harrods and around the Serpentine in Hyde Park where, instead of pond boats, raindrops played on the lake.

She stopped in front of a Knightsbridge antique shop window, captivated by a silver letter opener with a dazzling yellow stone set in a Scottish thistle. It was the perfect goodbye gift for Duncan, a token of thanks for the sweetest friendship she'd known—when it was sweet. She didn't want to hold a grudge, just hold the memory.

That night, the streets were wet and sitting at a table for one was lonely. She missed Duncan.

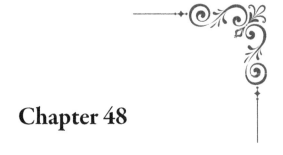

Chapter 48

"I need to know, then, thinking of the estate, are ye leavin' or stayin'?" John sat at his messy desk, China in the chair next to the desk, as they had countless times since she'd arrived. "It's nearly the year up, and I need to know. I canna run the estate waiting to know till the last minute—will we have a new owner, or no jobs at all?"

China wanted to scream; double knots twisted in her stomach. She'd thought this over a thousand times—and now John demanded an answer. Chicago was her home; she still had a good job; she couldn't just *live* in Scotland. Maybe she'd buy a penthouse on Lake Michigan in Chicago. Then she could come back to Scotland and visit friends—and family—fly them over to visit her in the off season. Or there was still that tantalizing thought of starting over.

The logical answer, the answer she'd always intended to give, threatened to rip her throat out. And now she had to say it.

"I'm leaving. Right after Christmas." Her cheeks blazed.

John leaned back in his chair and let out a long sigh, shook his head. "That's not what I wanted to hear, ye ken."

It wasn't what she wanted to say either, but she couldn't stay.

John tapped his steepled fingers together. "It pains me to say this, but I think it best, then, if ye leave before Christmas. If you recall, your year is ended ten days before ."

China's mouth dropped open—stupefied—then she snapped it shut. "You're kicking me out?"

"Nay, I want you to stay. Always have."

John looked like a thunder clap about to go off.

"I'm thinking of the hearts as will break when you're gone. Leave us to our lonely Christmas. It'll be a dismal time either way." He pushed back in his chair and stood, clearly dismissing her, his brow deeply furrowed.

Speechless, China got up and somehow found the door to stumble across the gravel yard on auto-walk. When she hurried into the kitchen, she kept her eyes averted from Sylvie at the computer and didn't stop when Sylvie said, "What's wrong, dearie?"

Marching straight to the study, she switched on the computer and pulled up the British Airways booking site. December 15 to Chicago, First Class—one-way. She hit Continue, then entered her credit card information and held her finger over the Return key. Tears slid down her cheeks.

Instead, she cleared the history and shut the laptop.

She changed into her hiking boots, piled on two layers of wool, and slammed the front door behind her—accidentally.

Over the bridge, past the waterfall, she hiked at a pace to burn off her misery, till she faced the scramble leading to where Duncan had found her that night. Drawn farther to the plateau of the cliff, China stood at the height from where her great-grandmother had fallen, where she'd sent her mother's ashes drifting to the earth.

Bitter wind dried her tears; China needed to think.

This year had been the most horrible—and the most wonderful—year of her life. The nightmare of her mother's death, etched in blood forever in her mind, might be reason enough to leave this place. But leaving Sylvie felt so wrong. The ache in her chest made her want to take it all back—stay.

China gulped in the raw air, filling her lungs with the frigid damp.

But it was Duncan...She'd never know if he could have been more than a friend. A muffled cry rose from her torn heart. It was too late.

The Highland wind knotted her hair and nipped her cheeks, yet she stood until lavender streaks tinted the sky and shadows spread over the hills—heartsick. She wanted to stay, but she just couldn't.

Turning away, she walked along the rim of the cliff to the rocky trail winding through fallen rubble.

About to step onto the path, movement on the track below startled her; Duncan was coming toward her—from the direction of Craggan Mhor. As he drew nearer, she saw his kilt swinging wildly, his stride long and steady—hands clenched at his sides.

It hurt that Duncan no longer wanted to be friends. She couldn't understand it. And she started to worry that he was angry for some reason and coming here to have it out. There was no going the back route down the cliff; he'd already seen her and quickened his pace. He didn't wave.

She waited, her breathing shallow.

Quickly closing the distance between them, Duncan finally slowed as he approached, his hands relaxing. Rough wind combed through his hair. Still he said nothing.

He stopped and stood right in front of her, so close she felt his breath. Looking straight into her eyes, his lips twitched with the hint of a smile.

China met his soft gaze, her heart on the edge of hope.

Slowly, he reached for her and cupped her face in his hands, his thumbs tracing her cheekbones. One hand strayed behind her head, and she felt his fingers catch in her hair.

He pressed his mouth to hers and kissed her—an aching, melting kiss.

Arms enfolding her, Duncan pulled her to him and kissed her long and deep. She pressed her hands to his back, aware of nothing but him.

He kissed her forehead, her cheek, her hair. Then he whispered, his lips tickling her ear, "I'm not letting you go till you say you'll stay."

A throaty moan escaped on her sigh.

Duncan drew back but held her tight, a concerned frown creasing his brow.

China leaned to him and brushed a butterfly kiss on his mouth—then held very still a moment, their soul-deep gaze unwavering. With a tilt of her head, she took in a long breath, about to speak—but then stopped, her heart beating against her ribs like a caged bird—or one ready to soar.

At last, her smile bloomed.

"Aye, I'll stay."

He jumped up to the level ground where she stood and wrapped himself around her like a cloak. If she thought she'd been kissed before...this kiss touched the deepest part of her heart. They kissed till they could barely breathe.

Reluctantly, they let the kiss end but remained entwined in each other's embrace. Duncan smoothed her windblown hair, and she laid her head against his shoulder, content, the wind dancing around them as the sky darkened to steely blue.

"Should we get back?" China said. "Sylvie—"

"Shh." He put a finger to her lips. "Sylvie knows where we are," he said with a sly smile. And he swept her off her feet and into his arms. "And I'm still not letting you go."

She laughed as she snuggled against his neck. "Braveheart."

Duncan tipped her toward his chest and squeezed. "It's a good job you're not dripping wet this time."

WHEN his arms ached, Duncan set China on her feet, and they walked the rest of the way to his car, hands clasped together.

China gave his hand a tug. "What did you mean: Sylvie knew where we were?"

"Truth is, Sylvie rang me up and told me to come straightaway and find you—or lose you. She said to look first at the stable, then up the cliff." Duncan slowed his steps to be sure of the footing. "And she called me a numpty."

"Oh, that might be one of the names Angus called me."

"It means idiot."

She laughed that trickly laugh he so loved to hear.

"And are you?"

"I think I was, but I seem to have come to my senses." He squeezed her hand. "Although, Sylvie said I had no more sense than God gave a goose."

They swung easily down the hillside, hand in hand. Duncan wasn't quite sure what he'd just done, but he had to do *something* when Sylvie called. And he was glad of it—if the pleasant bursting feeling in his chest was any indication.

Duncan had left the car at the bottom of the hill where the path veered upward toward the cliff. "How about we go back to Glengorm for a cold supper and a chat. I think we're long overdue for a chat, don't you?"

"It would seem so. I'll call Sylvie from your place."

He opened the passenger door for her before she could reach for the handle. She shot him a smile that, even in this low light, seemed to glow.

The headlight beams of the Range Rover bounced along the track to Glengorm.

Duncan had phoned ahead to let Janet know they were on their way. When they got to Glengorm, a candlelit dinner for two was laid out in the dining room. Janet had opened a fine bottle of Bordeaux and set it beside Duncan's place. Apparently, Sylvie and Janet had compared notes and figured a romantic setting was in order.

"I'm starving," China said, tearing the slab of Janet's bread in half. "Seems the Highland air makes me hungry. Or...," she gave him a sly-cat look, "was it you?"

He looked up from dolloping horseradish sauce on his plate with a what-do-you-think? tilt of his head and a you're-a-tease twist of his mouth.

They finished the bread and cheese and cold roast beef. He didn't want to linger at the table but get down to the chat. He was also mindful that he needed to check on Ross.

"Let's go through to the lounge," Duncan said, tossing back the last of his Bordeaux.

They padded down the hall in their wool-stockinged feet, having left their boots in the foyer.

"Coffee?" Duncan asked when they reached the lounge.

"Thanks."

While Duncan poured from the carafe on the sideboard, China settled on the old leather sofa and propped her feet on the ottoman, toes to the warmth of the peat fire.

He handed her a cup of coffee in the fine porcelain Janet had set out.

"I'll just ring Donnie and make sure Ross isn't pestering him too much."

Duncan finished the call. "Right, send him in then in about an hour's time. I'm in the family lounge."

He sat farther away from her on the sofa than he would have liked and stretched his legs toward the fire. China moved her feet to the side on the ottoman, and he put his feet up to share the space.

"I like this room," she said, her head resting on the back cushion, gazing at the frescoed ceiling.

"Me too. Apart from my study, I think I like this room best. Not quite so cavernous as the Drawing Room. One can actually get a bit of warmth from the fire." His socks were quickly absorbing that warmth.

"'Commit Thy Work to God.' Is that your family motto?" she read off the stone fireplace.

"The clan Sinclair motto actually."

She seemed lost in thought, staring into the fire.

"Duncan?"

"Hmm?"

"You've never said what happened to your parents."

He knew he'd have to answer this question sooner or later, and now was as bad a time as any. The few times he'd spoken of it, he had reduced the agonizing experience of losing his parents and the nightmare of Italian bureaucracy to a brief summary. Someday he'd tell China the whole story but not tonight.

"A drunk driver ran them off the side of a mountain."

China gasped.

"They were driving between ski resorts in the Val D'Aosta. Needless to say, I'm not keen to visit the Italian Alps."

"I'm so sorry."

"Aye. They never got to know Ross." Duncan had steeled himself to the topic of his parents. He nodded and said no more. And she didn't press him. Instead, she reached over and laid her hand over his and squeezed.

One of those longish silences stretched between them—and he let it. Should he broach the subject that weighed on him? He debated with himself and drank his coffee. He decided it was worth the risk.

"China, after your mother's memorial service, you asked to have a talk about what you called 'this God thing.' Could we have that talk now? Because you see, and this is going to sound frightfully archaic of me, but I'll never again be with a woman who doesn't share my faith."

That came out all wrong, and he was afraid she'd feel judged. "Only, I thought I got the idea you were wanting to know the Lord." He could feel the flush rise above his shirt collar. "I'm sorry, I don't mean to judge."

"I'm surprised Granny Nan or Sylvie didn't tell you." Her chin jutted slightly forward. "For your information, I've been reading the Bible, and they've been answering my questions...You know, they've prayed for me my entire life."

"William did too." And, Duncan thought, he had too in recent months.

"So let's just say for now that I'm not as much the numpty in that area as I might have been."

"Do you know what your name means?" Duncan asked.

"MacLeish? No, I guess I don't."

"The old Gaelic is *Mac GiolIa Iosa.* It means son of the servant of Jesus."

"Oh," she said quietly. "Then I guess it was inevitable. Only I'm a daughter—of the King, right?"

"Aye." Duncan found it a bit difficult to sip coffee through a smile. Thank you, Lord.

Only the crackle of a peat brick falling in the grate and the tick of the mantel clock filled another comfortable silence.

China appeared thoughtful for a moment, a crease forming in her brow, then said, "And while we're making conditions here, I have one." She set her cup and saucer on the side table and looked directly at him, her sapphire eyes boring holes in him. "I will never, ever—do you hear me? *never*—be with an unfaithful man again."

He gulped and just about spit out his coffee. A cough and an astonished laugh came out instead. "You've nothing to worry about on that account. I've had a bellyful of infidelity," he said, meeting her demanding stare.

"Oh?" She narrowed her eyes and cocked her head at him, looking ready to accuse.

"No, no. Not me. Harriet. It's a bit embarrassing really, being the cuckold. A few times over, as a matter of fact."

"No, not a fun club to be in. I'm sorry for you too." Clearly riled, she tossed her hair over her shoulder. "For a while I thought it was my fault. But it wasn't. Brian was just a self-centered, faithless…Hey, maybe we should introduce Harriet and Brian. That could be a sweet revenge."

"'It is mine to avenge…says the Lord.'" Duncan said gently.

"Oh, that would be good. God would do a much better job."

She must have been pondering that idea as she fell silent and took up her coffee again.

After a couple of sips, she said, "Why didn't you divorce her after the first time?"

Her question took him a bit by surprise; he'd never given serious thought to divorce. But without a doubt, he knew the answer.

"My boys. I didn't want my children to go through that. And, I don't know…hope maybe. Or a bloody fool."

He was sorry they'd got to talking about the exes, but it was probably unavoidable.

Duncan put another peat brick on the fire. When he turned back to her, he was once again dazed by her beauty. The firelight brushed her face with a peach glow and glimmered in her eyes—her smile at him so inviting he wanted to kiss her—but didn't dare.

"That's enough about *them*, aye?"

"Amen to that," China said and patted the place beside her.

He sat near her and, with a finger, tucked a strand of hair behind her ear, his own smile brimming in his eyes. "I meant it, you know."

"The kisses?"

"Oh aye, I meant those all right." The new brick must have flared, because he felt much warmer. "I meant...that I don't want to lose you."

"Well, then, don't put me down."

He laughed. "But I'm not so young anymore. It's a bit much on the old arms." And she laughed as well.

China reached a hand out for his and said, "I realize you haven't proposed marriage, and even if you had, I wouldn't say yes today. But I *will* stay. Craggan Mhor is my home. I just didn't have the sense to admit it."

"You Americans. Never know what you're thinking, eh?"

She shook off his hand and gave him a gentle shove. He caught her up in his arms, pulled her across the small space separating them, and planted an unresisted kiss on her lips. He felt her go boneless as they kissed long and soft.

They drew apart, a bit winded.

"I don't like to say this—I don't like it at all," Duncan said, straightening his kilt, "but I think we should be careful."

"Careful?"

Would she make him spell it out? What he ached for?

She caressed the side of his face like the touch of a warm breeze and said, "I never thought I'd say this—but I understand—and I agree."

They sat a bit longer, Duncan's hand resting over hers between them. "I'd best take you home." He didn't know how to end this evening; he didn't want it to end. "Have you told Sylvie yet?"

"Not yet. In the morning."

"I'd like to see that. You'll be giving her the best early Christmas gift ever."

"To be honest, I wanted to see how our little chat went this evening. Not that I'd change my mind about staying, but you know—I wanted to be sure of you."

"And are you?"

She seemed to take an age to answer as she searched his face. "Aye...ye numpty."

Galloping steps sounded down the hall, getting closer.

Ross burst in at the door, red-faced and all grin. Trooper came to a stop, his head planted in China's lap.

"Hey, Da. Miss MacLeish." Ross plunked down on the sofa next to his father. "I had ever so nice a time with Donnie. We got all the bridles oiled. They look like new."

Duncan tousled Ross's hair and set him in a playful headlock. "You're my best stable boy, aye."

Trooper left China and tried to wag his way between Duncan and Ross. Ross wiggled out of his father's clinch and, with a big grin, stuck out his hand. "Then pay me." Trooper dropped his muzzle on Ross's palm.

"Cheeky." Duncan grabbed for his son; Ross dodged, giggling. "What say we take a drive before bed and run Miss MacLeish home?" He shot China a questioning look but noticed her smile at Ross never wavered, so he assumed she was fine with the plan.

"Hey, Ross," she said. "Call me China."

"Aye, Miss MacLeish. China."

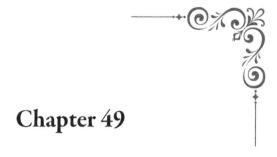

Chapter 49

Sylvie added raspberries to the online grocery order, then gave a glance at the schedule for the day. The guests were fed their breakfast and out of the house to go on about their day—and China wanted to see her in the lounge.

Sylvie felt uneasy that this was not good news. Maybe she shouldn't have interfered; Nan had tried to warn her off. But Sylvie knew that John was going to press China for a decision, and when China had come in from John's office looking in such a state and then slammed out the front door not ten minutes later—well, Sylvie couldn't think what to do but ring Duncan. And China had been vague when she phoned from Glengorm last night. Sylvie didn't know quite what to make of it. She wiped her palms down her apron, took it off, and hung it on the peg under the bells.

Andy started off with her down the hall. "You go to your bed, ye wee beastie." He sat, cocked his head at her, and refused to budge. "Go on, then." She pointed to the kitchen. But Andy cocked his head the other way. With a huff, Sylvie gave up and left him sitting on his behind.

China was curled up on the sofa, coffee in one hand, phone in the other, intently reading. She looked up when Sylvie walked in.

"Morning, Sylvie."

"And to you, dearie. A lovely mornin' it is. I'd forgot the sky was blue, aye."

China set her phone aside. "I was reading Luke. All the healing Jesus did...I don't understand why he didn't heal my mother. How many prayers does it take? Surely your prayers were good enough, even if mine weren't."

Sylvie perched beside China and patted her hand. "I wish I knew. But then, we'd have a very wee God if we could figure him out. All I know is he loves us and has a plan for us."

"You mean, like predestination?"

"Nay. I don't how it all works. God has foreknowledge, aye. Yet we have free will. It's all very confusing—for a time anyway. Then ye get the hang of it. The more we read his Word and pray, the more we know him. It seems to come round."

With a serious look, China set her mug on the table. "Sylvie, there's something else I want to talk to you about."

Sylvie's stomach dropped and dread crept up to grab hold of her heart.

China took both Sylvie's hands in hers. "I've decided to stay."

"Och, Lord be praised!"

"And Duncan and I—"

Sylvie clapped both hands to her breast and let out a girlish little squeal.

China laughed. "What did you think I was going to say?"

Sylvie stopped short. "Well, that you're courting, aye? Are ye not? Och, please say ye are."

"I guess that's a good word for it—courting. Yes, we're courting. But, Sylvie, I promise. I'm staying. This is my home,...and you're my family."

Sylvie threw her arms round China and rocked the two of them side to side. "I'm so happy for you. I'm that happy for *all* of us." Sylvie clamped her hands on China's shoulders and faced her. "Och, won't Nan be overjoyed?" The words tumbled out. "Come with me to tell her, aye? Have ye told John yet?"

"No, family first."

Little claws scratched at the lounge door that Sylvie had left ajar, and Andy sprang into Sylvie's lap, placed his paws on her chest, and swiped her face with a kiss. He wriggled out of Sylvie's arms and attempted to do the same to China. Then he hopped to the floor, stood up on his hind legs, paws raised, and let out a sharp bark.

"Aye, Andy's praisin' the Lord too, ye ken."

WORD whizzed around the village that Miss MacLeish would be staying on at Craggan Mhor. Normally, people she passed on the street or said hello to in the shops were polite, but now, people seemed to get the gift of gab.

China had to excuse herself from Flora Beaton in the post office, said she really had to finish her shopping to get things back to Sylvie. Maude Grant said she was over the moon that China would return to the charity shop once the season ended. And Alex shrilled her delight for all to hear at the Wildcat.

China walked on air.

But there was something she had to do.

THE cemetery was a mile out of the village, down a single-track lane hemmed in by low rock walls thick with ivy and brambles. Sheep grazing in the field took no notice of China as she drove by.

It wasn't difficult to find Uncle William's grave. Look for new grass on a low mound of earth, Sylvie said, and a humble gravestone of red Highland granite.

China propped a holly wreath against the stone. The crimson berries stood out like drops of blood against the glossy green leaves. "Dearly Beloved," the stone's inscription read.

Two magpies landed in a nearby crabapple tree and began picking the shriveled fruit, chattering at China between bites. Across the road a dog barked, a man whistled a sharp command, and a sheep bleated.

The Scotch mist cast a wet haze in the air, one Sylvie said would drench an Englishman but nary be noticed by a Scotsman. China pulled up the collar of Uncle William's mac and set the brim of her wool hat lower on her forehead.

Hands thrust deep in the pockets of the old coat, China remembered the day she had read Uncle William's letter. And China thanked God for her Uncle William.

Her inheritance was the most precious of all gifts that money could never buy.

Chapter 50

To get a break from the ever-present guests at Craggan Mhor, China and Duncan drove to Edinburgh together. China met with her solicitors while Duncan attended Callum's rugby match. It was Duncan's intention to tell Callum that he and China were dating, and China was worried. Ross had been thrilled, but she expected Callum to be less than thrilled.

At the solicitors', the legal action to transfer ownership of Craggan Mhor and all of Uncle William's estate into China's name was set in motion to take effect December 15. The solicitors would also look into endowment options, in addition to those Uncle William already had in place. There was a ridiculous amount of money at her disposal, and she was determined to give a lot of it away. No doubt Uncle William would have wanted the bulk of it to stay in Fionnloch and the area—maybe a library and an addition to the community center for starters.

That evening China and Duncan walked from their hotel on Gloucester Place to the Royal Mile and ate at a pub near St. Giles' Cathedral. The blackened woodwork and the fringed red velvet curtains draping the alcoves gave the place an elegant bordello atmosphere. But the smoked salmon was superb.

"So how did it go with Callum?" China asked.

"They won their match." Duncan's dimple created a small round shadow in his cheek, but his eyes held little spark.

"That's great...But you know what I mean."

"Callum scored the winning try."

China sagged. She put on a wan smile, torn between being glad for Callum and fearing the talk with his dad really hadn't gone well. "That bad, huh?"

"I'll admit, he wasn't thrilled." Duncan's expression seemed both pained and annoyed. "But he wasn't rude."

"I just don't want to be a problem for your kids. They've had a lot to deal with."

"You know," Duncan set the butt ends of his knife and fork on the table with a *thunk*. "Their mother hasn't contacted them since she was here in March. That's nearly eight months. And I don't quite know what to do about it."

China pursed her mouth tight and shook her head. "I don't blame Callum."

"No, I think he's the most hurt of the boys. Ross was only eight when she left. Callum took it harder; I'm afraid he knew what it was about."

"Maybe he and I could write a tell-all book about our mothers."

"Just give him time."

She nodded. "I seem to have plenty of that now."

They finished their meal and walked to the foot of Edinburgh Castle. The ramparts and the walls shone golden in the flood of lights set in the ground. They sat on a bench to take in the night beauty of the castle. China shivered, and Duncan put his arm around her, drew her tight to his side.

"I've decided to host a Burns Night Supper at Glengorm," he said.

"And I've no idea what you just said."

He laughed. "Twenty-fifth January. We Scots like to celebrate Robbie Burns's birthday. You do know of the poet Robert Burns?"

"Duh. I may be American, but I'm not stupid."

"I think you'll really enjoy it. It doesn't get more Scottish. Piping in the haggis and all."

"Haggis?" She wrinkled her nose and puckered her mouth, imagining a foul smell.

"It's formal."

She brightened considerably. "For-mal?"

"Yes, very. Black tie. Ballgowns. Dancing and all. You might want something rather Scottish."

"Ooo, now that *is* fun." China knew just the dress. She'd show him Scottish. If there was time to have it made. "You don't give a girl a lot of notice, do you?"

He laughed. "You mean you need more than two months to find a frock?"

Her Mona Lisa smile didn't give away a thing.

"You'll get to meet some of my old school chums." He gave her shoulder a squeeze. "And my sisters."

Chapter 51

A light Christmas mist dotted Duncan's bedroom windowpanes as he dressed for dinner at Craggan Mhor. Standing in front of the mirror on the armoire door, he tugged at the tan silk cravat, then yanked it off altogether and draped it over the valet. He picked up the green velvet box on the dresser and dropped it in a pocket of his sports jacket, strode out of his bedroom and down the hall, rapping on each of the boy's doors, calling, "Don't want to be late, boys."

Ross chattered like a magpie while Duncan loaded the bags of gifts into the boot of the car. He wondered if he could take Trooper along; would China like the birdhouse he made for her. And on and on.

Callum slumped in the front seat, earbuds and wire to his phone barely concealed. Duncan let it go till they got to Craggan Mhor when he asked Callum to please leave his mobile in the car. Wordlessly, Callum complied, tight-lipped.

Duncan popped the boot and handed a bag of gifts to Ross. He turned to hand the other to Callum but saw only the back of him, standing near the front door of the house.

The lounge got noisier when Duncan and his boys walked in; Andy and Fly barked, and everyone called hellos and merry Christmas. But it was the mistress of the manor, looking ravishingly Scottish in a long, red tartan skirt, who captured his attention. How he longed to plant a claiming kiss on her, right here for God and everyone to see. Instead, their eyes met as she lightly touched him on the arm and said, "Merry Christmas, Sir Duncan."

China's velvet voice threatened his resolve to not kiss her just yet. "Merry Christmas, Miss MacLeish."

She smiled up at him. When she turned to rejoin the party, he placed his hand at the small of her back, needing to feel her warmth.

Turning back to him, she whispered, "I want to give you my gift after dinner. Privately." He nodded and felt heat spread through his chest. Her scent faded as she drifted away from him to the sofa.

Ross sprawled on the floor in front of the fire, happily mobbed by the dogs. But Callum had plunked in an armchair, feigning interest in a book that Duncan knew he wasn't reading but using to cover a sulk. He'd speak to Callum later.

Drink in hand, Duncan sat beside China and put his arm on the back of the sofa behind her where he could brush her shoulder. He remembered sitting in this room a year ago, waiting for word on the runaway niece. Things had changed indeed.

"Right, then." Sylvie bent to pick out two presents under the tree. "Shall we open gifts?" she said, handing one to each of the boys. Callum grinned and set his book aside. He returned Sylvie's kiss on the cheek and thanked her. Ross sprang up and flung his arms round Sylvie. "Well, go on," Sylvie urged them.

The boys ripped off ribbons and paper and found knitted wool scarves: Callum's striped in his school colors of navy, red, and white; Ross's in the blue and white of the Scottish Saltire.

"Oh, cool!" Ross waved his scarf like the flag, then looped it round his neck.

"Did you make this?" Callum asked Sylvie, his grin wide.

"Aye. I made yours, and Granny Nan made Ross's."

Callum draped the scarf over his neck. "It's just grand. Thank you."

Ross handed around the rest of the gifts. A mound of discarded wrapping paper grew, into which Andy dove, chasing after the new squeak toy that Ross threw. Nan's woolly scarf to China perfectly matched her eyes in color. And China gave Callum a rugby ball and gave Ross a new riding helmet.

"Oh, thanks! You'll ride with me, won't you?" chirped Ross, giving China a quick hug. Callum muttered his thanks with no eye contact to China, and Duncan gave his eldest son a stern I'll-talk-to-you-later look.

Ross grabbed his gift for China. He had wrapped it himself and it looked it: taped haphazardly, the perch of the birdhouse sticking through the paper.

"I made it myself." He presented it to her with a grand flourish of outstretched arms.

"Thank you, Ross." China tore off the paper. "Oh, it's wonderful." She held up the green-and-blue-painted birdhouse.

"It's a robin house," Ross said.

China looked rather quizzically at the house, then at Ross, before realization dawned and she laughed. "I almost forgot which country I'm in. An American robin would never fit in this house." She planted a kiss on Ross's scarlet cheek. "That's very sweet of you. Thank you."

She set the birdhouse beside the small pile of gifts next to her and took up a leather folder from the side table. Duncan smiled, knowing what this was about.

To each of the staff, she handed an envelope bearing William's seal on the flap. "Merry Christmas...and thank you...I'm so grateful to you," she said, eyes brimming."You all have a place here as long as you want...Forever, I hope...And you have a place in my heart. Thanks to my Uncle William."

Angus made a gruff noise and sniffed.

"And I promise I'll never leave Craggan Mhor. You can't make me."

John smiled, bent and said something to Fiona, and she too smiled.

"You can open the envelopes later, if you would."

Duncan knew each envelope held a £2,000 draft and a note of appreciation. China had been concerned it wasn't enough, and she didn't want to put anyone on the spot opening the gift in front of her.

Gift-giving over, John made the rounds, refilling drinks, and Callum picked up his book again. Duncan stiffened, about to go and tap his son on the shoulder and say, Can I have a word? which was not meant to be a question at all. But China put a hand on Duncan's arm and said in a low voice, "I don't mean to butt in, but do you mind if I speak to Callum?"

"Are you sure?"

"Yes. I'd like to try."

"Right, then."

China got up and leaned toward Callum, not too close, and said something to him. Callum shot his father a pleading do-I-have-to look, to which Duncan cocked his head and gave his son the raised-eyebrow look. Callum huffed and slouched after China in the direction of the study.

They were gone long enough that Sylvie started to fidget and went off, she said, to see to how the girls were getting on with dinner. Duncan thought maybe he shouldn't have agreed to this chat. Callum could be rude when he was angry.

After a time, Callum returned, eyes cast down, his cheeks pinked. China followed, looking unexpectedly calm. When she sat beside Duncan, their hands found each other's out of sight between them, and China gave his hand a light squeeze.

His son's eyes were a bit red, Duncan noticed, when Callum looked up at Sylvie's announcement that dinner was ready.

Duncan lingered to be last to leave the lounge, indicating that he wanted to speak with China. "What did you say to Callum? Do you mind my asking?"

She smiled serenely at him. "I told him about my mother. That I understand what he's going through...And I told him I had no intention of hurting you."

A lump welled in Duncan's throat. He felt his own face pink, and he had to look away.

"And Callum gave me a lovely Christmas present," China said.

"Oh?"

"A smile." She reached up and kissed him, soft and short. And very sweet.

He couldn't possibly convey to her what it meant to him that she cared for his children. He swallowed hard, at a loss for words, so he took her hand, and they went in to dinner.

AFTER dinner, China and Duncan slipped off to the study while the others played charades. Light from the green glass shade of the desk lamp and the dim wall sconces cast warm shadows in the room.

From the center desk drawer, China withdrew an old leather hinged box. She extended it to Duncan, the length of the box just fitting into both palms held out together; she hoped he would like it.

"I was going to give this to you when I left. I got it in London."

"A goodbye present, eh?"

"Something like that."

He opened the box. The antique dagger-shaped letter opener rested on brown velvet. The round shaft of the hilt was topped with a thistle stem curving into a loop, a sparkling Cairngorm stone at its center for the flower.

Duncan took the letter opener out of the box and ran a finger over the pitted silver. "It's beautiful. Thank you." He touched the stone. "But why this as a parting gift?"

China laughed. "I thought you might remember me—prickly like a thistle. And I hoped, in time, that we'd write. Well, email anyway."

Duncan toyed with a tendril of her hair, winding it gently around his finger before freeing it over her shoulder. "Prickly, eh? And now I can barely contain myself for wanting to touch you." He rested his hand cupped on the side of her neck and stroked a thumb along her jaw.

She leaned her head to hold his hand there a moment. "Careful, we've got a party to go back to."

"Aye," he sighed.

He set the letter opener in the case, then reached in his pocket and held out his gift.

"We seem to be giving each other old things," he said.

China flipped up the lid of the square box. There lay an exquisite brooch, a round stone, amber as a Highland stream in sunlight, at its center. The silver setting resembled a small Scottish shield wrought in thistle flowers. The large Cairngorm stone glittered with the same fire as the stone in the letter opener.

"It's lovely," China breathed. "Thank you."

"It was my great-grandmother's."

A thought strayed in that China didn't want but couldn't ignore. Duncan must have seen the cloud in her eyes.

"I've never so much as *shown* it to another woman," he said. "It wasn't right till you."

China smiled. "Then it's even more beautiful."

"May I pin it on you?"

"Of course."

He pinned the brooch to her sweater, his touch heating her cheeks.

Duncan clasped her hands in his and held her gaze with his arresting green eyes. "China MacLeish, I love you with all my heart."

China could have melted into a puddle at his feet but stood straight and returned his gaze. "And I love you, Sir Duncan, with all *my* heart—and then some."

He brought her hands to his lips for a long moment.

"We'd better get back to the party," she said reluctantly.

"Aye, while we can." He let go of her hands and gave her a wicked grin.

Chapter 52

January 25, Burns Night—and China's dress was perfection. She smoothed her hands over the midnight blue velvet snug on her torso, past the dropped waist, where she grasped the tartan skirt between thumb and forefinger on each side to hold out the skirt. She twirled again to hear the rustle of silk taffeta. She'd never had a ballgown and had never even imagined having a couture gown.

She fixed the mirrored armoire doors so she could see the back of her dress. The iridescent dark blue, green, and black tartan was gathered at the back in folds falling vertically to the hem. A sash of the same fabric rested low on her hips and tied in a double faux-bow that gave the effect of a bustle—a fairy-tale dress.

Not bad for forty-two she admitted as she appraised her reflection—no gray hair in the messy-style updo. China wound a loose curl around a finger and smiled, remembering Duncan doing the very same when they exchanged Christmas presents. She adjusted the off-the-shoulder neckline and gave a tiny tug to the skinny sleeves.

The brooch on the dressing table caught her eye. She wanted to wear it but didn't want to flaunt the family heirloom in front of Duncan's sisters. He'd said Catriona could be a bit sharp-tongued. Duncan would understand.

She sat at the dressing table and inserted the delicate sapphire and diamond drop earrings. Tonight she wanted to look especially nice for Duncan; he was so excited about this party and his sisters' coming home. She leaned back to check the effect in the mirror.

Her face was unrecognizable, in some ways, as the woman she'd been a little over a year ago. Then, she wore tension like a brittle mask; now, her eyes sparkled like the jewels in her earlobes; her mouth bore the relaxed look of being deeply and frequently kissed.

The unnameable terror she used to feel—bottomless, irrational, monster-in-the-closet fear—was gone. China sighed and shook her head. Years ago the fear had turned to anger that she had wielded like a sword. No more. Deep sadness would always be there, that mother-ache. But she was thankful her mother had come home—to Craggan Mhor—to her.

She touched the Cairngorm stone in the brooch, amazed at how her life had changed. The warmth in her heart spread to her lips, and she smiled. So this was love.

A light rap on the door, and Sylvie poked her head in. "Donnie's here for you." When China stood, Sylvie let out a small gasp. "Och, you are the bonniest thing ever stepped out of the mist."

China twirled for her. "Thank you, Sylvie." She pressed her cheek to Sylvie's.

Slowly descending the stairs, China let her dress trail behind and fall down each step with the sound of silk and crinoline dragging on carpet.

Donnie draped the blue velvet cloak around her and stood to attention as he held the front door open. "Ye do look right queenly, Miss MacLeish."

"Oh, Donnie, how many times do I have to tell you—call me China." She grinned at him. "But thank you."

She rode to Glengorm in the backseat of the Jaguar, feeling quite chauffeured, and as Donnie drove, China thought of the briefing Duncan had given her about his sisters. Catriona, the elder of the two, lived in Frankfurt with her German banker husband and their three Teutonic children. They seemed to have houses all over Europe, and Catriona and the children were often on holiday. Duncan assured China that Catriona meant nothing by her sarcastic wit and that she was, in fact, generous and kind-hearted. Isobel lived in a Paris garret, albeit a sumptuous garret, with four dogs the size of large rats, and she cranked out volumes of wildly successful children's books. Her laugh was legend.

Donnie circled the front of Glengorm House and stopped at the front door. He hopped out and offered a hand to China. The cars parked in front looked like the showroom of the exotic car dealership in Chicago China had once gone to for fun: an older Rolls Royce, a variety of Jaguars, a Bentley, a Range Rover or two, and several Mercedes. Glengorm House glowed. As she stepped out of the car, China expected a movie director to yell from the shadows, "Lights. Camera. Action."

DUNCAN was there the moment she arrived, stunning in his full Highland dress. The backdrop of Glengorm added to the effect, making Duncan so jaw-droppingly gorgeous, China hoped she could keep her mouth closed and not drool.

The butler took her cloak, and she and Duncan stood alone in the foyer. Neither of them moved in what seemed like an enchanted moment.

"You are absolutely beautiful," Duncan said, his voice husky, as if he were speaking into the dark.

She twirled. "Do you like it?"

"I like *you*." He moved closer. "I'd crush you in my arms and kiss you till you begged for mercy, but I wouldn't want to wrinkle your dress." He brushed a finger across her bare collarbone and up her throat, stopping under her chin. China shivered to her toes. He tilted her face up to him and lightly kissed her.

"Tease." She dabbed the pink gloss off his lips with the tip of a finger.

"It's only teasing if there's no promise." He tucked her hand into his crooked elbow and led her into the party.

Promise? He must not have seen her quizzical look.

THEY entered the Drawing Room, China on Duncan's arm, and all heads turned toward them. A barely audible gasp echoed in the room, and China wondered if maybe she'd left muddy footprints. Her gown rustled softly as they made their way around the room for introductions.

"And this is my sister Catriona and her husband, Gerhardt."

China smiled warmly at Catriona and extended her hand.

For an instant, neither of them moved till Catriona laughed and thrust her hand to meet China's. "Sorry, I forgot—you're American. In that sensational tartan gown, I thought you were one of us." Catriona leaned forward and smooched the air on either side of China's face, her auburn hair a cloud of expensive-smelling perfume. "Lovely to meet you."

China wasn't sure if she should return the kisses. "Thank you. I'm pleased to meet you too."

Gerhardt gave a slight bow and kissed China's fingers. "A pleasure, Miss MacLeish."

"Please, call me China."

"I'd be most pleased to call you China," he said in impeccable English, "but I'm afraid you'll be asking that of everyone all evening. They're a rather stuffy lot."

"Oh, not to worry." Catriona took China by the elbow. "You'll have them eating off your palm by the end of the evening. Come and meet Isobel...Duncan, relax. I'll bring her back." Catriona patted her brother on the shoulder as she breezed by.

It wasn't difficult to find Isobel. Catriona steered them toward a rollicking laugh dressed in jewel-toned patchwork velvet festooned with ribbons and lace. Isobel's lush chestnut hair hung halfway down her back, a deep purple streak rippling from the crown of her head.

"Isobel," Catriona lightly touched her sister's arm, "I want you to meet China MacLeish."

When Isobel turned to face them, China was astonished by how elegant she looked. In spite of the gypsy getup and her rowdy laugh, Isobel was regal. Nearly as tall as China, Isobel regarded China with her brother's green eyes, and her face crinkled into a huge smile. Isobel handed her drink in Catriona's direction, grabbed China's outstretched hand, and pulled her into a hug.

"I am *so* pleased to meet you. May I call you China?"

"Please do."

"Duncan's been telling us all about you. Call me Izzy."

Catriona laughed a sweet laugh. "*We* call her the colorful sheep of the family."

Izzy gave her sister a mock-scowl, retrieved her drink, and started to lead China away by the arm.

"Isobel," Catriona warned, "you're not to walk off with China. I promised Duncan I'd have her back shortly."

"Later, then." Izzy leaned toward China. "After all the screeching of bagpipes is done and the unintelligible poetry spouted."

China gave an agreeing nod. "And I want to hear about Paris."

"*À bientôt.*" Izzy turned back to the knot of friends she had been chatting with.

China turned and nearly bumped into Duncan's waistcoat buttons.

He put a steadying hand on her arm. "I didn't think I should leave you ladies alone together too long."

Catriona affected a pout. "Really, Duncan, a promise is a promise." Catriona stood on tiptoe and stage-whispered in her brother's ear, "I like her." And, knowing that China heard, she gave China a friendly-feline smile and swished off, her gold charmeuse gown swinging as she went.

Duncan wore a rascally grin. "Feeling a bit stunned?"

"Your sisters are really something."

"They are indeed."

He held out his arm to her again. "Ready to go in to dinner?"

She drew her hand down his bicep—accidentally on purpose—before settling her hand in the crook of his arm.

CHINA almost jumped out of her skin. As she and Duncan crossed the threshold to the Great Hall, a piper revved up to full screech. It was all she could do to avoid covering her ears. But she had to admit, it was quite a dramatic effect as the guests paraded in.

Seated next to Duncan in the middle of one long side of the table, she stole a glance at him while he remained standing till his guests found their seats. He looked so handsome, his cheeks flushed and his smile welcoming, that China found herself in danger of staring like a lovesick fool.

The room seemed charged with anticipation, and after the rustling of ballgowns quieted, Duncan welcomed the guests. Then he introduced her as his honored guest, Miss China MacLeish, formerly from across the pond in Chicago and now, he was happy to say, his neighbor at Craggan Mhor.

Duncan said grace and took his seat. He lifted her hand and pressed a kiss to it, not seeming to care who saw them. Way down at the other end of the table, China noticed Catriona break into a pleased smirk aimed at Duncan and her.

And the Burns Night Supper was underway.

Duncan had warned her that there was an order to the dinner and that she wouldn't understand much of it, Robbie Burns being quite unintelligible to the uninitiated. So she had determined to just smile and nod when it seemed appropriate.

After the soup course, Catriona rose, and all eyes turned to her. She recited the Burns poem about a mouse, the old Scots language lilting like a song. What little China understood sounded depressing, but Catriona was fun to watch, gesturing with abandon.

Someone must have cued the piper again as the skirl of bagpipes blasted from the hall and drew closer—and louder. Following the piper came the chef, imported from Inverness Duncan had told her, bearing the haggis on a silver tray. Everyone stood to attention and clapped in time to the music. China thought the men might salute or daub a tear as the haggis passed by. The chef set the haggis on the table in front of Duncan, and mercifully, the pipes wheezed to a stop. China tried not to think about the yellowish blob on the tray being a stuffed sheep's stomach.

When the guests were seated again, Duncan delivered a Burns poem to the haggis. At the word "knife," he made a show of sharpening the knife, then plunged it into the haggis and slit the thing end to end. At "Gie her a haggis!" the guests leapt to their feet and applauded. Then Duncan toasted the haggis, knocked back his Scotch.

More rustling and sitting, and the haggis platter was whisked away. An army of servers entered, and plates of the main course were set before the guests.

China leaned over her plate and sniffed at the haggis. "So tell me, what's really in this?"

"Oh, sheep bits, onions, and oatmeal," Duncan said.

She squinted at him.

"Best not get too specific till you've tried it." He motioned her to go on, try it.

She took a small bite while Duncan watched her, obviously amused.

"Hmm. Kind of like hamburger casserole. But with oatmeal." But not something she wanted very often, she thought, realizing she couldn't spit out the unidentifiable bit she'd just hit.

He laughed. "Did you find one of those bits, then?"

She would have elbowed him in the side if they weren't at a formal dinner.

The guest to China's right was an old school chum of Duncan's and a charmer. His wife had a dry sense of humor, and China enjoyed the banter that flew between Duncan and them. And Lady Something-or-Other on Duncan's left peppered China with questions about her life in America and asked how China liked it here in little Fionnloch. "Sit back will you, Duncan," she said, "so I can see China." She waved a hand at him that, if she'd hit him, might have left a dent in his nose the size of her enormous emerald.

The dessert course, a layered trifle served in crystal compotes, had China stifling a giggle. "It's called Tipsy Laird?" she said. "And is he?"

Duncan winked at her.

Dessert cleared away and coffee served, Duncan leaned in close and said, "And now the fun begins." whisky glass in hand, Duncan again stood and made a toast to Robbie Burns.

Then Stinky Finch stood. All the standing and sitting reminded her of one of those carnival games where the object was to bop the clowns that popped up.

Stinky gave a speech to the lassies, ending with the definition of a wife: wonderful, interesting, fascinating, and elusive. "So here's a toast—to the lassies. What would we do without you?"

"Aye, lassie," Duncan murmured, his shoulder brushing hers.

Then Izzy gave a loud throat clearing and stood. "And now, to the laddies." She shimmied to her full height. "Have you ever noticed how women's problems begin with *men*?" She planted her fists at her waist and surveyed her audience. "*Men*opause. *Men*tal breakdown. *Guy*necologist."

Hoots from the women and groans from the men rose.

"Oh, come now, gentlemen," Izzy said in a most admonishing tone, "you've heard those words before.

"But," Izzy held up a forefinger, "we love you, laddies. You're very much like a bottle of wine: a touch fruity, a bit dribbly, sometimes sour, and when the right one comes along...a pleasure. But if he's not Mr. Right, like I told an old beau, 'Put a cork in it!'" And on Izzy went.

China laughed till her sides hurt.

"A toast to you, laddies." Izzy held her Scotch high. "You ask what you'd do without us? You'd do the washing up is what." Izzy trumpeted a laugh that set the whole party into howls.

After the laughter trickled away, an old gentleman launched into an elaborate thanks for the evening. Quite possibly his upper lip didn't move once during his entire speech, his bristly gray mustache not so much as quivering.

Just when China feared there would be a thanks-for-the-thanks speech, the guests hopped to their feet, joined hands, and sang "Auld Lang Syne," swaying side to side around the huge table.

The last note drifted to the ceiling far overhead, and Duncan invited the guests to dancing in the Ballroom.

Duncan pulled China's chair back and held out his hand to her, looking very courtly, as if he were a lord and she were a lady.

She couldn't help it—she giggled out loud.

THE ceilidh band struck up a Scottish waltz, and Duncan led China by the hand to the center of the dance floor, other dancers filling in around them. Duncan noticed the sideways glances and smiles cast in their direction. This was a very public declaration of his love for China, and he had intended just that.

"I picked this tune to start, thinking you might be comfortable with a waltz," he said.

"Ballroom dancing was compulsory at school. Do you want me to lead? I can do either." China offered both hands for him to choose.

"Thanks. I think I'll manage." He closed his fingers over her right hand.

They fitted like they'd always danced together. He whirled her round and she followed; he changed direction and she followed, the heat of her back warming his palm. Her gown swished and swung as she turned. He could have been dancing with a princess—if America had royalty.

When the waltz slowed to a stop, China continued to rest her hand on his shoulder, her cheeks rosy. "You're quite a dancer," she said, her indigo eyes glittering in the chandelier light.

"Compulsory at my school too." He so wanted to kiss her. "Only we brought the girls in from another school."

The fiddler launched into a reel.

"Are you up for trying this? Scottish country dancing."

"Just push me where I need to go."

China was often not where she was supposed to be, but she laughed and danced wherever she was. "It's a lot like square dancing. Also compulsory," she said as they lined up to strip the willow, men on one side, ladies on the other.

When the dance ended, China dropped her hiked up skirts and doubled over laughing.

Catriona claimed Duncan for the next dance. She waved at China. "Don't go far, my dear. He'll be looking for you."

Duncan partnered his sister in a promenade, but his attention was on China. She raised her eyes to him, as if she knew he was looking at her. Every day he was more in love with her.

After the last chord of the tune, Duncan made his way back to China, who was quite engaged in conversation with Stinky Finch and his wife.

The dancing carried on till well after midnight when guests started saying their goodbyes. He doubted his sisters would go up to bed yet, but he hoped at least they'd go away.

"China, if you don't mind staying till all the guests have gone, I'll take you home," he said.

"Home?" She smiled. "Yes, it is."

They stood side by side in the foyer and saw the guests out, the butler closing the door after the last couple. Izzy, Catriona, and Gerhardt had gone up.

Duncan took China by the hand. "There's something I want to show you in my study, aye."

"Sure, but I might turn into a pumpkin pretty soon."

DUNCAN closed the doors of his study, and they melted into each other's arms—kissed as long as he dared.

They drew away from the kiss but couldn't draw away from each other, his hands lingering on her slender waist, hers softly cupping the back of his neck.

China looked up at him, radiant with the heat of their kiss. "Was that what you wanted to show me?" She flashed a teasing smile.

"No, but I've wanted to do that all night."

She trailed her fingers over his shoulders. "Me too."

He did a quick check of the room; a peat fire flickered in the great hearth, and a pale glow from a dozen candles lit the room. Just right, he thought. Good of Gerhardt to lend a hand.

His fingers laced in hers, he led her to the window alcove where the moon shone framed in the diamond-paned windows, purple clouds covering all but a slice of the winter moon.

"My, this is romantic," she said, taking a step closer to the window.

Duncan stepped up behind her and gathered her into his arms. He squeezed ever so gently, savoring the spicy scent of her hair and being so close to the woman he loved. China leaned back against him and rested her hands on his encircling arms.

The clouds floated past to reveal the full moon, spreading moonlight farther into the room. He felt her body move with a deep breath in and a sigh out.

"So *this* is what you wanted to show me—Glengorm in the moonlight. It's truly beautiful."

"Aye...but it's *this* I want to show you."

He released her, and she turned to him. Duncan undid the clasp of his sporran and reached into the old sealskin pouch. Dropping to one knee, he held out a small box on the palm of his hand.

For the thousandth time, her beauty stunned him: the candleglow on her cheeks, her eyes wide and dark, her joy a warmth to his heart. He could scarcely open his mouth for staring at her but managed to gather his wits about him.

Slowly, he opened the box for her to see.

"China MacLeish," his voice thickened, "my love...will you be my wife?"

She gasped and sank to her knees, both hands clapped to her mouth, her skirts puffed in a tartan mound.

Duncan took the ring from the box, and China extended her trembling left hand, pooled tears wetting her lashes.

He smiled crookedly, swallowing his own tears. "Does this mean yes?"

Two tears traced her cheeks as she met his eyes. "Yes," she whispered.

The ring, a Cairngorm stone set in a circle of diamonds, slipped on to a perfect fit. And a single tear slid down Duncan's cheek.

He stood and helped her up. And for several heartbeats, he held her hands and drank in her shining gaze.

"Yes," she murmured again. "Oh yes."

She laid her hands flat on his chest where he thought his thumping heart would surely knock them off.

Pressing his hands over hers, Duncan bent to meet her lips.

Chapter 53

"Hurry up, woman," Angus said, his chin poked in the air so Sylvie could tie his bow tie. "I dinna want tae be late. The weddin' guests willna seat themselves, ye ken."

"You'll no be late." Sylvie pulled on the ends of the bow to adjust it. "But you will look a proper Highland gentleman." She raised a staying finger to him while she checked her work.

"Ye auld besom." Angus flipped the beribboned bonnet onto his head and was about to leave.

"Wait! You forgot your boutonnière." Sylvie waved a long pin in front of his nose. "Hold still, will you." She pressed the white rose to his lapel and pinned it in place. "Right you are, then. Off you go."

Angus turned on his bandy legs, knobbly knees jutting out below his kilt hem, and marched out the kitchen door—whistling a tune.

Sylvie inclined her head to the fragrance of the pink and white roses in her corsage. She smoothed the periwinkle chiffon overskirt of the long, most beautiful dress she'd ever had and gave the satin jacket a straightening tug.

"Hullo the hoose," Alex shouted over the upstairs bannister. "Here comes the bride, aye."

Sylvie hurried down the hall to the entryway where John gazed to the top of the stairs, looking for all the world like he'd just seen an angel.

A little sob wedged in Sylvie's throat.

There stood China, her silver and white figure-clinging gown shimmering in the light. She looked a proper Scottish bride, a MacLeish tartan sash held in place on one shoulder by the Sinclair brooch. Sylvie was quite certain Duncan would go weak in the knees when he saw the woman he was to marry.

China glided down the stairs, Stacy and Alex holding the train of her dress. She beamed and looked like she might cry, all at once.

"Oh, my dear." Sylvie's hands fluttered toward China, not knowing if she should hug or kiss her for fear of mussing her.

China pulled Sylvie into a hug. "Aunt Sylvie, what would I do without you?"

"Well, now," John said, "seems you're stayin' for sure, aye?"

China laughed, releasing Sylvie. "If you don't kick me out."

"Nay, though I'm that pleased to be giving you away." He winked and offered his arm. "Your Rolls awaits you."

Settled beside China in the back of the Rolls Royce Silver Shadow, their hands clasped together, Sylvie marveled at her niece, the woman she thought she'd never see, now dear as a daughter. Her chin trembled as she thought of William and how happy he would have been on this day.

CALLUM handed a silver and onyx cufflink to his father.

"Thank you, laddie." Duncan inserted the cufflink, casting a glance at his son. "Something on your mind, Callum?"

"Nothing."

"Bit of a long face for nothing, I'd say." Duncan gave Callum a gentle smile and donned his waistcoat.

"It's just that...Will I have to call her Mum?"

Duncan's fingers stilled as he did up the silver buttons, and he looked deep into his son's eyes where he saw the worry of a young man whose life was about to change. "Would you like to?" he asked.

Callum looked away. "Not really. But I don't want to upset you...or her."

Duncan took Callum by the shoulders, much broader shoulders than just a few months ago, and said, "You can call her China. She'd be delighted." He gave Callum a quick pat and released him.

"But Ross says he wants to call her Mum."

Duncan's smile broadened. "And do you mind if he does?"

"No, I guess not."

"Good lad." Duncan pulled his son into a bear hug and clapped him on the back. "Callum, I'm so proud of the man you're becoming."

"Thanks, Da." Callum grinned impishly.

"Cheeky boy. Da, is it? Sounds like you've been hanging around Donnie, eh?"

Callum ducked his father's attempt to tousle his hair.

Easing into his coat and straightening his sleeves, Duncan had a look out his bedroom window. "And now, I think you'd best get down there and help seat the guests. There's quite a crowd milling outside the marquee."

Callum turned to leave, then turned back. "Dad, I'm happy for you...and I like her...China."

As Duncan watched his son's retreating back, he nearly sobbed.

CHINA woke to feel the June Highland breeze play along her cheek. Duncan lay curled beside her in a tangle of bedclothes, his arm resting over her middle. She watched the valley of muscles across her husband's chest rise and fall.

He stirred but didn't wake, his face so close she felt his warm breath tickle over her ear and into her hair.

She glanced at her wedding dress draped on the back of a chair, his kilt tossed next to it—and she smiled at her sleeping husband.

China tipped her head toward Duncan and so lightly touched his forehead. She closed her eyes and thanked God. As a child, she had felt sacrificed on the altar of her mother's moods, but yesterday she knelt before the altar of the Lord and pledged her heart to the man she adored—and who adored her.

Duncan's arm tightened around her, and he nuzzled into her neck. "Come here, *mo nighean*," he whispered, slipping his other arm under her and pulling her close. "China Sinclair...my own lassie."

She turned in his arms to face him and nestled against his chest, nothing between them. "Aye, Sir Duncan." And with a fingertip, she traced his smile. "Laird of my heart."

RECIPE

T IPSY LAIRD
(Scottish Trifle)

Tipsy Laird is often served for the pudding course at a Burn's Night Supper on January 25th or on Hogmanay, New Year's Eve. A Scottish version of English Trifle, Tipsy Laird is both a visual treat and easy to make.

Ingredients

- 10 oz (300g) pound/sponge cake, halved longwise, cut into thick slices or cubes

- 10 oz (300g) fresh raspberries

- 6 tablespoons (90ml) Scotch (whisky) or Drambuie (orange juice for a nonalcoholic version)

- 2 cups (500ml) thick custard sauce (see *Note about Bird's Custard Powder)

- 2 cups (500ml) heavy whipping cream (double cream), softly whipped

- Handful toasted, slivered (flaked) almonds

- Grated chocolate over the top (optional)

Directions

Assemble Tipsy Laird in one large glass trifle bowl or divide into individual glass compote dishes. Don't make the trifle too far ahead.

- Arrange cake slices in the bottom of the bowl

- Layer raspberries, reserving a few to decorate the top

- Drizzle liquor or juice over raspberries, making sure it soaks through to the cake

- Spoon custard over in thick layer

- Spoon whipped cream over

- Decorate the top with a few raspberries and toasted, slivered almonds

*Note—Bird's Custard Powder is an egg-free custard shortcut that has been popular with UK cooks since 1844. But the trick to getting it thick enough is to add *heaping* tablespoons of the powder. And, Americans, remember the UK pint is 20 oz, so adjust the milk.

This bonus recipe of Tipsy Laird is a taste of what's to come—a wee cookbook of recipes inspired by *Love Inherited*.

Enjoy!

ACKNOWLEDGMENTS

Novel writing is one of those endeavors of which I've said, "Had I known how hard it was, I'd have never started. But I'd have missed out!" I'm indebted to the people who helped me complete *Love Inherited* so I didn't miss out on it.

Thank you to my brilliant readers: Betsy Fagen, Diane Glorvigen, Laura Jacobson, Anita Klumpers, Peggy Konkol, Lisa Lynch, and Gary Lynch. Each of them contributed in unique ways to making the story and my writing better. They were my grammar and punctuation cops, reality checks if I flubbed a detail, and objective and insightful eyes on the plot and characters. And friends.

Thank you to my consultants: Dr. Bill Heifer and Brooke Eastin. If I got any medical details wrong, it's my error, not Dr. Heifner's. And Brooke, my horse expert, did warn me: "No knowledgeable horse person would tie a horse by the reins unless it was an emergency. If the horse freaks out it can cut its mouth with the bit before the reins would break." So don't tie your horse by the reins just because I wrote it in a couple scenes for expediency.

And lastly, certainly not least, thank you to my husband, Dave. Support, encouragement, putting up with frozen pizza, helpful critique—prayer—he did it all. Thanks!

ABOUT THE AUTHOR

CRISTINE EASTIN writes contemporary women's fiction spiced with romance, threaded with life's heartaches, and enriched with faith and hope.

Cris grew up in Minnesota where life centered on family and friends, outdoor activities, pets, music, and reading. She also wrote short stories and terrible poetry. Then the fun writing stopped and she attended the university. She earned a doctorate in counseling from the University of Wisconsin-Madison.

A psychotherapist for over thirty years, Cris has a passion for encouraging people. She tells patients who feel dried up inside, "You can't pour from an empty pitcher." Writing for fun again, Cris hopes her fiction not only entertains but pours into readers' deepest needs.

Cris and her husband live in Wisconsin, not too far from the grandkids.

She's a member of American Christian Fiction Writers (ACFW).

Visit Cris at her website: CristineEastin.com[1].

---

1. http://www.cristineeastin.com

ALSO BY
CRISTINE EASTIN

A WEE SCOTTISH COOKBOOK

FEAST ON TWENTY RECIPES inspired by the Highland romance novel *Love Inherited*. This companion cookbook spans the meals of a Highlander's day from breakfast to a drink by the fire. But more than serving up food, the author folds in tidbits to place dishes in context of the story and the Scottish culture. Beginning with humble porridge, there are soups to warm the tummy, a hearty stew, main dish pies, and chicken drenched in liqueur. Vegetables, bread, oatcakes, delectable desserts, and a centuries old whisky concoction round out the twenty recipes. In *A Wee Scottish Cookbook*, ingredients are given in US and UK measurements for cooks on both sides of the pond.

FIFTY DAYS TO SUNRISE

HER LIFE IS A LOVE story, but then...What's a woman to do when her husband dies three thousand miles from home? Scream, cry—or run.

It's 2003, a year and a half after her husband's death. Fifty-three years old and alone, Lissa Maguire's seething with grief. She has to cope but makes a self-destructive mess of it.

Lissa's parents ask her to spend the summer in small-town Gifford, Minnesota, helping them move to an apartment. Cleaning out the attic of her childhood home, Lissa discovers her old diaries, and her potholed road to healing begins.

But when an old friend turns up, she's confused.

"TOLD WITH A RARE AUTHENTICITY and grace, *Fifty Days to Sunrise* is much more than a story but a hallowed place with people who are so finely crafted and multi-layered they feel more like family and friends. Cristine Eastin has given us an honest, memorable look at grief, love, healing, and home. Readers will want more of these characters and this author!"—Laura Frantz, author of *A Moonbow Night*

REVIEWERS' PRAISE FOR *Fifty Days to Sunrise:*

"What a wonderful heart-wrenching book! Grief is a journey that cannot be rushed."

"I sincerely felt like I was right there, in the midst of the family...I found myself crying, laughing, and struggling along with Lissa, her parents, siblings, and friends."

"*Fifty Days to Sunrise* has something to offer a wide variety of readers. Because of its deep insight, comforting atmosphere, and encouraging message, it would be an excellent choice for a book discussion group or as a tool of bibliotherapy...At its heart, the book is optimistic and hopeful as it unflinchingly examines grief and affirms the promise of recovery."

"Nice to read a faith-based book that holds your attention and makes you feel good."

Made in the USA
Monee, IL
07 January 2021